Charmian Clift was born in Kiama, New South Wales, in 1923. When she was eight she filled an exercise book with poems and illustrations, but it was not until she was about twenty that she realised that she wanted to be a writer.

In 1946 she joined the staff of the Melbourne *Argus*, where she met the war correspondent George Johnston; they were married the following year. In 1948 the couple's collaborative novel, *High Valley*, won the *Sydney Morning Herald* prize, and they continued to collaborate after moving to London in 1951. In 1954 the family settled in Greece where, over the next ten years, Charmian Clift wrote the two travel books *Mermaid Singing* and *Peel Me a Lotus* and her two novels, *Walk to the Paradise Gardens* and *Honour's Mimic*.

After returning to Sydney in late 1964 Clift began writing a weekly newspaper column which quickly gained a wide and devoted readership. These essays have been collected in the anthologies *Images in Aspic*, *The World of Charmian Clift*, *Trouble in Lotus Land* and *Being Alone With Oneself*.

Charmian Clift died in 1969.

Also by Charmian Clift

Peel Me a Lotus
Walk to the Paradise Gardens
Honour's Mimic
Images in Aspic
The World of Charmian Clift
Trouble in Lotus Land
Being Alone With Oneself

Also by George Johnston

My Brother Jack
Clean Straw for Nothing
Cartload of Clay
The Far Road

By George Johnston and Charmian Clift

High Valley

IMPRINT

The Sponge Divers

CHARMIAN CLIFT & GEORGE JOHNSTON

Angus&Robertson
An imprint of HarperCollins*Publishers*

The brief quotation from Homer's Iliad *is from the
translation by E. V. Rieu, The Penguin Classics,
Penguin Books, Harmondsworth, Middlesex, England*

*AN ANGUS & ROBERTSON BOOK
An imprint of HarperCollinsPublishers*

*First published in the United Kingdom in 1955 by Collins
This Imprint edition published in Australia in 1992 by
CollinsAngus&Robertson Publishers Pty Limited (ACN 009 913 517)
A division of HarperCollinsPublishers (Australia) Pty Limited
25-31 Ryde Road, Pymble NSW 2073, Australia*

*HarperCollinsPublishers (New Zealand) Limited
31 View Road, Glenfield, Auckland 10, New Zealand*

*HarperCollinsPublishers Limited
77-85 Fulham Palace Road, London W6 8JB, United Kingdom*

*National Library of Australia
Cataloguing-in-Publication data:*

Johnston, George, 1912–1970

　The Sponge Divers

　ISBN 0 207 16902 0

　I. Clift, Charmian, 1923–1969. II. Title

A823.3

*Cover illustration by Louise Tuckwell
Printed in Australia by Griffin Press*

*5 4 3 2 1
96 95 94 93 92*

For the Kalymnians

AUTHOR'S NOTE

Kalymnos is a small island with a large and particular problem. It is necessary therefore to emphasise that *The Sponge Divers* is entirely a work of fiction and, while the problem of the island is in broad outline more or less as we have described it, all the incidents related to that problem and all the characters in the novel are entirely the products of the authors' imaginations. To the real inhabitants of Kalymnos, both the town and the island, any resemblance in our characters, directly or by inference or by the inadvertent use of a particular name, is purely coincidental. Our respect, admiration and love for the people of this Ægean island and our gratitude for their wholehearted hospitality require this note.

KALYMNOS, 1955
Charmian Clift and George Johnston

CONTENTS

Sea of the seamen, sea of mine:
Be as rose-water, calm on his hair.
O my sea lover,
Let another dawn break for you.
Sea! Sea!
Be as sugar, be as honey!
For my sea lover my nights are sleepless:
He is sailing, winged like angels.
Sea of mine, bring my love back.

O poor Kalymnos! Poor Kalymnos!
Sea if mine, you have blackened her mountains.
Blow, following wind, blow!
They have gone, the strong ones, the brave ones;
They have gone, the fresh, the blooming ones . . .
O my sea lover, for you I am sleepless!

I am very small, sea of mine,
And black does not suit me.
O sea of mine,
I am sleepless, sleepless . . .

Thalassaki Mou,
old Kalymnian Song

PART ONE

Manoli

I

It was in Athens that Morgan Leigh met Telfs and first heard about Kalymnos—in a Cretan *taverna*, the Xania, down near the cathedral, drinking the black wine of Crete and watching four men with handkerchiefs in their hands, mincing and leaping and spinning in a wild, mad dance as heady as the wine.

Telfs was at a corner table by himself, drinking retzina with a morose and dedicated concentration, paying no attention to the barbaric music nor the violent twirlings of the men. A solitary figure he seemed, uncommunicative, unfriendly. His long egg-shaped head, bald and brown, appeared to have been chipped out of wood as a preliminary study of the grotesque by some sculptor not quite certain of his ability. It was a curious face—big mouth and bright caustic eyes and ears that stuck out, and very young things and very old things all mixed up together. An intelligent face, and a lonely one. It was not until towards the end of the evening, when Telfs came across to his table with the copper beaker of retzina in his hand, that Morgan saw the other things in his face.

The American walked steadily and poured the wine without spilling a drop, but he was drunk—drunk enough to be talkative.

" You English? " he said suspiciously.

" Not English," Morgan said. " Australian."

Telfs nodded, as if something had been explained to him. " I know Australia," he said. " I was out there in the war. I knew a girl there."

Morgan grinned. " Lots of Americans did."

Telfs shrugged. " What do you do ? " he said.

" I write. Or try to."

" Is that why you're in Greece ? "

Morgan nodded.

" Writing about what ? "

" I don't know. I'm not sure. Not yet anyway. I suppose you could say I'm looking for something."

" You want something to write about ? " He had a rough gravelly voice that gave all his questions an edge of accusation. " Go to Kalymnos," he said. " In the Ægean, the Dodecanese, ten miles off the coast of Turkey. Go there."

" Yes ? What is there in Kalymnos ? "

" The whole goddam world ! " Telfs glared at him. " The whole goddam world, *all* of it, changing. Everywhere is changing, sure, but most places you can't see it. Too many things moving at once, too much clutter, everything too gummed up with too many things. But you can see it in Kalymnos. Past, present . . . and a future, I guess. If there is a future of sorts, anyway. All there right in front of your eyes. The world changing." He spoke with a husky, desperate vehemence, as if the change he was talking about was something terrible, terrifying, something you had to talk about very quickly, lest it catch up with you.

" Go down there," he went on, " and take a look at God with the Byzantine face. Not our chubby, pink-faced God with his mealy mouth and turn-about collar, presiding over a safe little party of curates sipping weak tea and nibbling thin cucumber sandwiches. The big God with the dark, hard face ! " Telfs was thinking of Nikolas, the kid Nikolas with his withered legs strapped up in irons and *his* picture of God, the only God he had ever seen: the fierce, stern, bearded face carved in ivory on the bishop's crook. And Telfs was thinking of how often he sat in Mina's little house on the rock hill near the blue church of Saint Vassilias, overlooking the green harbour of Kalymnos, trying to explain—he, who had lost all sense of Christianity twenty years before !—trying to explain to the child the two faces of God . . . and Mina outside in the sun near the jasmine tree, sewing.

He called for more wine, the pale retzina for himself, the black wine for his companion, and began to talk about Kalymnos. Now, with Mina in his mind, he talked more quietly. But his words carried a sort of pleading undertone, as if he were anxious for somebody else to share his awareness of what he had known.

"It's just a seaport," he said. "A little Greek seaport, all crazy colours and light and sunshine, and storms too, storms that come boiling out of the air, in that corner of the Ægean where the world began. That's Kalymnos. It sent its war galleys to Troy. And all history has trampled over it for three thousand years. . . . But the boats have always gone out and come back and gone out again. It's got a pulse, a particular pulse. But now the pulse rate is slowing down. It's all coming to an end. I guess that's what gives it its special fascination. You can see the end of the world there, all wrapped up on one little island of fourteen thousand people."

"I don't quite see what you mean by——" Morgan began, but Telfs cut him short with a quick, impatient gesture.

"Listen," he said. "There's only the port, see. It's a sea-faring town, it always has been. The island itself is nothing much more than one great big rock. It doesn't hold pasture, it doesn't grow food—not to speak of, not to keep fourteen thousand people alive. It lives on its divers and its boats. It lives on sponges. It's lived for a hell of a long time on sponges. But then some smart guy comes along and he spins a synthetic sponge out of a test tube in a laboratory. It comes easy out of a test tube, a whole lot easier and cheaper than groping around in thirty-five fathoms, groping for just one more sponge, hoping you can stand it, waiting to die maybe, or waiting to be crippled for the rest of your life." Telfs swilled the last of the retzina around the bottom of his glass. "Did you ever wonder why sponges cost plenty of money?" he said. "You've seen the poor bastards shuffling round Athens in their rags, hung with sponges to sell? Walking mountains of sponges with a couple of feet sticking out the bottom, and frayed trouser cuffs. But do you ever see anybody buy one?" He shrugged. "Well," he said, "that's Kalymnos."

They went down together on the *Karaiskakis*, with the goats and hens and a trussed pig, and the decks crowded with steerage passengers vomiting in the scuppers at the first roll of the swell off Ægina, and the sailors sitting on the hatch covers singing *Sousourada*, and a kid with a pale, sad face playing a mandolin in the darkness. There was a big moon that night, and one after another the islands slid by, black and magical in the rivers of quicksilver.

Homer Vraxos was in the first-class bar, talking about highballs and American blend whisky and the money a smart guy could pick up in Detroit and how all Greeks who didn't get abroad to make dough were bone lazy. " They're animals, the Greeks," he said. "Animals ! They can eat, they can drink, they can talk—and that's all. Animals ! " All the time he was talking he fiddled with the tasselled gold watch fob hanging on his round little belly.

He had been up to Athens for shirts and three new suits. He was short and fat and oily and he stank sourly of garlic and the oil seemed to sweat through his big pores, and all his clothes from the loose-draped coat to the two-tone shoes were an extravagant caricature of American outfitting. And he was patronising to Morgan because he wasn't an American and faintly contemptuous of Telfs because he was but didn't dress like one.

" I got a tailor now in Athens who fixes me fine," he said, with a complacent glance at the knife-edged, stitched-in creases of his cinnamon-coloured trousers. " Well, maybe it's not Stateside, but it's the next best thing. So what if the guy charges plenty ? It's all investment, that's the way I reason it." He nodded sagely, although he made no attempt to explain the purpose of the investment.

He talked endlessly of the plumbing in the States and the lack of plumbing in Kalymnos and of the Kalymnian tailors who couldn't run up a sack to fit a bushel of flour.

" Thirty years in the States, sir, and an American citizen," he said proudly to Morgan. " Well, I guess it's what you're accustomed to."

" Nuts ! " said Telfs, and went out on deck.

Morgan stayed with Vraxos for another round of drinks, partly to compensate for his companion's rudeness, but held mostly by the odious fascination of the man. Vraxos kept lifting up his glass and saying " God bless America " and " God bless Australia," but he still pronounced it " Afstraleea." He had been born in Kalymnos, he explained to Morgan, and he had gone back there to live on his American pension, and now he was looking around for a wife.

" It's got to be something young for me," he said, leering. " Sixteen, maybe. That's when they're lush, that's when the bitches can open you out, make you feel young again."

They came to Kalymnos through the light before dawn, pale and grey as an oyster shell, with a yellow smudge behind the black outline of Kós and the morning star hanging like a lantern over the peaks of Oromedhon. The passengers going on to Kós and Rhodes were still asleep, wrapped in their blankets, sprawled in the tangerine peelings and the scraps of soggy newspaper and the caked vomit of the scuppers.

At the anchorage the water had a strange deep blueness, and, looking down from the railing, Morgan could see the sand pattern and the bleached rocks with the black fish flicking above them, and for half an hour he stayed with Telfs watching them unload the freight—sacks of Porto Rican sugar and Canadian flour and empty fish boxes returned from Piræus—watching the Kalymnians in their jerseys and black caps manhandling the crates and sacks into a broad-beamed caique with a great curving prow, high and black.

On the end of the breakwater the red eye of the lighthouse blinked improbably against the paling colours of the town. Beyond the breakwater the masts of fishing craft and sponge boats stood like a forest of young pines.

" Well, there it is," Telfs said.

" It's wonderful," Morgan could see the first patches of sunlight on the rough high edges of the mountains, huge, bare mountains, all rocks and sage patches scarred by the reddish gashes of precipices. Below the cliffs the town huddled, close to the edge of the sea that gave it life and reason. It looked like a kid's painting of a town, the sort of painting they would put up in exhibitions of child art to illustrate the perceptiveness of the young mind before some damn-fool teacher came along to strangle it with convention. Cubes of different colours, crazy colours, wonderful colours, not laid on flat and clear but all washed out into streaks and blotches, like an amateur's water-colour—bright blues and pinks and very pale blues like the faded eyes of old fishermen, and yellow and orange and grey and white and green—all piled on top of one another, with the rugs hanging vivid and gay from the balconies.

A town in abstract : toy blocks with little square windows ruled in white, spread between the rock wall of the mountains and the harbour, green as a jewel and shining in the sun.

Morgan had a curious sense of *arrival*, of reaching something that possessed a special significance, of coming to a particular point in his life that had already been established and fixed im-mutably. Not a home-coming, for the town seemed strange to him and alien and like no other town he had ever seen before. More an awareness that here in Kalymnos there was something awaiting him, something yet to be disclosed.

" It's not at all like what I had expected," he said softly. " And yet it's exactly right—and so much more."

" The feeling you've been here before ? " said Telfs. " It was what I had."

"No. Not like that. Nothing like that. Just that it seems important somehow. I've been reading about it. They say it was the grandsons of Hercules who took the ships out of here to go to Troy."

" The thirty hollow ships from Kós and the Kalymnian Isles." Telf grinned. " Take my advice and don't get yourself all balled up with a sense of reverence. It won't do you any good. It doesn't mean anything. Not here. It's only the *now* that counts. Well, I guess it's time for you to go ashore. The baggage is on. I'll come over from Kós in a day or two to see how you're settling in. I'll be seeing lots of you—I get over pretty often."

Going ashore in the boat, Morgan sat next to Homer Vraxos, smart as paint in a new gaberdine raincoat, but no longer talkative.

" It's a pretty town," Morgan said, as the boat rounded the breakwater.

" It's a dump," Vraxos said sourly. " You'll see, brother ! "

In the little yellow house on the quay, above the sponge room, Morgan Leigh unpacked his bags and set out his books on the window ledge, and twenty round-eyed children came crowding up the tunnel of the stairs to watch him.

It was on the afternoon of that first day that Paul Pelacos called.

There was no rap at the door, no formal invitation, nothing but a soft discreet cough from the doorway of the big room. He looked across to see, smiling at him, a tall, slender man, handsome, in age somewhere in his middle fifties, very correctly dressed in a dark suit and wearing a raincoat with that air of assured negligence that spoke of other coats at home, other raincoats.

" You must forgive the intrusion," he said. His English was as faultless as his apparel. " My name is Pelacos. I heard you had come in the *Karaiskakis*, and I have taken the liberty of calling. To offer you a welcome to Kalymnos." The smile flashed again in his dark, well-cared-for face.

" Why, thank you. It's very good of you."

" That is the first of my reasons, to welcome you. The second, to see if there is any way in which I can be of help to you. The third, to invite you to have coffee with me."

" I'd enjoy some coffee very much. As for the other, I think everything is fine. For the moment I don't imagine——"

" Ah, the room is pleasant, yes, but sparsely furnished, I think." Pelacos surveyed the apartment earnestly. " Hanging space for your clothes, for example. You will need that. And there will be other things, of course. Yes, I shall see to it. If there is anything you want, please let me know."

" But there's no need, really. You're much too kind. I can——"

" It is a tradition with Kalymnians that the stranger should be made to feel at home. Hospitality has always been the first law of Greece." Pelacos smiled. " Come, there is a quite pleasant café just along the harbour front where we can take coffee and talk."

Paul Pelacos wore his attributes rather as he wore his raincoat, with a nonchalance that suggested adequate reserves of all his qualities : his charm, his obvious breeding, his wealth, his standing. When he said, " My family has always lived on Kalymnos," the image that sprang to Morgan's mind was not of a sponge merchant with muttonchop whiskers, but of a Paul Pelacos with pointed beard and shield and plumed helmet and bronze greaves on his legs, sailing off in an open galley to Troy.

" My great-grandfather," said Pelacos, " was a merchant in London, in Cripplegate." And behind the great-grandfather was ranged a host of shadowy Kalymnian ancestors, trading with the Turks and the Frankish pirates and the knights of the Crusades, sailing off to Byzantium and invoicing figs and dates from Smyrna.

" So you are here to write about us, Mr. Leigh." Pelacos nodded and smiled. " I had an uncle who was a writer. Only in Greek, of course. He was never translated. I imagine it was just as well—it always seemed to me that his talent was no match for his literary exuberance. A prolix man, with an imagination of the most florid character. At Oxford I dabbled myself a little . . . a piece or two for *Isis*, an occasional offering to the fortnightlies. At one time I thought . . ." He shrugged. " Then my father died and there were all the responsibilities of our company here and in London, our agencies, our fleet of sponge boats. . . ."

While he talked his hands were never still, graceful hands, beautifully kept. The right hand decorated his conversation with a series of precise, formal gestures ; the left hand twirled a thin gold key chain.

" If you are to write about Kalymnos," he continued, " you will need a valedictory pen. There is nothing to be composed now but our epitaph. Kalymnos is dying. A lingering death but a comparatively peaceful one. No death throes, no wild paroxysms."

" Yes, that's what I understand," Morgan said. " It doesn't really seem possible, although it is what Telfs told me."

" Ah, Telfs ! You know the doctor then ? "

" Doctor ? "

" Why, yes." Pelacos seemed surprised. His finger on the

key chain was suddenly still. " But did you not know ? He is a doctor, and, indeed, a very accomplished one. I cannot understand why he does not practise."

" He never told me."

Pelacos laughed softly. " He is not the most communicative of men. Except when he takes rather too much retzina—we have an excellent retzina here, by the way—and then he can become quite garrulous, and profoundly entertaining, I must admit. I should like to see much more of him. A pity he chooses to live at Kós, rather than here. Being a medical man, he prefers, I imagine, the island of Hippocrates. It would have more meaning for him."

" I understand he comes over here quite frequently," Morgan said.

" He does, yes. He takes a particular interest in a crippled child who lives up behind the big church, the son of a poor woman, a widow. Mina Vraxos."

" Vraxos ? There was a man on the ship coming down from Piræus. Homer Vraxos."

" Her brother-in-law. You will find, I believe, they are not very friendly towards each other. But one day you will meet Manoli and you will understand. His boats are out at the moment, diving off Crete."

" And who is Manoli ? "

Pelacos bent his head and studied the thin gold chain held tautly between his fingertips. He seemed to be laughing silently.

" Ah, you will meet Manoli," he said. He looked up. " Now let me tell you of the defeat of Kalymnos. One needs an outlook slightly morbid to appreciate it, but it is, I think, an interesting story."

There was still warmth in the late autumn sun, and the afternoon had that special quality of beauty that only the Ægean possesses. Light seemed to come upwards from the sea, lifting the islands into the pale air so that they appeared to float upon the water. Far across the strait the mountains of Kós were capped with ribbons of light cloud ; offshore a line of fishing boats showed their pointed red sails like the wings of exotic birds.

"There is a very curious irony in our defeat," said Pelacos quietly. "We have been a tenacious people for over three thousand years, and nothing has been able to dislodge us—no force, no brutality, no suffering, although we have known all three in full measure. I am astonished sometimes when I think of all those who have come here—here, to this simple little seaport. The Carians, and the Dorian men with their rule of iron. Medes and Persians, Greeks, Macedonians, Romans. The Franks and Turks, Venetians, Genoese, the Crusaders. More recently, and with more refined brutalities, the Italians, the Germans." Pelacos paused, staring down at his key chain, fingering it interestedly, as if he had just realised he possessed it. "All these," he went on, "came to us with violence and strength. Ironically, it was a peaceful man who defeated us, a chemist, an industrial chemist, working somewhere. Does it really matter where? The United States possibly. France? In a laboratory somewhere a man created a sponge out of his retorts and test tubes. He defeated us."

"But you are wealthy, and you are in the sponge trade. Your ships still go out."

"Of course. But my family has always been in Kalymnos and naturally we shall stay." He smiled dryly. "The winter climate here is excellent. Much better than Athens. Or London. It would always be a pleasant thing to have a villa in Kalymnos for the winters."

A gang of men was unloading big baskets of mandarins from a white caique berthed at the centre quay.

"From Vathý," said Pelacos. "It is the only part of the island where there is land capable of any substantial cultivation. The rest, as you see"—his gesture encompassed the bare, grim mountains overhanging the town—"is rock. Arid rock. The rock behind us, the sea around us, nothing else. When my father was alive there were thirty thousand people living on this island. A simple people, but prosperous and happy. To-day there are not fourteen thousand people and there is much poverty and unhappiness. Many people are poor. They do not have enough to eat. All of them are desperate to go away—to your country, Mr. Leigh, to the United States, to Canada. To the

new countries, the young countries, where there is hope for
them."

Telfs had said it with a sort of hostile fury. Pelacos spoke
of it without emotion, looking at the problem in abstract,
accepting it as a fixed natural law that something should be born,
should flourish, grow old, die. The inevitable self-destruction
that was latent within all growth.

". . . could counter it with economics, I suppose," Pelacos
was saying. " The natural sponge is still better than the synthetic,
and if we could market our sponges at a cheaper price . . ."
He stretched out his hands, fingers spread. " But how can we ?
How can we, when men must go down to the bed of the sea
and pluck out each sponge, one by one, with their own hands ?
Each year it grows more expensive. Now it costs a thousand
pounds for a licence to dive off Cyrenaica. All the time expenses
are going up. It is only a matter of time, a few years perhaps,
before the industry is dead." He smiled. " More coffee, Mr.
Leigh ? Or perhaps something to drink ? Cognac ? I cannot,
I am afraid, wholeheartedly recommend the *ouzo*."

" Thank you." Morgan shook his head. " I don't really care
for anything more. I'm very grateful to you, and I hope that——"

Pelacos waved a deprecating hand, and almost immediately
excused himself. Morgan watched him cross the street to where
a slight, dark young woman was talking to an old lady in black
shawl and skirt. Pelacos walked as he talked, with an assured
grace, still twirling the gold key chain round and round the
index finger of his left hand. After a few minutes he returned
to the table, smiling, the young woman accompanying him.

" Mr. Leigh," he said, " this is my daughter Irini."

He spoke warmly, and with affection ; in spite of this Morgan
could not help feeling that there must be many more daughters
at home, equally beautiful. " Irini is twenty-three," said Pelacos.
" She lived in London for many, many years." By mentioning
his daughter's age Pelacos, for the first time in the conversation,
had undeniably revealed himself as Greek. " She will be able to
explain much to you about Kalymnos. She loves the place even
more, if it is possible, than I myself do."

" How do you do, Miss Pelacos." Morgan smiled down

at her. She was very small, very trim, with cropped black hair and quick dark eyes, more French in appearance than Grecian. She seemed inappropriate, somehow, among the black-shawled women of Kalymnos; it was easier to imagine her in tight-ankled trousers and a black sweater in the bright streets of Paris, near the Sorbonne. " You might have quite a task explaining things to me," he went on. " Everything here is completely new to me."

" But you are not new to Greece ? " she said.

" No, not to Greece. But this is different. Different and new—and rather wonderful."

" It would please me very much if I could help," she said shyly. Her voice was soft, like a child's, at variance with the sophistication of her appearance; her eyes, too, were the eyes of a child. It would be easy, he thought, to delight her . . . and as easy to hurt her.

Again he had the feeling, the feeling that had come to him at dawn on the deck of the *Karaiskakis*, that there was some special significance about his coming to Kalymnos.

2

TONY THAKLIOS opened his eyes cautiously, chubby pink finger-tips rubbing his temples to see whether the retzina of the night before had left him with a two-aspirin or a three-aspirin headache, and when he had satisfied himself about this his left hand groped beneath the pink pillow to make sure that the leatherbound lexicon was still there. The lexicon, his American passport, and his wife Calliope were, in that precise order of importance, Tony Thaklios' most treasured possessions.

The lexicon was safe beneath the pink pillow, his wife Calliope slept soundly beside him, the passport was secure in the safe in the small shop below the house. And it was only a two-aspirin headache. He glanced tenderly at the sleeping woman, smiled to himself, and climbed from the big built-in bed. He went to the side wall first, the pink wall with the family portraits in thick frames and the coloured picture of Miami, and crossed himself and kissed the little icon of Saint Anthony, and then, walking on tiptoes against the chill of the tiled floor, he moved to the window and opened the shutters. The light that filtered in, grey and cold, appeared to flow towards him from the quiet harbour below. It was light in the process of formation, compounded as much from the starry night as from approaching day. Along the sea wall the sleeping caiques waited, motionless, all their bright colours subdued; the row of high, imperiously curved prows pointed to the hills of Kós, behind which the sun would rise.

About the boats there was a sense of . . . a sense of . . . ? Tony Thaklios frowned. Again the word had eluded him. On the very tip of his tongue, and now—Jesus Christ! Could he *think* of it? Frowning and muttering, he tiptoed back to the bed for the lexicon and brought it to the window. For a long time he fingered through the pages, pausing at intervals to seek inspiration from the unco-operative sky, and then suddenly: " God damn! " he said, his round face irradiated by triumph. " *Expectancy!* " About the boats there was a sense of expectancy.

With a firm tread now he returned to the bed, stowed the lexicon beneath the pink pillow and took up his stub of pencil. Very carefully he printed the word *expectancy* on the white wall, among all the other hundreds of disconnected English words written there, the words that had eluded him. " *Expectancy,*" he said, studying his pencilling with pride, and then he went back to the window to watch Kalymnos awaken.

It was a habit he had acquired in Georgia and Florida, and now there was no hangover powerful enough to deny him the pleasure of his sunrises, of watching the daily rebirth of the town's activities. In all the years he had lived in America he had thought of coming back some time to Kalymnos, to the place of his birth, and watching the town awaken to its days. Now that he was here with Calliope and the little shop with the spools of thread and envelopes and writing paper and kids' toys and general merchandise, he was not to be denied it. With Calliope and the shop and his pension and a little interest in sponge buying, with his retzina in the *tavernas* at night and his sunrises in the mornings, he was a pretty happy man. Particularly the sunrises, the awakenings. They gave him a gratifying sense of omniscience. *Omniscience.* He smiled as he rolled the word around his mind comfortably. It had eluded him for a long, long time, longer than any other word, but now it was there in bold pencilled capitals right above the corner post of the bed.

Omniscient and happy, his headache forgotten, Tony Thaklios leaned his elbows on the window sill, breathing the cold, clean morning air, watching his world come alive.

There was always a dark furtiveness about the first movements —a stirring of the cats around the bakery along the street and old Beanie shuffling along beside Saint Christos to unlock the market gates, old Beanie with pieces of hessian sacking wrapped around inside his shirt to keep the cold out, but always with a smile as he said *Kalimera* as if each day were a joy to him.

And always before dawn there were the fishing boats coming in, seven or eight of them coming in a long line from the black cliff of Point Cali with their engines throttled down to a slow, sleepy beat that seemed like the pulse of the morning.

George, fumbling for the padlock on the door of Vassilis' dark little tailor shop near the Customs House, heard the slow *thud thud thud* of the boat engines, and it made him think of fish— huge platters of golden pink *barbunia*, soaking in oil, the sort of fish he used to catch by the basketful when he was younger, before his eyesight had begun to fail.

Well, if old Vassilis stuck to his promise of the night before, when he had been benevolent over his bottle of *strega*, there would be a few extra pennies each day, and he would be able to buy a kilo of two of *barbunia*, perhaps three, for himself and Maria.

It was very dark inside the shop. He had to feel his way around to take the cloth covers off the three big sewing machines and lay out the threads and the buckram and the ironing blocks and Vassilis' own piece of thin blue chalk, and he barked his shin against the bench leg trying to find the charcoal to put in the big pressing iron.

It was too dark for him to see the framed pictures on the wall of King Paul and Queen Frederika or even clearly to make out the white calendar of the Nomikos Line. He was very much attached to the calendar and at the end of the year, when it could be of no further use, he would ask Vassilis if he could have it for his own wall. Often he would stare at it when the bright sunlight would come in through the doorway of the shop, for then he could pick out every detail of the picture of the blue and white ship sailing past an island with palm trees growing.

Vassilis, he felt sure, would give it to him. Never having been to sea, Vassilis had no particular interest in it except to mark the dates by, whereas he as a young man had sailed twice to Cardiff as a fireman.

When you came to think of it, in spite of his meanness with money, Vassilis had been very kind to him, giving him work when his eyes were so poor : just the cleaning up and tacking and looking after the irons, admittedly, but this was very considerate when you realised that somebody had to thread his needles for him when he was tacking. Oh, Vassilis would give him the calendar all right, no doubt of that.

From the bake-house in the lane behind the *Rapseion* he could hear the clink of the coke rake against the bricks, and old Dimitri coughing and hawking as if his guts would come up—he always complained of the phlegm in the mornings—and there was a warm smell of bread on the air.

By this time Maria would be getting her breakfast, a thick slice of the day before yesterday's bread dipped in olive oil and sprinkled with sugar. If Vassilis kept his promise there would be a whole round loaf of new bread as well as the *barbunia*.

And soon Manoli would be back from Crete, and there would be warm times again : endless games of *belota* in the coffee-houses at night, and retzina and singing.

George began to sing softly to himself as he fumbled in the charcoal basket, feeling for the small pieces that would start well.

The room of Homer Vraxos was quite dark, for the shutters were drawn and bolted. Two mice gnawed and scratched in the crusts and litter in the corner beneath the rack where the new clothes hung in their creases.

In a pair of soiled Sea Island pyjamas with a floral pattern Homer Vraxos slept, and dreamed of a girl who had come to him naked as the day she was born : a girl with great, thick braids of hair and her young breasts assertive, and as she came towards him she smiled and the palms of her hands rubbed up and down against her flanks.

A very young girl, a virgin. Homer Vraxos stirred in his sleep and sighed, and from beneath the bed coverings his hands came reaching for her, old yellow hands, puffy and short-fingered and adorned with thick gold rings, hands that reached up and clenched orgasmically. She came down on top of him, the whole length of his body, warm and eager, and he could feel her hair against him. Over in the dark corner beneath the new suits the mice nibbled.

Christos dreamed, too, but his was a waking dream, for he was up and limping around the dark cellar of his room, down in the basement below where Vraxos slept. He had heard the slow thud of the boat engines growing louder.

The winter to pass, and then the spring would come and the boats would be out again, and Christos with them.

Yes, his legs were bent and twisted, and they smiled at the way he pushed himself around the town on his sticks, but was there any among the supple, straight-limbed boys who could dive as well ? Save Manoli, was there any living man among them who could dive as well ?

And even Manoli . . . Could Manoli himself have done what he, Christos Papagalos, had done that summer day off Benghazi ? That unforgettable summer day with the sponge boats circling on tight helms through the oil-smooth water. Eighty-two metres the first dive—eighty-two metres, by Jesus, and measured to the centimetre ! Down into the blackness at the very limit of the air pipe. And then down again for the second dive at seventy-six metres, knowing the dog-fish were there. And old Kret the *colazaris*, who had charge of the gear and the boat and who fished the divers up, trying to take off the helmet, pleading with him not to make the third dive ; and down once more to seventy-nine metres with the big shark grazing the rubber of his suit, and the prayers going up with the air bubbles to Saint Stephanos !

By Jesus, he had been the *pallikari* that day ! All that night, in the big ship with the other divers, they had cried his name and drunk retzina until they saw the sun come up, hot as fire behind the red cliffs of Libya.

Over the slow jet of the paraffin stove Christos heated the water for his sops. His was a small room—with arms outstretched and the walking stick in his hand he could reach from one wall to the other—but it was tidy and very clean. There was not much in it to become untidy : the flat shelf of his bed and the cooking ledge and the painted cupboard and two chairs, and on the wall the bright little picture of Saint Stephanos, his patron saint, the patron saint of all divers.

They still talked of it, even though seventeen years had passed, and whenever some stranger asked, " How deep can the divers go and live ? " they would always say " Seventy-two metres is the limit." " For a *good* diver, seventy-two metres," they would say, and then they would always pause, holding the drama of it, and add, " But there was one man, many years ago . . ." And they would tell of the three great dives of Christos Papagalos.

It was ironical that the paralysis which had twisted his legs like the branches of a thorn tree had come to him in a dive that any stripling could have done, no more than forty-five lousy metres, off the reefs near Patmos. There was no accounting for it. All through the months in the hospital, lying awake at night, he had tried to reason it out, and he had prayed to Saint Stephanos for enlightenment. But there was no accounting for it.

Christos poured the steaming water into the earthenware bowl and broke the sale bread into it and sprinkled some sesame seed. The sesame seed was good for his voice, and without a fine, robust voice he might find it difficult to live through the winter.

For Christos Papagalos, in the months of winter when the

town was full, was the newspaper of Kalymnos. On most days he would go through all the streets, the big streets planted with trees and the twisty little up-and-down streets with their brightly painted houses, and he would cry the news of the things that interested the townspeople : the opening of a new shop or the bargains in an old one, the announcement of a wedding, the times the ships would be arriving from Rhodes or Piræus. Nothing from the outside world, nothing except that which might interest the people.

To-day he would be announcing the opening of the new shop of old Halludis, and all day he would be going through the town, very slowly on his two sticks, draped like some Oriental prince with embroidered lengths and tablecloths and ladies' jumpers and blouses, and all the women in their black head scarves would come up to finger the things.

Christos carefully poured a few more sesame seeds into the cup of his hand and sprinkled them into the sops.

By the time Christos had completed his breakfast and laced his boots tightly, a considerable stirring had begun to manifest itself along the whole length of the front street, and although few shutters had yet been pushed back there were curls of smoke from many chimneys, and among the shadows lights had begun to appear here and there.

The shawled women had begun to come out, soft-walking and difficult to see in their black, going to the wells and the public taps with their pitchers to fill.

The small boys were coming out, too, some waiting by the bakeries to fill their trays with bread rolls and sugar cakes, and others along the fishing wharf, down near the edge of the water, slapping octopus against the stone slabs. And the harbour had begun to stir, with the fishing boats unloading at the market wharf and over at the breakwater a long grey schooner from Amorgos warping in with a deck load of firewood. The men were also beginning to come down from the side streets, men in sea boots and blue jerseys and peaked caps, dark figures moving along beneath the salt trees, going to the boats.

It had rained in the night and the air was still damp. Old

Mike Grassis, who had slept in his clothes and boots because the fever was at him again, could feel in his bones every one of his sixty-six years. Ah, if only he could find some English aspirin he could fix it in no time at all and he would feel fine again. . . .

While he waited for Johnnie and Anna to come he went around to the bakery furnace and collected from the ovens the pastries he had made up the night before—*pastaflora* and *galatobouriko* and *baklava*. And the English cake ! Very carefully he carried them back to his house and set them out on the table, the English cake separate from the others on a small, clean square of white paper.

The urge to make the English cake had come to him the night before while he was tramping from *taverna* to *taverna*, from coffee-house to coffee-house with his box of pastries and feeling the damp night crawling into his bones.

Always when he was aware of the fever coming on he found himself thinking of the thirty years he had spent as a galley boy and steward on the big ships. Singapore and Durban and Halifax and Seattle he would think of, but mostly of Liverpool and Bristol and the English cakes. And if he had an egg or two he would always stay up late when he came home, mixing up an English cake for himself. If he could only get yeast now, the real yeast in the little brown cakes. . . .

The door banged open, and there were the children, Anna and Johnnie, their eyes wide with surprise as if this were something they were doing for the first time. The old man, playing the role that was expected of him, scowled fiercely and waved them away. The boy grinned, but his sister took a slow step forward, her eyes dark and hungry on the English cake.

" Yes, yes, it is for me," said Mike complacently. " Too rich for children. Fresh from the oven. Come, smell it, both of you."

The children approached it with an air of reverence, that proper show of respect and admiration which the timeless experience of childhood had taught them was both expected and profitable.

" Nice, eh ? " said Mike proudly. " An English cake. Very special. Closer now, both of you. Smell it. Anna ? "

The little girl nodded solemnly. " It is much better than the last one, *Kérios*," she said earnestly. " It smells better. And it is much, *much* higher."

Mike nodded contentedly. " Johnnie ? "

Johnnie closed his eyes and smiled as if at some ecstatic vision. And then he sighed.

The old man lifted a warning finger. " Ah, no tricks, now ! It is for me, you understand, for *me*. And I know. Oh yes, my little friends, I *know*. Give you one slice and you will eat it all. Not a crumb for poor old Mike. Not a crumb ! "

" No, no, no ! " Their protest was emphatic, but their eyes were shining, knowing that the victory was already won, as it was won every morning. To-day there was a special savour in the victory, a particular triumph, for it was the English cake.

The old man took the big sharp knife from the cuboard and cut the thick slices with great care, grumbling all the while, and then he sat back to watch the faces of the children. For two years now they had been coming to him and although he seldom saw them except for these few minutes each morning the daily visitation somehow filled the void that Themolena had left. His wife had been a very stout woman—the years since her death had dimmed the memory of how cantankerous she had been—and she had filled the little house with her presence. The passing of a woman so big had left much space behind, much emptiness. Johnnie and Anna had helped to fill it.

When the English cake, to the last crumb, had gone Mike sent the children away to get themselves ready for school, and into the bottom of the glass box with the blue metal edges, a box just big enough to be carried beneath his arm, he placed clean white paper and packed the round rosettes of the *pastaflora* and the *galatobouriko* and *baklava*.

The sea tang was rising in the air and with it a rich mingling of other smells : fish, coffee, burning charcoal, warm bread, oranges. The mountains of Kós were still dark and opaque but

above their summits there was a flush of pink and gold and much
higher in the sky the blue had appeared, a blue so deep that its
substance seemed more than air.

The sun came suddenly, blazing above Kós, and its light
struck the top edges of the Kalymnian mountains and spilled
in a flood of gold down the rocky slopes above the town, marking out the white walls of the cemetery and the dark-blue dome
of Saint Vassilias, warming the bright walls of the uppermost
houses terraced beneath the cliffs.

The flood of sunshine awakened Mina Vraxos. She dressed
and went down the outside steps to the shelf where the water
pitcher stood and the great earthenware bowl. She washed in
the cold water, with the sun warming her, and brushed her hair
and then went into the kitchen to heat the water for Nikolas.
It took only a moment or two to start the fire in the little grate :
a scrap of sponge soaked in paraffin and set alight and the lumps
of charcoal piled around it. Through the window she could
see her father Stavros in the garden near the young trees. Behind him, and below, was all of Kalymnos.

Planted firmly on its rock ledge on the orange-coloured
hillside, the house of Mina Vraxos was two simple cubes of
brick, the smaller superimposed upon the larger. It was a
pretty house with pink shutters and a jasmine tree in a tiny
courtyard, and the walls and steps washed with a very pale
blue, and there were a covered well painted green and a small
garden with herbs growing and radishes. From the windows,
small squares cut out of the thick stone, it commanded a prospect
of all the town below.

First there was the rough tumble-away of clay and stone
patches, and then the geometric pattern of the town, all seen
from above, only in the shape of its planes : close at hand the
oblongs of vivid green, where the thin grass grew on flat rooftops, ending at the high white wall that prevented the scattered
poorer houses of the upper levels from tumbling into the narrow
streets below. Underneath the sheltering wall the main town
huddled, a long, multicoloured crescent fanning around the curve
of the bay, all the houses precisely shaped and absurdly bright,
like the separate sections of a patch-work quilt. The houses

ended abruptly at the line of salt trees, looking like a tasselled green fringe to the quilt.

Behind the house were rocky slopes of weeds and thistles and wild thyme, providing frugal forage for a flock of skinny goats and innumerable quick-pecking fowls, and there was a single black pig tethered to a stake. Much of the sparse pasture was scoured away by jagged watercourses where torrents rolled the stones down when the rains were heavy. From the limits of this pasture an immense precipice reached into the sky.

The harsh cruelty of the background was softened a little by the fifteen young trees which Stavros had planted two years before and which now stood as high as Mina's shoulder. Two of the trees had been planted close together so that one day they might support a hammock for Nikolas, a larger hammock than the one he slept in now, made of canvas and notched slats and slung from the ceiling beams over the bed in the kitchen where Stavros slept.

While the oil for the fish heated in the pan, Mina went to the pink-painted window ledge to slice the bread. In the sun all the sea was shining and she could see the islands: Plateia, and Pserimos with its ragged cliffs, and Kós stretching the whole length of the skyline, and far away, pale in the morning, the lumpy mountains of Nissiros.

The glimpse of Nissiros in the mornings was always something that gave her a particular pleasure; somehow it had a different look from other islands. Was it not logical to think that it offered something that was not the same? Something different? Something better?

Sometimes when she climbed on the hills above the house, scrambling along the rough ridges behind the convent, the same feeling would come to her, for then, if the day was clear, she might see far in the distance the dim shape of Astypalaia like a picture in a dream. This, too, had the special magic for her, the magic of invitation, calling her.

But she would always turn back after seeing Astypalaia, because if she climbed higher she would be able to see the dark snout of Leros jutting out into the sea and the memory would come back again of that terrible day when all the bells had rung. . . .

Stavros was loosening the earth around the roots of one of the young trees, jabbing with a pointed stick and flicking the white pebbles away.

" Come ! " she called to him. " It is time for Nikolas."

When he looked across to her she was frightened again by the thing in his face, that bitter darkness that no longer merely reflected some passing mood but which had become a part of him, permanent and ineradicable. It was talking to the others that did it—talking to Dimitri and George and Gregory, talking to the others and watching mad Stephanos and growing old and knowing there was no end to it. Yet would the look have been there had she been a son instead of a daughter ? Or a wife ? Or anything but a widow ? There was no end to it for her, either, no end to it for all of them. . . .

Together they wakened Nikolas and carried him to the chair and laced his boots on, and even Stavros seemed cheerful as the boy joked about a dream he had had, a dream of flying across the tops of the mountains, all the way to Vathý.

" You must stop talking and eat your food," she said, smiling at him. " Or you will be late again for school. I will come down with you this morning. I must go to the market."

Her father's face darkened. " They will be ringing the bells to-day," he said ominously. " The bells. Ringing to Saint Stephanos. I did not tell you last night when I came back. There was another one."

" Who ? " Her voice was sharp, with pain in it. " Who ? Manoli ? Not Manoli ? "

Stavros smiled faintly. " How could Manoli die ? Besides, he is around Crete. This was Leros again."

" Again ? Like Paul ? "

He nodded. " Like Paul. The same. That big swell coming off the Anatolian reefs. Up and down, up and down." His thin knotted hands lifted slowly, as a sea lifts. " I suppose a chafing. The air pipe pulled away. Forty metres. Or forty-two. Nothing to speak of." He shrugged.

" Who ? "

"Dimitriadi's boy. Apostoli. The boy who came here at Easter, the one with the curly hair. A nice lad."

"Why?" she said. She could feel the anger and the hate clawing at her. "Why do they go at this time of the year at all? *Why?* It is so cold and they can do little, and the few sponges they bring back, what are they worth?"

"Apostoli," he said. "They are worth Apostoli if the price is good. And the price is good."

She looked away. Easter, and all the flowers and the shy boy with the curly hair who had brought the almonds for her. "When his mother was here," she said softly, "she told me that he would go next summer with the men, with all the boats, to Egypt and to Libya. And I thought how young he was. He was to go next summer."

"Well," said Stavros, "it seems now that he will not," and he rubbed his hands together, cracking the knuckles.

"They go now, when the weather is bad," she said fiercely, "because they are mad, stupid! They make their money in the summer and they come back and it is all gone. Poof! Gone on gambling and retzina. And then they have to go out in the wrong time of the year to try to make more money to get their names out of the shopkeepers' books for the bread and the oil and the scraps their wives and children have to eat. Bah, they make me angry! And three weeks ago, only three weeks ago, it was Constantine. Yes, Constantine. Pulled up dead, black in the face and dead, off Patmos."

"Like Paul," he said quietly, needing to be cruel to check her, needing to be cruel because his love for her was so deep.

"Yes," she said bitterly. "Like Paul." Like all of them. Paul, and his father before him, and Apostoli and Constantine. Or like Stavros, her own father, with his chest ruined and his body all twisted, and nothing for him to do but hawk his paltry baskets of fish around the streets. And one day it would be Manoli. One day they would come to tell her of Manoli as they had come two years ago to tell her of her own husband, when they had taken Paul's photograph to the church and all through the day the bells had rung, clashing and clanging until she had thought herself mad.

"Manoli gambles and outdrinks any ten men in the town," said Stavros, "and is he not away now, taking his boats out in the bad months? Is he stupid, too, like the rest of them? Does Manoli go because he is in need of money, or hungry for it? That's the way I would like to be stupid and hungry, owning five boats and not giving a damn for any man alive."

"Manoli is different," she said.

Stavros crumbled the bread between his fingers. "All men become the same in that life," he said. In his bruised, tired eyes the bitterness smouldered, but his voice was quiet. "All of them. Manoli too. You wait and see. Now he is lucky. Yes, for a long time he has been lucky. One day, maybe, he will not be lucky." Stavros hoped it would not happen to Manoli, but he remembered when his own luck had changed, that summer when Petros had drowned and his brother Giorgios had cut the throat of Vassilis Antoninous, the *colazaris*, in the night off Tripoli. "It does bad things to men, Mina," he said, "that six months at sea. Sixteen men in a boat nine metres long, living like animals, and never a foot on land unless to bury somebody in a grave of sand at Derna or Tobruk." He looked at her. "Do I have to tell you? Your grandfather was a diver, your father after him, your husband. And the boy here," he glanced affectionately at Nikolas, "when his legs are mended he will be a diver too—eh, Nikolas? The greatest *skafendro* of all of them, eh?"

Neither he nor Mina spoke to each other of what Doctor Telfs had told them: better to talk of the day when the boy was older, when perhaps . . .

"I tell you I will not hear the bells." His daughter's voice was subdued, but the anger was still there, and the fear and hate. "I can come back and go on the hills where I cannot hear them."

He shrugged. "They will still ring in your head," he said. "Come. The boy must go to school."

They went down the hill together. Stavros carried the boy in his arms over the steep, rocky part, where the pebbles gave an insecure foothold, and did not put him down until they came to the path by the wall that circled the lower town.

Mina walked behind them, tying the clean white scarf over her dark hair and then across her chin so that only the tawny oval of her face showed.

At the top of the curving flight of steps that dropped away between the coloured houses she waited with her father while the boy went down. He preferred to do the steps on his own. One hand against the retaining wall, he wrenched his small, thin body from side to side so that each of the withered, ironed legs could be placed securely on the step below before the meagre weight of his body went on it. When he came to the first wide landing he turned and waved up at them, smiling.

" Let him go all the way," said Stavros. " See how he does it ? Much easier than a month ago."

" Yes," Mina said composedly. There was no expression on her face as she shared the lie with her father. There was no difference in the way Nikolas was doing it. No difference at all. Nor any difference in the pain of watching it.

" When does Doctor Telfs come again to Kalymnos ? " Stavros' eyes followed the lurching figure of the child.

" Perhaps next week. He has been in Athens. He had to talk to a man."

" About Nikolas ? "

" He did not say. He will tell us when he comes."

" He is a good man," said Stavros.

Mina did not reply. Her father was aware of her feelings : words could not deepen her gratitude nor add expression to what she felt for the American. Words were for the times when she clambered to the hilltop and walked along to the edge of the cliff where the half-ruined chapel of Saint Peter overlooked the sea and the islands. There on the white walls, faded and almost obliterated by the damp, were the old paintings of the saints, paintings so old and so strange that people could no longer remember when they had been done. On one of the pictures the name had been erased, but the face was still there, peering from the mildew and the cracked plaster. She had come to think of it as the face of Telfs : it had the same strangeness, the same compassion and ferocity, although the likeness perhaps was not anything real at all, only something in her mind. . . .

" Come," said Stavros. " The boy will be down now, and waiting."

As they went together down the steps, the morning sunlight poured through the town.

From the balcony of the yellow house by the quay, Morgan Leigh saw them come out of the narrow side street curling down the hill—the tall, graceful woman in the white head scarf and the old stooped man and the crippled child. He did not see the face of the woman ; it was the way she walked that attracted his attention. Among the walkers in the morning she was something separate, moving differently from the other women, with a grace and assurance that reminded him curiously of Paul Pelacos ; there was the same absoluteness about it, but something more too, something simple and uncultivated and beautiful. That was it. Pelacos was a cultivated growth, the product of attentive care, of selective breeding ; this woman possessed the pure quality of naturalness, of belonging to the earth and growing from it like a flower on the hillside.

" Maria ! " he called.

The old woman had been cooking for Morgan and doing his cleaning and carrying water from the well behind the barber's shop since he'd come to Kalymnos, just six days ago, though it seemed he'd belonged there a longer time. She looked up, set aside her brooms and bucket and, nodding and puffing, came out to him.

" Maria, who is she ? " he asked, pointing down. " There, with the lame boy."

The old woman peered, wrinkled her nose and sniffed. " Mina Vraxos," she said disapprovingly. " A poor woman. She lives on the hill. It is her son with her, and her father." She shook her head.

Mina Vraxos. He remembered what Pelacos had told him about Telf's interest in the crippled boy—*this* boy. He tried to pick them out again among the people sauntering along the quay, but he could no longer see them.

Half the town seemed to be out warming itself in the sun, and a crowd was gathering around the town crier, a big lame man propped on two twisty sticks, bent over to one side like an old lopped tree, gnarled and crooked, that has begun to grow again. He was hung with garish lengths of fabric and gaudy garments on wooden coat hangers. In a great, booming voice he proclaimed the merits of his wares, punctuating each announcement with sly badinage and bawdy comments that provoked gusts of laughter.

Maria chuckled, her great black-draped body quivering. " Ah, Christos," she said. " Christos Papagalos. The parrot, eh ? He always makes the big joke of everything. He is a long story, Christos ! "

It was ten o'clock when the bells of Saint Stephanos began to ring from the black-domed church below the hillside where the fishermen lived. But the bells rang not with the slow and intermittent tolling that might mark the death of the boy Apostoli, but with a quick excitable clangour that brought the men hurrying into the street from their *belota* tables and backgammon boards, and turned all the eyes of the town questioningly towards the church and then out beyond the breakwater to the glittering sea.

A small boy fishing by the cliffs had seen them first, coming in a line around Point Cali, and he had dropped his tackle and scrambled up the rocks so that it should be the bells of Saint Stephanos that might first herald the coming of the boats.

Now, as Morgan watched, the small boys were pelting past below his balcony, running fast, shouting to one another, elbowing and pommelling, laughing, sprinting towards the breakwater ; and from behind the house the big bells of Saint Nikolas added their wild peals to the brazen clangour of the morning.

There was no need to call for Maria. She was already beside him, panting with curiosity and excitement.

" What is it ? " he asked.

She squeezed herself into the corner of the balcony, peering out to sea and sniffing, as if she might smell the reason for the bells. And then she nodded.

" The boats," she said, pointing.

Four boats, coming towards the harbour entrance. Grey with the sea tiredness, they came fast, with licks of white leaping at their bows ; grey and white and sturdy against the rich blue of the sea and sky. A big two-master led with its black-patched sails spread to the south-east wind, and in a line behind her followed the three grey diving boats, the *aktaramathes*, with their flags flapping.

" Manoli," said Maria, and grinned. " Manoli is back." Her right hand made a quick circling gesture in front of her immense bosom. " Oh, *po-po-po-po-po-po !* " she chuckled. " Manoli ! "

3

THE FIRST picture Morgan ever had of Manoli was the one that always stayed most clearly in his mind : the true picture, the true Manoli.

He was on the afterdeck of one of the diving boats, the *Ikaros*, warping in towards the yelping pack of children on the quay. He leaned against the high arch of the tiller, his fist on the engine wheel—a strong, big man, dirty and unshaven, wearing sea boots and a blue jersey with the elbow out, and his shiny-peaked black cap pushed back on his head above the tangle of black hair and the broad, brown forehead. Between the thick beard and the thicker moustache his teeth were white as wave crests. They were strong, big teeth, like everything about him —strength and bigness, that was the picture of Manoli. His eyes were narrowed against the sun flash on the water as the boat came in slowly, stern first. Morgan could see the deep creases in the dark face, around the eyes like knife marks in walnut wood and running like scars down both sides of the unshaven face, the marks of tiredness and strain and hard living.

His eyes seemed to be searching for something, for somebody, among the crowd of kids and sailors and port officials ; he gave no regard whatever to the shouts and the waving and the screams of the children.

Because of this and because of the attitude of the crew also, all stooped over the ropes and gear, talking together in low voices, their eyes turned away, all very preoccupied by the pull of the wet ropes against the bitts—because of these things, a hush gradually fell on the waiting crowd. Even the children were quiet, expectant, sensing it.

" Why does Manoli come in the *aktaramas* and not in the captain's boat ? " Zeffis the harbour master spoke to the man beside him without looking at him, his eyes on the big two-master still circling slowly inside the harbour with a slow, soft thud of the engine, waiting to anchor. Zeffis knew the answer, but the asking of the question pushed it back for a minute or two, back there where the big boat circled.

The stern of the *Ikaros* touched the quay, and Manoli reached over and took the nearest boy by the neck of his jacket and lifted him across to the deck as if there were no weight in the child at all. And then he handed him a great sponge—as big as an elephant's ear and shaped like one—and pointed to the truck of the mast.

The boy grinned and went up the stays like a monkey and lashed the sponge there, right at the top where the blue and white flag was snapping in the cold wind.

When this was done Manoli shoved back the cabin scuttle with the heel of his hand and reached inside for a bundle of faded clothing wrapped around with marline, and with this beneath his arm he jumped ashore, pushing through the quiet, solemn-eyed crowd with only a nod here and there to the men who greeted him.

It was Zeffis who asked the question. The bundle of clothing had told him what had happened. It was for Zeffis, because of his position, to confront Manoli and ask the question.

" Who ? " he said.

" Costas," said Manoli. " Costas Gravos. The week before last, off Kouphonisi." He pointed to the big sponge which the boy had lashed to the masthead. " It was his sponge," he said. " It was still in his fist when we dragged him up."

And everyone looked up at the big brown sponge tied to the mast, as if they might find Costas Gravos there, looking down at them, smiling.

"They're coming now, the women," said Zeffis quietly, trying to remember whether Katina Gravos had six kids or seven.

Manoli nodded and pushed past him and went down alone to meet them. It was like Manoli to do it himself, thought Zeffis, to do it himself and not send one of the crew. Most captains would have stayed on the big boat until the women had come and gone.

The women were coming around the back of the Customs House as Manoli went down to meet them : nine women, all dressed the same in black shawls and long black skirts and two of them with their aprons clutched in their hands, not all coming together but spread out, walking for a few steps and then breaking into a trot and then walking again. Their shawls were flapping in the cold wind.

They all stopped when they saw Manoli and clustered around him, and the high, thin wailing scream was borne to the watchful crowd as eight of the women broke away and came running towards the boats.

The other woman had flung herself to the ground at Manoli's feet, screaming and tearing her clothes and clutching up handfuls of dirt and throwing it on her hair ; and Manoli stood above her like a giant, quite motionless, looking down at her, the clothes of Costas Gravos still clutched in his fist.

It was a minute or two before some other women came and raised Katina Gravos from the dirt and led her away weeping, with the bundle in her hand.

Manoli went on then, striding down to the broad walk of the town, speaking to nobody until he came to Christos Papagalos. He said something to him, and the two of them went together into Mikali's *taverna* and sat facing each other across the bare board table, each with a kilo of retzina in front of him, Christos still draped in his gaudy fabrics and coat hangers, Manoli with the dirt and the oil and the salt on his beard.

While they sat together, drinking a lot but not talking very much because Costas had been a friend of both of them and a fine diver, Katina Gravos went through the streets of the town, wailing, with the children following her. And at intervals all through the afternoon the bells of Saint Stephanos tolled slowly, for Costas and the boy Apostoli.

There was the blue brick frame of the kitchen window around the oblong of the night, a deep blackness scattered with frost-bright stars, and the small room was lamp-bright and warm with the heat of the shallow charcoal brazier. The room smelled of pine carbon and the fumes of strong Kalymnian cigarettes. From the edge of the swinging hammock Nikolas peered, his dark eyes stiff and wide with sleepiness but never wavering from Manoli's face. The smell of the room, to the boy, was the smell of the big man in the blue jersey—a smell of engine oil and salt, the smell the wind had sometimes when it came up gusting from the harbour.

Manoli was crouched across the table, his shoulders pushed forward, his hand flat on the oilcloth with the thick fingers spread. His eyes were red with drinking and fatigue, and he was as unkempt and dirty as when he had come ashore from the *Ikaros*.

In the corner of the room Mina sewed, and behind her head the lamplight caught the edges of the crockery in the rack and the shining pans.

"Well," said Stavros musingly, "a hundred million drachmae in sponges. It's good enough. For winter, it's good enough."

Manoli grunted and lifted his forefinger to trace the pattern on the oilcloth. He was sick of talking of sponges, sick of the sight of sponges. All around Mina's kitchen there were scraps of sponges, the discarded clippings—sponges for cleaning the pans, sponges for washing, sponges as stoppers for the water pitcher and the big red *liyinei* that Mina filled each morning from the well, sponges for lighting the charcoal fire, sponges for mopping up the floor.

"For three months?" he said. "Jesus! Four thousand dollars, if the price holds. Divide it up, Stavros—a hundred dollars for each man. For three months of that life! And Costas dead."

"Why do you go in the bad months?" Mina asked quietly.

"She talks all day like this," Stavros said resentfully. "All day. Since I told her about Apostoli. As if talk could change it. What else is there?"

Mina licked the end of the thread and put it through the needle eye. "Three weeks, three dead," she said quietly.

Manoli shrugged. "They know when they go. There were nine in the summer. Winter or summer, it makes no difference. They know." He drummed his fingers on the table. "When I go I take twenty-seven divers. Why do I go? They need the hundred dollars, that's why I go. It's not much, but they need it. Do I ask them to go? They come to me." He rubbed his knuckles into his eyes and put his hands down again, flat on the table, and looked across at the hammock as if what he had to say was for the boy's ears. "One day," he said, "there will be no sponging to be done. Like it was in America, at Tarpon Springs, when the germ got into the sponges and rotted them away. Rotted them away on the bed of the sea, so they came out like chewed-up rubber and fell to pieces in your hand. Like that, perhaps. Or something else. The sea has lots of tricks. No sponging to be done, no sponges to sell . . . and then, by Saint Stephanos! they will be down on their knees praying—yes, you too, Mina—praying for the boats to go out, winter or summer, good weather or bad. Stavros is right. What else is there?"

Stavros turned to his daughter. "And they go with Manoli because he is lucky. The sponges cling to the tips of his fingers." But even as he said this Stavros wondered if Manoli's luck had changed. He had lost Costas. But when he had been a *colazaris* he had never lost a man, and in the five years he had been captain he had never lost a man until now. And a hundred million drachmae? It was good enough, but there had been better winter cruises. Why, two years before, when he had gone all the way to Alexandria for the winter and brought the *deposito* back full of wonderful sponges like silk, he had sent the buyers crazy, and half the town had lived like kings, and all through New Year's Eve they had sat in Nick's café and gambled a whole winter's work away as if it hadn't meant anything at all! "Do you remember Alexandria . . . ?" He abandoned the reminiscence even as he began it. Manoli had turned his head away and was looking at Mina.

The wine and the tiredness were like a thick wadding inside Manoli's skull. He understood Mina and he understood Stavros, but he was sick of talking of sponges. The wadding inside his head was numbing and prickling at the same time, and he just wanted to look at Mina and to think of her, to think of her just as she was there in the lamplight with her face framed in the white handkerchief and her eyes dark. She pricked her needle through the square of cloth and rolled it all up and put it on the bench beside her, and she rose as he pushed his chair back.

" Come," he said.

Together they climbed the narrow, twisting path that rose behind the house, skirting the overhanging precipice ; the loose pebbles dislodged by their boots clattered into the dark bowl below. They walked in silence to the little whitewashed church of Saint Peter, standing alone on the cliff top, and went along to the wall of the courtyard and leaned against it side by side, looking down at the black, restless sea.

She could see nothing of the other islands, nothing of Kós or of Nissiros, but she looked in the direction of Nissiros, knowing exactly where it would be, aware of its humped shape even in the darkness.

" Manoli ? " she said softly.

" What is it ? "

" Manoli, some time I would like to go to another island."

" All the islands are the same," he said.

" Not this one. This one is cruel, and it grows crueller."

" All islands are cruel," he said.

When they went back to the house the lower room was in darkness, and he went with Mina up the outside steps to the room above, and the pink door closed behind them.

It was midnight when Manoli went down the hillside to the sleeping town, but he went to the *taverna* and hammered on the door until Mikali, half dressed and yawning, opened for him and served him with a blue beaker of retzina.

4

It was the third week in December when Manoli brought his boats in, and all along the broad street there was the smell of Christmas, and the children were wearing the new clothes and the cowboy shirts that had come in parcels from America.

Between the cafés the little stalls were out with the cheap toys from Athens, tin whistles and plastic aeroplanes. The balloon men went up and down with their barrows, shouting " Fooska ! Fooska ! all through the day, and the farmers were there with long bamboo canes in their hands escorting flocks of turkeys past the appraising eyes of the townspeople. And there were mountain folk, too, curious shy-eyed men with fierce moustaches and broad-brimmed flat hats tied beneath their chins, all of them bowlegged in their baggy trousers and high brown boots. There was a villainous air about their moustaches that was not related at all to the puzzled timidity of their eyes, so that the moustaches looked false and the men looked as if they were children dressed up for a masquerade.

Each morning the animals would go past squealing and protesting—sheep and cows and pigs, and a curly-haired brown and white ram with tiny, precise hoofs and a wonderful head and horns. It was a heraldic animal from an ancient ritual, being dragged to the slaughter yard to be made ready for the feasts, and some of the other animals had garlands on their necks, as if they were sacrifices to an old god.

It was a cold, bright week. The wind had a bite in it and hung to the north, the Boreas ; never a cloud crossed the sky ; and the mountains had hard, metallic edges to them, as if they were encased in bronze.

Manoli stayed over at Lavassi, slipping his boats for overhaul in the crowded yard where the sea came in flat over the white pebbles, and it was not until Christmas morning that Morgan met him.

Telfs had come over, and they were in a crowded café, at a table with Paul Pelacos, drinking the sweet Lipsian wine of Christmas. And suddenly there was Manoli filling the whole doorway, his fist full of paper icons of Saint Stephanos. Behind him were Christos Papagalos and two lean, brown men wearing seamen's caps. Christos carried an embroidered bag with golden tassels on it, a bag bulging with money.

"For Saint Stephanos!" roared Manoli in a great voice hoarse with wine, and he went from table to table.

There was no diffidence, no pleading about Manoli's alms gathering for the saint. His method was simple and direct, beyond any danger of misunderstanding. One of the paper icons was slapped down on the table in front of every man. Christos came behind with the tasselled bag held open to receive the money. The two seamen, young hard-faced men, two of Manoli's divers, followed with their hands thrust into their trouser pockets, intently watching each man's offering, and the expressions on their faces indicated a willingness to assault anyone insufficiently generous to the saint. About the visitation there was more the character of a plundering foray by a band of corsairs than of an act of Christian humility.

At the table where the three men sat Manoli paused for a moment, his dark eyes weighing up the face of the man who was strange to him, and then he grinned and slapped a sheet of the printed paper down before each of them. "For Saint Stephanos," he said, his eyes on Morgan.

"Come, Manoli," said Pelacos. "Join us in a glass of *krassi*. One glass for Christmas. And for your name day."

"Later." He waved the thick wad of paper sheets. "When these have gone."

Christos collected the money from each of them, and Manoli led his band outside. They could still hear his shout, "For Saint Stephanos!" and the slap of his big hand against the outside tables.

Paul Pelacos burst into laughter. "The incomparable

Manoli," he chuckled. " He wins a fortune for the church every
Christmas. He himself decides how much money is needed. If
there is not enough contributed, he goes around the town again.
Sometimes a third time, even a fourth time. Each time, you
understand, he is a little more drunk, more capable of violence.
Everybody gives most generously. They say in the town that
two walls of the church and one dome are Manoli's." He smiled.
" They should make him a saint, except that he is such a villain."

" What a Savonarola he would have made ! " Telfs grinned.
He should have lived in the Middle Ages."

" My dear Doctor, he *does* live in the Middle Ages. Manoli
does not belong to our time, or, rather, he *does* belong—but
only in the way that the mountains up there belong, the sea
in front of us, the olive trees renewing themselves, the wild
herbs growing in the rocks. He is like that, only belonging to
the *now* because he is the eternal *always*." He twirled the gold key
around his finger, first one way then the other. " But you have
me interested, Doctor Telfs. You say the Middle Ages. But
what do you see him as ? A crusading priest with the flames of
fanaticism in his eyes—because he *is* fanatical, you know—as
a soldier of fortune perhaps, a stormer of castles ? What ? "

" I see him as the Middle Ages," Telfs said simply. " Something dark and strong, something compounded of old forces.
Something *happening*. And something yet to happen."

" Yes, yes." Pelacos nodded thoughtfully. " Manoli is
something happening, yes. Always he is something happening.
It is this immediacy of his that is so startling. Whenever you
are with Manoli you are strikingly conscious of the *now*, not of
what has happened or is likely to happen. As I say, the immediacy.
But I confess, Doctor Telfs, that I cannot see a renaissance
emerging from his medievalism, as you evidently can."

" I have a feeling about him, that's all," said Telfs. He
suspected that Pelacos was merely playing with words and ideas.
" It's difficult to explain." How could he explain the other
Manoli he had seen at the house of Mina Vraxos, the Manoli
who dreamed and had a twisted sort of poetry in his dreams ?
" I guess Manoli to me," he added thoughtfully, " is the
Kalymnian. The Kalymnian. Nothing else. That says it, I

guess." He poured wine into their glasses and studied Pelacos quizzically. " My turn now. You said that Manoli was a fanatic. About what ? "

" About life. About living. He takes life in both his hands and eats it as if it were a piece of meat."

" Sure, it's what I said. The Kalymnian."

Pelacos raised his eyebrows, smiling. " You flatter us, Telfs. We are not living any longer, we are dying. We are past middle age and all our attention is concentrated upon the approach of finality. We have aches and pains and our teeth have fallen out. We cannot bite on the meat as Manoli bites on it. Manoli has very strong teeth. Have you noticed his teeth, Mr. Leigh ? Very strong and white."

When Manoli returned to the café he had shaved, and his black moustache had been trimmed, and his jowls were faintly blue and shiny. He wore a clean blue jersey and a coat, and his black trousers were held in tightly at the waist with a scarlet cummerbund.

" *Chronia pollá*, Manoli," Pelacos said, lifting his glass to him.

" And long years to you, to all of you." He spoke surprisingly good English—stiffly, as if each word were considered, but with little accent. " You are Australian," he said, turning to Morgan.

" Yes."

" I knew them in the war. Two years I was with them in Palestine and North Africa. Good drinkers. Good fighters also." He emptied his glass and Pelacos immediately refilled it. " You were there ? "

Morgan nodded. " And in Greece. Greece and Crete. I was captured in Crete."

Manoli grinned, and Morgan could see what Pelacos meant about his teeth. " Ah, at Sphakia, eh ? I was there in a boat. We tried to get them off, but there were too many. And too many *Stukas* ! " He chuckled, as if he were looking back on some pleasurable experience of his younger days.

" You never told me you were a prisoner," Telfs said.

Morgan smiled. " You never told me you were a doctor."

" All of us," said Pelacos, " have certain things we are not communicative about. Our public faces are only papier mâché moulded around an inner core of reticence. Possibly Mr. Leigh suffered as a prisoner. I am sure he did. It is something he would prefer to forget."

Morgan shrugged. "It was a long time ago. It was an experience." He remembered how, when the release had come to him in Germany, he had been terrified of freedom, scared of being dragged away from the security of the bare, familiar cell he had occupied for so long. The prospect of liberty and of free choice, of exchanging the few simple props of his own imprisoned existence—the tin mug and one razor blade and his knife and scrap of mirror—for the infinitely complex mechanisms of the outside world, had almost overcome him. The thought of having to belong once more, to find time itself unregulated and shapeless, to begin all over again in a world that had turned three years onward, to face every complicated problem himself—how appalling it had been, and for a long time after how agonising trying to fit in.

Yet here on this island everybody was desperate to do what he had been afraid of doing : desperate to separate themselves from their own frugal securities, from the few old established things they understood, the things they could touch and smell, desperately eager for something that was infinitely complex and quite beyond their understanding.

In the few days he had been in Kalymnos they had come to him in scores, gentle, polite people but with eyes that were desperate and hungry. They had asked him about Australia, talked about that impossibly distant continent as devout men might talk of Paradise. They had no conception of what Australia was like. To them it was something of myth and magic, something golden, something beyond the rim of the world, where there were grass and forests and seas teeming with fish, where men had work and were happy and where there were no sickness and no hunger, where children laughed and grew big. He had tried to tell them what Australia was really like, tried to convey to them something of its harsh complexities, something of the jarring tensions which had driven him away from his own land to seek quieter things in an older world. He had tried to explain to them that men suffered and were happy in about the same proportion wherever they were. But they had only laughed politely, thinking he was joking with them.

"There are many people here who seem to want to go to Australia," he said to Manoli. "They keep coming to me."

"*Many?*" Pelacos threw up his hands elegantly. "Everybody! Everybody wants to go to Australia." He turned to Telfs. "Or America. Not so much your country now, Doctor, as it used to be. Now it is Australia that has become the land at the end of the rainbow, Cloud-cuckoo Land, the country of Prester John, a compelling Eldorado nurtured on starved imaginations."

"Starved children, too," said Telfs. "Don't forget that. The Big Rock Candy Mountain. I guess there always has to be a Big Rock Candy Mountain—for all of us. Though, God knows, I've been three times round the world hunting and never found it."

"Has the world, I wonder, ever been constituted so fantastically as it is now?" mused Pelacos contentedly. "Half the world insane with a desire to go somewhere else, where there is clatter and noise and excitement, and automobiles and washing machines and a cinema every night. And the other half just as desperate to crawl back into the quiet, warm shelter of the womb."

Shelter and security, thought Morgan. The absolute simplicity. A tin mug and one razor blade, a knife and a scrap of mirror, and the assurance of time. Was that why he had come back to Greece?

"When I said everybody I should have made an exception," said Pelacos. "Manoli has no wish to go. Manoli, I think, would prefer to defeat it here. Is that correct?"

Manoli shrugged and said nothing. His big hand reached across for the carafe, and he filled his glass again. It was like Mina dreaming of other islands, dreaming of other islands until the pink door had closed behind them, and in the darkness he had thrown her down on the big flat bed, with the sea smell still upon him and the smell of the room around them. The two smells—the wild sea smell that you brought in from far away and the soft, secure smell of the things that were always there, that always stayed in the same place—the two smells all mixed up together, belonging to each other.

He had not followed all the conversation, only some of it, but that was what they had been trying to say. Perhaps he and Mina understood it better than they did.

" To-night, you must drink with me," he said to Morgan, liking the eyes of the Australian and his big thick body, and the shared memory of the beach at Sphakia with the black smoke and the bodies on the sand with the sea washing the blood away. " And since everybody wishes to go to Australia you will tell me why you do not stay there, why you come here." He smiled across at Telfs. " And you will come, too, Doctor, to pace me with the retzina, eh ? And you, Pelacos ? You see too little of the *tavernas*."

Pelacos laughed and twirled the key chain. " We compliment each other, Manoli. You see too much of them." He shook his head. " You will have to excuse me. I am conserving my energies for the New Year. But on the eve of Saint Vassilias you and I, Manoli, will play cards and I promise to take a million from you."

" Like last year, eh ? " Manoli's laugh, a great bellow that seemed to shake the glasses on the table, echoed through the room. " Seven millions before the church bells rang. Like last year, eh ? "

In the afternoon Telfs took Morgan with him when he went up the hill to visit Mina Vraxos.

Telfs carried a basket with some mandarins and candy and a few toys he had bought in Athens for the kid and some sweet cakes baked in the shape of little men, like the gingerbread men his mother had made for him in Taconic when he was a child. Not so nice to eat, but they looked good and the kid would get a kick out of them. And some good Athens cigarettes for old Stavros Papastratos—the ones he liked best but couldn't afford to buy. And, carefully packed in a cardboard box, a nylon blouse and new stockings for Mina.

Stumbling beside him up the stony path between the

dilapidated cottages, Morgan carried the gallon wicker jar of retzina.

All around the houses the shabby, ragged kids were playing with penny ballons and cheap tin whistles and little tin frogs and crickets that clicked when you squeezed them between finger and thumb. " There's not a toy among them that costs more than a dime," Telfs explained. " It's a poor part, this."

The women went out in the sunshine, cooking at the open stoves. Big whitewashed cubes of stone supported the primitive little grates where charcoal glowed and crackled beneath the feast dishes—big pots of stew and bean soup and macaroni and pans of *sikoti* and *barbunia*. And the air was rich with the smells of oil and wood smoke and chickens cooking.

" It's a big day, this, the feast," said Telfs, pausing for breath at one of the stone stoves. The smell of *dolmádhes* steaming in the pan filled his nostrils. " Most of them eat meat maybe half a dozen times a year. It sure is a rough life here."

" It's why you stay on, though, isn't it ? " Morgan looked up at the last stiff climb that led to the little house beneath the cliff. " Because you think you can help a bit. That's why, isn't it ? "

" I guess it's one reason. Or maybe it's because I have a sort of morbid interest in disaster and decay. In calamity and causes. A sort of philosophical pathology." Telfs pursued the thought silently. That was it. A preoccupation with the intensities of suffering, the preoccupation that had sent him wandering around the world ever since the war ended, that had always kept him close against the simple hearth of humanity, where you could observe the glow of life amid the ashes. The glow was always brighter and more warming where the burning had been fiercest.

He had seen so much of it since China—since the day of the plague in Teng-yueh, when he had gone through the streets with a blazing pine brand setting alight the houses with the red joss papers pasted on the door ; since the cholera in Ch'eng-tu, when he and a pink-faced kid from Massachusetts faced a howling, death-scared mob in a temple of Kuan Yin suffocating with incense, and drove them out and down the street to the clinic for their inoculations, down the street where the corpses were

stacked like logs in a woodyard. And a whole lot of other
things—the famine in Calcutta, and typhus, and malaria, and
the bodies all bruised and mashed up by the stones in the earthquake toppled towns of Cephallonia. It was the earthquake
that had brought him to Greece. He had come down with one
of the United Nations outfits, but he had quit finally because it
hadn't been too easy for him to see the bodies and the crippled
kids and all the dark, starving faces in terms of forms in triplicate
and reports for the statistical bulletins.

Besides, it had seemed to him then that there was much that
had to be said. Somebody had to sit down somewhere very
quietly, away from the tangle, and study it and work it out and
make some sort of sense of it. There had to be an explanation,
a core of sanity and *reason*, if only you could find it. Maybe there
were other people all over the world who wanted to sit down and
work it out and make sense of it.

It was only a pretence now that it could be done, he admitted
to himself. Not even a pretence, really, because he didn't kid
himself any longer that he could work it out. But he stayed on
in Kós. Why ?

The place stank of poverty and suffering, and for a time he
had been able to delude himself that it was the right place for
him to be. There the problem could be reduced to a smaller
scale, as if the hell of hopelessness was something on a glass slide
to be put under a microscope and examined. Besides, it was his
particular shrine, the place where Hippocrates had begun it all.
For a while it had made sense, sitting there quietly in the ruined
precincts of the ancient shrine of Asclepius, the god of healing,
and for two months he had tried to work it out, write it down.

Or did he stay on only because it was the right place to be
because of Mina Vraxos—far enough away so that it didn't
nag at him all the time, and yet close enough for him to come
across when he couldn't help it ?

" Okay, let's go," he said abruptly, and trudged off up the
hill with the basket in his hand.

Manoli was her lover, that was what they said, and maybe
it was true. The big Manoli. It was difficult to imagine a woman
not being Manoli's lover if he wanted her. Maybe it was true.

If he asked her she would tell him, and that was why he never asked her—because if it was true he didn't want to know. If it was true and she lied to him, that would be fine. But Mina wouldn't lie to him.

The hell of it was that she was so desperate to get away. He could take her away or Manoli could take her away. But neither of them would. They all had to sweat it out here, the three of them together, waiting to see what happened.

He could see her now, standing on the topmost of the blue steps, staring down at them. He stopped and waved to her, waiting for Morgan to catch up, waiting much longer than was necessary so he could get his breath back.

"Well," said Morgan, glancing at him curiously, "do we go up now?"

"Sure, we go up," he said. "Go ahead."

He didn't want to confront her gasping and puffing like an old man. When Manoli came up he came singing. He could take the whole goddam mountain in his stride and never show a breath!

In the little room the bedding and the kid's hammock had been rolled up and stowed away, and there was a good-sized crowd of people sitting at two big round tables. The tables and most of the chairs, Telf guessed, had been borrowed from neighbours. On each table there was a big jug of retzina. The women sat all together at one table, eating little dishes of tomato preserves but the men's table was piled with platters of *barbunia* and smoked octopus and big bowls of stew and enormous disks of dark bread. It was a man's world all right!

Some of the people he knew, and others were strange to him—friends and distant relatives come for the formal Christmas calls—but there were smiles and greetings from all of them and a great flurry to find chairs.

Morgan was fascinated by the room. It was very clean and simple. Against one wall was a rack of pans that shone like mirrors and a small glass-fronted cupboard for cups and dishes. Tacked to the wall above the wide built-in bed was a gaudy, cheap tapestry of a lion and a tiger that had something of the

naïve charm of a Rousseau painting ; its subject doubtless was
chosen for the small, dark-eyed boy who sat, stiff and happy, on
a chair in the far corner of the room and clutched the model
caique that Telfs had brought from Athens. The walls, washed
a pale, streaky blue, were sparsely decorated. There was a frame
full of faded snapshots pasted on cardboard, individuals and
groups sharing a dim, out-of-focus anonymity ; and there were
four other framed photographs, stiff and old-fashioned, of
elderly men and women. The photographs reminded him of when
he was a small boy in Australia. There had been a photographic
shop which had been closed ever since he could remember, and
in the window were many old photographs of soldiers of the First
World War, very pale, yellowed photographs, all curled up and
fly-spotted. One day he had been looking at them, his nose
pressed to the glass, when another boy had come up to him and
said darkly, " All them fellers in there is dead, you know."
And he had hurried away from the shop and never gone back to
it again. There was the death colour about certain photographs,
as if all the blood had drained away long since : these photographs
on the wall had the death colour, as if you had taken the graves
from the cemetery and brought them into the house as a reminder
of mortality. He wanted to turn them to the wall.

Yet in a way they belonged to the room, to the carved
cornices of the cupboard and the tarnished bobbles on the tablecloths, for they possessed what the room contained more certainly
than the people who feasted around the tables.

Apart from the photographs and the tapestry, there was only
one other decorative element : a Currier and Ives lithograph of
a sailing ship in a carved-out, up-and-down sea, and for all its
improbability it seemed to belong, too. Underneath the print,
in old-fashioned lettering, it said :

THE CELEBRATED CLIPPER SHIP

DREADNOUGHT

*Off Tuskar Light, on her passage into Dock at Liverpool, in 13 days
11 hours from New York, December, 1854*

Mina Vraxos stood in the corner by the little stove, refilling the platters as they were emptied, spooning out tomato preserves from the big glass jar.

She was a tall, slender woman, dark and grave and of a singular beauty that for all the magnificence of her external appearance seemed to derive more from some quality within her. Whatever the essence of this distinction—and she had a distinction apart from any woman Morgan had ever seen—it was a secret, hidden thing. The sort of thing, elusive and fugitive, that you could sense sometimes in front of one of the Renaissance portraits of Florentine women, that made you aware of some quality, occasional but persistent, that set certain women apart from others.

It was this quality that Mina Vraxos possessed, subdued for the moment by her grave and patient externality, as if the fires of it were still there, but banked down, hidden, smouldering. For all the fine richness of her appearance—the high-planed cheeks, the dark eyes, the strong mouth, the proud arrogance of her bosom—it was Eliot's line that was in Morgan's mind as he studied her : " Some infinitely gentle, infinitely suffering thing . . ."

Occasionally, as somebody lifted a glass to jest with her, a quick, vivid smile would light her dark face, and for that brief, flashing instant one could sense the truth of Mina Vraxos in the whiteness of her small teeth and the warmth of her eyes.

They had not been there half an hour before Homer Vraxos came.

The sudden hush that fell upon the room at the appearance of his short portly figure in the doorway would have embarrassed anyone possessing a trace of sensitivity ; it had no effect whatever on the newcomer. His eyes, surveying the room, were sly and spiteful ; the slight bow he made was a gesture of mockery and contempt.

" And Mr. Leigh and the good doctor too, eh, seeing how the other half lives." His small dark eyes snapped maliciously. " Local colour, eh, Mr. Leigh ? Well, this sure is the place to come for it." His mouth pursed up, he hesitated on the threshold,

as if revolted by the thought of entering this crowded room
where somebody might rub against him.

He was wearing a wide tan hat with a pale, narrow band;
his smartest suit was made even more flamboyant than usual
by the raffish addition of a hand-painted tie, very wide and very
long, bearing a picture of a half-nude girl. Three tiny studs of
red glass were sewn on the tie, two for the nipples of the breasts
and one for the navel. Beneath the tie his pudgy yellow hands
fiddled with the tasselled golden watch fob.

Morgan was aware suddenly of the shabby, simple clothing
of all the other guests in the room; he understood why Telfs
had come in a pair of stained and baggy flannels and a checked
shirt that was patched and faded.

" Come in, Homer," said Stavros, his face dark with memories.
He motioned to a chair. " *Kathisé*," he said.

" Hell, no ! " Vraxos shook his head and glanced suspiciously
from his shiny shoes to the hens' droppings on the ground
below the steps. " Brother, this is the wrong side of the tracks
for me," he said to Morgan, and sniggered. Morgan realised
that he was a little drunk. " I don't get up this way too often,"
Vraxos continued contemptuously. " A few times a year to
make the duty calls. Christmas. New Year. Easter. The bastards
get resentful if you don't show up. But I ask you, brother, I *ask*
you ! Take a look at the place. Clay and rocks and hen manure
all over ! Not only hens', if it comes to that ! I ask you ! "

" Nobody asked you, Vraxos," Telfs said coldly. " Come in
and sit down." There was a cutting edge to his voice that made
Vraxos obey immediately.

Once inside the room Vraxos seemed less sure of himself.
His hat was still on, and he sat well forward on the edge of
his chair, arranging the creases of his trousers, rubbing the toe
of one glossy shoe against his pants' leg. All the faces watched
him, set and still : the women's faces in the black shawls ; the
men's faces without collars and ties, the men's faces over blue
jerseys ; and most of the faces unshaven and old and tired. The
faces watched him. . . .

" Jesus, what a dump ! " he said, braving it out, feeling some
security in a language that was not understood by the faces

watching him. " Jesus, in New York the public sanitation people would have plenty to say ! "

" Stavros is offering you a drink," said Telfs.

" I don't care for one. Thanks all the same. I don't care for the cheap stuff they get up here."

Telfs pushed the glass towards him. " You're going to drink it whether you care for it or not," he said. " Happy Christmas, Vraxos."

Vraxos shrugged, smirking. " Okay. I guess you can always close your eyes and kid it's bourbon. Happy Christmas, Doctor."

" It's not my drink. It's Stavros'—and your sister-in-law's."

Vraxos lifted his glass in a quick circle of vague salute and, after a mocking bow towards Mina, who was standing in the corner, watching him impassively, he emptied the glass and pulled a wry face and spat on the floor. " Holy Jesus ! " he said. He turned to Morgan with a grin that was all insolence and contempt. " So you've met my sister-in-law ? " he said. " Quite a dish, eh ? A bit long in the tooth now for my choice. If she was a year or two younger I'd make a play for her myself. If I could get past Manoli, of course. First Manoli to get past, and then the hens ! " He slapped his hands against his thick thighs and guffawed, " Boy, is *that* a steeplechase ! " he spluttered. " First Manoli, then the hens ! "

" Just Manoli," said the voice from the doorway, a thick, deep voice that caused every head in the room to turn. And there was Manoli, standing at the entrance, blocking the day out. He pushed in through the doorway, bending his head beneath the lintel ; Morgan had the ridiculous thought that the walls of the room would have to split apart to contain him.

" Just Manoli," he said, " and then the hens."

He was a little unsteady on his feet and he stank of wine, but when he moved he was like a great cat moving—all the strength of the man was bunched into one swift, smooth swoop that hoisted Vraxos from his chair. And before anybody could make a move, Manoli was gone, out through the door, carrying Vraxos by the neck of his jacket and the seat of his trousers, writhing and screaming.

There was a clatter of overturning chairs then, as everyone

scrambled from the tables and crowded to the door and window. They could see Manoli standing astride two stone ledges, holding Vraxos by the seat of his trousers at the full stretch of his arm, and as the fat little man squealed Manoli shook him slowly from side to side.

They began to laugh then, all of them—great, choking gusts of laughter, for below the suspended figure was the little wired-in enclosure for the hens. And they could hear Manoli saying in a soft, sing-song voice : " First Manoli, eh ? First Manoli, eh ? "

Then he let out a great yell and gave a swift, twisting wrench to his arm, and the whole seat came tearing out of the trousers, all the seat and half one leg out of the new, beautifully creased cinnamon-coloured trousers. And Homer Vraxos was down there howling, sprawled flat on his face in the clay and the muck and the hen droppings, with all the feathers flying in a cloud of brown and white, and the hens squawking and flapping on his head, and his fat, white buttocks glistening in the sun.

Twice he attempted to scramble to his feet but each time his glossy shoes slithered in the muck and he was down again, sobbing, while the hens flapped around him and the laughter rocketed. Finally he flung himself out of the enclosure, stumbling through the sagging wire, and then was gone up the hillside with Manoli after him, bellowing like a bull.

They watched until Manoli had chased him away, right over the top of the stony ridge, the white, bobbing globe of his backside like some queer fluorescent witch's light that drew Manoli on.

5

A SMALL embossed card tacked in the centre of the end wall proclaimed Mikali's *taverna* as of the Category D, and it was this card that often filled Mikali's brain with visions of the Belgian Congo.

Standing beside his shining pans at the white-painted charcoal stove, with his soft, neat hands clasped over the aproned curve of his belly, Mikali tried to keep his eyes away from the ceiling. Everything else about the *taverna* he had inherited from his father satisfied him ; it was the ceiling that drove his imagination on desperate, timorous voyages to the Belgian Congo. The rest was good. Each morning the floor received a coating of fresh white sawdust. The chairs and benches were clean. The clock kept time. The calendar always marked the correct day, with particular saints' days ringed in red pencil as reminders to certain of his customers. The long tables were covered with clean cloths of checked linen, cheap but fresh-looking. The retzina glasses were invariably washed twice and rinsed for the third time under well water until they shone like crystal. Bunches of bay leaves hung in the big, cool room where the retzina casks were racked, massive casks painted bright blue, so that it was a joy to go in there and smell the cool fragrant air. But the ceiling !

It was the ceiling that inexorably and eternally kept the *taverna* fixed to the embossed card of the Category D. With a morose masochism, Mikali lifted sad eyes to the hated ceiling : hundreds of sheets of paper pasted together, all bulging and sagging and falling away in one corner where the steam from the cooking pots had peeled it off its tacks. Once there had been a pretty pattern on the paper, but now it was all hidden under a new and revolting pattern of ugly damp stains, great brown blotches like the map of some sinister archipelago, like the stains that appeared sometimes on the flesh of dying men, like a strange menagerie of terrifying beasts. There was no end to the horrors that could be conjured from the imagination of Mikali when he looked at the ceiling.

He wiped his hands slowly down the front of his apron and turned to Tony Thaklios.

" Only a few more months and I'll be going," he said, nodding his head quickly, as if to reassure himself. The look of adventure in his sad, gentle eyes was hopeless and exhausted. " Two years in the Belgian Congo, maybe only one, and you can make plenty money. Then I come back and fix the ceiling and maybe get a Category C."

" Sure," said Tony, " it could do with fixing." For three

years now he had been listening to Mikali's story of the Belgian Congo—ever since Mikali had got that goddam magazine with the coloured pictures in it—and the talk of the adventure no longer really impinged on his consciousness. It had grown to be part of everything, part of the bulging ceiling and Mikali's sorrowful eyes and the footprints scuffed through the sawdust on the floor and the sad-eyed ragged kids with snotty noses coming to the door of the *taverna* to have Mikali fill the retzina bottles. And the stink of ammonia from the privy just outside the door.

"That toilet, too," said Tony abstractedly. His years in America had made him very conscious of sanitation, and every visitor to his own house above the store was taken to see his toilet. "That could do with fixing some day." But even the thought of the toilet only scratched his consciousness. He was concerned at the moment with other matters : how much retzina he could drink before Calliope came looking for him, and whether she would arrive before Manoli, and whether Manoli would be able to help him, and what sort of weather it was going to be the way his corn was playing up.

"They say nothing about the toilet," said Mikali darkly. "It's the ceiling. That's all they say about."

"When you get back from the Belgian Congo, I'd fix 'em both. Maybe you'd get a Category B." The ceiling didn't look so good, but at least it didn't stink.

It was Calliope who came first. He could see her out of the corner of his eye ; she was standing in the doorway with her arms folded, all her best clothes on because it was Christmas Day, but still wearing the white handkerchief around her head. She'd worn it ever since they had come back from the States ; it was her concession to the ways of the other Kalymnian women. She wore the scarf like a wimple. Tony was proud of *wimple*. When he had dug it out of the lexicon he had even surprised Calliope, and Calliope was no slouch when it came to the intellectual stuff. *Wimple*, it said : *a veil folded around the neck and face*. Well, that was the way Calliope wore it—and even now, when she was a grandmother, her face was sweet and handsome with a wimple round it.

Tony Thaklios was proud of his wife—the way she looked, even though she'd never see forty-five again, and the way she would come most evenings and stand right up at the counter and take a drink with the men and tease them and joke with them, just the way she would have done back in Florida, not like the other Kalymnian women who stayed at home and never showed their faces unless they were out marketing or off to a wedding or a funeral. Sure, he was proud of Calliope because she was a smart woman, the way she managed everything and still stayed young and pretty. And she had a sharp way of finding out things, like that time in Athens when she'd found out about Calliope being one of the Muses in the old, old days. And she had dragged him all the way up to Delphi so they could drink the water at the Castalian Spring, which had once been sacred to the Muses. That's what she had claimed, anyway, and although he would have preferred a half kilo of retzina he had jollied her along.

Yes, he was proud of Calliope, and fond of her, but he wished she wouldn't chase him around the *tavernas*, hunting for him.

" Here's Calliope," said Mikali, with nothing in his voice of warning or surprise. It was a thing he would say maybe six or seven times in an evening if Tony was drinking, because even when Calliope dragged him off home he'd come sneaking back again in maybe ten minutes or half an hour and stay on with the boys until Calliope called again. Besides, Mikali was preoccupied now and a little miserable, with the toilet to think about as well as the ceiling.

" Sure," muttered Tony. " I see her." He turned casually towards the door, and started with surprise. " Why, *honey !* " he said. " Hallo ! " And that was another thing : he wished that when she came chasing him she would look sour and shrewish and bad-tempered, and not come with her eyes dancing, as if it was a hell of a joke, so that he couldn't get sore with her without making a goddam fool of himself in front of everybody. " We've been talking, Mikali and I, talking about things. This toilet of his and the ceiling."

Mikali nodded a gloomy endorsement. In his imagination now all the ferocious blotches on the ceiling stank.

" I've been searching all over for you," Calliope said, smiling.

" Well, that's okay," said Tony. " I was just coming." He examined the copper beaker of retzina thirstily. " It's only we've got some things to work out about this problem of his, this toilet."

" Can't you postpone it, Tony ? " she said. " You're wanted at the house. It's important."

" Important ? You only got to use your nose to realise this matter of the toilet's pretty goddam important too ! Who ? "

" Homer Vraxos," she said. " He's waiting for you."

" That bastard ! " He said it softly, but she heard him.

" Well, he's waiting for you. There's been trouble."

" Why can't he come here ? Is the guy too lousy to buy a drink ? Besides, I got to wait here for Manoli."

" That's who the trouble is about," said Calliope. " It's Manoli."

Tony sighed. " Okay," he said resignedly. " Tell him I'll be right over." When Calliope had gone he held out the beaker to be filled. " That bastard Vraxos," he said.

" One day," said Mikali hopefully, " Manoli will kill him. One day he catches him smelling around Mina—the way he's always smelling around the schoolgirls at the Gymnasium, patting them and buying them sweets. One day there'll be plenty trouble for that Vraxos. Looking for a wife, he says, but he doesn't want anyone over sixteen. And him sixty-five, maybe older."

Tony shrugged. " It's the way it catches them sometimes when they get that age." He paused thoughtfully. " When I confront certain elements . . ." He left the sentence unfinished. It was his favourite beginning for a philosophical oration, but, having begun, he had no heart to continue. After all, he was a peaceable man and he had no wish to be tangled up in—there was a better word than that. What was it now ? *Involved.* Yes, he had no wish to be involved in some dispute between Vraxos and Manoli, especially when he had his mind fixed on other things.

" One day there'll be plenty trouble for that Vraxos," Mikali said again, as if by reiteration he might fulfil the wish.

" Sure, one day. But there's always trouble for Manoli. Every day. People ought to learn to get along together. It isn't all that hard." He emptied his glass, hesitated for a moment over the beaker, and shook his head. " Best I get back, I guess, and see what all this trouble is."

Outside the *taverna* a gust of wind howling up the narrow lane from the sea struck him like a blow. It had chopped right round to the south-west, the sirocco wind, and it was piping and howling above the rooftops. Through the street gratings, where the sluices ran, he could hear the sea growling. It always gave him an uncomfortable feeling, hearing the sea beneath his feet, way up the street behind the shops.

That was the reason his corn had been killing him all day.

In the police office across the pebbled square from Saint Christos the duty captain, Dimitropolis, sat at the big desk fingering his mechanical pencil. On the wall behind his head was the map of all the Dodecanese ; the desk piled high with irregular hillocks of documents, yellow, brown, grey, white and green. Dimitropolis was a big, swarthy man with small eyes and he looked like a Turk. Behind the desk he was a great immobile mountain of grey rising from the foothills of the littered documents, as if somebody had taken a section of the map from behind his head and modelled it in relief.

The massive size and stillness of Dimitropolis, the swarthy, globular face perched on his shoulders as if he had no neck at all, the unblinking gaze of the small black eyes—every aspect of the duty captain emphasised the antithetical qualities of Sergeant Phocas, who sat at the desk across from him.

In his twenty-six years' experience, Dimitropolis had never known another police officer quite like Sergeant Phocas. The sergeant was a Cretan by birth and quite small ; he was quick and effervescent, created, it seemed, from a volatile spirit rather than from flesh and blood. You had the feeling that he should be kept in a bottle, with a glass stopper. In spite of the grey uniform and the three white chevrons and the pistol in the holster at his belt and the blue and silver duty armband, his appearance was pretty rather than intimidating—almost girlish, in fact, with the soft laughing mouth and the small hands and the long black lashes to his eyes. Sergeant Phocas, moreover, giggled. When other men laughed—often when they scowled and were angry, too—Phocas giggled. And he was always nice to people, very polite and charming and nice. Why, even his *kombolloi* . . .

Dimitropolis glanced down at his own *kombolloi*, tossed on top of the papers on his desk—his conversation beads, a great string of them, each bead of amber and as large as an owl's egg, and at the end of the string a florid tassel of green and gold silk.

And there, across the facing desks, was Sergeant Phocas fingering his delicate, little string of tiny, pretty pink sea shells threaded on a piece of cat-gut.

Still, thought Dimitropolis, it was good the Phocas was the duty sergeant to-night, because in the handling of Manoli there was no one to compare with Phocas, for all his girlish ways and his giggles and that ridiculous *kombolloi*.

"Drunk, yes," said Dimitropolis, "but with Manoli that is nothing. This time it is the assault. Very bad. Vraxos will get Tony Thaklios to assess the damage."

Sergeant Phocas looked up from his sea shells and giggled. "I expected we might have something from Manoli to-day. When I saw him collecting for Saint Stephanos, drinking the sweet wine." The mouth curved, and his white teeth shone. "Yet we must remember that it is his name day, and we should——"

"The drunkenness?" Dimitropolis shrugged.

"He has been drinking heavily, even more than usual, since he came back. It is Costas Gravos he thinks about when he is drinking. That's why all his share of the cruise went to the woman, to Katina Gravos, and why——"

"It is not the drunkenness that concerns me. But the assault now. Ah!"

"Even Vraxos?" The sergeant smiled mischievously. "Remember what you have always said about Vraxos."

"We cannot have one law for Manoli and a different law for everyone else. And Manoli, with his drinking and his brawling and his roistering through the streets when all the town sleeps—no! The whole winter becomes a nightmare. For everybody. Just because you like Manoli——"

"Everybody likes Manoli."

Dimitropolis permitted himself the slightest of smiles. " Homer Vraxos too ? " he said.

The sergeant shrugged, as if Homer Vraxos' opinion did not interest him.

" And look what happens to all the children in the town," Dimitropolis continued. " Oh, yes, they are the *pallikaria* ! They all want to be Manoli ! *Boom, boom, boom !* All of them. I am sick of seeing five hundred Manolis tearing through the town like crazy wild beasts ! " He grunted and picked up his *komboloi* and flicked the big beads through his fingers two at time. " A night or two in the cell might cool him off for the New Year," he said.

The wall shuddered as a great gust of wind struck, wrenching the shutter from its bar.

Sergeant Phocas put the little string of sea shells into his pocket and walked across to the window.

The harbour had begun to seethe. Broken crests were toppling over into the roadway, and there were quick wind-driven water flurries across the asphalt, as if the skin of the earth were trembling. Over against the breakwater the big empty caiques were rolling like pigs, and below the window the sponge boats were lunging and rearing at their anchor chains. The gale was streaming in from the south-west beneath a ragged scud of cloud.

" *Po-po-po-po !* " said Sergeant Phocas. " This will be a night ! " And he giggled as he took up his greatcoat.

The storm that night was the worst for five years, and the big steamers stayed away—the *Heliopolis* from Rhodes and the *Kyklades* from Piræus, kicking and rolling far out to sea—away from the bleak, foamed rocks of Kalymnos. Their lights were a brief glow passing in the wind's lull, soon lost in spray and darkness.

The wind came flat across the water, screaming beneath the low ceiling of the clouds, so that there seemed to be four layers of rushing movement : the sea and the wind and the clouds and, in the gaps between the clouds, the full moon churning through the vapours.

Each wave crest was taken as it rose and ripped into shreds

of white. But as the violence of the gusts increased, the power of the sea asserted itself and the waves kicked higher, rolling clear across the top of the breakwater, bursting in running explosions along the buttressing rocks, flinging the spray higher than the lighthouse. In the harbour the surge began, banking up the water until the waves, a dirty yellow colour under the street lamps, were breaking across the broad walk, spreading muddy fans of foam all the way to the salt trees, floating the swollen, flaccid body of a drowned black pig actoss to the doorstep of Katrina's café. In the narrow streets behind the market the sluices choked, and the sea boiled to the house steps.

Along the front the café men struggled with their shutters, the spray stinging their necks, the wind jostling them. The night whined in the rigging of the boats. And then the noise of the wind was compacted into the ominous sound : a low, unbroken roar, as if all the air in the world were rushing away down a narrow tunnel.

Outside the yellow house on the quay Morgan staggered in the rush of the wind. Telfs was buffeted to one side, clutching at his flapping coat, and Morgan dragged him into the shelter of the doorway.

" Christ ! " Telfs gasped. " This is a hurricane ! "

" Look ! " Morgan grasped his arm as he yelled. " The boats ! "

The inner harbour was a crazy confusion : the sponge boats twisted and rolled, the tangle of their masts swinging great arcs against the sky, and on each, little groups of men struggled with mooring ropes and spare anchors, their bodies straining, grotesquely twisted, as they fought for their boats while the sea poured over them.

With the yellow waves across it, the broad walk of the town was like a tidal flat, and only the seamen of the town were there, some in sea boots and jerseys and some half naked and some in bare feet with their trousers rolled above their knees. From the side streets other seamen, helped by the ragged kids, were dragging chains and coils of rope and big four-pronged grapnels. In an old yellow oilskin, torn by the wind and flapping between his knees, Zeffis, the harbour master, ran backwards and forwards through the bursts of spray, yelling at the men in the boats. The amplifier from the cinema along the road crackled and spluttered absurd metallic dialogue.

Morgan was seized by an overwhelming excitement as he watched. About the scene there was something tremendously elemental : everything ran together in the mad black and yellow and silver of the night ; sky and wind and sea and night churned together in primordial chaos, in some cosmic disintegration that reduced everything to air and water and a dark, cold light. He could feel himself trembling as he watched the wild sway of the masts, the stars and the moon flash, the headlong rush of clouds, the surge and seethe and wind lash of the sea. And against it all the swing of the boats and the struggling groups of men, drenched by the sea and with the wind tearing at them.

A big sea, running along the flanks of the boats and filling a dinghy as it came, smashed against the wall. It tore three feet of stone from the coping and slid it across the road. The wave that followed took the *Sevasti*, the little caique that brought the paraffin from Rhodes. Morgan could see it high up, hanging in the air with the stern dragging, and then it was against the wall, splintering and rasping, and the empty oil drums clanged as they rolled away.

Zeffis led the men towards it, and Morgan was running, too, aware of a delirious madness, of the banging of the empty paraffin drums across the roadway, and of the hoofbeats of the Western film, and all the men shouting to one another from the boats, and Zeffis cursing and yelling. There was a wild demented music to it, contrapuntal to the hiss of the sea and the wind's deep roar.

He was aware, even as he ran lurching and staggering in the push of the wind, that this was Kalymnos. This was all Kalymnos ever was or ever would be : the wind and sea, and the boats and the men and the struggle. The storm had swept all the trappings away. " Okay, brother, but keep your hands away from those guns ! " the tin voice crackled from the cinema, and the storm swept that away, too.

Manoli was on the deck of the caique moored next to the smashed and floundering *Sevasti*, one of the Pelacos diving boats, the *Irini*. As its bow reared up Morgan could see the green weed folding down at the waterline and the name painted against the white planking in big red letters, and he thought of Irini Pelacos with her shy smile and her cropped hair. Manoli was stripped down to a soaked pair of white drawers and he was up in the bow by the anchor bitts, struggling to get the second anchor out and into a small red dinghy that Christos Papagalos was holding against the side of the boat by the sheer strength of his arms and shoulders. The *Sevasti* had begun to tear apart and the broken planking was kicking around in a yeast of yellowish water with a tangle of rope and two twirling paraffin drums.

Morgan took the leap as the stern of the *Irini* dropped away in the trough, with the deck rolling towards him and the impact of his body against the wet planking jarring through his arms and shoulders, and then the stern jolted up and tossed him against the deckhouse. He was only vaguely aware of the pain as his knees cracked against the wood; beneath his hands he could feel the rough, wet prickle of rope and he hauled himself along to the bow.

Manoli was wedged into the triangle of the bow, dragging at the anchor. His forearm was gashed open where he had been driven down on one of the sharp prongs. The ends of his fingers were torn and bleeding, and his right fist was a hammer beating at the stubborn links of the chain. Morgan went down beside him in the smell of salt and blood and wet iron.

Together, sweating and gasping, they freed the cable and dragged the anchor clear. Then Morgan clambered over the side and dropped into the tossing dinghy, and as Manoli lowered the anchor to him Christos fended off the floating planks and paraffin drums. When the anchor was stowed Christos settled the oars on the pins and began to pull.

For a long time they seemed to make no headway at all. As each wave tossed them up, Manoli's face was still there, right in front of them, taut with strain and with the soaked hair plastered across his forehead. Christos cursed as the oars jarred against the planks and tangled in the waterlogged ropes, and the dinghy almost stood on its end. Morgan, crouched in the stern sheets, clutching with both hands at the anchor chain, felt himself lost suddenly in a world where all dimension had been eliminated—a confused aqueous world confined within the convulsive spin of the small red boat, related neither to the sweep of the *Irini's* prow above them nor to the infinity of the sea beyond, a world whose components were pain and cold and the sting of the sea. On the palms of his hands he could feel the cold, wet rust ; the weight of the iron dragged at his muscles, and at the other end of the iron chain were Manoli's hands, torn and bloody.

Christos cursed all the time as he pulled—rich and wonderful curses concerned with the sea and copulation and tempest and generations of bastards, great oaths involving God and Saint Nikolas and Christ and the Virgin and Poseidon and the devil and his own mother. Sometimes he seemed far below Morgan, dragging at the oars in the stinging, wet darkness, and at other times all his massive bulk was thrown against the sky, with the sea lapping against him, with his head thrown back, and the muscles of his neck twisting like cords, his shoulders overhanging the beam of the boat and his trunk swelling up from the thwarts. Only his fists on the oars and the oars themselves seemed fragile. This was Cyclopean man ; there was no other Christos Papagalos. The man with the twisted legs who hawked his coloured embroideries through the town was a dream, a myth.

Slowly and painfully, inch by inch, they made headway against the storm, dragging the iron chain as Manoli paid it out from the bitts of the *Irini*. As the chain went down, the sea washed Manoli's blood from the links. It took them half an hour to cover fifty yards, and not until then did Christos give Morgan the signal to manhandle the anchor over the stern.

Manoli took up the slack of the chain and then they could see him on the bow waving and yelling to them, and they went back racing before the waves, and Manoli took a flying jump, into the dinghy when it was still six feet away, landing like a great cat, on all fours on the bottom boards.

" Over to the quay ! " he yelled. " There by the steps ! Two anchors to get out ! "

" She'll hold now ! " Christos gasped. " She was holding with one."

"Not the *Irini* !" Manoli shook his head and spat the salt water from his mouth. "Look! There's one adrift from the breakwater. There! That big bastard from Leros!"

They could see her in the flicker of the moonlight, a big two-master with a high clipper bow, a two-hundred-tonner, and empty as a cask, rolling as if she would wrench the masts out, coming down on the gale towards the crowded moorings and dragging her cables in the broken sea behind. Up on the bow a tiny figure waved a lantern.

"Jesus Christ!" Christos bawled. "If that bitch gets into the boats they're all goddam well gone!"

"I saw her sailing in off Pserimos," said Manoli. "She's built like a pregnant woman. She drifts slow." He grabbed the oars and standing up, and pushing against them, headed the dinghy towards the steps where Zeffis and a gang of seamen were loading chain and two heavy grapnels aboard a big white rowboat.

Manoli bumped the dinghy into her side, and Christos rolled himself over the gunwale and into the rowboat, falling across the wet chains and dragging himself to the forward thwart and settling the big white oar on the tholepin. Manoli and Morgan jumped in after him and they sat on the chains while Zeffis and the men wrestled the two big grapnels aboard. Manoli reached over the side and scooped water into the cup of his hand and washed the blood off his arm and began to sing "*Yherakina.*"

"*Kinise i Yherakina yia nero krio na feri,*" he sang. Then he bellowed, "*Droom, droom, droom, droom, droom, droom, ta vrahiolia,*" stopped suddenly and grinned at Morgan. "Thanks for the help," he said. "Can you pull an oar?"

Morgan hesitated. "Not like Christos here," he said. "But I can pull one."

"We'll need three for this bastard!" He jerked his thumb over his shoulder. It was curious that, having accepted the menace of the drifting ship coming down on the wind, they no longer looked at it.

"Yes!" shouted Zeffis. He tossed two coils of rope into the boat and pushed it off into the plunge of the sea.

And then they rowed, all three of them, Christos in the bow

and Morgan amidships, and Manoli at the stern oar with his bare feet hooked around the grapnels. They rowed until Morgan thought he would tear his guts apart, fighting into the seas with the kick and shudder coming all the length of the thick oar to drive the pain into his muscles; rowing until the flying water and the pain had blinded him and he could no longer see right down in front of his eyes the muscles of Manoli's neck and back straining and swelling. But he could hear Manoli spitting the water out and singing " *Yherakina.*"

When they reached her, the big schooner was still sixty yards from the sponge-boat moorings, wallowing in the broken water. She was a big, round, fat-bellied ship with thick planking, and when she rolled away from them they could see half the curve of her bilge and the crust of weed and barnacles. The high, arching shape of the hull made her seem like some caravel out of a remote time.

It was Manoli who took the leap for the chains beneath the bowsprit, with one end of the coil of rope knotted around his waist. He made the jump as they were tossed high on the crest of a big snarling sea, and for an agonising minute he hung there, swinging and kicking his legs in the froth, with the bowsprit slicing a crazy arc through the scud. He was still there kicking when the next sea came along, breaking right over him, but when it had rolled away they could see the dripping figure in the chains clawing its way along.

The lightning had already begun by the time Manoli had hauled the chains up, and while he and the man aboard the schooner made them fast to the windlass, Morgan and Christos rowed the grapnels out. There was scarcely any thunder—it was only a faint growling to the north, somewhere around Brostá— but the lightning kept the whole sky streaked with a queer yellow light, throbbing up from behind the craggy mountains and flickering from peak to peak. All the way up the valley to Brostá the hills were bright as day, but of a queer sickly colour as if the world had been dipped in sulphur. As Morgan strained at the oar he could see the tiny white chapels on the steep cliffs of the ancient *Choria.*

It was something from a nightmare, crazily medieval,

demoniacal—the wild light of the sky and the sulphurous world below it, all the improbable painted cubes of the town, the forest of lurching masts, and in the foreground the great lumpy shape of the rolling Leros schooner. And on the foredeck the two black figures at the windlass, their arms stretched above their heads, pumped desperately, up and down, up and down, like clockwork toys, like demons operating some weird infernal machine.

"Now!" Christos screamed it into the wind, and they dropped their oars and fell together into the stern, wrestling the grapnels overboard while the seas poured across them. The chains went out plunging and kicking, and the iron links bruised their sprawled wet bodies, huddled together. They were insensible to the pain of it.

It seemed they watched hours before the bow of the schooner began to move, swinging slowly, resisting the pull of the chains, and the waves piled up along the side of the fat curved hull and burst against the bow. But still she turned, slowly and inexorably, and through the spray Morgan could see the two chains rising from the water, taut and shuddering.

"They're holding!" he muttered thankfully. "They're holding, Christos!"

"Jesus Christ!" Christos mumbled hoarsely, with something that was almost a sob in his voice. "Jesus Christ! Jesus Christ!" Over and over he said it, and Morgan couldn't tell whether it was part of his cursing or something different.

Mikali had never seen such a crowd in his *taverna*, not even on feast days, nor heard such music and singing. And as for the dancing of the men—well, that was something that nobody in the town had seen since the Liberation.

There at the long table were Manoli, all bruised and with his arm bandaged up, and Christos and the man from Australia and Doctor Telfs, the American—all of them together at the long table with their arms around one another's shoulders drinking and singing the songs of Kalymnos, the songs about the sponge divers and the fishermen. And the men from the boats crowded every table and hammered their beakers for retzina.

Mikali was humming the tune to himself as he went into the bay-scented cellar to tap another cask. A few nights like this one, and there wouldn't be any need for the Belgian Congo.

At the end of the room, right beneath the Category D sign, sat the little man without a name, the little man from the mountains with the face like Pan, playing wilder and wilder music on the *tsabuna*, the mountain bagpipes fashioned from a whole sheepskin and with the blowpipe carved from an olive root. To Morgan, seeing it all through a haze of tiredness and pain and alcoholic enchantment, it was fitting that the night should end with the *tsabuna* and the faun-faced man, with Pan down from the magic mountain glades to play for them.

All the others must have been infected by it too—by the music and the wine, by the thrash of the rain outside and tempest and peril lingering in their minds, by the thin, twisted face of Pan over the carved olive root, by things that were too deep for name or definition—for each man as he drank spilled wine on the floor as a libation. To what Morgan wondered. To the earth and the sea and the old gods ? To some lost and secret mystery, too old for understanding ? Through all the night this cord had run, this dark, twisted cord had entangled all men with something beyond comprehension, with the beginnings of things.

It was past midnight when Sergeant Phocas came to the door of the *taverna*, and although by law Mikali should have closed the door two hours before, it was quite clear from the singing and the dancing that nothing could be done about it. The night, like Manoli, had moved into a category apart from law, and Sergeant Phocas accepted a glass of retzina and fingered his *kom_olloi* of sea shells happily as he smiled around him. Then he went away, giggling, to report to Dimitropolis, the duty captain.

PART TWO

Irini

I

THE HOUSE of Paul Pelacos stood half a mile from the sea on the road that led through the valley to Brostá. It was a big white house with a wall around it and high gates of wrought iron that had been imported from Venice.

It was a fine house and a beautiful one. When Pelacos had built it to replace the old mansion gutted by bombs in the war, he had commissioned an architect from Marseilles, and almost driven the Frenchman mad by his insistence on an absolute simplicity. An austere house, its straight lines precisely chiselled, its angles and proportions exact as a geometrical drawing, it had fulfilled for Pelacos an important cathartic purpose by eliminating forever the picture of the sombre and ponderous residence it had replaced : the house which his grandfather, under the influence of the solidly opulent respectability of Disraeli's London, had commissioned an English architect to design. It was a perfect testimony to the taste and cleverness of Paul Pelacos that the new house fitted with absolute harmony into the cubes of Kalymnos.

"I had it painted white," he explained to Morgan, "an absolute white, in the hope that others in the town might follow the example." He smiled wryly. "Alas ! You see. It had not the slightest effect." He waved a disdainful hand towards the coloured, prismatic scatter of the town.

"I must say I like all the colours," Morgan said. "I find the whole effect quite charming."

"You do ? " Pelacos seemed surprised. "For my part, I am afraid I consider it unthinkably garish. Not the paler colours so much perhaps—that pink dome on the church there is not offensive—but this hideous blue they insist on using. A legacy of our Italian overlords. They were here for a quarter of a century, you know, and the Kalymnians—we are a proud stubborn people—insisted on painting their houses blue and white, the national colours of Greece, as a gesture of defiance. Many went to prison for it, some, indeed, were executed. But they persisted."

It was Morgan's turn to show surprise. "But surely that was wonderful," he said.

"Of course. Splendid. In those days my own house was painted blue and white." Pelacos smiled dryly. "But the Italians have been gone from us for many years, and the people are still persisting." He went to the table at the end of the terrace and took up his drink. "My dear Leigh," he went on, "when I was a child every house in Kalymnos was painted white. Without exception. The whole town white, everything white except the domes of the churches, which were pink or blue—a much more attractive blue than this horrible laundry colour they use nowadays. It was unbelievably lovely, and in the moonlight quite bewitching. There was something luminous! something enchanting, about that whiteness in the moonlight. I should like to see Kalymnos like that again, all white."

Irini laughed softly and took a cigarette from the box and lighted it. Her father permitted her to smoke in the house; outside it was forbidden because it was not the custom of the women of Kalymnos to smoke. "I am afraid Father would like to have all Kalymnos solidified into what it was when he was a boy," she said. "Like something beautiful kept under glass, to be looked at." She smiled across at her father as she spoke. "He would like to press it like a flower between the leaves of a book, so it would keep forever. He resents all forms of change."

"Nonsense, child!" Pelacos chuckled, enjoying her chiding. "Nobody supports progress more staunchly than I. It is merely that the sensitive man laments the passing of loveliness, in all its forms."

"Well, I agree with Mr. Leigh." She turned to him. Leaning against the railing of the terrace, dark and small and slender, with the orange trees behind her, the fruit on the deep foliage glowing like lanterns in the waning afternoon light, she impressed the moment with a delicate and particular aura, beautiful and yet melancholy. The Golden Apples of the Hesperides, thought Morgan, conscious of the oranges burning behind her in the dense green leaves. " I prefer the coloured houses," she said, " as you do."

" Ah, yes," Pelacos put in quickly, " but that is because you paint. I had not told you about Irini's painting, had I, Leigh ? She has talent, too. She was at the Slade, and a year or two in Paris. Here on Kalymnos there is not a great deal of entertainment for a young woman ; she is fortunate in having her painting. It stimulates her mind, keeps her occupied. I should warn you, however, that her style is rather violent." He chuckled. " Paris, I understand, has this effect on the young. At all events, she came back from the Rue Bonaparte and the Saint-Germain-du-Prés and the Café deux Magots with all the patient rectitude of the Slade quite obliterated. She came back, in fact, with her hair cropped short, a palette of the most primary hues, and violence in her imagination. She read Sartre and smoked incessantly. Her preference ever since has been for tuppence coloured rather than for penny plain." He smiled at her and walked across and touched her lightly on the cheek with the back of his fingers. " I am old enough," he added, turning to Morgan, " to prefer the refinements of tone to the excitements of colour. Tone is subtle and civilised. Colour is savage."

" Oh, I think that depends," said Morgan quickly. The girl was smiling, but there was something vaguely untrue about the smile, as if it were embedded in some deep sense of hurt. Or did he imagine it ? " It's something you can't generalise about at all. If you take Della Francesca——"

Pelacos laughed. " My dear Leigh, I haven't the slightest intention of taking Della Francesca—who was a mathematician, anyway, and therefore the purest of all refiners. I was teasing her, that's all." He took a thin gold watch from his vest pocket. " There is another hour before dinner," he said, " and there are some documents from London to which I must give attention. I suggest, Leigh, that you allow Irini to walk you around the garden. It is at its pleasantest at this hour. Or, better still, let her show you some of her paintings. Then you may judge for yourself."

He bowed slightly and went inside, smiling to himself, twirling the golden key chain.

"Well," said Morgan, "which is it to be? The garden? Or your paintings? You must say."

"The garden. While there is still light."

Like everything else that Paul Pelacos owned, the garden was exactly right, neither too wild nor too tame. In spite of this Morgan had the impression that it owed its luxuriance and beauty less to nature than to the skill and ingenuity of Paul Pelacos. Each weed, each fallen twig, every rock and pebble seemed to have been laid in its place under expert supervision; the little stream that ran so naturally from wall to wall, falling melodiously across the stones and twisting through moss and nettles, undoubtedly had a faucet at one end and a cistern at the other; the vines grew to a dictated pattern; the oranges and lemons and tangerines had unquestionably been tied to the branches to create an exact effect. Morgan smiled to himself at his image of Paul Pelacos, making a final scrutiny, comparing each detail of it with the original design, adjusting a twig here, a thistle there, arranging a heap of pebbles, moving an orange a few inches to the right, and then nodding and twirling his key chain in complete satisfaction.

"It is a lovely garden," he said. "Do you feel as I do that oranges growing on trees never look real? They always seem to have been tied there."

She reached up gravely and plucked an orange and held it out to him. "See for yourself," she said. "No string."

There was a cool, green dusk in the orange grove, and the fragrance of the fruit and flowers and wet grass and earth was all part of the secret manifestation of approaching night. Her slight, white-garbed figure standing before him, solemnly offering the golden fruit on outstretched hand, was part of it, too, part of the mystery. Her smallness in the gathering gloom, the dark gravity in the large eyes looking up at him, the slender outstretched arm made her look like a child playing Atalanta in a school charade. Caught by the arresting poignancy of the moment, he was quite still, looking at her, and then he laughed lightly to break the spell and reached out to take the orange from her.

"Yes," he said softly. "No string. It's all real then? I didn't quite believe it. But have you ever felt something about this particular hour of the day? At dusk everything is possible, but nothing is believable."

"Now you must see the walnut tree," she said. Her eyes were quick and alive again. "It's Daddy's special love."

"I think I'd like to see your paintings, if I may."

"You may of course, if you want to." She shrugged. "But first the walnut tree. He will ask when we go in, and you must have an opinion to express. Daddy likes people to have opinions about things. It helps him to sharpen up the opinions he has already."

He glanced at her quickly, but she had turned her head away and was leading him towards the orchard.

The walnut tree was already in blossom. Morgan thought of London, with another four months to wait before the crocuses began to appear in Hyde Park, and he admired her choice of words when she said, "It is very, very venerable." Then he was taken inside to see the paintings.

There was something strange about the paintings, and something intensely sad. Pelacos was right: the girl had both talent and a taste for violence. It was difficult to believe that this rather fragile, gentle person had painted the turbulent scenes. The sadness lay in the fact that while the talent was evident there was not one picture among them that was really successful: all betrayed a pathetic, desperate groping for some suitable style and form, and in each canvas was the peculiar childish violence, as if all the groping and frustration, the agony of incompleteness, the awareness of an absence of fulfilment had exploded suddenly in a wild rebellious disorder that secretly must have infuriated Paul Pelacos with his impeccable sense of pertinence. Infuriated? Pained more likely, thought Morgan. To Paul Pelacos, fury itself would be an irregularity, a farrago.

"They are all of Kalymnos," she said, speaking softly and diffidently as if, sensing his perplexity, she felt an apology to be necessary.

" Yes," he said thoughtfully. " I see."

" Some of the more abstract ones . . . I thought . . . That was why I explained. They could be anything—anywhere." She stopped, watching him like a child awaiting censure. " Why are you frowning ? " she said.

" Was I ? " He smiled at her. " I was wondering. You see Kalymnos differently from your father, don't you ? "

" I suppose I do, yes. It's what I said. He sees it as something under glass, jealously preserved, the way he wants it to be. But I cannot remember it, you see, when it was all white."

Morgan smiled slightly. He gestured to the paintings. " You mean you really see it as something violent and savage, like this ? "

" Oh, yes," she said simply. " And cruel."

" Cruel ? " He pursed his mouth. " Harsh, perhaps."

" Deeper than harsh. Cruel."

How *could* she see it, he wondered, from this green oasis her father had created—this walled-in garden of sophistication and pedigree far from the beat of the sea, where the smell of damp moss and the soft music of the little artificial streamlet masked out the realities. The mountains were cruel, and the ocean was cruel. They were the realities. And the hardship and poverty and peril that attended the realities, they were cruel, too. There were dragons outside in the darkness, yes, but Pelacos had tamed the dragons and put them out to work for him.

It was odd to think that not only the wealth of Paul Pelacos, but all this girl's breeding and education and background, the clothes she wore, the canvases she painted on, even the cropped hair and the sense of a scarcely comprehended violence she had acquired in Paris—that all these things derived from the sea, from innumerable oozy sponges wrenched out of the dark thalassic depths. Her father, on the first day they had met, had talked to him of the ingenuity of the industrial chemist who had created the synthetic sponge from the test tubes, but Pelacos himself was by far the cleverer alchemist. For Pelacos had taken the black fruit of the sea bed and refined it into this cool, melodious oasis, had fashioned it into the shape of this daughter, had transmuted it into the splendid white house with its fine pictures and imported furnishings, into his library of phonograph records, his Bach and Mozart and Scarlatti and Couperin, into his books and into the wines on his table, Lafite and Chambertin and Château D'Yquem. From the porous skeleton of an unseeing animal crouched in the sea slime, Paul Pelacos had created his own world, precise and ordered and complete.

And there was another surprising thing : nothing of this marine provenance invaded the oasis it had created. There was no smell of the sea about the little world of Paul Pelacos ; it needed no brine for its preservation.

Morgan suddenly found himself recollecting his visit, not two weeks before, to the kitchen of Mina Vraxos. There the tang of the sea had permeated every corner—the sponge scraps on the shelf and stopping the neck of the big red water jar, the old print of the clipper ship *Dreadnought*, the unshaven men in the blue jerseys, the platters of *barbunia*, the octopus drying on the branches of the tree outside.

How could Irini Pelacos possibly sense anything of all this —of all the infinite complexities of cruelty that lay beyond— from the shelter of the oasis ? Or was the cruelty of which she spoke some different thing, something turning inward from the perimiter of the oasis to affect her ?

He was conscious suddenly of his own long silence and of her dark eyes upon him, questioningly. He pointed to one of the paintings, a large canvas crowded with figures against a quayside and the fire and smoulder of priests' vestments in the crowd, a painting of fiery colour and thick black shadows and outlines, with something of the qualities of a Roualt suggested but never fulfilled. It was rather like a bold design for a stained-glass window that had not quite come off, that had failed and been discarded.

" And this ? " he asked gently. " This is—what ? "

" I did it last year," she said. " It is the Epiphany, when all the people go down to the harbour and the archbishop throws the silver cross into the water and the young men dive for it." She studied the picture dejectedly for a moment and then turned to him. " It is to-morrow again, the ceremony," she said, with a sudden childish eagerness. " I should like to try to do it again."

" I was going to ask you," Morgan said. " If it wouldn't

be too much of a bore for you, I was going to ask you if you would take me. I heard about it. And you did undertake to explain things to me, you know." He smiled. "Would you?"

"Yes." Her pleasure was obvious. "I'd like to very much."

Before they went into the other room to join Pelacos, he said to her: "Do you know Manoli?"

"Yes." She looked up at him inquiringly. "I have met him."

"One day you should do a painting of him."

"Of Manoli? Why?"

He stopped at the door and looked back at her paintings thoughtfully. "I think you might find he has all the qualities you are trying to express," he said. "I'm not sure, but I think he might have. One day you should paint him." He smiled. "It would be a way of finding out, wouldn't it?"

"Yes," she said, but he had the impression as he followed her through the doorway that his suggestion had not been particularly welcomed.

2

IN THE weeks that followed Epiphany, Morgan saw much of Irini Pelacos. Zelfs had returned to Kós and had taken the little boy Nikolas with him for some special treatment at the hospital. Paul Pelacos had gone to Athens on business. Manoli spent most of his days at Lavassi, attending to the overhaul of his boats.

Once or twice Morgan saw Mina Vraxos in the street, the white scarf around her face, and it was after one of these occasions that he clambered up the hillside until he could see the little blue house beneath the cliff. But instead of going up the last steep stretch where he had climbed with Telfs, carrying the retzina jar, he turned away down a narrow path and walked instead up to the blue church of Saint Vassilias and stayed for an hour in the old cemetery, sitting amid the queer, painted graves, watching Kalymnos.

There were fewer boats in the harbour now, but across the bay a forest of masts had sprouted in the hill-encircled cove of Lavassi, where the sponge boats had gone for refitting, and a rusty Greek freighter off the breakwater was unloading bales of rope and drums of gasoline and diesel oil and big coils of thick, white rubber tubing. Every day now there were freighters in the port—from Rhodes or Piræus, and once a Dutch motor ship from Amsterdam, bringing steel cable and an alien air of scrubbed stolidity—and the wharves were stacked with the stores and gear which the sponge fleet would take away on its summer operations. Johnny and Mike and Costas and Petros and the rest of the labouring gang in the cloth caps were toiling from sunrise until after dusk, hauling the stuff to the warehouses in the big heavy hand-carts. Morgan, watching them with their bodies twisted sideways on the thick drag ropes, watching the crouched, taut, gut-wrenching travail of it, hour after hour all through the day, realised that this was the way the Pyramids were built, the way emperors had mounted monoliths to their own glory. This was man's labour, fixed unalterably since the coming of the wheel. It was in this fashion that these men had rolled the stores down to the galleys setting out for Troy.

There was no time now for Costas and Johnny and Mike and Petros to sit around the steps of the war memorial, with the big barrows upended in a long line along the harbour wall, telling one another dirty stories in the sunshine. But they had money in their pockets, worth-while money. There was wild drinking every night in the *tavernas*, and they could forget the pains in their thighs and the thick callouses on their shoulders and the way their bodies were beginning to slope over to one side even when they weren't working, when they were just sitting around.

In the cemetery there was a deep quietness, only the drone of a bee and the stirring of the nettles in the wind.

The edge of the wind still bit, and there was a cold glitter in the sky that spoke of winter. Across the sea the mountains of Turkey were sharp-edged and steely, but a froth of white blossom had spread up the valley to Brostá, and on the twisted silver branches of the fig trees the green nipples were showing. Sometimes the wind would drop away and then come nervously across the water in soft, warm flurries, and there was a disturbing restlessness in the inference of the wind.

It was a restlessness that almost imperceptibly had infected the town with a sense of urgency, as if the ending of the triple feast of Christmas, New Year and Epiphany had brought an awakening to reality. The bells had tolled, the litanies been chanted, the candles guttered out, the emblazoned copes of the bearded patriarchs put away; all the rich Byzantine colouring had dimmed. It was the nervous wind that brought the realisation that the festival was over, that too much time had already been frittered in the indolence of winter, in drinking and gambling and in the interminable games of cards around the painted tables of the coffee-houses, in aimless promenading up and down the street, in waiting. One day soon, the wind whispered, spring will come and all the boats will go, and fifteen hundred men with them—and now there is much to be done.

To Morgan, looking down from the quiet graves, it was almost as if a gigantic sponge was being prepared and moistened to wipe the town clear of the accumulation of the vanished year— as Mikali might wipe the chalked retzina tallies of his clients from the big slate slab on his *taverna* counter, as the gamblers in the coffee-houses would wipe the *belota* scores from the cracked school slates.

As he walked through the town with Irini, he had become acutely aware of this quickening tempo : the accelerated pace of all the old year's activities, like the sand in an hour glass running more quickly as it comes to its final drop, and the growing excitability of the new things happening. There was a curious symphonic quality to it, one thing germinating the thing that followed, everything blending towards an inclusive purpose, all the activities of the town separated and yet belonging to each other. Almost a fugal thing, with infinite variations springing from a single theme.

Spread out below him were the town and the harbour and Lavassi across the bay, and all these things happening. In the stillness of the painted cemetery Morgan could almost hear the music of it drifting up to him.

The little, self-contained world of Lavassi, with the big rock overhanging the slipways and the grey-green aloes climbing up the cliffs and the chains of the caiques stretched out in the pebbly shadows. Manoli would be there—Manoli, who had brought his sponges in and sold them and now was back with his ships to prepare them for another foray . . . back where the painted masts stood like a thicket . . . back with the rasp and screech of the big saws and the thud of the shipwrights' hammers and the squeak of dry tackle reeving through new blocks and the smells of paint and creosote and wood shavings and pitch.

This was the year impending, the sea's year, related to the world of men in blue jerseys and black caps . . . to dark, smoky little workshops smelling of brass and rubber . . . yellow diving suits hanging in the racks like flat figures of giants cut from painted cardboard . . . black rubber and the big piles of leaden chest weights and the air hoses oiled like serpents, crimson and white, and the glint of the copper couplings . . . fourteen diving helmets, metallic curves shining in the sun, stacked outside the doorway in the cobbled lane and three yellow-beaked ducks waddling around them . . . Costas and Mike sweating past with the hand cart laden with paraffin drums and great, fat coils of hempen rope, white and soft to touch and smelling of warm, distant fields . . . the marline smell in the stores of the ship chandlers, and the sun coming in through the doorways and shining on the shackles, and the brass sidelights, and the casks of copper nails. . . .

This was the impending year, but the year that had passed had left a heavy sediment yet to be dispersed. In every warehouse the sponge clippers were working, not only in the vast sponge rooms of the big companies, where a circle of a hundred men would be sitting on upturned packing cases among the tawny hillocks of the sponges, shearing them and shaping them and tossing them into the great, square bin in the centre, but all through the town, in dark rooms and little cellars. In his own house Morgan awakened each morning to the sound of the shears snipping in the sponge room below. Often, as he walked with

Irini, he heard the familiar yet unexpected clicking of the shears in some narrow, twisty lane—a curious sound, persistent and insectine—and through an open doorway he sometimes glimpsed some small, dark interior and the yellow mound of the sponges and the circle of stooped figures; then the men would be motionless for a moment, the shears in their hands, and all the dark faces in the gloom would watch them as they walked past.

All around the bay, when the sea was calm, the barelegged boys were trampling the sponges clean; the big bleaching vats were out along the quay by the market, and whitened sponges were drying in the branches of the scraggy trees. If the day was warm and clear every square in the town and all the vacant plots of ground were thickly carpeted with the sponges drying in the sun.

To Morgan it was as if the whole town had declared itself —not only the town, but the whole island, all the people. He remembered what Telfs had said to him back in Athens, in the Cretan *taverna*, with the wild music twanging behind his words and the men dancing. " It lives on its divers and its boats," he had said. " It lives on sponges."

Pelacos lived on sponges, too, and Irini. And Mina Vraxos. And the men hauling the hand carts, pulling their guts out, and everything else in the town—all the ragged fringes, the riff-raff, the shoeblacks, the peanut boys, the well-dressed men with their raincoats worn across their shoulders like capes, the poor bastards hawking cakes of green soap around the town, the cripples, the tailors, the grocers, the café men stewing coffee over primus stoves, the itinerant musicians with their zithers and mandolins. And the man with the face like Pan who played the *tsabuna*. And the fishermen and Mikali in his *taverna* and the barefooted kids and the woman in black and the men with old faces and the backsides out of their pants. Everyone.

Down there now, in the warm sunshine, the trees and the verandas of the houses were festooned with sponges. In the Customs House the square, pressed bales rose higher and higher towards the girdered roof, and though the ships from Piræus came in and took the bales away, the men were still crowding the street with sacks of sponges and armfuls of sponges. Sometimes you would see a man walking along with only a single sponge, clean and white, and with the texture of silk ; he would carry it very carefully and with a sort of reverence, as if it were something precious, as if it were a jewel.

Morgan went down the hill slowly, taking the stony path on one side so that he would pass the house of Mina Vraxos, but the shutters were drawn across the windows and the pink door closed. Around the henna-coloured rocks the hens were scratching. He wondered when Telfs would be returning from Kós with the boy.

"Another wedding ? " Morgan stopped at the edge of the crowd. " Or the same one ? "

"It is the same one," Irini smiled up at him. " They've been singing and dancing all night and, they'll be singing and dancing all day."

"I must say I admire their stamina." Morgan laughed. In the sunshine against the mottled-pink wall of the café were the three musicians, the old man with the zither and the violinist and a wizened gnome-like creature plucking at an egg-bellied *bouzouki*. They had awakened him at dawn, the three of them, coming slowly down the street along the waterfront—the three of them in the pale, grey light, shuffling their feet in time to the music, and behind them the wedding party, singing and looking up to the shuttered windows, and one man waving aloft a big carafe of retzina.

The party had thinned out a little now, but four women, one with a baby in a shawl, and a dozen young men, drunk with wine and sleeplessness, still sat outside the café where there were four tables pushed together, littered with plates of food and glasses of wine. Three other men, in black caps and jerseys and with sprigs of white blossom behind their ears, were dancing on the roadway. It was the same circling, kicking dance that he had watched the Cretan men doing in the café in Athens, but these men danced awkwardly, limbs loose and uncertain with fatigue and intoxication, and they laughed together helplessly when one among them stumbled or fell.

The music came to a stop with a sudden upward screech.

One of the dancers, a lean young man with a brown face, staggered to the table, filled two glasses with wine and brought them across to Irini and Morgan. He had pleasant eyes and a loose, good-humoured grin.

" *Chronia pollá*, Antoni," Irini said gravely, then drank the wine and smiled and shook hands with him.

"He is a diver in one of Daddy's boats," she explained as they walked on. "This is the time of the year when there are many weddings. And baptisms, too. Soon all the young men will be going away in the boats, you see, and these are things that must be done before they leave. Some nights you can hear them singing and dancing all over the town. At times I wake hours before dawn, and away in the distance I can hear the music and the singing and the hands clapping, and the cocks crowing all around the hills. And . . . do you know something?"

"You have an overwhelming desire to throw off the bed coverings and run from the house and climb the hills to join them."

"Yes," she said. "How did you know?"

"It's what I should want to do. I warn you that if I ever awaken and hear it, I shan't lose a moment. Shall I come and fetch you? One night when it happens you should go, you know. It's important. It's all part of the symphony. A little rondo, I think—very simple and sweet, going round and coming back to where it all began."

"Symphony?" She stared at him in surprise. "What are you talking about?"

"Some day I'll explain it to you," he said, smiling. "It's a symphony all about a great sponge clearing the slate. This is the rondo—the wedding feasts, the music you hear in the night." What would happen to her, he wondered, if one night she did follow the beat of the melody? So small and white—she would be in white—and drawn by the magic, following the empty, twisting paths up the hill, and beneath her feet the pebbles in the moonlight and the shapes of the shadows and the changing, flat planes of the walls in moonlight. You could not see the colours in moonshine, you could only feel them; yes, Irini would feel the colours of the pebbles under her feet, and the colours of the flat, rough walls beneath her hands in the moonlight. And high up on a hill where the cocks were crowing, at the very top of an uneven flight of white stone steps, an open door and black figures against the lamplight. It would be magical for her, going in through the open doorway, into the room with the framed Swiss oleographs on the wall and the music and the figures all spinning and whirling together, and the smell of sweat and wine.

They walked on together around the harbour road that led to Lavassi; beneath his arm Morgan carried the box of paints and the folding seat.

" One day you will be married," he said.

" Yes, I suppose so."

" And will you have a wedding like that ? Dancing all night and singing in the street ? "

She laughed softly. " Can you imagine Daddy dancing down the streets to the music of a zither ? I think he would prefer Monteverdi—and martinis."

The faint acidity in her voice was not reflected in her smile. She was right, of course. Paul Pelacos would arrange it all impeccably—an imported husband of the finest quality, and something very sumptuous at the Brompton Oratory or maybe in Paris at a very little, very fashionable church, and Monteverdi on the organ. Or a proper and wealthy young man from Athens, the son of a shipowner or a banker, with suave friends and a house at Kiffisia. Yet how much more wonderful if the iron gates of the white house here in Kalymnos were flung wide and the sea wind blew in through the garden, and they went up through the gates dancing and singing to the music of the three old men, all the brown-faced young men in seamen's caps and the women in black shawls carrying the garlands of flowers, and dancing and singing until the cocks crowed all around the hills. . . .

When they came to Lavassi they went down the goat path and across the planked walk between the hulls of the caiques and the long, low, open sheds where the white ribs of the new boats gleamed like skeletons of extinct creatures in museums. They climbed together through the aloes and figs and the tumbled red rocks until they reached the end of the little promontory.

Below them was the curve of the sea and a criss-cross of rusty chains patterning the shallows, and overhanging the crowded shipyard a golden rock like a ruined castle and the bare hills folding away behind.

"There are Manoli's boats down there," he said, as she arranged her canvas and palette. "There, on the second slip." The four *aktaramathes* were all hauled up together, one behind the other, the one that had not been away gleaming in new paint, blue and white and red, and the others grey and sea-stained. The *Ikaros* and *Angellico* and *Elektra* and *Saint Stephanos*. Beautiful boats. Beautiful names. So much more beautiful, too, in the angular Greek lettering. "Did you give any more thought to what I said?" he went on. "About doing a painting of him? Of Manoli?"

She was already blocking in the sketch with swift, stabbing brush strokes. For a time he thought she did not intend to answer him, but finally she said, "How could I? Even supposing I wanted to, how could I?" Frowning down at the palette, she lifted some red pigment on the square bristles of the brush. "Do you think he would permit it?"

"He?"

"My father. Do you think he would allow me to paint Manoli, to be alone with him?"

"Good heavens!" Morgan laughed. "Does he have such a reputation as that?"

"Oh, not only Manoli. Any man."

"He allows you to be alone with me, doesn't he? Am I so much safer than other men?"

"You are quite different. You're not from here."

Good God! he thought. It couldn't possibly be *that*—the imported husband of the finest quality. No, it wasn't that at all. It was merely the way Pelacos thought, the way his world was built: the wrought-iron gates from Venice, the architect from Marseilles, the wines from France, the pictures on the walls from London, the companion for his daughter from Australia.

"Manoli is a fine man," he said, "whatever they say about him. Oh, he's tough and wild, yes. I don't even know all they say about him. But he's a fine man. Your father admires him, I think. But that isn't the point at all. We're not concerned with the character or reputation of Manoli so much as with his fitness as a subject for painting. I think it would be interesting to try —from your point of view." In a sense painting Manoli was hearing the distant music in the night and getting out of bed and climbing up the hillside, lured on by something old and big and strange. A cockerel arching its neck and crowing and three notes on a reed pipe high up somewhere in the darkness—Manoli, with the blood on his arm, spitting the sea out and singing. Pan's face over the *tsabuna* and the libatory wine spilling to the floor—and the glimpse of it, no more than a glimpse, in the tormented pattern of her paintings. It was a door that had not opened yet, not for her. Beyond the door were sweat and music and wine and the bodies twirling, twirling, twirling ; and the bald brown head bent over the clanging, singing zither; and on the faded wall in the lamplight the framed oleographs of painted lakes and glaciers and the absurd châteaux. *Printed in Zurich, 1886.* Older than the white house of Paul Pelacos, older than the oasis and the walled garden, older than the oldest things on earth.

He opened his case and offered her a cigarette, but she shook her head. " Would you like to paint Manoli ? " he said.

" Yes," she said simply.

" If I were able to arrange it perhaps your father would not object."

" Perhaps not."

" Shall I try ? "

" Yes."

She was bent forward over the canvas with the little frown of concentration on her face. Her small, neat head was in profile, and, with her short hair and the expression on her face, she looked like a schoolgirl who has been set a difficult exercise. Behind her was a spiky clump of aloes, grey-green and prickly, and the deep blue of the Ægean, and across the water the coloured houses of Kalymnos and the encircling walls of the mountains that imprisoned her.

" You hate Kalymnos, don't you ? " he said gently.

" Yes." She did not look up from her painting. " Yes, I do."

" You don't have to go away to escape from it, you know. You can escape from it here."

3

STAVROS WENT behind the market and left with old Beanie the round, flat fish basket and the metal scales he used to weigh out the kilos of *barbunia*.

" I have to talk with Manoli," Stavros said.

" But he is at Lavassi," said the old man. " With his boats. If there's a message to take, I'll go there for you." Old Beanie was like that : he was very old and not too strong but he was always anxious to help people, to run messages for them, to find old scraps of tin to mend stoves and chimney flues, to collect driftwood from the rocks for kindling, to fix fishing rods and kitchen pans. You could never get old Beanie to take money for the things he did to help ; he would only shake his head and look happy. He liked doing things for people. " It's a long walk to Lavassi," he said concernedly. " For you, with your legs."

" There's nothing wrong with my legs," Stavros said, scowling. " They take me round the town, don't they ? "

But the old man's concern had stung him and made him feel uncomfortable, and when he left Beanie's hut he did not go straight away to find Manoli. It would be better, he decided, to talk it over first with Dimitri, because Dimitri's house was on the way to Lavassi ; and anyway Dimitri had to be warned against saying anything about it to Mina. Mina would hate it when she heard.

Stavros walked on down the road beside the fish wharf, where the brown and white nets were spread along the pavement and the fishermen were sitting with their legs wide apart and their bare big toes hooked through the mesh as they plied the wooden needles. He knew the fishermen, all of them, and spoke to them, and he was conscious as he walked past of their eyes following him. Stavros walked this morning slowly and stiffly, almost like a clockwork figure, trying not to limp too much and with his shoulders well back to ease out the little stabbing pains that hurt beneath his ribs. Walking like this, very erect and with scarcely a trace of the limp, he felt good. Now, if he could walk up to Manoli like this, and tell him what was in his mind . . .

In the clay patches beside the roadway the new trees were grey and stumpy, sickly looking, not flourishing like the fifteen trees he had planted around Mina's house. By the time he reached Dimitri's street, walking well and with the thought of the trees in his mind, he had forgotten the discomfort which old Beanie's remark had given him.

Dimitri lived in a very narrow street running right down to the edge of the water, just hard earth between the houses and a drain running down and not two metres separating the facing walls ; but it was a pretty street, with all the little houses coloured differently and the white steps rising from the red earth, and the lines stretched across from window to window with all the rugs and mats hanging in the air.

In Dimitri's room the best brown-velvet cloth was spread on the table, the cloth with the pattern of fruit and the red tassels.

" You are expecting someone ? " Stavros asked, staring at the best cloth.

" No, no," Dimitri turned from the primus stove where he was making coffee. " It's pretty. Sometimes I put it on. I like to see it there." He turned to pump the primus, while Stavros studied the coloured picture on the wall of the big liner, the *Leviathan*, with the smoke pouring from its funnels and the Statue of Liberty behind it.

" To-day I feel good," Stavros said pointedly. Now that he was sitting the pain beneath his ribs was sharper. " Very good," he said, to disprove the pain.

" That's fine," said Dimitri, watching the coffee.

" I called in. I'm on my way to see Manoli, to talk to him."

" He's at Lavassi. It's a long walk for you, with your legs."

" I told you, I feel good." The darkness was in Stavros' eyes again, and there was a sudden surly defiance in the way he spoke. " Do you know why I see Manoli? Because he is looking for another diver, for when he goes away."

" Yes, I hear that. In the place of Costas Gravos." Dimitri shrugged. " Well, he can pick any one he wants. Any of them will sail with Manoli."

Stavros was hurt, and the pain cut deeper beneath his ribs, but he said, " You don't see what I mean. I'm going to ask Manoli to take me."

Dimitri turned then, with the tin coffee pot poised in his hand. " Take you? " he said, and laughed.

" Why not? " said Stavros furiously. " I was a good diver, as good as any of them."

" Ten years ago," said Dimitri, " when your legs were good." He turned his attention to the primus. " If he wants to take a cripple, Stavros, why should it be you? There are a thousand cripples in the town, more than a thousand. All of them were divers once." With great care Dimitri poured the coffee into the little cups, using his thumb to wipe the drops from around the edges. " When a thing is done, it's done," said Dimitri, carrying the cups to the table. " There's no point in fretting. Like me. I don't fret. It isn't worth it."

As he sipped the thick, black coffee Dimitri thought of the years he had spent in Gary, Indiana, after he had skipped ashore from the *Mauretania*—fine years they were, too—and the years he had travelled the world as a ship's fireman. The *Mauretania* and the *Leviathan*, and all the way round the Cape of Good Hope to Australia on the *Ceramic* . . . and the *Franconia*, taking the millionaires around the world. And the strange smell of the girls in Batavia, an odd smell, as if they had been kept for a long time in wooden boxes—soft, tiny girls without a hair on their bodies and that strange smell to them. . . . For a long time he had regretted not staying on in Gary, Indiana ; long enough, anyway, to get his pension. Then he could have come home. But he wasn't regretful any longer, not for that, nor even for the big ships coming in off Staten Island or hauling up the Mersey in the rain. He had liked the big ships. And now he was an old man, and there was nothing more for him to do than to walk up and down, up and down, swinging his *kombolloi*, drinking his coffees in the sunshine. Now he had forgotten it all—the big ships, the red and black funnels over the wharves, the smell of the girls, the words of English he had learned long ago, the hooting of the trains coming in to Gary. Only the *kombolloi* and the sun and the coffee and the old slow figures walking up and down. What was the use of fretting about all the rest? What was the point?

Stavros was different. Stavros was always fighting against it, trying to change the things that couldn't be changed, drowning himself in his own bitterness—as if it did any good.

"You wait and see," said Stavros stubbornly. "Manoli will take me. If I ask him he'll take me—because of Mina."

But Stavros knew as he spoke that Manoli would not take him. Manoli wanted strong things around him, big things, full of guts and blood. He had not really expected it, anyway. Stavros no longer expected anything. For a long time now he had been nobody, nothing—a black speck adrift in an evil wind. He had nothing behind him but pitiless memories, nothing ahead of him but the gradual decay into final, absolute failure, and the companionship of all the other old, broken, futureless men, the men who had given up, the men who didn't fret any longer. Like Dimitri. There was no escape from it. The whole island was a prison, and there was no escape from it.

"Thanks for the coffee," he said, pushing back his chair;
"Where do you go now?" asked Dimitri. "To Lavassi?"
"Sure. It's what I said, isn't it?"

Stavros walked down the narrow street very straight and erect, but at the sea front he turned his back on Lavassi, and went along to collect his fish basket and scales from old Beanie's hut. He was stooped over and limping heavily as he walked, and the pain burned deep beneath his ribs.

It was a mild evening and the four of them sat outside on the blue steps with the lamp hissing on the well ledge beside them. Manoli kept reaching across to the platter of small brown fish in Mina's lap. He ate them whole—head, tail, bones and all. On the lowest step Morgan sat with Stavros, the carafe of retzina between them, and it was Morgan who kept the glasses full. The carafe was a fine one, and Georgian ; Morgan wondered how it had found its way to this craggy, remote hillside at the end of the Ægean. Or the lithograph of the *Dreadnought* on the wall inside. The imprint said : PUBLISHED BY CURRIER & IVES, 115 NASSAU STREET, NEW YORK. It was the same all over Kalymnos—all the houses with their Swiss oleographs and queer, incongruous things : tinted photographs of an exposition in Paris, views of Chicago, coloured corals from the Bahamas, a stuffed macaw from Brazil in a glass case, a china mug commemorating the jubilee of Queen Victoria, a French *louis d'or* in a velvet-lined box with a steel engraving of Dreyfus pasted on the inside of the lid. The relics, no doubt, of many Kalymnian voyages, but their static incongruity had long since overcome all vestiges of human association ; the mementoes lingered on in the dull persistency of anachronism, no longer looked at with eyes bright with curiosity or alight with acquisitiveness, no longer the subject of any regard at all. Morgan had an image of Kalymnos as some lost island far away from the contemporary world, remote from the courses of the steamers, its rocky beaches receiving the flotsam of lost times, the detritus of worlds that had expired.

From the top step Manoli watched Morgan's face and his long, thin fingers stroking the curve of the carafe. He was glad he had met Morgan at Lavassi, glad he had brought him up here with him. He liked Morgan. There was something big and honest about him, and he had a curiosity about things that amused Manoli. He was an odd mixture of toughness—the night of the sirocco had shown his guts—and a sort of childlike, dreaming quality that Manoli admired without quite understanding. There was a sort of quietness about the Australian, as if he had come to an understanding with himself and with other people, and was prepared to wait to see what happened—not like Paul Pelacos, cutting himself off from things ; not like Telfs, the American, beating at things with his fists as if he could hammer the world down. . . . It was a pity the Pelacos girl had not come up with them also, just to sit down on the steps and eat the little brown *smarithes* and drink wine and talk and look down on the lights strung out around the bay.

He turned to Mina, chuckling. " Did you know that I am to be painted ? " he said. " By Pelacos' daughter. She's going to make a picture of me."

" When ? " Mina said.

" Oh, one day." He gestured vaguely. " Before we go."

" Why should she want to make a picture of you ? " Stavros asked accusingly. " Once I saw her doing a picture on the fish wharf. It didn't look like anything I could see. All of us were there and nobody could make head or tail of it. Maybe she'll paint you like that."

Manoli shrugged, smiling. " She wants to do it," he said. " Why not ? "

Why not ? He had been amused at first, and just as sceptical as Stavros, when they had come to him in the shipyard. It was Morgan who had asked about it, and for a moment he had been going to take it all as a joke, but then he had turned to the girl. She had looked so small, standing there beneath the big, clean sweep of the *Elektra's* bow with all the riggers and carpenters clustered around her, and in her face a curious look, earnest and shy, that made it hard to believe she was really Pelacos' daughter at all. So he had agreed straight away. When Morgan made the suggestion some of the men around had begun to snigger, and he could tell from the expressions on their faces—as if they had glimpsed the point of a joke but were all waiting to hear it expressed before they began to laugh—that they all expected him to refuse. Manoli sitting down on a chair having his picture painted by a girl—*po-po-po-po-po-po-po !* That was what their expressions had seemed to say. She had heard the sniggers, too, and she must have known what they were thinking because she had looked away quickly pretending to examine one of the big, rusty anchors on the slipway, but she hadn't looked away quickly enough to prevent his noticing how her eyes had winced. And straight away he had said, " Why not ? Of course." And then he had looked around at all the men, and the bastards, every one of them, had nodded quickly and approvingly as if his answer had been exactly what they had expected. Now, thinking about it, he was glad he had agreed.

" It all depends, doesn't it ? " said Morgan, renewing the conversation after a long silence. " Her father has to agree."

" Ah, Pelacos ! " Manoli grinned.

" Why should he not agree ? " Mina asked. " Manoli would make a fine painting. If she would like to paint him, what else is there ? "

Morgan looked up at her. How could she understand this set of values so remote, so distinct, from her own ? It was all simple to her : a pattern of life reduced to established fundamentals as natural as the sweep of the wind and the rising of the stars. The carafe beneath his fingers—to her something simple and natural, a container for wine ; to Paul Pelacos something utterly different, something to be coveted and admired, not wanted because it held wine but for its intrinsic beauty and worth, something to be treasured and locked away. How could Mina Vraxos understand anything of the complex arabesques which Paul Pelacos had twisted into the wonderful ornamental cage surrounding himself and his life—yes, and his daughter's life too ? Arabesque ? Yes, there *was* something Islamic about the Pelacos oasis : a decorative form in which the employment of the human element had been entirely eliminated. The lozenge and the whorl, the ribbon geometricised, vine and flower twisted into formalised conformity, as the wood of a straight and growing tree is steamed into the dead curve of a boat's keel. But nothing of the soft feel of flesh, no breath warming it. . . . Once, at Amber in Rajputana, he had wandered through the old zenana, where the Mogul princes had kept their women ; he remembered the slanted windows, devised so that the women could see the forbidden outside world moving in the courtyard below, but themselves could never be seen. . . .

The thought expired as he pursued it. He was arrested suddenly by the picture of the woman on the steps in the lamplight, by the sublime quality of her beauty. She was holding out the platter of *smarithes*, offering it, and at her mouth was a faint enigmatic smile, as if she was aware of what he had been thinking ; there was a gleam of gold along the tawny skin where the light caught the cheekbone and asserted the fine plane of her forehead, and the light gave a curious coppery lustre to the dark, straight hair, parted in the middle. It was the first time, he realised, that he had seen her without the white head scarf. As she leaned forward the folds of her dress fell in straight sculptural folds from her bosom.

There was an antique quality to her beauty. You could paint Manoli but you could not paint her. She was something that preceded painting. Sculpture, yes. In the relaxed stillness of the woman, modelled upwards from the stone step, the hands reaching out and down to offer the platter, there was something of the quality of one of the antique statues in painted marble. A *kore* bringing the votive offering to the temple, perhaps—the same cryptic curve to the mouth, the dress falling in the same precise, formalised lines, the same gesture of the outstretched arms, offering. . . . Offering ? Irini Pelacos in the dusky garden with the orange glowing in her outstretched hand—it was not the same ; it was something entirely different from this woman. Irini was the *kore*, the maiden, a virginal innocence ; Mina Vraxos was something far older, a dark, deep thing flooding out of the earth. Offering what ? Was she Demeter, perhaps ? If he took his gaze from her face would he find on the offered platter a single ear of dyed corn ? But the answer was there, surely, in her face, in the dark eyes looking down at him and the mystery that haunted the faint, upward curve of her mouth.

Morgan could feel the understanding of it gripping him inside, stirring at his loins, and he recoiled from it, disturbed and ashamed.

Manoli was saying something about the refitting of his boats, and Morgan had the uneasy feeling that he had been talking on the subject for some time, that the matter of Irini's painting had long been set aside. How long, he wondered guiltily, had he been staring at the woman ? The feel of the glass carafe beneath his fingers seemed to suggest that his hand had been there for some time, arrested in the act of raising it, the action frozen into a whole Pompeii of meaning. He lifted the carafe and filled his glass, and as he did so Mina Vraxos put the platter back on her lap and looked at Manoli.

"I was coming out to Lavassi myself to-day," Stavros said to Manoli casually.

"Lavassi?" Mina smiled. "It's too far for you. With your legs."

Manoli grinned. "It's too far for me, with my legs," he said. "Five times to-day. Back and forth, back and forth. And each time by once all the way to the Customs House. Papers, papers, papers! *Po-po-po-po-po*! He lives on paper, that Zeffis. Paper and rubber stamps. He eats them!" He slapped his thigh. "Coming back the last time, Christos said a funny thing. Christos Papagalos. He stopped there right outside the Mellekios sponge room, with all the buyers standing around outside, and do you know what he said? Bawled it out, too, as if he were crying it to the town. 'That Zeffis,' he said, 'that Zeffis never uses paper to wipe with, you know. All that ever comes out of him is paper!' That's what he said!" Manoli put his head down on his knees and choked on his laughter. "That Christos is a funny fellow, eh, a long story," he spluttered.

"Why did Christos have to go to the Customs House?" Mina asked.

"To change his papers," said Manoli. "This summer he dives with me. In the *Ikaros*, in place of Costas. I want to keep nine to a boat, nine divers. It's the best number."

"Yes, but why Christos?" Mina asked. "Why take a cripple?"

"Cripple?" Manoli stared at her. "This man isn't a cripple, he's a fish. Christos Papagalos can do seventy metres the way another man eats *barbunia*." The thought seemed to remind him because he reached across to Mina's lap and took another fish and swallowed it. "Cripple?" he said with a laugh. "Ask Morgan here. He saw him the night of the big storm."

Stavros stared down at the lights of the town and the smudge against the stars that was the outline of Kós. His face was in the darkness, turned away from the lamp.

"That's another thing," said Manoli, and he reached down and touched Morgan on the shoulder. "To-day I talked to

Zeffis about you. He'll fix papers for you if you want to come."

"In the boats, you mean?" Morgan stared at him. "In the boats with you?"

"Why not? You're curious about Kalymnos. You want to know how it works. You won't know unless you go in the boats. Zeffis will fix the papers. Oh, not for all the time, not for six or seven months, but for a few weeks maybe. We could put you ashore at Alexandria." He grinned. "Maybe we both go ashore for a night or two. I can show you some places in Alexandria."

Morgan was conscious of the face looking down at him, the dark strong face in the lamplight, with the shadowed creases in the cheeks like black scars : the face of Manoli, the face of the Kalymnian. It seemed to fill all the frame of his vision, like a close-up on a cinema screen. And Morgan was deeply aware of a sense of privilege, of the importance of the fact that it was *this* man who wanted him to come. But he was conscious, too, of the other face beside Manoli's ; the same strange smile was at her mouth, and for a moment his eyes searched hers, as if he might discover from them whether he should accept or not.

"Thank you," he said. "I'd like to go."

Manoli nodded and grinned. "Zeffis will be pleased. It's another mountain of paper he can make. There's time. It's ten weeks before we sail. Time for me to have my picture done." He took another fish and chewed on it happily, enjoying the thought of the picture and of Irini Pelacos. "Time for lots of retzina, time for singing and dancing. Eh, Mina? Time for everything, eh, Stavros?"

But Stavros did not answer. Stavros stared down into the darkness and saw nothing but the darkness, although the lights were there and the sheen of the night on the water, and all the bitterness had choked up into his throat so that he could not speak. So he *had* picked a cripple ! With all Kalymnos to choose from, he had picked a cripple. Stavros could feel his throat twisting up, tightening, as if the crooked legs of Christos Papagalos were wrapped around his windpipe.

4

WHEN PAUL PELACOS returned from Athens, he sent a note to Morgan's house, suggesting that the Australian might call on him that evening.

Morgan took coffee at a table by the sea and strolled around in the gathering dusk. He went through the back streets, making a long walk of it, feeling the magic of Greece touching him, as it always did at twilight. When the encircling mountains marched in closer to the town, sometimes ominously, sometimes protectively, he had the feeling that all time, past and present and future, had been dislodged from its true balance. Time itself became something crystalline and clear : a single absoluteness locked in light.

In the narrow, crooked streets the people moved slowly and without noise, diffidently, speaking in soft voices, as if aware that they were merely shadows, thin shapes which the light had created and which the light could change or obliterate. And the colours of the houses had a soft, incandescent quality, as if all the sunlight absorbed through the day had been stored up thriftily for this time of dusk, to extend the spell of it to the last lingering second.

Light was the true god of Greece, the essence—not the dark profundities of the Christian belief, but a golden effulgence, the young Appollo at the world's first dawning.

For the New Year most of the houses had been scrubbed with fresh colour washes, and each block of steps, each wall and well and stove stand had acquired its individual patina. In Greece, Morgan reflected, no colour was ever laid on evenly. Through the coarse brush marks of a new colour were revealed the faded tones of some earlier shade, and beneath that another and another, so that every wall, every fragment of wall, was a mingling of innumerable subtle shades and textures—never merely blue or pink or green, but all the infinite permutations of a single hue at once. Had accident or intuition developed these superb textures of stone and plaster and brush strokes ?

Morgan walked on slowly through the world floating in the solution of the light. On the surrounding hills each rock and stone seemed to be carved out of deep gold light, and the sky and the shadows of the ravines were two distinct tones of violet, gradually deepening and blending. Each component of the world around him was something discrete : an ultramarine door against the white rectangle of a plastered wall ; a lamp bracket, casting a long shadow across the stones ; a painted water jar ; a yellow boat upside down beneath an almond tree ; a man in a dark doorway softly singing, and a woman on a balcony looking down ; a brown donkey treading across the cobbles on soft cat feet, its wicker panniers high with grass.

Across the town the bells tolled for vespers. The tangled branches of the fig trees, white as bones, were crowded with the black lumps of the turkeys, roosting for the night. High on the mountain trail to Vathý—an abrupt zigzag carved into the overhanging crags—a man climbed upward slowly behind three donkeys, and above the crest of the mountain a single star had appeared. The man seemed to be climbing towards it, as if he would seize it and bring it back.

It was Irini who met him at the door of the big, white house. " He is in the study," she said. " I think he would like to see you there. Go in, please."

The study of Paul Pelacos was the inner core of his little world, the keep, the donjon of his citadel. Its fortifications were the shelves of books that filled two walls, the pictures, the framed photographs of Oxford groups, the magazines tossed on the side table—*The Economist, Fortune, Die Woche, Time, Occi*, the *New Yorker*, folded copies of *Akropolis* and *To Vima* and the rice-paper edition of the *London Times*.

" Ah, Leigh ! " Pelacos' greeting was warm. " How nice to see you again. You did get my note, then ? How good of you to come." He motioned him to a chair and went across to the mahogany cabinet. "Now what would you prefer to drink? Whisky? Gin? What shall it be?"

Morgan could see the labels on the bottles: tasteful, traditional labels of the finest European and American gins, whiskies and wines. What would Pelacos say, he wondered, if he asked for retzina. The impulse rose, too strong to be resisted.

"Do you know," he said, "what I would really like is retzina. I don't suppose——"

"Of course, Leigh." Pelacos beamed at him. "You have acquired the taste, then? Splendid!" He reached into the cupboard below and produced a decanter. "You will find this a very good one, too. I have it sent in cask from Samos."

"I have no complaint against the Kalymnian retzina," Morgan said. It was like Pelacos to have even his retzina imported, if only from another island.

"Excellent," Pelacos agreed. "But try this. I have always felt that the ancient poets had a reason for their songs in praise of the Samian wine. It has just that extra delicacy, a piquancy that our wine lacks."

"It is very good, yes." Morgan sipped it. The trouble was that Pelacos was almost invariably right.

Pelacos poured himself a Scotch and soda and settled himself comfortably in the big leather arm-chair, facing Morgan. In all Kalymnos, Morgan wondered, were there any other leather arm-chairs?

"Ah, retzina!" Pelacos nodded, chuckling. "I had a tutor at Oxford, an old man, quite obsessed about Greece. He had two ambitions. One to discover the lair of the Nemean lion which Heracles slew, the other to sit in the sun for the rest of his life, drinking retzina. Irreconcilable, of course. So he did neither. I could quite appreciate his point, but he should have seen that by drinking retzina he could have satisfied his historical sense. The cheapest, quite possibly the most plebeian of all drinks in the world, Leigh, and yet the true aristocrat. The father of all wines, the patriarch, the wine from Dionysus. And the method of keeping it with pine resin—from whom, I wonder? Theseus, sailing to Crete? Jason, going in the *Argo* to find the Golden Fleece? Agamemnon, taking the galleys to Troy? Somebody

in the boats, I suggest. It would have been their way of keeping the wine, the only way. I like to think it tasted exactly the
same as the wine we drink to-day, as that wine you're drinking
now."

"I shall drink it more reverently, then," Morgan said,
smiling. "It suprises me that you don't drink it yourself."

Pelacos pulled a wry mouth. "I am afraid it affects my
stomach. Dyspepsia. There is a greater refinement, I think, in a
good claret—and less heartburn. I detest disloyalty, but I
confess I am rather in accordance with that French priest who
came here in the tenth century and went away marvelling that
the Greeks pressed their wine not from the grape but from pine
forests." He laughed. "Still, it was we who gave them the
mystery of the vine. . . ."

Morgan let him talk on. Pelacos' conversation moved within
the white walls and the leather and the sober chintzes with an
easy familiarity, as if the selected words, the chosen thoughts and
sentences had inhabited the room for a long time. It was talk
that wore good leather slippers and a smoking jacket and could
take down any book from the shelves and know where to find
the appropriate reference. It was gentle talk, lulling him. Perhaps
that was Pelacos' intention.

He found his attention was more to the room itself than to
the words that moved within it. It was impossible not to admire
its taste and reticence—the moonlit witchery of the little Palmer
painting, the excellence of the Stubbs horse, the fresh luminosity
of a tiny Constable sketch that was doubtless ruined in the final
large and finished version, the airy grace of two Turner drawings,
framed side by side. Even the panel of Oxford photographs
beside the desk had the correct nostalgia of a reunion of dons.
The tutor who was mad about retzina was probably there in
one of the groups, although all the grey undreaming faces
against the cloisters looked alike, and in them was no hint of
sunshine or of wine. Morgan half expected a discreet tap on
the door to herald an aproned servant bearing tea and muffins
and hot buttered toast and thin sandwiches.

Yet in this room there were a harmony and a rightness as
complete, as unconvincing in their way, as the harmony and

rightness of the dusky world outside, the world of pure light
which he had wandered through on his way to the white house.
They could not be related to each other, that was all. The
chasm that divided them was too wide to be bridged.

"Ah!" Pelacos smiled. "I see what you are looking at.
The Boat Race. Nineteen fifty-one. That was the year Oxford
sank, rowed itself under. An absolutely foul day. I was at
Chiswick, and I remember . . ."

For a long time he reminisced about rowing and Oxford
adventures, and although his anecdotes were amusing and intelligent, Morgan found his thoughts straying again, this time to
the man climbing with his three donkeys over the mountains to
Vathý, to Mina Vraxos in the lamplight, with the smile at her
mouth, looking down at him.

It was quite dark when Pelacos came to the point of the
interview.

"Leigh," he said suddenly, "you know Darwin, I suppose?"

"Darwin? In Australia? Yes, I have been there."

"Describe it to me." Pelacos had turned his head away
and he was staring at the dark, black-shadowed window and
his fingertips were placed together. "Describe it to me——"
the way he said it, in his clipped, faultless English, it sounded
like a line from a Noel Coward play.

Morgan thought of Darwin, of North Australia, of ten
thousand miles away : of the Arafura Sea coming in pale and
milky across the wide, flat shelf of Ela Beach, and the sand at
the tidemark swarming with little red-backed crabs, and the
luggers sailing in from Melville Island ; of the funny little train
running down to Birdum through the mulga and the ghost-gums,
and beyond the red cruel plains of the spinifex and gibber ; of
pandanus palms over the sand-hills and the dust hanging in the
blue sky above the cattle muster. A world of black and ochre
and Indian red, of parching heat and demented rains : the
Adelaide River coming down roaring in "the Wet" and the
great grass springing ; tall, pale ant-hills in the moonlight, like
the broken columns of bizarre temples ; the stink of the tide
dribbling out from the mud flats and the hot ooze in the spiky
labyrinths of the mangrove swamps ; the beer swilling in the

pubs on Saturday afternoons and a radio blaring the race results
and the tinny tinkle of a phonograph, the smell of the Chinese
stores, the frogs croaking in the night . . .

"Describe it to me!" How could he possibly convey this
remote antipodean world to Paul Pelacos, sitting there beneath
his Oxford memories in the proved world of his own verities?
Yet Pelacos' command had struck a curious spark of homo-
geneity. There was a sudden, fluid moment in which everything
had seemed to fit together, all were parts of one another, belonging together: the world of Paul Pelacos, the Grecian nightfall
beyond the wall, the peasant climbing across the mountains to
Vathý and the land of black and ochre and Indian red on the far
side of the world.

"But what do you want me to describe?" Morgan asked
quietly. "And why?"

"Yes, perhaps I should explain." Pelacos turned to him.
His hand reached into the pocket for the gold key chain. "When
I was in Athens," he said, "I was consulted about a matter which
might be of some considerable importance to Kalymnos. At
the moment it is on the Ministerial level, a subject for consideration, no more than that. For this reason it must be treated
as confidential. I am quite sure you will——"

"Yes, of course."

"As you doubtless know, Leigh, there is a committee in
Athens that deals with the specialised problems of European
migration, taking the underprivileged, the people of the over-
populated countries, and settling them in new lands where they
can be given work and a new hope."

"I know of it, yes."

"I am informed," Pelacos went on, "that the committee is
now considering the problem of Kalymnos. This island—I
recall telling it to you when we first met, Leigh—this island is
dying. It is very poor and becoming poorer. There is not
enough work for the people, not enough money even when they
do work, not enough food. Most of them can afford only one
meal a day, and that a frugal one. If clothing has to be bought,
then they must dispense with food. They cannot have both.
For the children we see running around the streets to-day,

running in their rags and patches, there is no future. No future at all. Do you remember us—Telfs and you and I—discussing how everyone is so desperate to leave? *Everyone*."

" Yes. Telfs called it the quest for the Big Rock Candy Mountain. So many people keep coming to me, asking about Australia."

" Exactly. You are wondering about Darwin. Well, before the war, as I understand it, there was a substantial pearl-diving industry operating out of Darwin. Out of Darwin and also another port, the name of which, I am afraid, escapes me."

" Broome ? "

" Yes, yes. Broome. There is good money now in pearl shell—seventy pounds a ton was the last figure I heard—but the industry in Australia became moribund during the war. It must be revived. A new fleet must be built, new divers recruited. You begin to perceive what I am driving at ? "

" I think I do. That the Kalymnians——"

" There are no finer divers in the world, no finer seamen, than the men of this island," Pelacos said quietly. " The proposal which I discussed in Athens was this : that the sponge divers of Kalymnos should take over and re-establish the pearl-diving industry of Australia."

" But that would mean——"

" One moment, Leigh." Pelacos raised his hand. " That is the ultimate simplification. Could it be done ? That is the point. Could it ? We must find out. We must select a team of our divers, our best divers—ten men, let us say—and send them to Australia. If they can adapt themselves to the conditions there, to pearl shell instead of sponge, to all the multitude of different problems that will crop up—steep tides, for example, when all their experience is of a tideless sea—if they can do this, then the whole Kalymnian problem is solved. Our seamen and our divers, possibly even our boats, can move to the other side of the world, and their families can go with them, and . . . and . . ." Pelacos looked down at the gold key chain twirling around his finger. There was a faint smile at his mouth.

" And that is the end of Kalymnos ? " Morgan said softly.

" Yes, the end of Kalymnos. The full stop at the end of the

story that began before Troy fell. Or merely the opening of a
new chapter ? Who can say ? "

" A different story," said Morgan, " not a new chapter. If
it's somewhere else, if it isn't here on Kalymnos, it's a different
story."

" I wonder. Perhaps we should think of our experimental
team as rather like the covered wagons setting out to find a
new world in the American West, to establish a new thing that
would ultimately join up with the old thing. Yes, like the
pioneers in your own country, Leigh, breaking through the
mountains to the plains beyond. The distance is greater in this
proposal of ours, the contrasts possibly more sharp, the problems
stranger—but no more than that. The example is by no means
new. The principle is basic."

" But this is a tremendous thing," Morgan said doubtfully,
" too big a thing surely for many of them to accept. Leaving
all this, the simplicity of it, the things they love and understand,
all the associations. And the place itself—the look of it and the
smell of it, the little white chapels on the hills . . ."

" Oh, it will be hard, yes. It is always hard to turn one's
back on the things one loves and understands, on old associations.
But I wonder would it be quite so hard for the Kalymnians.
They have always been wanderers, going to the ends of the
world."

" But Darwin is so different," Morgan protested. " So
incredibly bloody different ! "

" So is the bottom of the sea, Leigh," Pelacos smiled. " Is
the world of Australia more fantastic, do you think, more
perilous, more bizarre than that queer green and purple world
of thirty-five fathoms, with the rocks and slime and the trees
of the ocean weaving and waving, and the sponges and the
mysterious black shapes ? Is it, Leigh ? The men of Kalymnos
go there every year. For half the year they *live* there ! Do you
think Darwin, for all its differences, will intimidate them ? "

" The men. But what about the women ? "

" Our society is less sophisticated, less emancipated than
yours. Here the men decide, and the women follow. You will
find Kalymnian women very obedient to their men." Pelacos

went to the cabinet and poured fresh drinks. There was a curious tenseness about him when he turned with the two glasses in his hand and said : " Once all men were nomads, Leigh, and I sometimes think that a creeping nomadism is returning to the world. One day, perhaps soon, men will turn their backs on the things they love and understand and they will fly to the moon. That will be stranger than Darwin, or the reefs off Benghazi." He carried the glass of retzina across to Morgan. " But our problem," he said, smiling, " is rather more immediate than that. It was suggested to me in Athens that I should submit the names of the divers who should go to Australia. That selection must be most careful. That is why I should like you to tell me about Australia and the conditions there—because these men will be our emissaries, and upon them will depend the hopes of all Kalymnians. They will take our future with them. They must be the best we can send."

" You want to succeed, then ? " Morgan said wonderingly.

" Naturally ! " Pelacos seemed surprised.

" Even if it empties the island of its people ? "

" Even if it does that, yes."

" Then you, too, will go to Australia ? "

" Good heavens, no ! " Pelacos chuckled. " Don't misunderstand me, Leigh. I have nothing against your country . . . but, no, I think I shall stay here."

" But your business ? Surely it would mean ruin for you, the end of everything you've built up. If the sponge trade dies and the boats go, doesn't the house of Pelacos collapse like a house of cards ? "

Pelacos stretched the key chain tautly between his fingers and smiled down at it.

" My dear Leigh," he said, " everything runs to its conclusion. As new things begin, old things must end. When all is said and done, our castles are ephemeral things, built in air. And all things, after all, are dependent on the peasantry of grass. Twenty thousand years ago there were men living in the valley of the Vézère, hunting the reindeer that browsed in the rich grasses. Possibly you have seen their carvings in the caves, and that miracle of Lascaux. Unaccountably the grass failed, the herds moved on, the men of the Vézère followed the herds and perished. The grass dries up and the people must move on. The grass withers in the Orient and the Tartar horde rides to the west—and survives. It is really very simple, Leigh. In Kalymnos the grass has withered. Now the people must move on. Whether to perish or to thrive, they must move on. To Santa Fe ? To Darwin ? To the moon ? Can I stop them from going ? Would you ? "

Pelacos paused, but Morgan did not answer.

" In any case," Pelacos continued, " it has already begun. Every year hundreds of our young men go away, and what is there to keep them here ? They go away and the erosion continues. The mountains around us, Leigh, how bare they are. How cruel and bare ! Pitiless mountains, scarred by storms. And no trees. Not a single tree. Yet once those mountains were green with forests. Did you know that Ovid wrote of the sylvan glades of Kalymnos ? First the erosion of the land, and then the erosion of the people. The younger men go, the adventurers. The grocer has fewer customers for his goods. The fisherman sells fewer fish. A café closes. The door of another little shop is nailed up. Have you observed that there are no luxuries sold here in Kalymnos, only necessities ? A few more people are hungrier than they were before, more desperate, their children more ragged. This is the lingering death, Leigh. I told you, do you remember ? The new proposal merely quickens the momentum, that is all."

Morgan heard him with a strange confusion in his mind. There was a sense of unbelief growing into a conviction and a sadness. Pelacos was right. Everything ran to its conclusion. It would happen because it *did* happen. The world was scattered with the ruins of things that had come to an end. Kalymnos had sailed against Troy, and Troy had come to an end, and since then more than three thousand years had passed, and through all the tremendous things that had happened, through all the history of Greece and Rome, through all Christianity, this little seaport in the Ægean had persisted. Jericho's walls had fallen, the pumice and the ash had drowned Pompeii, the sands had swept over salt-sown Carthage, and from the little harbour beneath these rocky hills the ships had still sailed out. Now there was to be an end to it. A total ending, and something new to be begun. He stared across at Pelacos as if it were the first time he had seen him.

All through breakfast Pelacos was preoccupied by the matters he had discussed with Morgan the previous evening. It was not until he was drinking the French coffee which in the mornings he preferred to Turkish that he said to his daughter, " Leigh was suggesting last night that you should paint a portrait of Manoli. You had indicated to him, I gather, that my permission would be necessary. Naturally, I told him I would have no objection. You would like to do it ? "

" Yes."

" Where ? "

" We thought at Lavassi, with a background of the caiques in the yard."

Pelacos raised his eyebrows. " Rather public, don't you think ? You'll have all the shipyard breathing down your neck, offering suggestions, every man jack for a mile around. That might be embarrassing for both of you, particularly as you are hardly likely to do a photographic representation of Manoli, which is what they will all expect, you know."

" I imagined you would prefer that to something more private. Something *intime*. I thought you would not approve my painting him in a room somewhere, just the two of us together."

Her father shrugged slightly. " You must do it wherever you think best, my dear. Manoli sober is a man of probity. I am a little surprised at his acquiescence, I must admit. I should have thought he would have been horrified at the suggestion and dismissed it without a second thought."

" He was very pleasant and agreeable," Irini said cautiously. There was an odd undercurrent moving beneath his words, as if his mildness were a lure to trap her into some admission. It was almost his " cruel charm " attitude—that was how a friend of hers in London had once described it—the cruel charm he had displayed the last time she had gone back from Paris and she had told him of the affair with Jacques, and he had been so

tolerant and understanding and had listened with a calm composure while she had unburdened herself of the whole sorry
business. There had been no recriminations, no scenes. He had
merely kissed her softly on the cheek and patted her arm and
smiled at her. But she had never returned to Paris; three days
later she had been on the airliner coming back to Kalymnos.
Neither of them had ever discussed Jacques again—but Jacques
was always there in the words that were never spoken, in her
father's faintly ironic praise of her painting, in his teasing of her
in front of Morgan when he had spoken to him about Paris and
its effect on the young.

"He was very nice about it," she said guardedly. "He
walked back with us from Lavassi."

"Oh, I'm not discounting Manoli's charm," he said agreeably.
"Nor his suitability as a subject. He has a fine face, Manoli, the
sort of face that would fit into any costume and any period. I
suppose it isn't everybody who has the sort of face that both
Picasso and Bellini could paint. Leigh, incidentally, is of the
opinion that you would do it very well. I told him your greatest
difficulty would be in getting Manoli to sit still for long enough.
I like that man Leigh. He is good value. Did you know that he
is sailing with Manoli in the spring, to Africa?"

"He told me, yes."

"I am pleased he takes such an interest in you, in your painting,
Irini. He could help you to settle in, you know. He has balance,
and a sense of sympathy."

"It's more than a year now since I came back," she said
quietly. "I think I have settled in."

"You have been very good, my dear. But what I feel is
that you have not yet come to an understanding with yourself.
Leigh gives me the impression that he has—with himself and
with other people."

"It isn't easy to come to an understanding with other people.
Here, I mean. The girls of my own age were married seven,
eight years ago. They have their families, their own preoccupations. I never meet other people."

He smiled. "If you paint Manoli at Lavassi, I assure you
you will meet them in droves, my dear." He paused and looked

at her earnestly. " Irini, my dear, life is made up of a series of balances, each one adjusted to the other. Paris was one world, this another. The problem—your problem, child—is to relate them to each other. I think Leigh might be able to help you do it."

She lowered her eyes and straightened the knife on her plate and pushed the bread crumbs into a little mound with her forefinger, but she had nothing to say, and for a long time both of them were silent.

Pelacos was studying Irini bemusedly when finally she looked up.

" What is it ? " she said quickly.

" Nothing, dear." He was himself again, smiling and bland. " I was looking at you. Your face this morning . . . you look so much like your mother. When she was young."

Irini shook her head. " She was so much more beautiful," she said. " Very beautiful."

" Was she ? " He said absently, returning to his thoughts. " Yes, I suppose she was, yes." It was painful to remember her as something beautiful, as something young like Irini, and beautiful. It was the other face that always crowded into the mind : the old woman's face, everything drawn down, fallen away—mouth, eyes, dewlaps, all sagging—the thoughts sagging, fallen away, too. The bomb that had come screaming down to tear the old house apart, to kill both his sons, to strip the name of Pelacos from everything except his own shrinking mortality —why had it not taken his wife too ? Why, having done so much that was merciless, had it not done also this one merciful thing, and taken her, not left her to sicken of memory ? And the cruelty of the years that had followed, with Irini in London so that she should not see what was happening. And then a final refinement of cruelty even in the mercy of death, pursuing her to the very grave : that she should have had to be carried up the hill so slowly, past all the crowded houses, carried up to Saint Vassilias in the open coffin so that everyone could see the face he had hidden from them for all those years, the face all fallen away into nothing.

"I shall be in the study this morning, writing," he said quietly. "Would you see that I am not disturbed until twelve o'clock?"

His hand fell lightly on his daughter's shoulder as he walked to the door. If only he could tell her what she meant to him, how much he loved her; if only they could understand each other!

5

"It's a funny colour," Manoli said. "It isn't purple and it isn't black. It's a sea colour, not a land colour, you see. It's hard to explain the sea colours. They have a sort of shine to them, a pale, thin shine, and I suppose that's what makes them different."

He looked across to her as if she could help him explain it. But she was peering at the canvas, her eyes half closed, and she didn't seem to be listening to him. Besides, how would she know the sea colours?

"Yes, please go on," Irini said, dabbing the brush at the canvas. She dared not look at him lest he stop talking. She had asked him to talk, to tell her about the sponge diving, more to ease her own embarrassment than to give him a sense of confidence.

Manoli, in fact, had from the beginning appeared completely at ease, rather enjoying the experience. At first he had been inclined to pose a little, sitting astride the upended fish box with a sort of animal arrogance, asserting the strength and vigour of his maleness even in repose—like one of those old-fashioned photographs of heavyweight pugilists, all muscles and wide ornate belts around their midriffs and strong contemptuous eyes above black moustaches. Like one of the lithographed posters, faded and yellow, that you still found occasionally pasted on the back wall of some cheap Parisian bistro. But as he had talked this self-consciousness had passed. Now he was sitting quite naturally, relaxed, talking to her.

There were only the two of them in the corner of the yard by the old capstan; the loiterers and the shipyard workers who had clustered around at the beginning had been curtly dispersed by Manoli, with dark warnings of what might happen to them if they persisted in being inquisitive. The corner of the yard between the prow of the *Angellico* and the ramshackle little corrugated-iron forge shed had filled up with sunlight and colour, and Manoli astride the fish box. Behind him were a corner of the shed and an old anchor, rusted to the purest raw sienna, with one of its flukes embedded in the earth, and behind the anchor a dark recess, a cavity of deep purple shadows and green nettles, and in the nettles were three ducks with orange beaks and iridescent necks.

Irini painted swiftly, blocking in the masses with a feverish desperation, as if it might break apart and scatter itself into a worthless kaleidoscope of colour before she was able to capture it. But she painted also with an enlivening excitement, with a joyous freshness she had not experienced since Paris. It was all going right, she told herself. It was all going right, right, *right*.

" Please do go on," she said eagerly. " I *am* listening. You must take no notice if I appear not to be. Because I am. Really I am ! "

Manoli grinned. " I was trying to think it out, that's all," he said, " this colour I'm trying to explain. How would you explain the colours of a fish when it comes out of the water ? I don't know."

" I couldn't describe it either," she said. " But I do know what you mean. Those ducks there behind you, look at their necks. It's that sort of thing, isn't it ? "

He turned to look at the ducks, and shook his head. " No," he said. " The sea does it differently. The sea colours don't have blood behind them. Water or jelly, and something else you can't describe—a dark, oozy something that has a shine to it. Look, when you see the sponges first, right down there at the bottom of the sea against the rocks, they're black. Not

just black like ink, not like your paints, but black as if there is
no such thing as colour. That's the way they look when you
reach towards them, when they call you."

"Call you?"

He laughed. "Well, not really, but that's what it's like, as
if they'd called you. It's the good sponges that call you. They
seem to have a kind of magnetism. They draw you over to
them. They do. You can feel them pulling. And they come
away in your hand so easily. Very soft and easy, as if they want
to give themselves to you. The good ones, I mean. It's only the
bad sponges that cling to the rocks, all rubbery, trying to resist.
You have to wrench at them and tear them off, and most times
they're not worth it."

As she listened to him, she was conscious of a secondary
excitement, something apart from the thrill of the painting
forming itself beneath her brush. It was as if a door were slowly
opening to disclose a world unreal and mysterious and fascinating;
she felt like Alice in the rabbit hole, taking up the bottle labelled
DRINK ME, shrinking and shrinking, and passing through the
tiny door into the fantastic world beyond. And across from
her on the fish box in the sunlight, in a blue jersey and a black
peaked cap, was this incongruous White Rabbit who was con-
ducting her to Wonderland, his big, brown face frowning as he
sought the images of his bizarre poetry. In his way of expressing
these images Manoli had little fluency, but his obvious devotion
to this queer pelagian world of his infused even the most simple
things he said with a subdued passion, so that it was all alive,
and real even in its unreality, and full of sensation and a curious
meaning, like Rimbaud's poetry. Yes, like Rimbaud. Manoli
would read *The Drunken Boat* and know its meaning instantly.

". . . and when you get enough sponges stuffed into the net
bag beneath your arm," he was saying, "you go up again. And
that's when this strange thing happens, because the sponges are
still alive, you see, and just as you're getting up towards the
surface, they begin to feel the light, and they hate the light and
they all start to pull down, trying to escape into the dark water
again. It's a funny feeling, as if the bottom of the sea is reaching
up to you, trying to pull you down again, all the sponges in the

bag dragging at you. Sometimes you have to fight to get them out of the sea. And that's when you see this colour I was talking about, this funny colour. Not black, not purple—and that strange shine. And the sponges are very soft, like . . . like . . ."

He hesitated self-consciously and pushed his cap back to scratch his head. Like the feel of a woman's flesh beneath your hands, that was what he was going to say : the very soft parts of a woman's flesh. "Very soft and smooth," he said, with a quick grin. "Like silk. And they have a wonderful smell when they come out of the water—not a perfume, not like that stuff you buy in the bottles at Alexandria—a sweet smell, not like any other smell you can imagine. The sponge smell. It goes away as they begin to die. You never smell it afterwards. You see, we put the sponges out on the deck of the boat, and they stay there all through the night and that's when they die, and the next morning they go over the side in the bags, and the sea washes them clean, washes out that colour I was talking about. There's nothing left then because they're dead. The colour and the smell and the feel of them, it's all gone once they're dead."

That was it, of course, Irini realised. There were two sponge worlds, the quick and the dead. She had never thought of the sponge as something living, something fighting against the light. She had seen the sponges, millions of them, in her father's warehouses, but they were dry, yellow things, the skeletons of a world that to Manoli was alive, that had colour and smell and texture and a weird sort of purpose. The sponges, the good sponges, luring the man towards them and then fighting to escape, recoiling from the light. Manoli could see a sponge as a thing struggling, hating, dying—dying on the deck in the night with the swing of the stars above and the noise of the sea around the boat. Manoli's was the dark fantastic poetry of an experience of which she knew nothing. Her father's warehouses were the museums, the glass cases of fossils and flints and scraps of bone, their link with the living things they represented long since stretched beyond the breaking point of understanding.

She remembered her father saying to her once, " Here in Kalymnos it boils down to about twenty of us, twenty families. We are the merchants. We stay at home to buy and sell. All the others, the foolish ones, the men who take the boats out, they are the venturers."

The venturers? They were the poets—venturing, yes, but into a territory beyond the reach of the merchants, beyond the reach of Rimbaud's hallucinations, into their own secret, silent world of the dark and the bizarre. And the merchants? They were not the merchants. They were the curators of museums, the custodians of morgues. Had her father, she wondered, ever smelled the sponge smell?

"The painting?" Manoli said happily. "Is it all right?"

"Yes, I think so. I hope so, anyway."

"Not finished yet?"

"Oh no, not yet." She looked at him quickly. "I am sorry. You must be awfully tired, just sitting there. But there will have to be two or three other mornings, I'm afraid. To finish it. You wouldn't mind, would you?"

Manoli grinned. "Three mornings, four, five—you say."

"You have been very, very good," she said. "Daddy told Morgan that my greatest difficulty would be in getting you to sit still for long enough." She smiled at him. "I like to hear you talk, that's the *real* difficulty. I want to stop painting and just listen to you. It's rather strange, you know—I mean, our family being in the sponge trade for so long, and my not knowing anything about it, not anything at all."

"You have to go in the boats," said Manoli. "You have to go in the boats to know."

"One day that's what I should like to do, to go away in one of the boats and paint it all. Paint the things you've been talking about."

He shook his head. "They won't take a woman in the sponge boats. It's unlucky to have a woman aboard. You wouldn't get a crew to sail." It was true, too. You couldn't mix women with work. They were two different things, demanding opposite attentions, needing different parts of your body. It wasn't just superstition, either; it was right to keep women off the boats.

"There was a case here," he said, "about ten years ago. In one of your father's boats, the *Seleni*. Maybe you know about it. It all happened because of Vassilis Antoninous—he was the

colazaris, and a good one, too. Well, this Vassilis, he took a girl,
a cousin of his, because she wanted to go to Karpathos and they
were sailing past Karpathos on their way to Africa. They had
bad winds all the way south and the men got mixed up about
the girl being aboard. There was some funny talk about the girl
and Vassilis. They landed her at Karpathos and then went on,
but it was a terrible summer. All the good sponges kept out of
the way of the divers, so that everybody got bad-tempered and
hated each other.

" Everybody except two brothers who were diving that year
in the *Seleni*. Petros and Giorgios their names were—they
were at school with me—and Petros was a fine, strong, pig-
headed lad, and he was going deeper and deeper looking for
the sponges. One day he went too deep and drowned. His
brother blamed Vassilis for it. Being the *colazaris*, Vassilis had
charge of the air pipe and the signal rope, and he was the one to
plan the dives and say how deep they should go, and he shouldn't
have allowed Petros to keep diving so deep, so in a way Giorgios
was right in blaming the *colazaris*. But really he was blaming
Vassilis because of the girl he had taken to Karpathos and all
the trouble she had caused, and the bad luck.

" There were plenty of arguments, and then off the coast of
Tripoli one night Giorgios got Vassilis down on the deck
among the few lousy sponges they'd gathered and he cut his
throat and threw his body over the side. He was a good *colazaris*,
Vassilis, but he shouldn't have taken that girl aboard, even if she
was his cousin."

" Might it not have happened just the same," said Irini, " if
the girl hadn't gone to Karpathos ? "

Manoli shrugged. " It's the way it did happen," he said.
" It wasn't the end of the trouble, either. The *Seleni* came back
very late in the autumn because they kept sailing all up and down
North Africa looking for the sponges that kept away from them,
and as you can imagine they weren't in any hurry to get back,
either, to have the police asking all the questions. They were
diving south of Crete when their best diver got paralysed. That
was Stavros. He's the father of a woman I know. Maybe you
see him sometimes walking around the town selling fish. The

people you see walking around the streets, they've got stories to tell, most of them."

" Yes."

" Well, that's the way this story ended up because of sailing the girl to Karpathos. Two men dead and one paralysed, and Giorgios spending five years in prison and dying there." Manoli shook his head, but then another thought came to him and he said, " Your father was good about that. It was his boat, the *Seleni*, and he paid all the hospital expenses for Stavros and he sent to Athens for lawyers to help Giorgios, but he still went to jail for five years and died there. It didn't help Stavros, either, because he was the best diver your father had, and now he sells fish. You see him around with his baskets of *barbunia* and *kalamaraki* and——" He broke off awkwardly. " You're not painting," he said. " Is it finished for to-day ? Or do I talk too much ? "

" I think perhaps it's enough for to-day's sitting," she said, smiling. She felt perfectly at ease with him now, no longer shy or embarrassed. " But really I was listening to you. That's what I said. When you talk, I want to stop painting and just listen."

" It's a fine thing to be able to make paintings, to do things like that."

" Do you want to see what's done so far ? " she said.

Manoli looked at her for a moment and then he shook his head. " You show me when it's finished," he said. " You tell me when you want me to see it." He stared thoughtfully beyond her, at the white arch of the *Angellico's* bow and the black criss-cross of all the masts and rigging against the blue sky. " When I was a boy I used to draw a lot," he said. " I liked drawing things. But one day I was out in a boat with my father and he let me look down through the *yalass* and there was the bottom of the sea, just as clear as a picture, everything waving and floating and bright. After that I didn't ever want to draw again."

He rose from the fish box and stretched his arms, grinning down at her, and she was acutely aware of the boy Manoli, all legs and dreams, looking down through the *yalass* at his world of magic. Aware also of the maturity that had sprung from it,

the big, lithe maleness of the man stretching in the sunlit air
among the caiques, of his strength and gentleness, of the passion
and the poetry that were there behind his furrowed eyes, of dark,
hard skin and white teeth, of the black hair oiled and brushed
for the sitting but with the wind and the salt still in it. Manoli
was the sea, the bigness and wildness of it, the tenderness of its
poetry, the grotesque mystery of it. It was all there in the shape
of the big man grinning down at her, stretching in the sunshine.

"Sunday night," said Manoli, "I give a party. I'll ask
Morgan to bring you. You'll meet people—this Stavros I was
talking about. You'll meet people with stories to tell. It's good
to know why people are the way they are. They've got stories to
tell, most of them. If I ask Morgan, will you come?"

"Yes," she said. "Yes, please."

Not until she was walking back to the town did she realise
that for the first time since she had returned to Kalymnos she
had made her own decision, without consulting her father,
without wondering what he might say.

"He wouldn't look at the painting," Irini said. "He said
he'd rather wait until it was finished, until I wanted to show him.
I thought that was rather nice." She laughed softly. "Although
I was quite pleased with what I had done, and wouldn't have
the least minded if he *had* looked."

They were walking slowly together around behind the
Customs House. In the dusk she had taken his arm and he was
conscious of the warmth of her body and her smallness beside
him.

"He has a happy touch about things like that," Morgan said.
"I've seen him with old people, and with children. You forget
how wild and tough he is. There's a kind of instinctive sensitivity
about him that smells out the sensitivities of others, makes him
aware of them. It's an odd trait, when there's so much else about
him so brutally immediate, so distinctly animal."

"Like Ferdinand the bull, stopping in the middle of his
charge to smell a flower?"

He chuckled. "Not quite that, no. But you take his friends.
Most of them are the derelicts, the wrecks, the burned-out

people, the ones nobody else has very much time for. Have you
noticed that?"

"I don't know him as well as you do. I don't know him at
all, really." It was not true, she thought with a secret pride.
She knew the poetry that was in him, and she knew what he
was, and why. "Until to-day I was terrified of him. I had a
picture of him as a great, swaggering, drunken brute, always
brawling, always in trouble with the police."

"Well, you know Stephanos," Morgan said, "that poor,
crazy old devil who wanders up and down all day long muttering
to himself. His wife and five sons were all killed together in the
bombing, and ever since then—that's ten, eleven years ago—he's
been shuffling up and down, up and down, trying to get someone
to listen to the story. It's a terrible story, I know, but he's been
telling it ever since 1944 and nobody listens any longer. Human
sympathy has a statute of limitations. Not for Manoli, though.
Manoli takes him to a table for a coffee or buys him retzina and
listens to him. He's heard it all a thousand times before but he
still sits there with the poor devil and listens to him as if he were
hearing it for the first time. It isn't just kindliness with Manoli—
I don't think he is a kind man, in the sense we know kindliness
—nor sympathy. It's something deeper, an understanding."

"It's the sea," she said softly. "It's the sea in him. It's
what happens when the sea is inside you. I'm not sure how
you explain it, but that's what it is."

He glanced at her curiously, and for some minutes they
walked on in silence. They went up the wide steps to the little
plateia outside Saint Nikolas. There were doves in the tree
beside the bell tower and a foam of almond blossom over the
high wall, and the chanting came muted from the inside of the
church, where the candles glittered in the dusk.

"What did you do with yourself, to-day," she asked, "while
I was painting?"

"Oh, I wrote for an hour or so, but nothing jelled, and then
I walked around, up the hill behind and along the cliff top to
the little chapel. To Saint Peter's." He spoke of it casually,
giving an air of aimless sauntering to something that had been
positive and intended, something deliberate; and then, because

he had a sudden feeling of guilt in deceiving her, he said : " I
could see Lavassi and I thought about you, painting him. I met
Mina Vraxos at Saint Peter's. She was praying for her little boy,
the crippled kid. Telfs is bringing him back from Kós to-day."

" She's his mistress, isn't she ? "

He stopped and looked at her. " Whose mistress ? " he said.
" Manoli's."

" Is she ? I don't know. She's very beautiful."

" At this party on Sunday, shall I meet her ? "

" I imagine so. It's Manoli's party."

6

Telfs settled the boy up on the foredeck of the caique on a
coil of rope, with his back against the blue bitts, and beside him
the basket with his clothes and the mandarins and a water melon
for Mina.

" He will be all right there," said Paul, the deck hand who
looked like a Sicilian bandit and wore bright shirts and had
charge of the galvanised iron bucket for passengers who were
sick. " The ropes rest his legs. To-day "—he shrugged—" *ti
pota*—it will be calm all the way to Kalymnos. Yesterday . . .
po-po-po-po-po-po ! " He thought of yesterday and all the earthenware pots and dishes smashing in the hold and the seas coming
clear across the deck and the old women down on the floor of
the cabin wailing, with the vomit swilling all over them. In
January the Ægean could be cruel as poverty and vicious as a
scold's tongue. Paul was glad it was calm for the boy with the
bad legs, although normally he enjoyed the bad weather best,
for the chance it gave him to gymnast around the decks and
bully the passengers.

He looked at the child curiously, at the smiling curly-haired
boy propped against the faded blue coaming with the basket
beside him.

"The hospital?" he said to Telfs. "Good, eh? They fix him up fine, eh?"

Telfs shrugged. "It was pretty much what we expected," he said, wishing that that was all it had been. "These things take a long time."

"Sure," said Paul. "Oh sure, a long time. But he always smiles, that kid. Always smiling, eh?" He grinned at Nikolas and went away to see the cabbages aboard and the last of the terra-cotta dishes.

It was a fine sunny morning, and with nothing else to do half the people of Kós appeared to have come down to see the boat go. It was always the same, there was never anything to make it different, but here they were again, standing around, gawping, chewing on sunflower seeds and spitting the white husks out, getting in the way of everything. "*Bros!*" Paul yelled at them. "*Bros, bros, bros!*"

The sea was a pale green and flat as glass in the harbour, and in the water there was a facsimile of every stone and patch of moss on the old, yellow walls of the knights' castle. The boats were motionless at their moorings. In the still clarity of the morning Kós was like a harbour in aspic. Kós was like that, Telfs reflected, like something from yesterday which time had sealed, like the ferns and flowers embedded in Victorian glass jewellery, like old paperweights with the coloured patterns buried in the heart of the glass.

The blue, airy clarity of the morning stretched far across the quiet sea to the Turkish coast, to the sugar-loafed cone of Ceffaloúcha, to the pink nipples of the Anatolian mountains, to what seemed to be grains of rice scattered at the foot of the steep, clay-coloured hills—the white, clustered houses of Bodrum, that squalid little Turkish town built on the venerable ruins of Halicarnassus, where the great Herodotus had been born and where once had been the tomb of Mausólus the King of Caria, the wonder of the ancient world. All gone now, overwhelmed by time and the light and squalor. Still, the kid had enjoyed the stories of Herodotus, the old legends and the travels and the battles.

"Whenever you are here, you are always looking over there,

to Halicarnassus," Nikolas said, smiling up at him. "You did
mean what you said, didn't you? Your promise?"

"To take you there?" Telfs nodded. "One day, yes."

"When my legs are better?"

"Sure, that's right. When your legs are better, Nikolas.
It's steep and rocky over there, and kind of rough. You've got
to have good legs." He peered over the side of the caique.
Paul was yelling at the crowd as he cast off the aft mooring
line. "Okay," said Telfs. "We're about to go. It'll be a good
trip. Calm."

"Oh, but I don't mind it when it's rough," the boy protested.
"It's more exciting when it's rough."

"Sure," said Telfs absently. Sure, when your legs are better
I'll take you across to Halicarnassus. . . . All the stories I've
read to you will come alive. . . It won't matter then whether
it's rough or calm. When your legs are better . . . And now
it was in the bone right down below the knee: tuberculosis,
the filthy bacillus that could throw up minute nodules more
gigantic than mountains, bigger than the sugar loaf of Ceffaloúcha, big enough to stop a small boy's journeying to Halicarnassus. The journey wasn't to Halicarnassus now, not any
longer, but to Athens—and perhaps to amputation. Maybe this
was the hardest part of the journey, having to take him back,
having to tell Mina.

The caique was out of the harbour now, its exhaust thudding
in slow drumbeats, with the echo coming back in soft, regular
slaps from the low pebbly shore where the windmills were strung
out all the way to the point. From the bow you could see right
down through the water: everything sliding, the keel and the
green water and the shoals and the pale shadows on the sandy
bottom, and the jellyfish tossing flaccidly as they rolled away.

Telfs sat down beside the boy and took the tattered, paper-
covered copy of *Iliad* from his jacket pocket.

"Okay, now let's see," he said. "Where did we get to?"

"The battle for the ships," said the boy eagerly. "Where
Idomeneus the Cretan King puts on his armour and joins in the
fight."

"Sure." Telfs opened the book and began to search for the

page. It was queer that it had all begun with the bank notes, with the kid's not knowing anything about the pictures engraved on the Greek bank notes. That was stranger in a way than his never having heard of Troy or of Homer, or even of Theseus or Perseus or Heracles. That was the way it had begun, with his pointing out to the kid the pictures on the bank notes, the charioteer of Delphi and Apollo and Athena and the Medusa, and then telling him the stories.

"Taunting him thus," he began to read, "the lord Idomeneus seized him by the foot and began to drag him through the crowd. But now Asius came to the rescue. He was on foot in front of his chariot, which the driver kept so close to him that his shoulders were fanned all the time by the horses' breath. Asius did his utmost to despatch Idomeneus. But Idomeneus was too quick for him. He hit him with a spear on the throat, under the chin, and the point went right through. Asius fell like an oak or a poplar or a towering pine that woodmen cut down in the mountains with whetted axes to make timbers for a ship. So Asius lay stretched in front of his chariot and horses, groaning and clutching at the blood-stained dust. His charioteer, losing such wits as he possessed, had not even the presence of mind to turn his horses round and slip out of the enemy's hands, but was caught by a spear from the cool-headed Antilochus, which struck him in the middle. The bronze corslet he was wearing was of no avail : the spear-point went home in the centre of his belly. With a gasp he fell headlong from the well-built chariot, and Antilochus, son of the noble-hearted Nestor, drove his horses out of the Trojan into the Achaean lines."

"It really was true, wasn't it ? " the boy said.

"Why, sure it was true," Telfs said emphatically.

"And they were all brave, weren't they ? The Trojans, too ? Just as brave as the Greeks, even if they didn't win ? "

"Just as brave. I guess it was a time of brave men."

"That's when I would have liked to live," the boy said softly, his eyes shining. "I would have sailed to Troy, too, with all the others, in a black ship far bigger than this one. And I would have had a spear and a gigantic shield and bronze greaves on my legs, not the silly things I have to wear now."

The man and the boy looked down together at the irons clamped around the shrunken legs, and Telfs could see the X-ray plate against the square lamp in the clinic.

"I suppose being brave is just about the most important thing in the world, isn't it?" said Nikolas, anxiously.

Telfs looked across to where the red-sailed fishing boats were sailing off the coast of Turkey, among scattered islands lifted above the sea. "I guess so," he said. "I guess that's about it."

He lowered his eyes to the book. "With one accord they all closed in and rallied round Idomeneus," he read, "crouching behind sloped shields." Maybe the kid would never make the journey to Halicarnassus, but he could still go to Troy. . . .

7

ON MONDAY morning there were mixed opinions about where Manoli's party had been held; nor could everybody agree upon its specific character.

Mikali, with a mountain of dishes to clean and every glass he possessed to be washed, with the orange peel and peanut shells and fish bones and lobster claws to be swept from the trampled floor, with a fine to pay that would postpone the Belgian Congo for at least another six months, with two chairs smashed and the leg off one table—with all these things confronting him on a bleak Monday morning, Mikali was unhappily convinced that his *taverna* had been, if not the entirety of the hurricane, at least its storm centre.

Morgan and Telfs, with images of crowding dark faces and the shadows in the lamplight black against blue walls, and the dancers twirling on a hillside, thought of it as it was in the house of Mina Vraxos.

To Mina Vraxos there had been no party—only a ribbon

of noise, a flow of faces, the music beating against her, numbing
the pain of what Telfs had told her.

Christos Papagalos remembered it as a great, moving brightness carved through the night, a roaring and a singing that had
burned through the town like a blazing pine brand.

Tony Thaklios, shaking three aspirins into the trembling cup
of his hand, his mind tormented darkly by a vision of Calliope's
arm around him as he tripped and stumbled down a black
hillside, not a light showing in the town below and all the stars
churning in a whirlpool that stung his eyes, was convinced
that Manoli's party had indubitably taken place in hell.

To Manoli himself, stretching luxuriously on the plank bed
of the prison cell and chuckling to himself, it had been a party
confined only by the boundaries of the town and the limitations
of the human appetite : a satisfying party, ending as the satisfying
parties usually did—here on the plank bed of the prison cell
with Sergeant Phocas sitting beside him on the hard chair,
fiddling with his pink sea shells and giggling.

" It was going too far," said the sergeant happily.

" Is it worth having a party if you don't ? " asked Manoli,
dabbing with the policeman's handkerchief at the cut on his
forehead, from his collision with the corner of a wall.

" Yes, but four o'clock in the morning is going too far."
Sergeant Phocas giggled. " And the *tsabuna* as well ! *Po-po-po-
po-po-po-po !* You had half the town out of bed. Christos
Papagalos and you, with the two biggest voices in the town !
It is going too far to bawl at the top of your voices at four
o'clock in the morning, and with the *tsabuna* to make matters
worse. And then, of all the songs you have to sing you pick
' *Psara-poula !* ' Not something soft and gentle, not a lullaby,
but ' *Psara-poula !* ' " He giggled. again. " *Kyrié Eleison*, they
could have heard you in Kós ! "

" We were not singing for Kós." Manoli grinned. " We
were serenading Homer Vraxos. He had not been to the party.
It was Christos who felt he should have a share in it." He burst
out laughing. " Christos wanted to climb on the roof with a
pail of water, did you know that ? He wanted to pour it over
him when he came out on the balcony to listen to our serenading."

Manoli shook his head sternly. " I would not let him do it."

" Good," said Sergeant Phocas.

" Christos might have hurt his legs. It would have been a nasty climb for a man with weak legs."

The sergeant giggled.

" Besides," Manoli continued, " if he had done that, maybe there would have been cause for complaint."

" There is complaint enough already. There were thirty-two people at the mayor's office when it opened at eight o'clock this morning. Thirty-two! From all the way along the street. Manoli! Manoli! Manoli! When I came past, I could hear them chittering like birds. It was as well that I arrested you, eh ? "

" It was, yes," said Manoli cheerfully. He stretched his arms behind his head and studied the ceiling happily. " I am beginning to like this cell," he said. " You always put me in this one, the same one."

" Christos prefers the other," said Sergeant Phocas dryly. " This time he has company—the *tsabuna* man. Possibly he enjoys it less when it is crowded." He giggled. " Captain Dimitropolis will be happy when he learns that you like it here. Maybe he will allow you to have a couple of your favourite icons on the wall, some better furniture, a rug or two."

" It was a fine party," said Manoli contentedly.

" Tell me about it." Sergeant Phocas' small fingers were busy with the pink sea shells.

" Half the town was there," Manoli said proudly. " At Mikali's *taverna* first—or was that later ? "

" There will be a fine for Mikali, maybe half a million drachmae."

" Why ? "

" Two hours after closing time, all that noise, not keeping his customers in control."

" When the fine is fixed, I'll pay it," said Manoli. " He's saving his money to go away. To the Belgian Congo." He grinned. " Well, at Mikali's *taverna* first, and then crowding up the hill to Mina's house, and sitting outside all around the walls, singing. Fine singing, it was. And the dancing ! *Po-po-po !*

Even old Beanie was dancing, out there under the moon with all the chickens and the turkeys awake for a mile around. There must have been a hundred up there on the hill, maybe more. I didn't know I had so many friends."

"You were paying for the wine and the food and the music," said Sergeant Phocas. "It's a reliable way of bringing a list of friends to a good handsome figure. Now tell me about the food."

"Ah, the food!" Manoli crossed himself. "Lobsters," he said. "Big lobsters as long as your arm. Mikali did them in the garlic sauce. It would be worth paying his fine just for that sauce. *Sikoti*, a whole lamb, *palamethes* broiled on the wire, the big fish from Anatolia, fine oysters from Leros, big ones. And *fooskas!*" He sighed contentedly, thinking of the *fooskas*, the hairy black fruit of the ocean bottom, tasting of the sea, the meat of them orange and crimson in the pale oil. "By Jesus!" he said. "There were a hundred there, Sergeant, but not an empty gut among them. Mike Grassis came up with his box of pastries, fine pastries too, and their bellies were too full to look at them."

He chuckled at his picture of old Grassis, forking up the discs of *palamethes*, with the oil and the lemon juice dribbling down his chin, and Mina's hens around him, clucking and scratching and pecking at the neglected pastries. "The Pelacos girl said she'd never seen a party like it," said Manoli. "Not even in London or Paris."

"She was there?" Sergeant Phocas looked up from his sea shells.

"Sure," said Manoli. "She's painting my picture," he added, as if that were sufficient explanation. "She was saying about the party when I walked her back home."

"*You* walked her home?"

"Why not?"

Sergeant Phocas shrugged. "No reason," he said. "I didn't think Paul Pelacos would allow his daughter to go to a party like that, to a *taverna*. Perhaps he won't be happy when he hears about it from the mayor, about all the complaints. Vraxos will run to him, you'll see."

"He's always running to someone, that Vraxos," said Manoli

contemptuously. " He's all water and wind, like the barber's cat."

" I often see her around, the Pelacos girl," said the sergeant thoughtfully, " but never in a *taverna*, never at a party like that."

" Pelacos keeps her shut up too much. She's young. It's healthy for her to meet other people, to sing and dance a bit. It's healthier than being shut up and just walking around with nobody to talk to."

" Yes, but she's different from the rest of us here. That way she does her hair, that's the way they do it in Paris. It's nice, I think, for a change. I often look at her and think it's strange that she was born here. She isn't like the rest of us at all."

" Maybe it's that hair," said Manoli. " It's a different look, that's all. Women are pretty much alike, but it's living in Paris and London and places like that that makes them look different."

At first she had not enjoyed the party. There was the guilt of not having told her father pricking at her, the deceit that she mistrusted because it could become a habit once begun. And there was the consciousness that her presence made it awkward for all the others, all the people crowding into the big *taverna* and being stiffly deferential all of a sudden on seeing her sitting there at the long table between Manoli and Morgan. The faces coming in through the door all warm and open and expectant, and then the inhibition of her unexpected presence freezing them into stiff caricatures of pleasure.

Some of them she knew slightly—like Tony Thaklios the storekeeper and his plump, pretty wife Calliope, because she had talked to them in the shop when she had gone in to buy things ; and the funny little pastry cook with the wizened face, whom she remembered selling sugar buns to her when she was quite a little girl ; and the old man they called Beanie, because he always had a smile and a bow for her and a cheerful " Good morning " whenever she passed the market ; and some of the captains and divers from the Pelacos boats ; and Christos, the big crippled man, because there was nobody he didn't know and make jokes with.

But most of the others were just faces, faces that had the

special anonymity of being neither familiar nor strange—the faces of a small town that you saw passing and repassing in the street crowds, at the market, in the shops, around the café tables, faces that you recognised but did not know. In big cities like Paris or London you selected your few familiar faces and all the rest was a blur, running behind them, not mattering at all. In a small place like Kalymnos the blur became a mosaic. All the pieces forming the picture of the town were separate and distinct ; you accepted the totality of the picture without having to examine the pieces in detail.

There had been a crazy artist in Paris who had come back from Italy obsessed with the thought of the first bombs falling on the monastery at Monte Cassino, obsessed with the picture of that instant of impact, the walls splitting apart and the air filled with the flying fragments of frescoes and mosaics, all the separate bits of saints' heads and crowns and faces and hands and crosses exploding apart, spinning through the air. For a year he had tried to paint it and then they had taken him to the hospital. . . .

And here was the established pattern of Kalymnos breaking apart, the anonymous faces of the detail coming towards her, staring, smiling, saying words to her, but stiffly, as if they were looking at one another through glass.

It was Manoli who smashed the glass with the hammer blows of his exuberance, whirling everything away into a wild, rambunctious orgy of feasting and singing and dancing, of music and wine. Manoli, clapping his hands and stamping his feet, shouting for more wine and faster music. Manoli, bounding boisterously from table to table, dragging the men to their feet for dances that spun ever more feverishly to the piping of the *tsabuna* and the twanging chords of the zither. Manoli, with the red handkerchief in his hands, twirling and leaping, his hands slapping the heels of his boots like pistol shots, his fingers clicking the rhythm, ending each spin with his feet thudding on the floor and his great, harsh cry ringing across the room. Manoli, with the sweat on his dark face and joy in his eyes, a great scarlet lobster claw in his fist, beating out the time for the songs of the sponge men, the songs of old Kalymnos and the sea. Manoli,

chewing on the whole carcass of a fish and spitting the bones
to the littered floor. Manoli, with his head thrown back and his
eyes closed and the copper beaker of retzina in his hand, singing
the love songs of Naples in his rich, deep voice with all the
tenderness of a child. Manoli, hammering the table for still more
wine and crying his toasts across the room : " *Si-yia! Si-yia!* "
Manoli, sitting at the corner table with the four old men—the
oldest men she had ever seen—and handling them very gently
and keeping everybody quiet while they sang the old ballad of the
imprisoned Klepht in their thin, cracked voices. Manoli, grinning
at her and lifting his glass to hers and calling, " *Si-yia !* " And all
the faces turned to her, warm and smiling, as she raised her own
glass and said, " *Si-yia!* " And then she was singing herself,
and nobody was anonymous any longer, and the smoke and
the smell of sweat and wine billowed up to a ceiling of paper, all
blotched and sagging.

" *Si-yia! . . . Si-yia! . . . Si-yia!* " Whirling her away,
whirling all of them away, through the narrow streets and up
the hill with the flashlights flickering on the cobblestones, and
the shadows racing with them across the flat masses of pale
moonlit walls, and Manoli leading them all on, singing.

This was the dream that had come to her in the night, when
she heard the wedding feasts, the music in the hills and the
cocks crowing. It was the same impetuous rush up, up, up into
the dark sky, higher and higher, clutching at the stars and moon-
beams. And in the high night Dionysus was singing to the
frenzied Bacchae, and it was not electric flashlights that the
men were carrying, but blazing torches smelling of the pine
woods.

It was an experience numbing senses already reeling with
wine, flooding all the mind with inhuman essences, so that going
in through the pink door of the blue house on the hill was part
of a dream or no part of anything—all the crowded faces and
the curious pictures on the walls . . . the silent beautiful
woman in the corner with the grave sad face . . . Morgan and
Manoli . . . a child swinging in a canvas hammock . . . all the
faces swimming together and the wine throbbing in her head.

There was no explanation of how she had come to be walking

up the dark mountain path with Manoli. It, too, was part of the dream or no part of anything, part of the dazing magic of the moon, part of that frenzied impetuous flight up into the sky as high as you could go, following the music. Higher, higher—the loom of the precipice bulging blackly above them, the mountain, the cliff's edge, the music. But the music was below them now, the singing and the hand clapping and the thin pipe calling and the cocks crowing. All below them now, embedded in the warm womb of the night.

It was all part of the dark coil that began with Jacques in Paris, with the easel crashing to the floor as she struggled with him, the big jar smashing and all the brushes spilling out and his foot trampling on the tube of viridian and squirting it across the carpet like a spit of poison. And her shivering terror when he had left her crouched amid the rumpled bed linen—not for what had happened, but for wanting him again. And she had gone trembling to the dictionary to look up the definition of *nymphomania* and stumbled back to the disordered bed and sobbed herself to sleep. Jacques in Paris, again and again and again, and then the dark coil tightening like a steel spring in the parched red prison of Kalymnos, tightening around her. " You don't have to go away to escape from it "—that was what he had said. " You can escape from it here." She loved him, too, for understanding her, perhaps she loved Morgan more than anything in the world, but this was the other end of the coil, here on the dark mountainside with Manoli. This was where the coil would spring open, releasing her.

There was no sense of time. It was after midnight, she knew, because all the lights of the town had been switched off and the houses were queer, pale shapes, like tinted tiles embedded in pitch. Half-way up the mountainside a lantern shone on the tiny dancing figures and the music came up to them, and on the grassy ledge near the chapel of Saint Peter, Manoli sat beside her, humming the tune to himself, not speaking.

" O God ! " she whispered and clutched him, feeling the strong, hairy arms beneath her hot fingers and the wine reeling in her head, smelling his maleness, the wine smell on him and he sweat and the sea.

Manoli knew it was for her sake, not for his, and he leaned over her gently.

The grass was damp beneath her legs, the dewy grass and the smell of thyme and sage woven into the cool night air like a continuing thread of the song he had been humming. But now the stars were gone, all the glitter of the stars obliterated by the black shape of the man leaning over her, and her head was cushioned on the sweet damp herbs, and she could feel his hands upon her, moving up.

Beneath Manoli's hands her thighs were soft, silky, faintly damp, the feel of the living sponge taken from the water, and there was a wind stirring up from the sea. The smell of her body in the grass and the herbs and the night were all part of the wild sea smell from far away.

Irini opened her arms, opened her whole body to him, his weight pressing her down into the damp, yielding fragrance, and she could feel the sea pouring into her, the rushing black strength of it, the dark, passionate, impetuous sea.

PART THREE

Mina

I

" I don't know," Telfs said thoughtfully. " There is a chance, I guess. We can try. He has to go to Athens anyway." He frowned. " What the poor little bastard needs is a year or two in a proper place, with rest and care and the right food. He can't get it here."

" They do what they can," Morgan said. " I've seen her, and Stavros too. They go without things so he can have some Dutch butter or milk and eggs."

" Sure, they're okay. But they don't have what the kid needs, that's all. If they have to buy him aspirin, have you seen the way they do it ? They buy one tablet. Just one. Stavros goes without coffee and they buy one tablet."

The path was only a mule trail, cutting around the edges of the desolate hills, the white rocks slippery after the rain, the tiny wild flowers stiff and wiry above the clay puddles. In the valley behind, the nut trees were in blossom, creamy white and a pale pink against the stone-pitted sage of the mountains, and the sun on the white walls of Santa Katerina had the premature glare of summer. The others were a quarter mile ahead of them, moving past the corner of the old rock wall where the trail turned down and away to the shining bay of Piso—Mina with the big basket of food and Stavros with the retzina and the fishing rods and Manoli walking ahead of them with Nikolas astride his shoulders.

Morgan said, " Look, I've got a little money, not awfully much, but if there's anything I can do, anything special the child needs——"

" It doesn't answer the problem," Telfs said gruffly. " The real problem is this goddam island. It's cruel, vicious, un-

sympathetic. It destroys people. At the moment Nikolas is a
bodily problem. That's routine. Poliomyelitis, t.b., vitamin
deficiency—they can occur any place. But what about later?
When the destruction of the soul begins? Look, Morgan, let's
face it: we can't ever make the kid a hundred per cent again.
At the best he'll limp around the rest of his life. At the worst
he loses a leg—maybe both, if the disease gets into the other.
Sure, he'll have plenty of company here. Fifteen hundred men,
in a population of fourteen thousand, who don't walk right.
That's quite a statistic! Okay, that's the diving, not polio, or
t.b., and another one won't make any goddam difference. But
what a future for a kid of eight to look forward to! You take
care of yourself, son, and if you're a very good boy when you
grow up you can have a walking stick too."

"But what's the answer? Mina has nothing. Stavros has
nothing."

"He's got to get off this goddam island, that's the answer.
He's got to escape from it altogether. All of them have to."

"How can they? There isn't any place in the world would
take them. Stavros is too old, and he'd never get past a medical
examination. Mina has a crippled child and no husband. What
chance have they got?"

"If this Australian experiment works out, won't they have to
take everybody, cripples and all? Maybe that's the answer.
They couldn't just take half of them and leave the rest to rot
here."

"What Australian experiment?" Morgan asked guardedly.

"This plan to use the Kalymnians in the pearl fisheries out
there. I thought you'd know about it."

"I do, as a matter of fact. But I had the impression it was
not generally known."

"Not generally known? Hell! Half the town is talking
about it. You mean you haven't heard tell of Vraxos' committee?"

"Vraxos? Homer Vraxos?"

"Who else would have a committee?"

"It isn't anything to do with Vraxos. How did he find out
about it?"

" He's got that sort of nose. He smells out. He was in Athens last week. Some friend of his tipped him off."

" According to my information it was a Government matter, at the Cabinet level—very confidential."

Telfs grinned. " Well, that's as good a way as any of having the whole world know about it. Vraxos nosed it out and came back home by the next boat. Now he's hollering around the town organising a committee to pick the divers who should go."

" But surely that is Paul Pelacos' responsibility ? "

" It seems Vraxos would rather it were done by what he calls a representative group of citizens. That's what he says, and I suppose there's something in what he claims, but that isn't the real reason he's so eager to poke his nose in."

" What is the real reason ? "

" He wants to make damned sure Manoli doesn't go. He hates Manoli's guts."

" Yes, but they'd *have* to send Manoli. There's nobody on the island to compare——"

Telfs looked at him curiously. " Why are you so sure that Pelacos would pick Manoli. He's a good diver, sure, and a fine captain. He's a drunk, too, and a wild, crazy bastard when he wants to be."

" But they want *divers*, don't they ? Not ambassadors ! Or tract sellers ! This is a test team, the best they can get. They're going out there to *dive* ! They've got to pick people like Manoli and Christos because they're the best."

Telfs laughed. " Maybe it's as well you're not representing your government in this. You've picked two so far. One's a drunk, the other's a cripple."

" That isn't the point. They're the two best men on the island for what is wanted. Pelacos will see that."

" I wouldn't be so sure," Telfs said. " Since that business of the painting . . ." He grinned, and went ahead around the edge of a brown bog. " Let's get up with the others," he called back. " This is a hell of a note to be beginning a Sunday picnic on."

Morgan walked behind him, thinking of what Telfs had

said. It was not logical surely to attach too much importance to Pelacos' mild complaint—complaint was too emphatic a word—his mild expression of opinion about Irini's restlessness since the painting had been completed. And in any case Pelacos' integrity and sense of duty would ensure that his selection of the divers and their captain would not be influenced by any personal doubts or animosities. Irini's restlessness, that was a different thing altogether, related to Manoli only in that he had provided the key with which she had opened the door. Her reluctance to go back through the door and lock it behind her was perfectly natural. Of course she was restless.

"I should be easier in my mind if she did not see too much of Manoli"—that was all Pelacos had said. "It is this sweeping dynamic quality of his. Irini is young. In this rather restricted environment, perhaps susceptible. Since the painting was done she has seemed unsettled, restless."

Well, Morgan commented silently, she had not seen Manoli since the day she had shown him the finished painting, and that had been three weeks ago.

Morgan would have liked her to come to the picnic to-day, but knowing Manoli would be there he had deliberately refrained from asking her.

He and Telfs were fishing together on a rock ledge above the sea when he brought up the subject of Mina again.

Not five miles from the crowded harbour of Kalymnos, the little bay of Piso had an empty, timeless serenity. The few white cottages on the shore were locked and shuttered, awaiting summer's occupancy. In a hidden cave below them the sea groaned softly, and offshore a single dolphin arched and plunged in the blue, ruffled water. On the lip of the high cliff opposite a lean *chopanis* in a leather jacket leaned statuesquely on his twisted crook, watching the sheep cropping amid the boulders of the cliff face, and his shrill whistling drifted across to them. The rain had left the morning pale and scoured, with a milky magic that made Morgan half expect to see an old, beaked galley come riding in around the point with a slow beat of oars. It was a sea morning, everything drenched in blue, a morning for the Nereids and the Tritons, blowing their conches.

" This problem of Mina and Nikolas," Morgan said, his eyes on the cork float bobbing in the water. " Why doesn't Manoli marry her ? "

" Manoli ? " Telfs stared at him.

" Yes. He could marry her and take them all away. Stavros, too."

" He could, yes. But that depends on Manoli, doesn't it ? " He looked towards the beach, where Manoli was stretched out on the pebbles in the sunshine, sleeping. The child was playing at the water's edge, and in the tangle of the fig trees there was a blue drift of smoke where Mina was preparing the food on a stone hearth beside the little, white chapel. " I don't think Manoli has any intention of going away," said Telfs. " Maybe that's why he doesn't marry her, because he knows darned well she'd want to."

" You ought to keep your eyes on that float of yours," Morgan said, chidingly. " You just had one on."

" On a nice day there's no point in fishing if you have to go to all the bother of catching fish. I can leave it there now for a long time. There won't be any bait left." Telfs eased his back comfortably against the rock. " There's another thing, too," he said. " Mina isn't a virgin. It's kind of important here. These people put a top price on virginity, and when it comes to marrying——"

" But, Manoli ? Surely he wouldn't—— "

" Oh, Manoli's his own law. I was just pointing out there could be a whole lot of reasons why he doesn't marry her. Maybe he's asked her and she won't have him. He wouldn't be everybody's dream boy, you know—not as a husband."

" He's her lover, isn't he ? "

" Is he ? "

" So Irini claims. I don't know."

Telfs shrugged and pulled the line in. There was no bait on the hook. He turned his face away, bending over the rock and taking a long time to cut the cube of white meat from the dead squid and fasten it to the hook. The cutting was neat, the fastening awkward.

" There's another thing I wanted to ask you," Morgan said.

" This animosity between Mina and her brother-in-law, what's behind that ? "

" Vraxos is a bastard. A dirty bastard. Would you care to be friendly with him ? "

" I detest him. But this seems to go deeper than that. There's more to it than that, isn't there ? "

" There's a whole lot more. But it's Mina's story. You'll have to ask her. Oh, Vraxos made a pass at her once when his young brother, Mina's husband, was away diving. The brother —Paul, his name was—he would have killed Vraxos if he'd known, but that was the cruise he didn't come back from. He was drowned off Leros. There's a whole lot more to it than that, but it's Mina's story."

" Did you know her husband, this man Paul ? "

" Sure. He was a fine man. Not like his brother. Nothing like him."

" That's why Stavros hates Vraxos, because he knew what happened ? "

" Stavros never knew, no. He has other reasons."

" And Manoli ? "

Telfs shook his head. " He didn't get friendly with Mina until after Paul died. She never would have told him. It was all through then." He pushed himself up from the rock and began to haul in the line. " I said it was Mina's story, and you keep asking questions. Why are you so interested ? It all happened two years ago."

" I was just thinking that if Mina and the boy have to get away, and Manoli won't marry her, perhaps I could take her away myself."

Telfs' fingers were suddenly still, the gut line was taut against his hand. For a long moment he stared at his companion, and then, in a low voice, he said : " Why not ? " and shrugged. " Time we went back," he said, " and helped along that food."

He allowed Morgan to go past him, picking his way cautiously along the smooth, wet rocks felted with green weed and black with the spikes of sea urchins.

Stavros sat with his back to the nubbly bole of the fig tree and watched them: Morgan, walking with his daughter up the narrow, stone-choked ravine where once a river had run, and Telfs and Manoli, scrambling out along the rocks with the fishing rods over their shoulders.

Of the four men, only he was useless. He could neither climb the ravine with his daughter nor negotiate the steep rocks encircling the little bay with the men. He could carry fishing rods and the retzina jar and pack the things away in Mina's basket when the meal was done. He could sit with his back against a tree and watch them. He could think.

It was all very well for Dimitri to protest that there was no point in thinking about things, no point in fretting. Dimitri had given up, yes; yet he still had dreams of the big ships. Surely he did. He kept the picture on the wall. And how could you help thinking when thoughts surrounded you all the time, plaguing you? Thoughts and memories—you never lost them; they could never be discarded like old clothes when they became ragged and worthless or you grew out of them. Old clothes were more reasonable than old thoughts; they would go when you wanted them to. But thoughts persisted. They were always there, buried in the bottom of your mind like the black weed on the sea floor. It was only that as you grew older all the thin, pretty weed drifted away, drifted away into a very deep recess, where it would stay until senility came calling for it. Then nothing remained but the coarse, cruel growths: weeds sharp and black-blistered and blotched like sick skin, weeds that cut and stabbed and choked and entangled.

Stavros thought of that second season's diving—he had been only twenty then—when for the first time he had gone with all the boats and with the older men to North Africa. It had been a wonderful adventure, exciting and beautiful—because the thin, pretty weed had not drifted away then; the thread was still unbroken that linked boyhood with maturity. The thin weed was part of boyhood; you found it spread on the sand or clinging to the wet sea rocks, and you picked it up, admiring its prettiness, rubbing it between your fingers.

The thin, bright thread was still there that second season, and treading the strange, soft sea floor of the African shelf had been only an extension of the games he had played with the other boys along the wide *plateia* or in the tossing summer water off the rocks here at Piso. It had seemed so strong and taut, the thread linking his own aloneness at the bottom of the ocean, with the wild, warring companionship of boyhood.

The stone games and the stick games and the water games—they had all been keyed to the impending world of adult adventure. The fights, the boastings, the climbs, the bold bravadoes, the whispered talk of girls, the pig fat rubbed into the arms and legs and belly to make the hair grow thick and black, the snapshots taken with arms folded and hands furtively pushing against biceps to make them appear larger, the delicious terrors of diving into the outsurge near the lacerating, bruising rocks, holding the breath for just one more agonising second to stay submerged longer than any other boy, the sweating, constant pain of being the *pallikari*—all this tumultuous world of boyhood play had been keyed to the imminence and inevitability of heroic manhood.

And in that second season, at thirty metres on the shoals off Derna, the actuality of this manhood had emerged—and it had seemed only a continuation of the juvenile play, part of the same imaginative, heroic adventure. The thread was still unbroken.

It had been a day, Stavros recalled, of burning heat, with the coast of Libya a red mirage and the pitch making wet blisters between the deck planks and an oven heat inside the copper helmet as he awaited the signal from the *colazaris*. Sitting there on the wooden rail beside the ladder, he had felt his crotch filling up with sweat, the hot sweat flooding his loins as if he had wet himself : after he had gone down it was still hot in the suit at thirty metres. Even down there, through a hundred feet of water, the sun was shining, all dazzle and dapple on the pale sea bed, and around him was a world of a queer, deep, shining blue like the luminous enamelled skies of the church paintings, but without the angels flying.

He had been down for fifteen minutes, lost in this blue and weightless world, when he had seen the outcrop of rock ahead, growing out of the deep blue as if something magic were forming in front of his eyes. And he could sense the sponges drawing

him on and he had gone in and pushed the weeds aside with his
hands. The weeds swayed away from him slowly as if they were
not weeds at all but dark vertical currents in the water. There
had been no feeling to the weeds as they swayed away from him.
No feeling and no weight to anything, and no sound as the
weeds parted. He had gone in, feeling the shoal slanting away
beneath his boots, and the soft darkness had wrapped around him,
thicker and thicker, until the blue was gone and he had looked
back and the weed was folding in behind him like a dense curtain,
no thickness or substance in the weed, only this black liquid wall
closing behind him as if he were drowning in the sable squirt
of some gigantic octopus. And the terror had gripped at his
guts and he had turned and stumbled back, thrashing the imprisoning weed apart.

It had released him without any feeling or sound, swaying
away unresistingly, and with the air whistling in the release valve
the deep soft blueness had formed around him again with the feel
of the sea bed sliding away as he went up—and he had known
then that the thread was broken. The soft surrendering weed
had severed the thread. After that day he had never been afraid
of the weed or the blackness again. But after that day there had
been no more boyhood. . . .

He could see Mina high up on the sunlit side of the ravine,
nimble and graceful among the white rocks, and Morgan climbing more slowly behind her, a big, quiet figure, moving easily.

In the year Mina was born the priests had closed all the
churches as a protest against the Italians, but the *despot* himself
had been there for the baptism in the little house on the hillside.
The *despot* had been there in his fine robes, and in the candlelight
five priests with thick, black beards, and other faces packed into
a circle around them—the faces of his four sons peering over the
wooden railing of the bed platform, where all the other children
were gathered, and the faces of the divers and the captains and
their friends and relatives, all the faces hot with wine. And the
great joyful shout from every one of them as the *despot* had
taken the funny, little, naked figure and plunged it into the great,
brass bowl and then lifted it, thin and drenched and wailing,
lifted it in both his hands high above his head, up into the dark-

ness almost to the beamed ceilings. And behind the robed and bearded figure holding aloft the screaming dripping baby, the figure of his own wife Mina, anxiety and pride and joy all mixed up in her sweet face as she waited with the warm rug in her hands to receive her daughter.

His wife Mina—the girl he had found in Siphnos, the daughter of a poor man, a miller, but the loveliest of an island famous for the beauty of its women ; the girl who had come to him without a cent for her *brika*, but who had given him the richer dowry of her beauty and four fine sons and a daughter. That night, when the baby had been wrapped again and put away to bed and when the *despot* and the priests had gone down the hillside with the lanterns bobbing, the wine had flowed and the old man with the mandolin had composed the song about his having made five children in six years, and everybody had clapped and stamped at the verse predicting that he would be the father of twenty children.

But that was thirty years ago, and there had been no more children after Mina. Thirty years ago, when olives were ripe and songs joyful and the sea was young. Thirty years ago, before the pretty weed had begun to drift away. . . .

Stavros, his father had named him. *Stavros*—the Cross.

Fourteen years ago . . . when young Mina was sixteen, in Leros, fresh from school and astonishing him with her bravery, not crying at all as she crouched in the red earth beside him. All of them were huddled together in the back of the cave with the earth shaking to the bombs and the dust coming down on their heads, quite fine and soft like summer rain, and sometimes a stone or a clod filling from the roof of the cave, as if the soft body of a baby had been dropped among them. Forty-three days of it, stretched out into days and nights and hours and minutes, with the black planes coming in wave after wave over the island and the bombs screaming down : the planes with the black crosses on their wings coming out of the sky like hawks, down, down, as if they would plunge right through the earth and out the other side. Where was the other side of the earth from Leros ? Not Hades. Hades was there, with the earth shaking and the black smoke hanging in the valleys and the flame licking higher and

higher, and the black darting shapes of the planes running through
the smoke and fire. And in the night the roar of the guns from
the German warships offshore, and next day the parachutes
flowering over the hills, and the boots and the dark uniforms
trampling through the shattered streets.

They had fed the people at first, giving them bread and food
—not much, but sufficient to keep them strong enough to build
the airfields needed for the attack on Crete. It had seemed bear-
able for a while, after the forty three days of bombs and hearing
the tales from Kalymnos, where there were no airfields to be
built and no food for the people and they were dying of starvation
in the streets. . . .

Morgan and Mina had reached the crest of the ravine, and
they both seemed very tall against the blue sky among the thistles.
Everything was tied together—Stavros and his sons, beating the
stones into the runway of the airfield at Leros ; and the planes
taking off from the runway that Stavros and his sons had
built and flying to Crete to capture Morgan ; and now
Morgan, walking along the cliff top in the sunshine with his
daughter.

Threads . . . but new threads now, thick and black and
knotted, linking everything together. Where now was the bright
thread that had snapped in the weed-veiled water off Derna ?

The priest coming to them in the night, that was another
thread, knotting things together—Elias, the old *papás* from
Vathý, coming to them in the night and whispering to them in
the grove of cypresses near the little chapel of Saint Demetrios,
telling them of the flight of thousands of Kalymnians to Turkey,
telling them how those who had remained were dying, twenty
and thirty of them a day dead in the streets, and others shot
because they had resisted the Germans or would not co-operate
with them, and the children starving. Fearful stories he had
whispered to them, there in the dark secretive shadows beneath
the cypresses.

Elias the *papás* leading them through the fields and across the
dark, rocky hills to the creek where the caiques were hidden—
the thread knotting them all together, knotting everything
together : the figure of the old priest striding ahead of them in the

night, his black cylindrical hat firm on his head and his robes flapping around his legs.

Elias, the same *papás* who had blessed their boat when he, Stavros, had sailed first to Africa—his thick beard was white with age now and reached to his waist and his fingers trembled on his staff of olivewood. Elias the *papás*, who had been there in the little house at the baptism of Mina, sleeves rolled up and vestments hooked back like a woman's apron, dipping his elbow into the big brass bowl to test the temperature of the water. Elias the *papás*, old and infirm, leading them in the night across the black ridges, his tall figure rising up against the stars and his staff clattering on the pebbles, leading them down the other side to the boats drawn into the secret reed beds.

The women and the children whispering and the boats hauling out with only the soft lap of the water in the reeds and the quiet creak of rope and timber, and then the seven caiques nosing together out of the harbour with the engines thudding softly. Everything quiet and secret until the grey light before dawn revealed the Anatolian cliffs, and then the world splitting apart in fire and water as the destroyer turned its guns on them. . . .

In the soft grass beneath the fig tree with the drone of the bees around him, Stavros wept quietly. It was only when he was alone like this that he could weep, and, choking with the smell of the sea and smoke and blood, see it again and hear the noise of it : the caique following them, with his four sons aboard, splitting apart, flying into the sky in shattered fragments, the flash burning the picture of it into his memory so that it was everlastingly there in the charred part of his brain, the black fragments splitting apart, flying into the air forever. And then the tearing crash of the planks beneath his feet, and the sea dragging down the drowned face of his wife, and the bloody, headless trunk of Elias the old *papás* hanging over the sagging rail and dipping in the waves like a sack of sponges, and his round black hat swirling away on the water. And Mina, on the drifting plank beside him, and the pain in his fingers as he clutched her.

Not many of them had got ashore, only Mina and himself

and a dozen others, and two of those had died of sickness and starvation on the way to Bodrum. For a long time he had feared that Mina too would die, from exhaustion and grief at the loss of her mother and brothers.

Had Homer Vraxos betrayed them? It was a question that still persisted, haunting the mind, even though the inquiries after the war had found no cause for complaint against him. In Bodrum they had first heard the whisper that Vraxos had betrayed his people, that he had talked too much to secure his own safety and ingratiate himself with the Germans, had betrayed Elias the *papás* and the secret of the boats. But there had been no way of knowing the truth of it. It could have been no more than a malicious rumour circulated by those who had no liking for him, by those who had suffered their own terrible losses and were resentful that Vraxos himself had come to Bodrum two weeks later in a boat that had got away from Leros and come all the way to Turkey without harm. There was no way now of knowing the truth of it—it had all happened so long ago.

In Bodrum the whispers had persisted for a long time, although nobody ever directly charged Vraxos with the crime, because he had a way of ingratiating himself with the officials responsible for the provision of shelter and food and he might have made it very difficult for his accusers ; and besides, he had been such a pitiable wretched figure when he was not with the officials, whining about the conditions and pretending to be ill to get more than his share of the food and clutching his American passport lest somebody steal it and forever cursing the day he had been misguided enough to return from the United States.

They had all been crowded then into an old, stinking barn with little to eat but slops and crusts, and Vraxos always came crawling into the corner where the Kalymnian people were huddled together. And he made a point of pressing in close beside Mina, who was still very weak and sick, pretending to be solicitous for her comfort and warmth, pressing in and rubbing himself against her as he leaned across to feel her forehead or stroke her hair. Stavros used to watch him, because he disliked the man and mistrusted him, and one night when Mina was sleeping he had seen Vraxos fumbling around her, and for all his own grief and misery he had taken the bastard by the neck and dragged him out through the crowded barn and thrown him into the pig yard.

He had not seen Vraxos after that night until the war was over, although in the refugee settlement at Gaza, where they had all been properly cared for, some Kalymnian people had told him how Vraxos had gone to Cairo with his American passport and pleaded that he wished to return to America to do his share in the war, and they had flown him back. From what Stavros could gather he had not made much contribution to the war, but had stayed near Detroit making ice-cream and lemonade for the factory workers at Willow Run—and by all accounts making a lot of money too. He had stayed on there until after his wife had died, and then he had come back to Kalymnos to look for a new wife.

He kept telling everybody he wanted a young one, and that was why he was always snuffling around the girls at the Gymnasium, the girls who had just grown tall and who were walking good with their breasts out. Homer was always buying them cakes and candy, and probably wondering what they would be like in bed after they had left school. But he had been doing that for three years now. He didn't seem in any hurry to get the new wife.

For a whole year after he had first come back from America they had seen a lot of him ; he visited the house often because his young brother Paul—he had been a good, fine man—was married to Mina. Although maybe it was Mina who had interested him most, because whenever Paul went away with the sponge boats Homer still came regularly to the house, sniffing around Mina, making jokes about how she shouldn't have married Paul because he was away from home so often. Paul was poor, he would say, and he was rich ; she should have waited for him to come back from America. If she hadn't married Paul, he would say, sniggering while he said it, then maybe he wouldn't want a young girl who was a virgin at all, but would marry Mina instead and take her off to America.

He was always harping on the subject of virgins. It was a twist in his mind. He couldn't keep off it for long.

It used to make Stavros uncomfortable listening to him, and watching him hanging around Mina, because it always reminded him of the night in the barn at Bodrum, and the same suspicions would come harbouring in his mind so that he would enter the room half expecting to find Vraxos with her.

Then Paul had died, leaving Mina with the little pension the government provided, which was barely enough to look after Nikolas, and it wasn't long afterwards that Manoli had begun to visit them, and he had made it obvious that he didn't like Vraxos sniffing around. After that they weren't troubled by him any more. . . .

Stavros lifted himself slowly from the grass, easing out the stiff pain beneath his ribs, and began to scour the tin plates with a tuft of grass and stack them in the basket.

It was odd, the attraction Mina had for men, when you considered that she was poor and no longer a virgin and had a crippled child and a father not much better. It was funny, too, that there were four men who *could* marry her and take her away if they wanted to—Vraxos and Manoli and Telfs and Morgan—but it wasn't likely that any one of them would. Perhaps, in a different sort of way, they were all like Vraxos— just wanting to smell around.

Stavros took the knives and drove the blades into the earth to clean them. For a long time he was down on his hands and knees beneath the fig tree with one of the knives in his hand, plunging it into the ground harder and harder until the cramp in his fist made him drop it.

" There are so many different worlds in Greece," said Morgan quietly. " Here you could never believe that the sea is just there, beyond that crest of rocks. This is a world quite apart from it. It belongs to the shepherds. Nothing has changed here for four thousand years."

He sat on the flat rock below her—he had chosen the position deliberately so that he would not see her as he talked ; it would have unsettled him too much to be looking at her—and from the stony ground around his feet he plucked a fistful of the tiny mountain flowers, *kookluthia*, dolls' flowers, their blooms as minute as match heads, spread across the rough surface of the earth in Lilliputian splendour. The country rolled away to the high, blue sky in a series of stony, gorse-roughened ridges eroded by the bleached, rocky tumble of dry stream beds. All the valleys and hills were bare of trees; this was a desolate empty wilderness where time, it seemed, would be marked, not by the quick mortality of people, but by the infinitely slow erosion of whitened rocks. Yet, as everywhere in Greece, you were startled by the *apparition* quality of the people. The desolation was inhabited, the emptiness astir with human activities. You never saw them coming; they simply appeared, *there*, as if they had suddenly grown from the empty earth— a *chopanis* astride a rock, whistling to his sheep; an old, stooped woman in black against the stony skyline, carrying faggots on her head; a boy, crooning to his little herd of goats and kids; three crones with their skirts bundled up, searching for herbs. And if you took your eyes away for a minute, they were all gone and others had materialised from the rocks—a fiercely whiskered man in high brown boots with an adze on his shoulder; a girl coming through the thistles with a milk can on her head; a child bearing a new-born lamb.

"It is why I come often to these places in the hills," Mina said. "Up here you can be sure of things."

"Of some things, yes." He was sharply aware of her presence behind him; it was almost the feeling he had sometimes of a person staring intently at him when his back was turned: the impulse to swing around and look at her was almost irresistible. But if he did, would she too be gone, like the woman with the faggots and the shepherd on the rock? "Perhaps only of the rocks and weeds and flowers," he said. "How can you be sure of others—that shepherd there, the old woman?"

"Oh, yes, you can be sure of them," she said, with a curious, simple certainty. "They are always here. They belong here."

"They belong to the port across there, to Kalymnos," he said. "If the port died, if it were suddenly spirited away, would they still be there, do you think? Where would they sell the wool and meat and milk, the honey they gather, the herbs, the faggots?"

"They were here before people sold things to one another.

There is something in the mountains that belongs to the mountains. It never changes. That is why I like coming here, to find out that there are things which always belong. One day I will take you walking on the hills behind Santa Katerina, past the olives. You can see Astypalaia from there."

"If you went away from Kalymnos, you would miss the mountains, wouldn't you?"

"But I am not going away from Kalymnos," she said, and there was a note of surprise in her voice that made him turn his head at last and look up at her. She had knotted the white head scarf around her neck, and her hair shone against the sky.

"One day perhaps somebody will marry you," he said, "and he will take you away."

She smiled. "I am an old woman. I am thirty. Our men marry their women very young, when they are sixteen and seventeen. I am an old woman. I have been married before, I have a sick child to care for, I have no *brika* to offer. Is there a man, do you think, foolish enough?"

Her eyes were warm as she smiled at him, but her words were spoken with an almost childlike earnestness, with an absolute conviction of the truth of what she was saying. In her question there was no coquetry, no invitation to some pretty compliment. To her, there would never be a man foolish enough. The handicaps were insurmountable. Her own beauty, her physical appeal—if she considered them at all, which was doubtful —were in no way related to the prohibitive factors forming her worthlessness as another man's wife. Physical beauty was not something you offered to a husband; either it came with the other things or it did not, and in its presence or its absence there was no particular importance. The important things you offered to a husband were maidenhood and the promise of healthy sons; and you offered *brika*, and *brika* should be a house and furniture and clothing and linen for the beds and table and a little money and the assurance of comfort. Could she, past her youth and with her innocence soiled, come to a man and expect him instead to take from her shoulders the burdens that were hers: poverty and a sick father and a crippled child? Would any man be foolish enough?

T.S.D.   L

Morgan looked up at her in the soft sunlight of early afternoon, realised the implications that were behind her question. In her humility there was a deep and unassailable truth: to her, it was the way things were and nothing could alter them. Yet how swiftly, how completely, they *could* be altered if she were to escape from the rigid conventions of her environment.

" You are a very beautiful woman," he said, making the statement as simply as she had made hers. " You would have that to offer. It's not unimportant, you know."

For a moment she looked at him, then laughed softly and turned her head away.

" If you were not here," he persisted, " if you were somewhere else—London or New York or Paris or Sydney—the things you talk about wouldn't matter at all. In places like that the attitudes are different. I think you would find there would be many men "—he smiled—" many men foolish enough."

He could imagine the stir she would cause, taken from this environment where even fat old Maria, his own cleaning woman, despised her because she was poor and would never get another husband. Yet hers was a very rare and singular loveliness, matured in suffering and by the subtle transfiguring qualities of the surroundings that now imprisoned her. It was a beauty that seemed to contain all the depth of these surroundings, from the topmost rocky peak, where the white church of the Prophet Elias glittered in the sun, to the mysterious stirrings of the sea's profundities. Yet it was a beauty no longer justifiable in the setting that had created it. It was imprisoned within stone, and it could never be warm again until some Pygmalion breathed life into it.

He could do it. There was an exhilaration, an excitement cogent and overpowering, in the realisation. Almost by a flick of the fingers he could perform the transformation. *He* could be her Pygmalion, his kingdom broader than Cyprus ever was!

He could imagine taking her to London, to New York, to Australia—the effect she would cause walking into a room, the brittle conversations shattering into silence, the eyes staring. It would not then be a problem of finding a man foolish enough, but of preventing all men from being foolish.

"I do not think I shall be going to those places you talk
about," she said simply. "One day, perhaps, to another island,
softer than here, not so cruel." She paused, then said wistfully :
"I think I should like to go to Nissiros. There are little streams
there, and trees. All the wood we burn on our fires, it comes from
Nissiros. Did you know that ? I should like to go there."

"Or to Astypalaia ? " he said softly.

"Or Astypalaia, yes."

"But these are merely other islands. It would make no
difference to *you* whether you were on Nissiros or Kalymnos or
Astypalaia. It would just be like walking into another room of
the same house. The room would be different, but the walls
around you the same. Can't you see that ? "

"I must go away from Greece, then ? "

He shrugged. "It depends what you are looking for, I
suppose. But if there is to be any fulfilment for you, yes, I think
you must."

"Tell me," she said, "what you were looking for when you
came back to Greece." She spoke quietly, but with a particular
emphasis, as if the explanation he gave might also explain herself.
The innocence of the request carried with it a startling acuteness ;
it was like a question carefully contrived by skilled counsel to
disarm a witness into an admission. And what should he admit ?
That he had returned to Greece for precisely the same reason
that took her walking in the mountains to the height from which
she could see Astypalaia ?—so that he might sit on a quiet rocky
hilltop under the sky and be sure of things again ?

"I came back to see if it were true," he said simply.

"If what were true ? "

"A dream I had. It's a long story." He plucked a stalk of
grass and chewed on it and leaned back against the rock upon
which she was sitting, and he could feel the soft point of her shoe
against his hip. "It began during the war," he said, "when we
came to Greece. I fell in love with the country, and with the
people. With that violet sky in the evenings above the Acropolis
and the colours changing on Hymettus, with lots of things,
right from the beginning. I remember that first day, when we
went ashore from the ships at Piræus—all the songs and the

cheering—and then going up to Athens. God! what a welcome
they gave us, the kisses and the flowers and the girls smiling——"

"But you had come to help us," Mina said. "Of course we
were glad."

"Oh, no, it wasn't that," he said softly. "It was later. When
we had been defeated, licked, routed all the way down from
Larissa and Lamia and through Thermopylae. We'd had hell
knocked out of us and we were on the run, and still they cheered
us and smiled and put flowers in our hats." He shook his head
slowly, as if it were still something to wonder at. "And then
at Nauplia, the evacuation, when it was time to leave. They
knew what we were abandoning them to. There couldn't have
been any doubts in their minds—they knew what had happened
in the north. But they were all there with flowers and smiles and
kisses, cheering us into the boats. Just the same as when we
had come to Athens, just the same, except that we were going
away, leaving them."

He could see it still, through the sunlight and the white
dapple of the rocks in the sage : the ragged, black line of the
shore ; and the huge outcrop of the Palaméthi, jutting into the
dusky sky ; and the dim lights moving along the water front ;
and the high, thin voices of the singing girls ; and then, across
the still water, the voices shouting, over and over again, " *Nike !
Nike ! Nike !—Victory ! Victory ! Victory !* " No recriminations, no pleadings, no tears, only that one word shouted through
the agonies of defeat. And the remnants of his platoon, crouched
on the dark thwarts of the boats, huddled together with their
rifles slung ; all the haggard, exhausted, unshaven faces, suffering faces, filthy and taut with the long weeks of battle and defeat
and retreat ; and Casey the sergeant, weeping beside him—Casey,
the biggest bastard in the battalion, who had been a crocodile
shooter up on the Katherine and who within two months was
to be blown to pieces in the retreat across the mountains of
Crete—Casey, the big tough sergeant, crouched beside him,
blubbering like a baby and mumbling over and over again,
" They're bloody wonderful ! They're bloody wonderful . . . ! "

"Please go on," said Mina softly.

"I used to think about it a lot," Morgan said, " in the prison

camp and the years afterwards, drifting around the world, and
then back to Australia. That violet light over Athens, and the
noise of the goat bells coming up from the valleys near Lamia,
and that evening we sailed away from Nauplia. . . . But after a
while it stopped being real. It wasn't anything any longer that
I had actually seen, that had actually happened. It was just a
dream I once had—a dream of a place that was like all the world
could be, if it were only given a proper chance." He smiled at
her. " So I came back to see if it were true," he said.

" And you have been disappointed ? "

" Disappointed ? No."

" Then *you* do not want to go away from Greece ? "

" But there's no reason why I should," he protested. " With
you it's different, it's——"

" Come," she said, and she smiled as she reached her hand
down to his. " We must go back to the others. And it is much
harder going down than climbing up."

He held her hand as they went down, although she moved
from rock to rock with the agility of a shepherd, as if she belonged among the rocks. Pygmalion ? He smiled wryly at the
brief vanity of the thought. Mina Vraxos at a cocktail party
in Claridges ? Mina Vraxos in furs and a low gown, being
photographed at a first night, with all the grey, tired faces
peering ? To take this wild, strange, beautiful creature of the
rocks and the prickly sage and the sun and the smell of thyme
and honey and the sea, and to throw her into the howling pit
from which he himself had fled !

This was where she belonged, here among the white rocks
with a piping shepherd astride a red rock on a cliff dropping
sheer to a jewel-blue sea, here where she could come to be by
herself and be sure of things. *Pygmalion !*

They were almost at the foot of the ravine when she stopped
and turned to face him. Her feet were wide apart on a flat shelf
of stone, her head tilted back a little, her arms stretched out and
down behind her body ; the wind was in her hair and was
moulding the coarse grey cotton of her dress against her breasts
and thighs.

" You must not forget what I told you," she said, and

laughed softly. " One day I will take you walking. Past Santa Katerina, past the olives. To the real mountains. You will see what I mean."

" I think I do see," said Morgan, and as they went back together along the old river bed her hand was still in his.

2

MIKE GRASSIS wrapped the two slices of *baklava* in a square of greaseproof paper, and, because it was for George's wife, he cut a slab of the English cake also and wrapped it separately in clean white paper and put it beside the *baklava*, but he took from George only the two drachmae which was the price of the *baklava*.

" Tell Maria," he said complacently, " that it is not very good. If I could get the proper yeast—ah, then she would see some real cakes ! " He coughed and changed the subject before George could start thanking him for his generosity about the slice of English cake. " Has that stingy bastard Vassilis come across with the extra money he promised you ? "

" Not yet," said George, blinking shortsightedly. " But he will. He is a good man, Vassilis, a kind man really, but if he cannot get the money from the people he makes the suits for, how can he pay extra to me ? They'll pay up when the banks release the money to the captains for the new season's stores, and then I'll be okay." He spoke with a confidence he no longer felt, but he didn't like to think about the stinginess of his employer nor of that long sequence of Saturday night disappointments when he had to go home to Maria and tell her the money was still the same, not a drachma more. And his wife sometimes would scold him for not standing up for himself, but he didn't like to ask Vassilis about it too often in case he got angry and stopped giving him work altogether. " Maybe next year," he said happily, " we'll all be in Australia. That's where there's plenty money for everybody. Did you know in Australia all the wages are fixed, and they even pay you when you take holidays or get sick? Did you know that? And when you get to sixty-five, you stop work and they pay you money the rest of your life. You just sit back, take it easy."

"Sure," said Mike dryly. "And in heaven you get a clean nightshirt every day. There'll be pie in the sky when you die." He didn't want clean nightshirts every day, or pie in the sky. He'd settle for a heaven with a shop with a double-fronted window and four glass cases and his name in fine big letters over the door, painted by a proper professional sign painter. And a good deep oven in the back and a storeroom full of fine yeast and good Canadian flour and the right sort of rose water and essences for making the syrups. Heaven, to Mike Grassis, would be a place where you didn't have to climb out of bed at five in the morning to cart your mixtures to the baker, where you didn't have to drag yourself around the town for eighteen hours a day with a heavy metal box under your arms, digging a black callous deep into the heel of your hand and making you ache with the fever so that in the night you were up five or six times to make coffee or smoke cigarettes. "You've had Vraxos around talking to you?" he said.

"He's been talking to everyone. He takes a big interest in this Australian business."

"That bastard takes a big interest in most things. Sometimes I sit on the john reading a scrap of newspaper and I look up and expect to see Vraxos there, snooping in to see what I'm up to. That's his stuff over there, for his little girls." He gestured to a tray of cakes, with chocolate on the top and twirls and rosettes of the white frosting which he squirted out of a spill of paper. Vraxos paid three drachmae each for the special cakes, and he never made any fuss about paying, the money was there right on the line, but Mike never really cared about making them. He always felt a bit dirty somehow, making the cakes for Vraxos' schoolgirls. He always made two extra cakes when he was fixing them for Vraxos, and he gave them to young Johnnie and Anna, and somehow that made him feel better about it. . . .

"I never liked Vraxos, either," said George. "Not only

Vraxos—all those other fellows back from the States, walking up and down all day in their fancy American clothes, not talking to anyone else, trying to make everyone think they don't belong to the place any longer."

" I been to America," said Mike. " Seattle, San Francisco, Wilmington, New York, Boston, plenty places. I don't walk round the place like a cigar-store Indian."

" You're different."

" Tony Thaklios and Calliope, old Dimitri—do they do it ? Thaklios had his own café in Florida, but do you ever see him strut around as if he's got the Statue of Liberty tattooed on his behind ? That's where Vraxos gives me a pain—right in the behind ! "

" Well, it isn't right to judge a man just by the way he wears his clothes," George protested. " I didn't like him myself, I tell you, but he's taking a big interest in this Australia business just because it's for the good of everyone, and it's our duty to support him." He spoke with what for him was a singular vehemence. It was not the way he generally spoke ; usually he agreed with anything anybody said, because then they didn't get angry and make trouble. If you protested too firmly about things, that was a sure way of making bother for yourself. And, besides that, it was essential that he convince himself about the good that Homer Vrazos was trying to do for the people, because if he didn't trust him then the whole thing broke apart and he was back where he was before, trudging up the hill on Saturday night to tell Maria that the money was still the same.

" You want to tell me," said Mike acidly, " that Vraxos does this just because it's good for everyone, for other people ? You want to make me laugh, that's why you tell me, eh ? "

" If it's handled right we'll all be able to go to Australia, that's what he says. There'll be plenty work for everyone, good money, nobody will have to go hungry."

" Sure, it's what I said—pie in the sky." Mike grinned sardonically. " Me, I'm sixty-six, sixty-seven next May. You mean they pay for me to go out there just so I sit back and take it easy, and they pay me money the rest of my life ? "

" Vraxos has made a whole lot of people in the town think

differently about him," George said doggedly. "Most of the people believe what he tells them." He paused for a moment, brooding darkly, and then his face brightened; as if he were producing his trump card, he said, "Even Stavros."

"Stavros? He wouldn't listen to anything that bastard told him."

"He's listened, all right," George said triumphantly. "Why shouldn't he listen? Out there in Australia he'll have proper work and good money, and he'll be able to look after himself. Why, out there he even gets paid if he's sick. And in a few years, when he gets to be sixty-five, he just sits back and takes it easy."

"Bah!"

"We've all signed, anyway—Stavros too!" George spoke eagerly now—because the trump card had worked and Mike Grassis could find nothing to say, he could only grunt—and all the confidence and trust had flowed back into him.

"Signed?" Mike said suspiciously. "Signed what?"

"This petition that Vraxos is getting up. He's getting everyone to sign it, and then he takes it to Mr. Pelacos."

"He brings his petition to me," Mike said darkly, "and I tell him where he can put it. I know just the place."

"I wouldn't want you to think, Mr. Pelacos, there's any thought of interfering," Homer Vraxos said ingratiatingly. "There's nobody here wouldn't put all his trust in you. Why, I guess most of us would say the Pelacos family *is* Kalymnos, and that wouldn't be far from the truth. It's only that some of us, we've been abroad, we made good some other place. I guess we consider we know the ropes better than others. We'd like to see the people get the same sort of chance we had. Those that aren't bone lazy, maybe they make a lot of dough out there."

He smiled encouragingly, but Pelacos only nodded and studied the key chain held between his fingers. It made Vraxos nervous. Why didn't the bastard say something? Just sitting there behind the big desk, playing with his goddam chain and nodding—just as if Homer Vraxos was a bad smell or something that didn't have any right to be there! They were all the same, these stiff, snooty, cold-blooded bastards with their thin noses and fancy houses in Athens, and flying back and forth all the time to London and Paris, and considering themselves so much better than anybody else.

"I don't mind telling you, Mr. Pelacos," he went on engagingly, "I got quite a surprise when they told me you were to make the selection. I don't mean you to take any offence about that, but I did get quite a surprise."

"Why?" asked Pelacos quietly.

"Well, you know what I mean. It's in the petition we sent."

"The petition you sent, Vraxos, quite apart from being grammatically grotesque, is so ambiguous that I can make neither head nor tail of it. That is exactly why I asked you to come here. And that is why I am now asking you—*why*?"

Vraxos stared down at his polished shoe for a moment, so that the rage and hatred boiling inside him should not be revealed in his eyes. The condescending, patronising swine!—That's why I'm asking you, Vraxos! Sit up straight, Vraxos, and answer my questions! Get down on your belly on the carpet, Vraxos, and lick my boots!

He looked up and smiled obsequiously. "I was pleased that it *was* you," he said, "but I naturally thought it would be a matter for *all* the people to decide. Well, for a committee. It's important to the town, Mr. Pelacos. Maybe it means life or death to lots of the people."

"I am aware of its importance, Vraxos," said Pelacos tiredly. "What I deplore, deeply deplore, is this quite premature discussion—as if it were an established project—of something which, apart from being extremely confidential, is no more than a tentative proposal that may never amount to anything. Now we have the circumstance of the whole island discussing it, the whole island in a ferment, taking it for granted that it will all come to pass."

"Well, if it's handled right, Mr. Pelacos," said Vraxos meaningly, "I guess it will."

"Nonsense! With the uproar that has been caused in the last week it would not surprise me in the least if the government

washed its hands of the whole business. Public meetings!
Petitions! Committees! Do you realise, Vraxos, that there
are people already who are selling their houses and their furniture
in the confident expectation that *everybody* will be sailing off to
Australia? Selling now, presumably, in the belief that prices
will fall as soon as all the others begin to sell!"

"I guess that's good business, Mr. Pelacos." Homer Vraxos
chuckled slyly. "You're a businessman. You wouldn't want
to hold off selling until a glut came along."

"All Kalymnos is unsettled, restless, drunk with these
ridiculous hopes and expectations. I tell you, Vraxos, it is
completely premature, and exceedingly dangerous. What will
be the temper of the people, do you imagine, if they find that it
was all a pipe dream? The tragedy of the poorer folk, misled
by this false hope? I tell you that whoever spread this story
has done us all a grave disservice."

Vraxos shrugged and spread his hands. "You know how it
is, Mr. Pelacos. Some guy visits up at Athens, and he gets to
hear some rumours and comes back and spreads them around.
Some guys can't keep their mouths shut. That's why it's nice
we have this talk. I get around among the people more than you
do—you're a busy man with your own affairs to look after, and,
besides that, I can get with people you wouldn't like to mix up
with. You just say if you want me to put a stop to all these
stories. You just say. If I can help you, Mr. Pelacos, you
know you can always rely on me. People listen to me because
I was in the States thirty years and I'm an American citizen,
and——"

"Yes, yes, Vraxos, I would be grateful for anything you
can do, but let us please come back to the point of this petition."

"Well, you've got to understand how the people feel, Mr.
Pelacos. You're a very wealthy man, but this is mostly an
island of poor people. There's a whole lot of suffering, men
out of work and starvation. Maybe sitting in this room of
yours, you wouldn't see it so much. . . ." Vraxos surveyed the
room again. He had never been inside it before, nor any room
quite like it, although it reminded him a bit of the suite in the
hotel at Cleveland that year of the convention, when the girls

from the burlesque show had come up and everyone had got drunk and the girls had changed into the men's clothes and danced around on the beds, wearing only the men's hats and shirts and the big convention badges, and old, fat Stan Farnsworth trying to pin the badges where they oughtn't to have been. . . . "Maybe you don't see it like I do, Mr. Pelacos. You're able to send your daughter to London and Paris to school, and——"

"I don't think my daughter's education is strictly concerned with the subject, Vraxos. Nor does it have any real bearing that I can see on the matter of Kalymnian poverty. I do not oppress the people nor underpay them so that my daughter may be educated abroad. My business, Vraxos, is buying sponges. I buy them in an open and competitive market in which anybody is at liberty to bid."

Sure, thought Vraxos, big fish eat little fish. But he did not express the thought.

"Oh, don't get me wrong, Mr. Pelacos," he protested quickly. "I didn't mean anything like that. Miss Irini is a lovely girl, a real credit to the town. I often see her walking around. What a *pretty* girl she is, Mr. Pelacos. Only yesterday, coming back from Lavassi, I'm walking behind her and I couldn't help admiring the way she looks, the way she carries herself. Oh, no, you mustn't get me wrong, Mr. Pelacos. I was only trying to point out the contrasts."

"I am aware of the contrasts," Pelacos said wearily. He dropped the key chain to the blotter and with his thin finger tapped it into a coil. Lavassi? Had she been to Lavassi again? He was suddenly tired of the discussion, tired of the presence in the arm-chair before him of this unpleasant portly little man with his horrible clothes and cunning eyes, tired of Kalymnos. "Let us assume," he said brusquely, "that I fully understand the position of the people and their anxiety that the experiment in Australia should be successful, if—I repeat, *if*—it is ever permitted to become a concrete reality. Your petition, I take it, proposes that the team of divers whose names I am to submit to the government should first have the approval of some committee?"

"Something like that, Mr. Pelacos." Vraxos nodded and smiled agreeably. "Sort of a representative group of citizens, responsible people. Just to make absolutely sure the right men are picked—steady men, reliable, trustworthy." He examined his yellow fingernails. " Some of the more conservative people— not me, of course ; I was in the States thirty years—some of them are a bit worried on account of this talk about Manoli and your daughter, and——"

" What talk ? " Pelacos said sharply, so sharply that for a moment Vraxos' courage failed him.

" Ah, I wouldn't pay attention to it, Mr. Pelacos." Vraxos laughed uneasily. He had to go on with it now. " You know how people talk in a little town like this. No night life, nothing to keep them——"

" What talk ? "

" About you getting your daughter to make the painting of him, and the two of them going to parties together and——"

" If there is any suggestion of impropriety——" Pelacos began coldly, but Vraxos shook his head and grinned and waved his pudgy hand in the air.

" Jesus, it's not like *that*, Mr. Pelacos. Nothing like that. But you know what lots of people in the town are like. They're away back a thousand years. They'd keep their women in veils, locked up, if they had *their* way. Well, some of these people, they think Manoli might be trying to get in with you by playing up to Miss Irini, so he can take the men out to Australia. Everybody trusts *you*, Mr. Pelacos, you got to understand that, but Manoli's popular with a lot of people, and he's no fool. I got nothing against Manoli and he's a good seaman, a good diver, maybe, but I imagine what it would be like if *he* was picked. I got a lot of time for Manoli—he tickles me the way he roars through the town like a one-man Elks' convention—but if he went to Australia . . ." He chuckled. " Well, I don't have to tell *you*, Mr. Pelacos. The whole scheme would blow apart the first bar he got to." He laughed quickly and was suddenly serious, leaning forward in the chair. " What the people feel, Mr. Pelacos," he said earnestly, " is that we got to send good ambassadors as well as good divers."

Pelacos tapped the coil of the gold chain apart and lifted it between his fingers. " I realise the responsibilities, Vraxos," he said quietly, his eyes on the chain. " And if this committee is formed you may give it my assurance that the team to go to Australia will be the best and most responsible that can be selected. You may say also that I am prepared to submit the list to them. As for Manoli . . ." He shrugged and looked up. " His claim for selection will be considered in exactly the same way as everybody else's. Our aim will be to send the best and most responsible team we can."

" I only quoted Manoli as an example," said Vraxos blandly. " I got nothing against him, you understand. I like the crazy bastard, if it comes to that. It's just there's been all this talk around the town."

3

FEBRUARY WAS the month of wind, of Boreas and sirocco, blustering from north and from south, booming around the houses and through the narrow streets. The children put away their stick games and made their kites—kites of split bamboo and string and newspaper, with long frilly tails of old rags from the tailors' shops, the sort of kites Morgan himself had made when he was a boy in Australia.

To Morgan there was something immensely stimulating about the kites, about these kites, the kites of Kalymnos— something brave and young and crazy in their soarings and plungings. And there were kites everywhere. They danced along the broad walk behind galloping, screaming children ; sailed serene and stiff-tailed from the high slopes above Saint Vassilias, stately as old ladies in long gowns ; and then frolicked away on the wind like skittish girls. There was nothing here of the stuffy, sedate kites of Kensington Gardens, which rode high in the air and yet were earthbound to costly winding reels and to elderly men with faces like closed purses.

These were young and mettlesome kites, jigging on the arms

of the wind, rebellious and unpredictable, aerial wantons making
a mere pretence of being tied to lengths of frayed and knotted
string.

Once, as Morgan watched, a kite freed itself and soared away
across the town and over the masts of the caiques, spinning higher
and higher towards the sun, and it hung there for a moment,
quite still in the air, then dropped like a strange winged creature
into the sea. And on the faces of all the people watching was
the same expression, as if they had seen something happen that
was sad and beautiful and wonderful, as if they had been onlookers
at the death of Icarus.

The theme of the kites, riding the brusque winds of February,
ran all through the town. In the symphony a new movement
had developed. The theme of the January awakening was still
there and also the sweet little rondo of the wedding feasts, but all
subdued now, buried beneath the infectious exuberance of the
kites.

It was as if the wind were tugging at all the restlessness of
the town, blowing old things away so new things could take
their places, scattering the blossom from the trees so young
leaves could start. It banged the shutters on the windows of
the storerooms, where the beef and pork were salting in the
vats for the summer cruises of the boats ; blew a soft, disturbing
smell into the nostrils of Mike Grassis, reminding him that soon
he would have to put aside his pastries and begin to make the
galetis for the sponge men, the small loaves of bread that would
be baked and fried and baked again to harden them for the
barrels that would be rolled one day to the boats ; blew sparks
from the forges at Lavassi and tossed the echoes of the shipyard's
work far along the shore to the fish wharves ; blew dust in the
air and the black shapes of shadows across the mountains ;
blew new things into the mind of Irini Pelacos, wild things,
despairing things. . . .

Morgan watched her now with a peculiar personal concern.
There was something lost and strange about the girl, a restlessness
that went far deeper than the February infection of the kites.
She had done no painting since the portrait of Manoli had been
completed ; once or twice he had suggested subjects to her, and

although she had talked gaily of how best they might be treated, she had not seemed really interested.

And then, on the last day of February, came the Monday of the *maskaras*, the great carnival of the *Apokryes*, and she had gone with him to the sea front at Brostá to watch the singing and the dancing on the old threshing floor. . . .

"You know, you were foolish not to have brought your paints," he said. "It's quite wonderful."

"Yes," she said absently. "They should always wear clothes like that, the old dresses."

They were seated on a grassy ledge above the olive grove, and below them was the threshing floor and the musicians and the vividness of the girls dancing in the old costumes and the men in the home-made flamboyance of masquerade. A few were dressed as pirates and shepherds and mountaineers and *Evzones*, but most of them had adopted a queer Satanic garb— to the black skin-tights of the *ferneze* divers they had attached long, rag tails, and over their faces they wore crimson devils' masks, and they moved lithe as animals around the girls, high on their feet, prancing with a masculine vitality almost disturbing in its frankness. Around the broad circle of the dancers the people were gathered in hundreds, drinking wine and singing, all stirred by the same curious nervous agitation as their feet shuffled quickly, from side to side and backward and forward, in the jigging rhythm of the Kalymnian steps. The singing and the hand clapping and the shuffle of the feet came to them on the high ledge, all the sounds threaded on the piercing squeal of the *tsabuna*.

"Everybody on the island appears to be here," Morgan said, although he knew that it was not true, for there was still no sign of Mina Vraxos among the excited faces packed below. For half an hour he had been conscious of an almost juvenile expectancy, waiting for her to come. Probably, because of the boy, she would arrive later, when the buses bringing the people of Kalymnos across the island were less crowded.

"Will Manoli be coming, do you know?" Irini said.

"Manoli?" He glanced at her quickly. "I've no idea. 1

shouldn't think so. They're putting a new engine in one of his boats. Did he say anything to you?"

"I've not seen him," she said quietly. "Not for weeks."

"Oh, it's a very busy time for him." He laughed. "He treats those boats of his like spoiled children. I was at Lavassi on Thursday, and, do you know, I found him in the carpenters' shop sitting by himself, carving wooden blocks for one of the boats. Carving them in the shape of little fish. He'd finished two of them and painted them blue and white—they were drying on the bench beside him. Very pretty." He shook his head wonderingly. "He's an extraordinary fellow."

"Yes." It had been nearly a month since she had seen him—not counting the day she had completed the painting and shown it to him and he had nodded admiringly and walked backward and forward looking at it and grinning. Morgan had been there, and Doctor Telfs, and she did not count that as the last time because that was a public occasion, relating Manoli to the pigment on the canvas but not relating him to her. The last time she had seen Manoli was the night he had brought her down from the mountain top, leaving her at the big wrought-iron gates and swaggering along the empty moonlit street, not looking back and singing as he went.

"Could we come back here later, do you think?" she said suddenly. "It will be more amusing anyway towards evening. It's given me rather a headache, the sun and all those figures spinning. I'd like to get away from the noise for a while, to walk somewhere. Would you mind?"

"Of course not. Where?"

"Let's go across the mountain to Myrtiés. It shouldn't take long, less than an hour."

As they went up the narrow path between the villas, he looked back towards the threshing floor, but he could not see Mina.

There were few people on the road to Myrtiés: some late-comers hurrying towards Brostá, their greetings quick and gay as if a sense of rapture contained within them had tripped the springs of their tongues and their faces already bright with the carnival infection of *Kaloeri*; a solitary shepherd with resentful eyes enthralled to the stony pastures of his flock. The trail otherwise was deserted; the cry of the *tsabuna* had emptied the glens and mountainsides as effectively as the piper had emptied Hamelin of its children.

Once beyond the limits of the village fields, with the high, bare cliffs closing in on either hand, they were quite alone. Here on the northern side of the island the landscape possessed an oppressive bleakness, a quality harsh and austere that even the crags around Kalymnos did not have; Morgan could understand why the townspeople came here only in summer when forbidding outlines were softened by haze and heat. Now, in the windy clarity of February, the true cruelty of Kalymnos was revealed, the cruelty of which both Mina and Irini had spoken to him: a cruelty not of deliberation but of indifference. The people emptying the countryside for the day of festival had not turned their backs on their surroundings; this austere land had long since turned away from humanity, heedless of its joys and cares and pathetic little pleasures.

Yet, in the wild, cruel emptiness of the place there was an intimidating grandeur that was stirring and compelling, a mysterious quality to which one was forced to respond, and for a long time, as they climbed slowly up the trail of red clay and white embedded pebbles, they were silent.

They rested at the crest of the first ridge, beneath a rocky outcrop shaped exactly like a ruined castle in which nature had forgotten nothing save the portcullis.

It was Morgan who broke the silence, reaching for a topic cautiously remote from their aloneness among the silent mountains, as if he had deliberately gone back for reassurance to places where people were gathered together and human activities performed.

" Is your father still worried," he asked, " by all the agitation in the town ? "

She shook her head. " Not so much, I think. It seems to have died down. There's been nothing from Athens, you see, nothing to confirm the proposal. I imagine most people have decided now that it was only political talk. And there's a man called Vraxos who's been awfully helpful about it all. I don't like him very much. He's a rather unpleasant, fat little man, and he has a nasty way of looking at you, but he really *has* been awfully helpful, checking all the rumours and calming people down."

" Yes," Morgan said noncommittally, and took out his cigarettes. For a time he smoked in silence and then he said, " Your father has been a little worried about you, too. You realise that, don't you ? "

" Yes."

" He thinks you're restless, a bit on edge, as it were."

She shrugged. " He's been very much on edge himself." She laughed lightly, but there was a forced, artificial quality about it. " Do *you* think I've been edgy ? "

" Yes." He looked at her, but she turned away and shrugged again, and in the gesture there was an air of defiance, child-like and pathetic. " Is something the matter ? " he asked quietly, and his eyes were kindly as he studied her small averted head with the dark, glossy hair cut jagged at the nape of her neck.

On an impulse he reached across and touched her hair lightly with his fingers ; it was almost as if the fleeting pressure of his hand had flicked a switch, for she swung around and stared at him, and there was a hint of tears in her eyes as she said, " I'm perfectly all right. There's nothing wrong with me at all. I'm *perfectly* all right." Her voice was high and tight with strain. " Hadn't we better be getting on ? " she said brightly. " When I said it would take less than an hour I wasn't counting rests."

She walked away quickly, and he followed her, frowning. She neither talked nor looked back at him, but he was resolved that the matter should not be allowed to rest there. His solicitude for the girl demanded that the subject, now that it had been so indecisively opened, must be explored to its limit ; it could not be permitted to stand uneasily between them as something unresolved. He suspected, moreover, that her headache at Brostá had been a fiction, that she had asked him to walk with her to Myrtiés only so they could talk about whatever it was that troubled her.

By the time they reached the edge of the pass overlooking the olive groves and ugly villas of Myrtiés, her composure had returned.

"Let's not go down," she said. "It's an awful climb back because it's not even a path, only a rough stream bed, and anyway the view of Télendos is loveliest from here. Shall we go and sit over there, under that little pine tree?"

From the grassy bank beneath the tree the view was magnificent: the immense stretch of the blue bay and the shore of Kalymnos hooked around it like a bare arm, muscled and sunburned, and only a mile offshore the gigantic rock of Télendos rising massive and spectacular from the sea, its summit thrusting at the sky, its precipices scarred with gold and vermilion and black.

"It's so beautiful it frightens me," she said softly. "Even when I was a little girl and we used to come here for picnics, Télendos used to frighten me. I used to think it was so big and quiet and was just out there in the sea crouching, waiting for something. One day, I would think, it will start moving, and it will march across that little strip of water, and it will be so big and heavy that the whole world will be crushed beneath it."

Morgan was aware that she was talking like this only to re-establish the link that had been broken in the mountains, to rebuild with words, with the quick eager excitement of explaining things that were strange to him, the bridge that would carry them both from Brostá to whatever it was she had to tell him. He had an intuition that what she had to say would hurt both of them, hurt her more unbearably perhaps than it would hurt him, but there was no avoiding it. Télendos must march across the narrow strip of sea and crush them.

"Long, long ago," she said, "long before real history, the most beautiful woman in the world was Queen of Télendos. In the morning, when you get the light and the shadow on that cliff there, you can see her face. They say that when she died all the earth shuddered with grief and all the rocks tumbled away so that her face would stay there forever on the cliff. It was an earthquake really, of course, because her city fell away and sank beneath the sea. It's still there, the sunken city. One day when it is very calm you must come in a boat with a *yalass* and look down through the water. You can see the city, all the houses and the walls, down there in the water with the fish swimming around. It's strange and wonderful."

"We must get Manoli to bring one of his boats around some time and go down and really explore. Heaven knows what we shall find. Sunken treasure? Atlantis?" He smiled. "Shall we ask Manoli about it?" He had brought Manoli's name into the conversation deliberately, knowing that Manoli was the key to what she had to tell him. Give me a lever long enough, Archimedes had said, and I will move the world. Give me the name of Manoli and I will shift Télendos.

She was silent for a long time, staring across the water to the massive, scarred island, and then she said quietly, "You know, don't you?"

"What?"

"That Manoli made love to me?" There was no emotion in her voice, nothing but a pensive quietness as if she were recalling something that had happened a long way back in time. The expression on her face, the intonation of her voice, were exactly the same as when she had talked of her childhood terror of Télendos.

"I didn't know, no," he said. "I suspected he might have. It was that night of the party, wasn't it, when you went with him up the mountain?"

"I wanted him to make love to me. I *made* him! He was just sitting beside me, singing. I don't think he wanted to particularly. I don't think he cared. He was drunk and I was drunk, and he was just sitting there singing and looking down at the lights and the dancing at that woman's house. I *made* him, I tell you!" All the detached, lost serenity had gone. Her voice was low and fierce, and her hands were shaking. "Can't you understand, Morgan, that I *made* him?"

"I can understand, yes," he said, the pain of her confession cutting at him. "I hope he was kind."

"*Kind?*" She recoiled a little and half lifted herself so that she was on her knees, leaning back from him, and she was shaking her head very quickly, and her mouth was quivering and there was a wild, terrible unbelief in her eyes, as if she had seen a ghost. "*Kind!*" The world was almost strangled in a sudden, quick sob. " He was *cruel !* He was cruel and savage and . . . wonderful ! I didn't *want* him to be kind. I don't want anybody to be kind. Can't you see, Morgan ? It's what's driving me mad ! I want to be beaten, flogged, rolled in stones—anything but this . . . this awful *solicitude* ! " And suddenly she was in his arms, sobbing, talking incoherently, her hands clutching at his shoulders.

He held her against him, saying nothing until the paroxysm had quieted, until the shuddering had passed from her small, warm body, until her hands no longer gripped him.

" I should have asked you before," he said gently. " That night of the party, Irini, I hadn't realised you'd gone away with Manoli. I was talking to Mina and Telfs, and when I saw that you and Manoli were no longer in the room, I imagined you must be outside watching the dancing. And I went outside, but you weren't there. Stavros told me you'd gone up the mountain with him. That's when I suspected it."

" You didn't come looking for me ? " She was quite still in his arms, limp and quiet, as if the paroxysms had left her exhausted, spent.

" There wouldn't have been any point, would there ? I had seen you looking at him earlier."

" But later, the next day—you still didn't say anything."

" Well, I think I knew, really. I felt guilty about not having taken you home, and I should have apologised, I suppose. But I didn't want you to feel you had to explain anything."

" You're very thoughtful, aren't you ? " she said softly. " And very kind."

" Am I ? There wasn't any reason why you should have had to explain, not to me. There wouldn't be any reason now, Irini, except that he's hurt you."

" I *wanted* him to hurt me. That's what I told you : I wanted him to be cruel." She spoke of it now without any force or passion.

" I know you did, Irini, up there on the mountain. But he's hurt you since, you see, and that isn't the same."

For a long time she was silent, and when she spoke her voice was low and reflective, as if she had just awakened and was trying to describe a dream she had had : " When he took me home, Morgan, he just said good night and turned his back and walked away singing, and he walked on and on until I couldn't see him any longer in the darkness, and he never looked back. And the following week, when you went with me to show him the painting, he just talked as if . . . as if nothing had happened. And I felt sick and dirty because——"

" You mustn't say things like that."

" I did. I felt sick and dirty because up there on the cliff-top he hadn't really wanted to, and I'd made him, but it hadn't meant anything to him. And I haven't seen him since. Did you know that three times I set out to walk to Lavassi to see him ? I thought I might find out if it *had* meant anything. He might be different, I thought, when you and Doctor Telfs weren't there. But each time I got only as far as that bend in the road where you can look down on Lavassi, and then I turned back, because I knew he wouldn't be any different."

A quick shudder passed through her body, like the spasm that ripples across a horse's flank.

" Irini, you've got to understand Manoli," he said. " You're Greek and I'm not, but neither of us is Greek, really. You're not any longer, because of London and Paris. But Manoli is *pure* Greek, the essence of it, the masculine personification. That's what Telfs means when he says that Manoli is the Kalymnian. He doesn't have an interior life, Manoli, as we do. With people like us—oh yes, we're all messed up, the most hideous complicated tangle, most of us, but we're all of a piece. Whatever we do—however apart from us it may seem at the time—is related to *all* of us, to the whole strange tangled entity. But it isn't like that with Manoli. Manoli is two people, living separately in two distinct worlds. One world is the sea, his boats, his sponges. I think that's the real Manoli. Don't you understand why I talked to you at Brostá of his sitting in the carpenters' shop carving the little wooden fish for his boats ? That's his real world, and he lives in it like a child. It is a child's work in a way. It isn't complicated in the way that we are complicated, it doesn't have threads connecting it with any interior mechanisms. It's adventure and magic and brave, strange things happening, and it's making things look pretty and having toys, and it's being strong and big and bold. But then there's the other Manoli : wild and unreliable and mischievous and rather spoiled, eating life, as your father once said, as if it were a piece of meat."

He paused, but she was still and passive in his arms, saying nothing.

" Irini," he went on softly, " you said you wanted me to be cruel. Well, now I'm going to be. I *have* to be, Irini, for your own peace of mind. Listen, what happened up there on the mountain mustn't mean anything to you, because it didn't mean anything to him. It didn't, you know. You were no more important, nor any less important, than the flagons of retzina or the man playing the *tsabuna* or the dancing or the big lobsters or waking Homer Vraxos up or paying Mikali's fine or going to jail to sober up. You were just one bright little fragment of coloured glass which was shaken up together with all the other differently coloured pieces to make a pretty kaleidoscope pattern of his party. Nothing more than that, Irini."

For the first time she stirred in his arms and turned to him. Her eyes were as he remembered them on that first afternoon he had come to Kalymnos : the eyes of a child. He had thought then how easy it would be to delight her, how easy to hurt her.

" Like a dog and a bitch on a dusty road, is that what you mean ? " she said. " It was like that, wasn't it ? "

He shook his head. " Not like that at all. That isn't being fair to him. He has a queer tenderness, a sensibility, an odd streak of strange poetry in him. He would have understood, I think. But it wouldn't relate, there wouldn't be any threads connecting it to the interior mechanism."

Was there any thread anywhere for men, she wondered, connecting it with interior mechanisms ? Or was it always just a thing that happened on a hilltop, in a rumpled bed ? A thing with an ugly name that wasn't related to anything ? Was it always just that, copulation, nothing else ? *Copulation, fornication, sexual intercourse*, all the words were loathsome and horrible, and ugly, like two animals coupling on a dusty road, words that didn't relate to anything but which to a woman had a vindictive bite to them. It had been the same with Jacques. It

had been no more than that to him, for all the pretty phrases
he had wrapped around it, the heavy lids closing over his Parisian
shoe-button eyes as he made his avowals of what he had called
his " intellectual passion," his thin, pale hands closing over hers
in the taxi that had taken her to the airline terminal. Not even
out to Le Bourget, but only to the terminal—and it was she who
had paid the driver. And before her plane had landed at London
Airport he would have been in another bed, a different bed but
just as rumpled, saying the same hot, panting words, wrapping his
coloured cellophane around the bitter ugliness of the world.
Copulation !

Gently she disengaged herself from Morgan's arms and
moved away from him a little, her fingers absently arranging
the pleats of her skirt.

" You don't love him, do you ? " he asked.

" Manoli ? No. No, I don't love him." She took a twig of
pine from the grass and examined it intently and scratched at
the stippled brown bark with her thumbnail as if there was
something astonishing to be discovered in the pale-green damp-
ness of the sapwood that lay beneath. " It isn't what we've been
talking about, is it ? " she said. " That's something different,
isn't it ? "

" It is, yes."

" Because it's really you I love, Morgan," she said quietly.
" It isn't Manoli, it's you." She made the statement reflectively,
almost with diffidence, as if she had expressed a thought merely
to test its veracity, to see whether it could still be believed in once
it had come out into the open. A solitary bee paused above the
clump of wild thyme and droned away into the quiet emptiness
of the afternoon.

" I love you," she said. " But you're too kind. I don't want
you to be kind." She was sitting stiffly against the thin trunk
of the tree, looking at the shredded twig. " There's something
wrong with me, I think. There must be. I want things to be
cruel and brutal and savage, as Manoli was, and yet I want them
to have threads too."

Morgan stared across the silver shine of the bunched olives
to the blue arm of the bay and the mass of Télendos rising from

the water. From the little fishing village on the island a small
boat was putting out under a red wing of sail. He tried to think
of Mina. Had she come yet to Brostá ? Would she be looking
for him ? He tried to think of Mina as he waited for Télendos
to move. . . .

" Oh, God ! Can't you see, Morgan ? " she cried suddenly,
and she flung herself against him, her head buried on his chest
and her hands clutching at him in a desperate suppliance. " It
can't always be filthy and horrible, can it ? " she sobbed. " It
can't always ! "

He went down with her on to the soft carpet of the pine
needles and he knew that Télendos had marched across the
water and the whole weight of it was on top of them, crushing
them into the earth.

4

At the end of the week, when Telfs went in the *Kyklades* to
Athens to consult with the specialists about the treatment for
Nikolas, Morgan accompanied him.

It was necessary, he told himself, to obtain an Egyptian
visa for his passport so that he could leave Manoli's boat at
Alexandria ; and there were some matters to be attended to at
his bank.

At the same time he was honest enough to realise that he
had fallen in with Telf's suggestion mostly because of a sudden
desire to escape, if only briefly, from Kalymnos. By writing two
letters the visa could have been obtained and the bank details
settled ; letters, however, would not have provided him with
the pause he needed to examine the new situation that had
developed out of the afternoon above the Gulf of Télendos.

In the cosmopolitan stir of Athens, in the lurching clatter
of the yellow trams and the whine of the trolley buses coming
down to Omonia past the garish cut-outs of Jane Russell and

Humphrey Bogart, in the evenings with Telfs, eating prawns and lobsters beside the crowded anchorage at Turkolomani, watching the days die royally in gold and purple on the slopes of Hymettus, or revisiting the Cretan *laverna* where he had first met the American, Morgan was aware that he was deliberately evading the self-examination which he had told himself was the purpose of his escape.

Kalymnos seemed much more than a few hundred miles away across the sea. It was a story one had read about, not an actuality one had experienced. Its houses and mountains were painted on a canvas backdrop, its characters for a brief interval had retreated into dark, mysterious recesses. Ultimately they would emerge again with compelling conviction, but for the moment the safety curtain was down : a screen of asbestos blocked off belief in them.

Only Mina Vraxos, to Morgan, seemed to have any sort of probability ; the curious detachment from reality she always appeared to possess made her seem more logical once the setting itself had lost the veneer of its reality. Nonetheless, it was disturbing to discover that when he did try to force himself to consider Kalymnos his thoughts were always inclined to by-pass the more immediate and specific problem of Irini and to hover instead around the enigmatic question of Mina.

By the time he left Athens, Morgan was aware that he had sailed around Télendos, evading for the moment its treacherous rocks and uncharted reefs ; but a sort of spiritual inertia persisted and for ten days he stayed with Telfs on Kós, climbing the rugged central spine of mountains and making long, exhausting walks along the flat, salty coast that looked across to Turkey. March was three parts gone when he returned to Kalymnos, and two of Manoli's boats, the *Angellico* and the *Ikaros*, were moored in the harbour below the window of his house, spruce and shining in new paint and rigging, a glossy, clear varnish on masts and gaffs and booms, the weather cloths around the bulwarks of stiff, new canvas, white in the sun. Sheets and halyards were all of new rope reeved through white blocks and the little blue and white fish that Manoli had carved himself.

Morgan found himself looking through the window, as he

unpacked his bag, at the new paint, white and crimson and blue, on the hull of the *Ikaros*. He was conscious of an almost boyish impatience at the thought that there was still almost a month to wait before he would be sailing in this boat to the coast of Africa.

His reunion with Irini, contrary to his uneasy expectation, was not in the least awkward, or embarrassing. She was obviously overjoyed at his return, but in her welcome to him there was no sort of intensity, no implication that the quality of their association had changed into one that might have all sorts of new demands to make. It was almost as if the earlier intimacy had proved something so entirely to her satisfaction that no further proof of its truth was necessary—more, that a renewal of intimacy might even be destructive of the cause of her content. It seemed as if for the first time in her life she had discovered something that was *certain*, something that must be preserved just as it was, without further elaboration or modification.

The change in the girl, the contentment that appeared to have banished frustration, the attitude of compliance so different from her earlier rebelliousness, had been observed also by her father, in spite of his preoccupations.

" Do you know, Leigh," he said one evening at coffee, " I'm not at all sure that I haven't underrated Irini ? She did a painting the other day, a line of those little cottages behind the girls' school, and, by heaven ! I doubt that Utrillo could have done it better. Tone, texture, colour, light—all quite remarkable. I asked if I might have it for my study, which seemed to give her great delight."

" I've always felt," said Morgan, " that she has a very considerable ability."

" Quite. Until recently, however, the confusion of her mind has rather walled it off. You were perfectly right, you know, about her painting Manoli. There was a period of uncertainty that followed—it worried me a little, I confess, although I realise now it probably was just the coalescing of new factors—but since then she has come to grips with it in a most satisfying way. I am enormously grateful to you, Leigh, for your influence on her."

" There's nothing to be grateful for," Morgan said awkwardly. What would be the thoughts of Pelacos, he wondered guiltily, were he to know the truth of this influence, were he to realise how fierce had been the heat in the crucible of his daughter's transformation ?

In the few weeks remaining before the boats would leave for Africa, Morgan spent much of his time with Manoli. The refitting of the two remaining diving boats, the *Elektra* and *Saint Stephanos*, had been almost completed at Lavassi. The big *deposito* which would carry the stores and gasoline and water and bring back the harvest of the sponges, a chunky sturdily built schooner named *Okeanos*, had been winched up on the rollers to the pebbly beach behind the Customs House, where it stood high on its blocks while gangs of men worked all through the day, caulking the seams with oakum and replacing the worm-infested planks, and there was always a swarm of children around the braziers where the pitch for the seam caulkers was boiling. The third point of activity was at the town quay, where the stores and engine oil and diving gear were already being loaded aboard the *Angellico* and *Ikaros*. Christos still limped through the town draped in ladies' jumpers and embroidered tablecloths, but he seemed to go more quickly on his sticks, to devote less time to the ornamentation of his announcements with badinage and bawdry, so that by mid-afternoon he could be aboard the *Ikaros*, helping with the gear. Stavros always took the longer route home, down the side street beside the bank, so that he should not have to pass the quay and see Christos working on Manoli's boats.

Each of the boats had its own *colazaris* to supervise the work, but Manoli was more than the captain of the *Okeanos*, the flagship, as it were, of the little fleet, he was captain of all of them. He worked with an indefatigable energy and enthusiasm and a scrupulous attention to the most minute detail which astonished Morgan until he realised that this was much more than a seasonal task to Manoli : it was an annual reaffirmation of certain truths which he had accepted during the thirty-nine years of his life. To Manoli, the yearly foray to the African sponge beds was in the nature of a pilgrimage ; his devoutness made it imperative that his preparations should be without error or blemish.

Morgan, watching him day after day, grew to understand why men liked to sail with him. It was not merely that Manoli's infectious gusto lent them determination that his—their—boats should be the smartest and the best equipped when the fleet put out. They had a deep and almost childlike confidence in his judgment—even, Morgan observed, about such trivial matters as where the casks of *galetis* should be stowed or the cleaning of a carburettor or the right way of applying a vulcanised rubber patch to a worn diving suit—because all of them shared a common property of experience and they were aware that Manoli, having endured discomfort and known peril himself, was solicitous both of their comfort and their safety.

At the age of eight Manoli had for the first time sucked in all his breath and dropped from the rail of the boat off Pserimos, his thin, unformed boy's arms clutching to his chest the big stone that would carry him down to the bed of the sea, naked and alone. At thirteen he had sailed away to the coast of Africa as a boat boy; in the twenty-six years since then—apart from the years the war had devoured—all his life had been a dual thing, each of its separate years notched into the two seasons of staying at home and going away. He had been boat boy, deck hand, skin diver, then *skafendros*, *colazaris* and captain. If life had taken him into the sleazy brothels of Alexandria and Casablanca—because it had been the sort of life that demanded such escapes—it had also ushered him into a strange and wonderful kingdom where few men trod. Seated beside him on a rough, sun-warmed bench at Lavassi, Morgan would listen enthralled while Manoli talked of this world to which he himself had for years been in thrall; and then he could understand why the men, faced by some problem or involved in dispute, would always say, " Well, ask Manoli. He'll know."

Of the hidden, secret world of the sponge beds he spoke with an easy familiarity, as if it was an apparent thing, something visible before his eyes in all its shapes and colour and texture— the forty-metre beds of Alexandria where the silky sponges grew; the long, flat shelves of Cyrenaica where at twenty-five metres a diver could stay below for upward of an hour, plucking sponges almost as a vicar's wife might pick flowers from her garden ; the dark, deep shafts off Benghazi, where the thick strong sponges clustered at the limit of the air pipe, where no diver, however strong, might for more than three minutes withstand the killing, paralysing pressures.

The dangers of the profession and its poor rewards Manoli accepted without condemnation. His men resented them bitterly ; they hated the economic necessity that forced them into the crowded, comfortless months at sea ; hated also the merchants with their fine houses and big cars, waiting without risk to themselves or the slightest diminution of their comforts for the boats to come back in the autumn, bringing the sponges which they could buy casually between cups of coffee and later sell for ten times what they had paid and for a hundred times, a thousand times, what would be paid to the men who had plunged to the bottom of the sea to get them. They hated the six or seven months without a foot on land, without the companionship of women or the comforting assurances of a *taverna*—months with nothing but the cramping imprisonment, aboard a plunging boat not thirty feet in length, of ten, twelve, fifteen men, with pro-pinquity and peril making friction of each hour. They hated the sourness of the water, the weevils in the *galetis*, the rank meat and fetid cheese, the endless meals of octopus, the taste of engine oil in stale cigarettes. They hated, above all else, the deadliness and the certainty of every summer's threat—to take its toll of them, to return some to their homes as cripples, to return some not at all.

And for what ? they would ask bitterly. For a wage of thirty dollars a week—if you were lucky !

Manoli's carelessness towards the factors that embittered the men was not, as Morgan at first thought, because his economic situation was different from theirs. He had independence because he was his own master, but he had not wealth in the sense that Paul Pelacos had wealth. He, like Pelacos, made money out of sponges ; but Manoli, except in so far as his boats were concerned, had no sense of providence. With money he was spendthrift : he shared generously with the men who sailed with him and the men who dived for him, and most of what was left went back into the boats, for he was lavish in the provision of stores and fuel and equipment. The rest was consumed in his voracious appetite for living, in gambling and drinking, in music and feasting. It was perhaps his indifference to money that voided him of any sense of true charity. He could spend a million drachmae in one, single, riotous night, and he would always make a special point of seeing that the poorest of his friends—George and Old Beanie and Stavros and Grassis and the rest of them—were there to share his hospitality. It would never have occurred to Manoli to wonder what a million drachmae might mean to George and his wife Maria, to consider that old Beanie could live on them for almost half a year; nor would Manoli ever have thought of offering George a hundred drachmae with which to buy food or a new coat. On the other hand, George, who worshipped Manoli, would never have expected it.

Manoli's indifference to the economic disparities of the industry did not mean that he was unaware of them, but his job was to go out and get the sponges and bring them back, and what happened after that was no concern of his. The total dependence of Kalymnos on the men who sailed away in the boats and risked their lives at the bottom of the sea was for him a matter of sardonic amusement.

" Have you tasted the bread here? " he asked Morgan one day. " Good bread, very strong. It has blood and salt in it as well as flour." Unlike his divers and his crews he harboured no rancour for the few wealthy merchants who lived like feudal princes on the hard-won harvests of the sea. They were un-important people, tradespeople, as colourless as side-street grocers; he had a vague contempt for their sedentary softness and he pitied them for the unending dullness of their lives. They were contained within a ghetto of drab monotony beyond the walls of his own flamboyant kingdom. They did not matter.

Manoli's kingdom was entirely a masculine world into which women were not permitted to intrude. Occasionally at Lavassi a woman would cross the end of the shipyard, carrying a pitcher of water to one of the cottages on the hill, and all the work of the yard would cease for a moment—all the brown, gnarled hands, scarred and black-nailed, would bunch on the ropes and hammers and mallets, and the men would be quite still and silent, watching her as if some remarkable apparition had appeared.

Even Morgan found in this man's world a curious sense of security, of certainty. There was a camaraderie of the boats, a unanimity of purpose that made one at the end of every day reluctant to relinquish the associations; it was more tempting to go on to some water-front *taverna* where the continuities could be maintained and mellowed over beakers of retzina and platters of brown *smarithes* hot from the pan.

He could understand how Manoli could engross himself for weeks at a time and never think of Irini—nor of Mina.

And then one night—they were drinking together, just the two of them in Mikali's *taverna*—Manoli said, " Well, we sail next week, next Thursday." He rubbed his hands together and grinned, and then, as if it were related to the subject, he said, " You promised to walk with Mina to Santa Katerina ? "

" I did, yes," Morgan said. " One day I'd like to."

" Not one day. On Sunday. Mina wants to go on Sunday."

" Sunday, yes. That's fine."

" There's something she wants to show you," said Manoli. " That's what she said."

Morgan smiled. " The top of a mountain, I think it is. She talked about it once before."

" Mina's mountains ! " Manoli laughed. " She's crazy about mountains. Anyway, she wants to go on Sunday."

" Sure. We can all go together."

" Not me," said Manoli. " I've got things to attend to on the boats." He smiled slightly. " Besides that, I've seen Mina's mountains."

Nearly two months had passed since the day at Piso when he had climbed with Mina up the ravine, and now this day, although the appearance of the countryside had altered, seemed no more than a continuation of it. It was as if they had walked out of the ravine and, instead of taking the stony trail back to Kalymnos, had turned aside into a warm and mellow valley.

Against the deep-blue sky the pencils of the cypresses around

the monastery had a dusty darkness, and the branches of the
nut trees, so recently pricked with blossom, were heavy with
foliage. Shadows fell into deep pools and ink blots, the panniers
of the donkeys were high with yellow grass, the day drowsy
with heat. To Morgan, walking with his jacket over his arm,
there was an almost irresistible invitation in the glimpse of the
blue bay of Piso on their left.

He stopped to mop his forehead and said, half jestingly,
" What I should like more than anything in the world at this
particular moment is a place to swim."

" There is a little beach on the other side of the mountain,"
Mina said gravely. " You can swim there if you wish. But
nobody swims here before May."

" Do you swim ? "

" Yes."

" But not before May ? "

" No, not before May." She smiled and they walked on.

" Why did you want me to come with you to-day ? " he
asked curiously.

" Just to walk with me. So you would understand."

" You told me at Piso that day that when you took me here
I would see what you meant."

" But surely you *do* see ? " She seemed slightly surprised,
as if she had not expected him to demand more than he had
already been given. " It is very beautiful and peaceful. It is a place
where you can be sure of things, as I said."

" Sure of *what* things, Mina ? "

Her answer when it came—and it was so long before she
gave it that he no longer expected a reply—took him by surprise.

" Up here, walking," she said, " I am sure of you."

" Of me ? "

" Yes. Back there, at Kalymnos, I do not know you, and
therefore I am unsure of you. Here among the rocks I do know
you, and I am sure of you. Is that hard for you to understand ?
I cannot explain it more than that."

" No, I think I understand," he said thoughtfully. " I have
the same feeling about you, as if I have to move away from you
to get you into focus, or transplant you into some entirely

different setting, an uncrowded setting, where I can see you all
by yourself. When I was in Athens, you seemed the only real
thing about Kalymnos. All the rest of it was unreal, something
I had dreamed. And yet in Kalymnos you are out of focus again
—everything around you is real and you are not. You don't
belong to it."

"There is the beach," she said quietly, "where you could
swim if you would like to."

They had come to the crest of the ridge and the ground
dropped away down a series of rough, rolling hillocks to a
small, secluded cove hooked within the arms of two masses of
red rocks fallen from the cliffs. The beach was of grey shingle
and no more than twenty yards across. Enclosed by the toppled
rocks, the water was mirror-calm—a pale, transparent green in
the shallows, deepening into peacock and purple around the
perimeter of rocks. A narrow, twisting goat path led down to
the shingle.

Mina seemed to take it for granted that he would want to
go down, because she walked on, guiding him through the
spiky thickets to the goat path. How easily she moved, how
certain her judgment of where the rocks were firmest, the thistles
least annoying; it all seemed familiar to her. She went ahead
of him in silence but he had the illusion that she was some
Calypso singing him down to the sea. It all went back to the sea,
the understanding of it. As Morgan followed willingly behind
her, he had already glimpsed the understanding.

Near the beach she moved faster, going ahead of him from
rock to rock in quick, agile bounds that left him far behind,
lagging and clumsy among the tumbled stones. When he reached
the edge of the shingle she was standing on a shelf of rock
above the water, her fingers unfastening the hooks of her bodice,
and as he watched the grey dress fell around her ankles. For a
moment she looked across at him, smiling, and she turned away,
the slim, olive column of her body motionless against the sky,
and then the water broke apart into a sunlit shower of diamonds.
Far down in the green, crystalline depths he could see the pale
shape moving like a Nereid among the rocks and weeds. For a
moment he was afflicted by a feeling of intense desolation. This

was where the dream ended, the image was dispelled : the fugitive gleam of her body twisting in the water among the dark weeds, going deeper and away from him, going away from him forever, sinking into depths beyond his reach.

He had no sense of immodesty as he took his clothes off and dived into the water. She had swum out around the sheltering arm of rocks—she swam with a strong easy rhythm, her body belonging to this aquatic environment as naturally, as gracefully, as it belonged to the mountain rocks—and Morgan swam towards her with easy, powerful strokes. And as he swam he felt the understanding of what it was.

It was something related to the immediacy of their being together in the secluded little cove, separated from all that belonged to another world. But this, the mutuality of their presence, was only the smallest part of it ; the rest could be understood without being explained. It was all the moments of significance coalescing into a single truth that one accepted as a matter of faith, without having to explain it : the night in the *taverna*, after the sirocco, with the face of Pan and the libations of the wine and the smell of the dark, twisted things that were beyond comprehension ; her face smiling at him in the lamplight as she offered the platter of fish ; the magic of a man with three donkeys climbing in the twilight towards a single star up the zigzag trail to Vathý ; the cockerels, roused by music, crowing in the night on darkened hilltops ; a woman in black, carrying faggots against a stony skyline, and the whistle of the shepherds, ringing down the cliffs—things that were old and eternal and possessed by an aching loveliness, things of wonder and melancholy and strangeness.

Morgan, lost in the cool, green mystery of the sea shallows, seeing past his eyes the swim of weeded rocks and the crusting limpets and the fleshy swing of the fronds, glimpsing her pale figure moving in the water, was aware that this was an experience of singular rarity, an experience that belonged in the lost, secluded places outside the perimeters of time. " Come with me," she had said, " and you will see what I mean."

For half an hour they swam, separate and engrossed, never talking, as though each of them found distinct bewitchment in

the cool, green, crowded sea, and then, as if in all that time a
harmony had prevailed between them, they swam together back
to the shingled shore.

Only then did Morgan, seeing the wet, naked beauty of the
woman standing before him on the grey pebbles, find a cruel,
demanding hunger wrenching at him. He made to move
towards her, but she shook her head and smiled at him and went
behind the rocks to dress herself.

After they had dressed, they clambered around the rocks
to the end of the little promontory.

" I had a letter this week," said Mina, " from Doctor Telfs."
She spoke with a deliberation that made it clear to him that
what had gone before had reached an ending ; the things that
had happened and the things that had not happened had been
put away together into an impregnable vault where they might
be remembered, but never touched again. " He has had the
final report from Athens," she said, " about Nikolas."

" Yes ? " he said guardedly.

" There is a chance of curing him. But it might take three or
four years, perhaps even more. And he must go away from
Greece. To London, or America."

" I see. They can do nothing in Athens ? "

" Nothing more than they have already done. They saved
him from dying. They made it possible for him to walk, in a
fashion. Now they can do no more. If he is to be cured he must
go away—for a long time." Her face was grave and composed.
The suffering that was in it was not a new thing ; it was a
quality constant in her beauty, drawing it down below the surface
of her appearance, embedding it in her heart.

" This is why you wanted to walk with me to-day ? You
wanted to talk about it ? " The reason had already been disclosed
to him, but it was necessary for him, too, to accept a world that
lay beyond the single truth of things.

" Yes." There was a quick warmth in her smile that told
him she understood, and was grateful. " It was you who said
I must go away from Greece."

" And now you must, I suppose." He frowned. What had
once seemed plausible, even necessary, was now scarcely compre-

hensible. You could rob the Parthenon of its marbles, wrench them from sunlight and the shadows on pale rocks and set them up again in a cold, bare room amid fog and soot and darkness, and the beauty of the violated temple still remained. But could anything of Mina survive, anything of the woman's truth and beauty, if taken out of this April afternoon? " It is farther than Astypalaia," he said thoughtfully.

"Farther, yes. Much farther. But I must go."

" Yes."

" I think I shall marry Homer Vraxos," she said.

" Homer Vraxos ? " he said dully, as if he were repeating the sound of words in a language strange to him, words that had a meaning if you could understand them but were otherwise beyond comprehension.

" He is willing to do it," she went on evenly. " An approach has been made to me, a cousin of his. Not now, next year perhaps. He is my brother-in-law and the *despot* must permit it. He is willing to pay for Nikolas to go away before then so he can be cured."

" Not Homer Vraxos, no," he said, as if he were talking to himself. " No. I don't believe it."

" He has wanted to marry me, I think, for a long time, for two years, ever since his brother died. The Church will permit it, he says, because he is an American citizen. . . . He has a passport. . . ."

A passport. *E pluribus unum* . . . God Bless America . . . in Connecticut the trees were leafing and the golden rod is spattered through the fields and the long-legged girls in sweaters are sipping chocolate floats at the corner drugstores . . . and I will take my passport in my hand and lead you into a promised land flowing with milk and honey and chocolate floats and long spoons in long glasses and long-legged girls in long sweaters and everything glitters with the golden rod in the green fields, and there you will die listening for the sound of the *chopanis* whistling down from the old, grey rocks.

" You must not do it, Mina," he said quietly, because quietness was the only spell against the sorcery that had grown out of the sea magic, and only in the field of quietness could you see the picture of the woman whose son was withering away, the woman with no *brika* but her own beauty; only in this fashion could you bring the right picture forward so that the passport was blotted out.

"Do you remember at Piso," she said reflectively, "when I asked you if any man would be foolish enough? Well, now there are two. In his letter to me Doctor Telfs said he would make me his wife so that he could take me away."

Telfs! Vraxos! Not one passport, but two!

"I wrote and told him I could not let him marry me," she went on. "He is a good man, a kind man. Sometimes I think he is almost a saint—and in a way I love him very deeply. But don't you see that he would marry me because of pity? Pity. For he is not the sort of man who *could* marry. He is a saint, finding deserts to walk through, and wildernesses, looking for the lost people, the forlorn ones. If he married me, one day he would want to go to different deserts, and I should be there holding him back from what he wished to do." She shook her head slowly. "We must beware of pity. It is dangerous and terrible, and it makes everything cloudy so you can't see anything clearly any more. That is why I believe I shall marry Homer. It is not pleasant, but it is not clouded either. Because he has no pity, you see. None."

"I can't let you do it," he said. "You don't see what it means. Mina, *I* can take you away. I'll marry you. I want to marry you. This other thing will kill you, destroy you. It isn't a solution at all—it only seems to be."

She shook her head slowly. "When we came out of the water," she said, "you began to come towards me and you wanted to be my lover, and I knew you did and I refused you."

"Yes."

"If I had let you do it, Morgan, you would have thought it was because I wanted you to take me away. And I did not let you do it because it would have spoiled what had happened. There were two reasons, you see."

"Would there have been any reasons at all if I'd told you before that I wanted to marry you? That's all that matters, isn't it? I love you. That's enough, surely?"

" Come," she said, rising, and she held out her hand to him and led him back across the rocks to the seclusion of the little cove, and they lay down together beneath the cliff.

" Let it be here," she said softly. " Let it be here, now, nowhere else. It must all be clear, not cloudy like the other. This is where it belongs."

And afterwards, as they lay side by side among the rocks with the sun on their bodies, she said, " It would never be like this again, you see. I would change, and it would all be different. Everything would be so different that you would never be able to believe that this had ever happened. It belongs *here*, not some other place. You must not ask again to take me away, because that would change it and spoil it. I shall go away with Homer Vraxos."

5

THE SEA was a deep blue, with a long, swinging rhythm to the swell, too long for the ground swell which by sundown would meet them off the coast of Africa. When the boat lifted, Morgan could see to the southward the ochre shelf of Egypt with the mirages shimmering above it.

The *Ikaros* had a sweet run in the waves, heaving and sliding with a smooth and leisurely regularity that made him think the movement had been rehearsed in the ten days of sailing down from Kalymnos until now it was perfect. Elias the *colazaris* was at the tiller with the wind blowing his hair back, and the bending of his straddled legs was keyed to the run of the ship. The other boats had their own distinct rhythms, each woven separately into the swing and slide of the sea—the *Okeanos* ahead, her masts moving in slow sway like a metronome on the pedestal of the shouldered seas, and the *Saint Stephanos* on the starboard beam, running smoothly, and astern of them the *Angellico* and *Elektra* ; and far away to port, black specks rising and falling against the hot, pale sky, five other Kalymnian boats sailing with them in company until they reached the sponge beds.

Manoli's five boats and five others—ten of the fleet of sixty sponge boats which less than a fortnight before had sailed out beyond the breakwater with the echoes of their thudding exhausts ringing back from the rock cliffs of Point Cali. The boats had been blessed by the *despot* in his robes, the hymns chanted and the prayers said ; the women had sung the old, sad Kalymnian songs of the sufferings the sea had brought, and, as the boats had put out, they had taken off their white handkerchiefs and donned the black scarfs of mourning which they would wear until their men returned seven months later. Morgan had watched until the arm of the breakwater encircling the almost empty harbour and the people crowded along its length had dwindled and vanished, and then he had turned his eyes ahead to where all the sea between Kalymnos and Kós was alive with the boats running and plunging to the southward.

And now there were only ten of them ; the others had scattered, some sailing on courses that would take them directly to Libya or Tripoli, and others swinging away to test the beds of Kassos and Karpathos and Crete, or sailing different routes to the waters of Egypt.

Morgan could see Christos sitting on the foredeck where the other divers were checking the gear, and he went along the heaving deck to join him. He enjoyed Christos, his inexhaustible good nature, his endless stories, his appetites as Rabelaisian as his wit.

It was still a matter of some astonishment to Morgan that fifteen men—nine divers, the *colazaris*, the engineer, the boat boy, two deck hands and himself—could live in reasonable contentment aboard a boat so small, particularly as the mid-ship quarters were stacked with gasoline drums and diving gear, and there was only a confined space on the decks below the flapping weather cloths. How much of the contentment would survive seven months of such confinement was, of course, another matter.

Once at the sponge beds, if the weather was good, the four *colazares* and the divers from all the boats would go aboard the big schooner, the *Okeanos*, at the end of each day's diving,

and they would eat there and sleep and sometimes drink retzina.
But now Manoli was anxious to begin the summer's work, and
there was no time for pause as he drove the five boats southward.
The nights were mild—nights of a clear and starry brilliance
—and they could all sleep on deck—all except old Tomás the
engineer, who crawled each night into the plank bed of his
tiny engine-house to sleep blissfully in the stinking fug of hot
engine oil and gasoline fumes, his thin, undernourished body
shuddering to the thud and thump of the big, greasy engine
which for months might never cease running.

Christos was propped against the anchor bitts, his twisted
legs spread wide on the deck, and he was forking into his mouth
big hunks of dogfish from a heaped platter between his legs.
He held a forkful up to Morgan and grinned.

"To-morrow we begin diving," he said. "To-day we eat
like pigs. I told myself this morning that all through the day I
would eat. I would stuff myself like a great, fat pig. You see
that I keep my word."

"*Po-po-po-po-po !*" A skin diver named Costas laughed and
winked at Morgan. He was a tall, lean young man ; his narrow
chest did not seem to have room to contain lungs that would
take him, dragged down by the thirty-pound stone, through a
hundred feet of water to the sea bed, and keep him there for two
minutes. "I can see no difference," he said, "from any other
day. You always eat like a great fat pig, every day stuffing your
guts as if you'd never seen food before. Besides, what is to-
morrow ? " He shrugged. "Chicken feed. The first day is
always chicken feed. He will go to those banks east of Matruh,
you see if he doesn't. Twenty-five metres, thirty—no more.
Five summers I've sailed with him, and if he comes to Egypt he
always goes there first, to those banks east of Matruh."

"I dived those banks when you were still messing your
pants," Christos said good-humouredly, and picked a fish-bone
from between his teeth. "I did eighty-two metres off Benghazi
before your father—may God keep him and Saint Stephanos
forgive him his misjudgment !—turned over in his bed one
night and put it in and made a lousy skin diver. One time the
papás tell me a story from the Bible about a man who spills his

seed upon the ground, but, by Jesus ! this was a bigger waste ! "

"Take a walk around the deck, parrot, and see what's happened to your legs." Costas grinned. "Let's all be the great big *skafendro*, the *pallikari* boy, and toss our legs away and end up with half a body. *Po-po-po-po-po !* Listen to the parrot talk ! I tell you, Christos, it'll be chicken feed to-morrow. Twenty-five metres. You could eat that whole lamb we had at Easter and still go down."

Christos smiled at Morgan. "You will always find a child like this," he said, "who *will* prattle when grown men would like to talk. He is a thin, miserable, naked fish who jumps into the sea clinging to a stone because he is afraid of the suit and the helmet and the machine that pumps the air. He is afraid that it will kill him or paralyse him, so he jumps into the sea with his arms wrapped around a rock, just as the savages did. And when he is down, a little prickle in his ears, a touch of blood at his nostrils, and, *whoooosh !* up the bastard comes as if all the sharks in all the oceans of the world were biting at his tail ! " He nodded. "And this is the soppy, snivelling creature who sits there, calm as you please, prattling on, trying to tell me— me, Christos Papagalos !—the way I should go diving. It is my good nature, nothing but that, which prevents me from picking the bastard up, here and now, and tossing him over the side to join all the other wriggling fish ! "

There was a burst of laughter, in which Costas joined and Morgan too. Living with these men for the past ten days, he had come to understand their badinage, to appreciate their talk. They were going to their work, joking and laughing as they went, rolling southward through the dark-blue sea and making a holiday of it. But to-morrow they would embark again upon the real purpose of their lives, and for the six or seven months that followed they would be tormented by the hardships of it, haunted by its perils. Awareness of danger lay there all the time, even beneath their jesting and their ribaldries.

"Twenty-six years I've been going down," Christos was saying, "and there are some things you learn that have got the truth in them. I eat to-day because I won't eat to-morrow. Whether we dive at twenty-five metres or seventy-five, you don't catch me having anything in my belly until the day's work is over. A cigarette maybe, a sip of water, but nothing more than that. I remember once aboard the old *Tasoula*, diving of Sollum, and it was so damned hot—late August it was—the helmet made steam when it hit the water. You could hear it spitting, like putting a wet finger on a hot iron. And old Soklerides was sitting there next to me, waiting his turn to go down, and his lips all black and cracked and his tongue hanging out like a dog's, and just before the *colazaris* gave him the nod he called for a mug of water. I was going to say something to him but he was an older man than me and he'd been diving a good many years, but I thought to myself, ' You poor, silly, stupid bastard, that mug of water can be the death of you ! ' And sure enough, that's the way it was. There wasn't even a signal, not a touch on the rope, but the *colazaris* knew something was wrong by the slack feel of it. We hauled him up—by Jesus ! what a weight it was—and he was dead by the time we got the helmet off. All full of blood the helmet was, where it had squirted out of his ears and nose and mouth, and his eyes rolled right back so you could only see white. They were open but you could see only white. It wasn't a deep dive, either—forty metres maybe."

" Plenty men are killed and paralysed," said Costas, " who act the way you do—living half the year on one meal a day, not taking a glass of water into their guts before they go down. There's a whole lot of ways of killing yourself down there."

" It's whether you're lucky or not," said Lazarus, who had dived most of his life with the Symi boats and was only making his second season with Manoli.

" Nuts ! " said Christos bluntly. " You can be lucky, sure. But you can be careful too. A dead diver's a bad diver."

" It's luck mostly," Lazarus said stubbornly. " Look at old Fortunato."

" You want to quote me ancient stories, eh? " Christos said witheringly. " Next you want to tell me about Methuselah." He hawked richly and spat with a neat precision over the weather cloth ; the wind took the white gob and planed it away into the sea, where a gull dived on it. " Christ, you weren't even born when Fortunato was diving ! "

Morgan knew the story of Fortunato. It had happened fifty years before, but it had become almost a part of the Kalymnian folklore. Fortunato had been a skin diver, and one day he'd taken the big thirty-pound *petra* and dived in head first with the stone held in his outstretched hands; down he'd gone, right into the open mouth of a huge shark, and the stone had hit the bottom of the creature's gut so that it had vomited Fortunato out again. Fortunato had carried to his death the great scars of the teeth marks all down his face and body, but he had gone diving again the next season and he had lived on in Kalymnos until the Germans came, and then he had starved to death under their occupation.

All their talk, Morgan reflected, was of boats and diving— of men who had died and men who had survived. Unlike any other group of men he had known, they would never, when deprived of the companionship of women, talk of women or of sex. Even their dirty stories were crude and alimentary rather than sexual. They must have thought a good deal about their wives and families because their family sense was enduringly strong and they were devoted to the invariably numerous children who had sprung from their sturdy loins—the ragged, brawling, noisy, snot-nosed rabble of kids who infested the Kalymnian streets like vermin—but they seldom spoke of them. Perhaps they were content in the knowledge that while they were at sea they were working, and it was this work, however hazardous and inhuman, that stretched a rope of security back to the women and the urchins of the island town. While they were away their credit was good in the shopkeepers' books, their wives and children could eat; they had a sort of embittered accepting pride that was denied to those who had stayed behind to loiter in the summer streets, workless and hopeless and hungry. Their word for work, Morgan remembered, was *thouleiá*, and that was the word for slavery, too. And it was their work that enslaved them; it obsessed them and oppressed them; it surrounded them like a great imprisoning wall, blocking out the light, standing between them and any real contact with soft, warm things. They could talk of nothing else.

Even his mere ten days in the *Ikaros* had shown Morgan

how it might happen. He could feel himself being enmeshed in the terrible fascination of it. He wanted to keep the men talking, to ask questions, to listen to their explanations. When Christos had said, " To-morrow we begin diving," he had felt his throat choking and his belly filling with the queer empty feeling he remembered from the war when he heard the whistle of the bomb and waited for it to fall. It was here on the deck of the boat driving down to Africa that reality assembled itself.

It was no longer easy to think about Mina ; even the shape of her had retreated into some mysterious, mellow yesterday, into an afternoon of sea magic composed of a little viridescent bay with pale shadows on the sea floor and the sun on grey rocks. But that sea was not related to this, to the deep boom and rush of dark waters along the hull planks, to the high-swinging lift of the thick bow, to the gulls riding stiff-winged in a pale sky. There were two seas of different substances : the sea of magic and the sea of slavery ; and there were two suns, and one touched the grey rocks of Greece and the other scorched the sands of Africa. And this was the African sun.

" Feel it now ! " shouted Costas. " Feel the lift of it ! "

He was up on the stempost, his arm hooked around the forestay, and the others were scrambling to their feet, testing the new motion of the boat beneath their boots, and they all nodded and grinned as the ground swell hit them.

They could see the Egyptian coast quite clearly, brown and bare and eroded, with a deep red *wadi* coming down to the sea, and the *Okeanos* was half a mile inshore, hauling off to the eastward.

" What did I say ? " Costas grinned. " The banks off Matruh. Chicken feed ! "

Christos was hugging the starboard shrouds, one fist on the light board and the other cramming great chunks of dogfish into his mouth, like a man filling his belly against the fear of famine, and his dark eyes were alight.

Manoli's boats were the first to reach the Egyptian beds, but within a week many other vessels had gathered along the hot, red coast : boats from Kalymnos and Symi and Patmos, from Hydra and Spetsae and Rhodes, and at night Morgan heard the Greek songs floating across the water from the decks of the anchored *depositos*, where the men were trampling the black juices from the gathered sponges.

"They'll all be here this summer," said Manoli. "The price is high, a million drachmae an oka, a million and a half an oka for the best quality. There'll be a hundred and fifty boats, two hundred maybe, diving along Africa before June. You'll see."

The sun was setting over the Libyan coast with the garish splendour of a bazaar painting; it needed only the awkward, black silhouettes of pyramids and palm trees and camels to remove the scene completely beyond the bounds of credulity.

"We'll do ten more days around here," said Manoli, "then run down and take a look at Benghazi. You want to come along, or do we put you ashore at Alexandria?"

"I want to come along," Morgan said. "I want to see who wins that bet, Christos or Costas."

Manoli grinned. "Whoever wins, it'll be Christos who gets the wine. He always does. That bastard I love." He went across to the railing and slacked off the coir fender. "The boats are coming now," he said.

The *aktaramathes* were sailing in out of the sunset all abreast, as if racing to see which should be the first to reach the big schooner. There were only three of them, because the *Ikaros* was in reserve. Manoli always kept one boat back from the sponge beds, to give the crews an easy time and rest the divers and overhaul the gear.

About the operations there was a smooth, rhythmic efficiency, everything geared exactly to a method which Manoli had tested over the seasons and found to be the best. Each boat carried nine divers—six *skafendros* and three skin divers—and even with a boat in reserve and nine divers resting, it gave him twenty-seven divers each day to work the beds. He would allow each *skafendro* to make only three dives a day. In the shallow beds they might stay below for half an hour or more without particular danger; in the deep and dangerous dives, the dives of *profundito*, every *colazaris* had orders that no dive was to exceed four minutes. But whether the dive was an easy one or hazardous, Manoli would never permit more than three a day. " They will be doing it every day for the next seven months," he explained to Morgan. " It is a long time."

More latitude was permitted the skin divers, who might make upwards of fifty dives a day. Their safety lay in the strength of their own lungs. The big stone would carry them into the deeps, fifty metres, even sixty metres ; they held their breath, while they clutched and grabbed at the sponges, and then lunged upwards with the blood hammering in their skulls, lunged upwards to the light and air, clutching the slimy softness of the captured trophies to their naked bodies. Their work could blind them or deafen them, but it would seldom paralyse or kill them.

The *Saint Stephanos* was sliding alongside with the engine thumping softly, and Morgan could see the sponges on the deck, a mound of glistening, gelatinous shapes, a deep, blackish purple in the evening light, and the *colazaris* was grinning up at them and waving two big lobsters in his fists. Behind the *Saint Stephanos* the other boats were circling. They were thick, sturdy boats, but the high-curved bows and the back-sweep of the sheer gave them a particular gracefulness as they cut through the dark, glassy water, and they turned as tightly, as daintily, as London taxi-cabs. They were strong, handy, workmanlike boats with that special beauty the sea imparts to things fashioned from wood for the sea's work. Already the bright paint of Lavassi had faded into a bleached tonality more pleasing than the earlier brilliance.

" Those lobsters," said Morgan, chuckling. " Shall I go across to the *Ikaros* and tell Christos ? "

" He smells food before you can see it," Manoli said with a grin. " Look."

Christos was rowing the dinghy across from the *Ikaros* with great, sweeping strokes, yelling to them of a garlic sauce he could make.

That night, as a special privilege, they anchored the *aktaramanthes* and everybody came aboard the *Okeanos*, because the *Elektra* had brought in five lobsters as well and a basketful of *fooskas* and they had *fooskas* and the lobsters with the garlic sauce, and Christos made them laugh with his jokes and his gluttony, and in the warm wonder of the African night, in the smell of the sponges drying on the deck, a young diver with a high, thin voice sang " *Thalassaki Mou.*"

" It couldn't be like this, you know, if you went to Australia," Morgan said contentedly. " It wouldn't have this quality, whatever it is—I can't describe it, but it belongs here. You couldn't transplant it."

" Australia ? " Manoli frowned. " I don't pay any attention to this Athens talk. Talk, that's all the bastards can do in Athens. Two Athenians, one argument—that's what they say."

" It could be important though."

Manoli shrugged. " Boats are boats, wherever you go. And any place there are things to do. There are things to do here."

The young diver was singing the old song, the song of poor Kalymnos, and of the sea that had withered its mountains and left a girl too young and too small to be wearing black.

" We'll move down to Benghazi to-morrow," Manoli said suddenly. " Not ten days from now, as I said, but to-morrow. I can smell those sponges."

Morgan rowed slowly, standing between the tholepins and pushing at the oars so he might see the slight deflections of Manoli's head that would tell him whether to pull to port or starboard, to go ahead or to back water.

Manoli had jammed his hips into the little circular hatch in the bow of the boat, and his trunk was bent right out over the water; he had the big cylindrical *yalass* gripped in his two hands and through its thick glass bottom he could see down through seventy feet of water to the sea bed sliding below them.

Costas was sprawled on the bottom boards between them like some queer amphibious creature they had fished up from the sea. He was wearing the rubber *ferneze* suit, black and skin-tight, because there were dogfish below and because five times since they had begun diving at dawn, the sharp, slicing fins of sharks—big sharks—had been seen in the still, oily waters and the warning cry, " *Karxarias ! Karxarias !* " had been shouted from ship to ship. Manoli had ordered the skin men to put on the black suits and the masks because he didn't want the gleam of the white, naked figures in the water to bring the sharks around.

Each time Costas came out of the water he glistened like polished jet, but it took only a minute or two for the sun to peel the gloss and wetness off in steam, and then the suit looked grey and dull. It was like the fading of the shine and colours of a fish after it had been landed, and the dry rubber looked as if it might have an unpleasant feel, like the skin of a peach against your lips. . . .

Costas sprawled contentedly on the bottom boards, all his muscles relaxed and his head pillowed on the big stone that carried him down and he whistled quietly to himself as he thought of the dogfish and the sharks. He glanced behind Morgan at the pile of good, black sponges he had gathered, and wondered whether Christos had made as many in his earlier dive. Twenty-two minutes, Manoli had said. He could have made as many, he could have made more. They were puny shelves, but there were sponges about. Costas could see the *Ikaros* circling half a mile away, too far to make out who was diving and who was in the line waiting.

" *Endaksi*," Manoli said quietly, and tilted his head back. Morgan pulled against the oars to check the boat, and Costas clambered up and reached over to take the *yalass* from Manoli and he swung it in a slow, slanted arc.

Morgan could see through it, too, across Costas' shoulder ; it appeared to bore a circular hole of brilliance through the opaque skin of water, and to frame the mysterious, shimmering pattern of the sea bed, all swirls and stipples and pale Marie Laurencin colours applied in a queer dreamlike abstract. Then Costas steadied the *yalass* and Morgan, leaning forward, could see the bruised darkness of weeded rocks and the sponges clustered.

" Ah ! " Costas said softly. He pushed the *yalass* back to Manoli and lifted the big stone from its nest of coiled rope and gave it three swinging heaves to get the turns of the rope around his left wrist, and then he took his breath in. There was nothing demonstrative in the way he took his breath in, no show of ability, nothing of the professional strong man displaying some special prowess. Costas just straightened his long, lean body slowly, taking breath in all the time, but quite silently, and swinging the big *petra* from the rope around his wrist as if the swing of its pendulum was a measure for his lungs. And then he gave a bigger swing and the stone was above his head, clutched in both hands, and he was over the side, head first into the water.

Morgan had already seen Costas make seven such dives from the small boat, yet he still watched with a sense of awe as the figure plummeted away, the dark, wriggling rush down through the sea and the splash frothing away and the bubbles boiling up like a comet's tail. And then no more bubbles, only the dark, thick skin of the sea closing quietly over its wound. Nothing could be seen of Costas—only the rope kicking, kicking, kicking off its coils and running out, the coils spinning off and the rope hissing down into the sea, and then a last weak kick as if the life had been crushed out of it and the slack of the line sagging in the quiet, concealing water.

Manoli squirmed his body out of the little hatch and rolled the *yalass* into the bottom of the boat and grinned happily at Morgan. " It's down there what I've been looking for," he said. " There's a shelf of rock that falls away. It goes very deep, very dark. You can't reach it with the *yalass.*"

It was difficult to believe that Costas had ever existed, that he was down below them—seventy feet below them !—scrambling among the rocks and sponges. The rope sagged in the water, loose and meaningless, as if there was nothing at the end of it.

Manoli stood up and put his fingers in his mouth and whistled to the *Ikaros*, a shrill, penetrating whistle that would carry across the half-mile of water. Morgan looked astern and he could see Elias the *colazaris* waving to them. The boat was circling slowly on a tight lock.

" They've got a man down," said Manoli. " They'll come when he's up." He jerked his thumb over the side. " There'll be some big strong bastards down there," he said triumphantly, as if he had planted the sponges himself. " Maybe we get all the boats over and run it for half a mile along."

Costas burst the surface with a rush that took his body out clear to the navel, the sponges hugged high on his chest. He bundled them over the gunwale, five good sponges, and the sweet, pungent smell of them was in Morgan's nostrils as he reached down to drag Costas into the boat. He came in black and glossy, his legs kicking and his chest heaving, and for a minute he lay panting in the bottom of the boat like some queer thalassic creature helpless and dying in the destructive air. Morgan began to haul in the *petra*, coiling the wet rope beside his feet in a careful two-foot circle.

"There's a hell of a great ridge down there," said Costas. "That rock shelf drops away over on the left."

"Sure," said Manoli. "We see it. Pretty soon we get the *Ikaros*, maybe the others too."

"It shelves for a while, fifty metres, maybe, before it goes deep and dark. It's big rocks and weedy, but there's sponges. Maybe I do two more dives on that fifty-metre shelf, just to see."

Manoli shook his head. "We'll run it with the *skafendros*," he said. "I want to take it deeper. You've been diving twenty-five metres all morning. You do some damage to yourself if you start jumping fifty without a break. You take it easy. You've done all right." He grinned at the big glistening mound of sponges in the stern sheets. "Christos didn't take that many on his first run this morning."

"That bastard Christos!" Costas stared dolefully towards the *Ikaros*. "He gets down there in these deep ridges, he wins that bet all right—you see if he doesn't."

The feeling had been with Christos ever since sunrise that it was to be something special, perhaps even something like the day, eighteen summers before, when he had done the three great dives. These were the same beds, the Benghazi beds, and it had been just this sort of day, exactly this sort, with a smooth, oily sea heaving to an almost imperceptible swell under a heat-bleached sky, and the three boats running the bank together, all turning on precise and separate circles as if they were the cogs of some complicated machine moving in the black oil of the sea.

The morning dive had accentuated the feeling. It had been a leisurely, rambling dive on the shallow thirty-metre bed, and the sunlight was right down on the sea bottom so that everything was a wonderfully strange pale-blue and you could see ahead for a hundred metres before the blueness thickened into a sort of dense wadding, like clouds that had been given the colour of the day. He had enjoyed it down there, feeling the strength return to his legs as the weight went out of his body. Down there he didn't need sticks to haul himself around on ; down there he was crutched by the push of the sea and his body became whole again. . . .

Christos Papagalos was possessed by a deep sense of contentment as he sat with his back to the wooden diving ladder watching Iannis the boat boy rope the heavy boots to the lap rubbers. He grinned at old Tomás, waiting with the copper helmet and the big spanner ready to screw down the shoulder bolts.

"That engine of yours sounds sick again," Christos said accusingly. The engine was thudding with a sweet, constant rhythm, but it was a joke he always had with Tomás because the engine was coupled to the air pump and if it failed that was *kaputt* to any diver who was down below.

"Sure," said Tomás agreeably. "I hear it spluttering all morning. Maybe there's water in the gasoline. I guess it'll hold out for as long as you're down. If it doesn't we'll lower you a bottle of retzina." He shrugged and moved in to put the helmet on Christos, holding it crookedly so he could twist it into the lock rings.

But before the helmet went on Manoli came up to give Christos his instructions. The sun was high overhead, and the heat of it beat down on the deck and Manoli had stripped off to a brief pair of cotton drawers.

"Take the thirty-metre shelf first," he said. "It drops away on the left. Costas says fifty metres maybe before you reach the edge of the ridge, where it gets weedy. Big rocks and weedy. Don't take anything yourself before you get there, because it's over the ridge you'll find the big bastards. If you see anything shallow or down on the fifty-metre shelf, give Elias four pulls on the rope and we'll send skin divers down. I want you to go over that ridge and look for the big bastards."

Christos saw that the colour of the water had changed since

the morning dive. It was a deeper colour, greenish, and you couldn't see so far; over to the left, where the ridge began, there was a sort of muddiness, as if something had stirred up the water, and there were dark levels of brown and purple running through the green, and in the darkness the pale, running flick of the dogfish. Christos felt he could have done without the dogfish. They weren't very big and weren't giving him any trouble, but the bastards had a way of bringing the sharks around.

Christos gave four tugs on the rope and waited against a low buttress of rock; it wasn't thirty seconds before two of them came down, one behind the other, Costas and Dionyssos, spearing down all straight arms and legs in a descending silver jet of bubbles, and he watched them crouching there, tearing the sponges off the rocks, and swinging their arms to unhitch the *petras* and then lunging upwards, kicking their legs to get over to one side so they wouldn't tangle with the *petra* ropes. Because of the light in the water they seemed to go up in a big outswinging curve, black, wriggling shapes growing smaller and smaller and then disappearing in a green church of water. It seemed quite an appreciable time after he had lost sight of them before two tiny pricking explosions of light, one after the other like candles winking, told him they had broken the surface.

Christos moved over to examine the ridge. It was like a low wall of rock thickly impasted with a smooth, dark weed, and with a deeper drop on the other side, ten or twelve feet maybe, but then the slope flattened out and it receded more gradually through dense but broken growths of weed fanning out of tall, jagged pinacles of rock. Christos suspected that the slope would run down to a deep cleft, because there was an impenetrable blackness beyond the rock pinnacles, as when you look into a pit.

He hooked the air line more securely beneath his crotch and up and over his left shoulder, and he went over the ridge very carefully, bringing the air line in behind him. The weed seemed less thick up to the right, and he was glad of that because his instinct told him that was where the sponges were. He could feel them drawing him.

The hull of the wrecked ship came at him suddenly, as if

it had been materialised instantaneously from the sea substances, but that was only because of what the sea had done to it, crusting it over with its own colours and materials and draping it with its weeds. It looked as if it had been a wooden ship, but now you couldn't even be sure of that ; it seemed more like a shape made out of sea rocks. You couldn't even tell whether it was some ship that had been torpedoed in the war—a lot off Benghazi had been—or an ancient galley that had been down there for a couple of thousand years or more. That was how the sea treated the things it claimed. It fixed them all up the same way ; ten years or two thousand years, it was all the same once they were down.

There was a lot of slime around the wreck and the dogfish were closer, but Christos could hear the sponges calling and he could see one, a good one, growing against the big gap where the hull of the ship had broken away. It was down low, just above the thick jelly of the slime, and he stooped over and took it, squeezing the milk out of it with his fingers as he dragged it away. He could see the pale milk jetting out of the black nostrils of the sponge and floating away ; he always liked to squeeze the milk out because that spread the spores around and made sure of next summer's sponges.

He went in carefully through the gap in the hull, making sure that the air line came in behind him, and he could see the sponges about ten feet ahead, rising in a big cluster from the slime.

It was funny the way the good sponges liked to live on the things that didn't truly belong below the sea, on wrecked ships and ruins, even of things like wine jars. Once, off the coast of Syria, Christos had found himself confronted by a whole ruined city buried beneath the sea, big square houses, some of them two and three stories high ; and it had been a queer feeling, walking through the wide, lost streets picking sponges from the walls.

He had taken two of the sponges and squeezed them and stuffed them into the netting bag around his neck when he felt the slime begin to move. It didn't move much, just a slow slip to one side—scarcely enough to rock him on his feet—and then a gradual subsiding, as if it was all settling back again. It was so slight that he would have thought he had imagined it but for the dark sediment stirring up around his feet and thickening so that he could barely see the sponges although they were only the reach of his arm away.

He groped forward again, but there was a faint giddiness in his head and the sediment seemed to be turning red.

Christos took a hitch on the signal cord with his hand and gave it one tug to warn Elias that there seemed to be some trouble and he was going to investigate it, and that would mean that Elias would bring the *Ikaros* right above him so they could drag him up if anything was wrong.

He backed away from the sponges very slowly, both hands between his legs, feeling his way back along the thick rubber length of the air line. It didn't seem to have any slack to it, so that as he went back he had to crouch right down on his haunches to feel it, and that was when he felt the air line going down into the thick jelly of the slime. He dragged at it, cautiously at first and then with a fierce desperation, but it didn't move a fraction of an inch. The subsidence he had felt couldn't be explained, but it was clear that it had shifted something on to the air line, something heavy that had pressed the line into the slime and clamped it there.

Christos went on his knees and began to grope with his hands, burying his arms to the elbows in the muck, but the rubber tube went straight down, unyielding as a rod of iron. The air had almost stopped coming through, just a faint whistle, as if somebody far away was trying to attract his attention, trying to tell him maybe that the dogfish were around—hundreds of dogfish, big ones, spinning around him in a circle, faster and faster, swimming in a way he'd never seen dogfish swim before, but that was probably because they were marking this circle around him so the sharks would know where to find him. Down in the deep parts the sharks liked to see something pale and spinning. Deep parts? Fifty-two metres maybe. He'd gone over the ridge that Costas had talked about, but the sponges had called him up along the shelf and he'd never gone near the deep cleft . . . fifty-two metres. Chicken feed, that was what Costas had said. Around these parts he'd dived eighty-two metres, and they still talked about it.

He lowered his buttocks into the black, moss-soft jelly and tried to drag at the line, pushing into the slime with his feet, but there was no feeling in his legs and nothing to press against. The circling dogfish had changed into a band of bright red running behind his eyes, as if his eyes had spun right round in their sockets and he was able to look inside his own skull at the blood pouring through his veins. His hands could no longer feel the signal line, but that didn't matter because they wouldn't be able to haul him up to the *Ikaros*, not when the air line was holding him.

The red band exploded into sparks and darting flashes of colour, and then all the colours faded and there were only queer shapes forming, growing darker and darker; but there was no pain at all. It was strange to think that this was how it happened, without any pain at all.

He sank slowly into the slime without any pain and with no fear, with nothing but an overwhelming sense of wonder.

" Steady it now," said Manoli. Tomás gave two fingers to the long-angled engine wheel, and there was no sound but the dying ripple of the water against the side.

Elias lifted his hand again on the signal line, his expression abstracted, like a man feeling a fishing line to see whether something is nibbling, and he shook his head slowly.

" Still slack," he said softly.

Manoli nodded and glanced at the air line. It went straight into the sea, vertical and rigid. The white drawers now lay on the deck, and Manoli was on the second step of the diving ladder, naked, with one of the *petras* hanging from the three hitches around his wrist; and Costas was behind him in the black suit, with his own *petra* hugged into the crook of his elbow. He had pushed the mask up on the top of his head and it looked like some ridiculous carnival hat, and he kept licking his lips and spitting over the side as if his mouth was dry.

" Let me take it first," he said. " I've got the black on. Those sharks—they're big bastards."

Manoli didn't appear to hear him. He was staring into the water, as if he could see clear to the sea bed, and suddenly his muscles bunched as the big stone swung up over his head, and they could see the pale shine of his body rushing away as if it were running down on the white cable of the air line.

They were crowded at the rail, peering down, all except Tomás, who kept his fingers on the engine wheel, and it was Tomás who saw the two dark fins come slicing in around the bow, one quite close to the ship and the other about forty feet away, sliding up through the water and then diving slowly.

" *Karxarias,*" he said softly, not shouting it because Elias was standing right beside him.

Costas heaved the *petra* on to the top step of the diving ladder and climbed up. The rope running down to Manoli's stone hung in the water beside the ladder, quite limp.

Manoli pushed both his feet against the crusted hull of the wreck, unaware of any pain as the sharp shells split the flesh open, and dragged with both hands at the air line. He could feel it moving slightly beneath the slime, not coming away, but moving a little. He had maybe another fifteen seconds, no more. In his head there was a black dizziness and all the inside of his chest was burning, and he pushed his feet with all his force into the razor edges of the shells, wrenching at the air line with a bursting desperation as he felt it pulling clear.

Costas and the big shark came almost together: Costas a dark shape plunging down beside him in a churn of water, and the pale outline of the shark sweeping towards them in a wide, descending curve as it smelled the blood from his torn feet. It was Costas who came over the top of him, reaching down to free his wrists from the *petra* and pushing him sideways through the slime, and Manoli was shielded by the black, thrashing body of Costas as the shark made its rush at them through the dark boil of slime and sediment.

PART FOUR

Pelacos

I

Irini looked again at the open envelope beside her plate, the curious squiggles of the Arabic writing on the stamps and the Benghazi postmark, the bold clarity of his handwriting. She had never seen his handwriting before but she had known instantly that the letter had come from him, even before she realised that it had been posted in Benghazi. The paper of which the envelope was made had a strange, thin, far-away look.

" Shall I go on ? " she said.

" Please." Her father's eyes were on his plate.

" They put Costas aboard the *Angellico*," she read, " but it was a day and a half into port, and the poor devil, I'm afraid, was in awful pain. No morphia, no drugs of any sort, and he had lost too much blood before we could get the tourniquet on. He died an hour before they got in. Manoli stayed on with us, although his own arm was pretty savagely mauled. We worked with all three boats but it took a whole day's diving to get the body of Christos up. He had somehow got himself inside the hull of an old wreck, and it seems his weight had dislodged a section of it, which had come down on the air line. The poor wretch was half buried in slime, and the sponges he had taken were still in the bag around his shoulders. We took his body ashore in the *Ikaros* and buried them both together at Benghazi. They were fine men ; I liked them both very much. Christos, I think, will be greatly missed by everybody there. I never knew anybody who wasn't fond of him."

Pelacos nodded. " He was a fine fellow, yes. Your grandfather, Irini, gave him his first job. He was with our boats for years, and then after the paralysis . . . I don't know, we seemed to lose track of him. He would not take compensation from us, and later, when we wished him to come with us again, he told me he did not want to be tied down to any particular company. He preferred to free lance, as it were." He sighed. " Yes, poor Christos . . . Does Leigh have any more to say about it ? "

" He goes on to explain why he has decided to stay on with the boats for the whole summer," said Irini. " That's only a repetition of what I read you earlier. Then he says : ' It's the most devilish bad luck for Manoli, losing two of his best men so early in the season, because, you will remember, he lost another man, Gravos, on his winter cruise. It's pretty shattering for him, of course, to have lost three men in only a matter of a few months—particularly as he had a very special affection for poor Papagalos. If it was anybody but Manoli, I imagine his depression would infect everybody. I'm not suggesting that any of us is happy at the way things have begun, but Manoli is himself diving every day and that's put heart back into the other divers, and the work goes on. You can see how impossible it would be for me to leave the boats at this stage. I am aware that I don't belong to them, but it might seem as if I were deserting because their luck had run out. And besides that the *Ikaros* is shorthanded now, and there are a hundred little ways in which I can help. I pull the boat for Dionyssos, the other skin diver, and you would be astonished at what an excellent cook I've become. I must send you my recipe for a sort of *bouillabaisse* I've concocted. It's a way of using up the *galetis*, which are beginning to gather the taste of engine oil and are otherwise inedible anyway. . . .' " She looked across to her father. " The rest isn't important," she said.

" Thank you, my dear. I'm sorry Leigh won't be with us for the summer, although I do see his point of view entirely. Now that they've almost completed rigging the *Astra*, I was hoping you and Leigh would have some enjoyable sailing together in the summer."

" She's only an eighteen-footer. I can sail her by myself."

" Of course." He smiled at her. " I was not doubting your nautical skill, but it will be rather lonely for you."

" It won't be different from last summer," she said quietly.

" It will be better, really, because this summer I shall have the boat."

" Yes." He took a peach from the bowl and fingered it and began carefully to pare the skin. " Will you be writing to Leigh ? " he said.

" Of course." Her impulse was to fly from the table now, to hurry to her room, and write and write and write. And having written, where should she send it ? To a thirty-foot boat, some-where in the Mediterranean along the coast of Africa ? Where was the postman who would deliver it ? She would write a long letter, a page each day until Manoli's *deposito* came back with the first crop of sponges, and then when it went away again to take the new stores and water and oil it would take her letter to him, a long, careful letter telling him everything.

" When you write," her father said, " you might let him know about the team going to Australia. Quite conceivably they may know nothing about it. If their boats had moved away from Alexandria when we sent down to bring the men back it's unlikely that they would. I should like Morgan to know. He has been very interested in the idea. Tell him we flew men out to Australia, and they are all in fine fettle."

" He'll be rather surprised, won't he, that Manoli wasn't selected ? "

" Possibly, yes." Pelacos considered the matter for a moment. " There were a number of reasons, which I am quite sure Leigh will understand. I shall let you have the names of the divers who went—he will know some of them—and you must be sure to point out that they are ten first-rate men, absolutely first-rate on all counts. Oh yes, and tell him that a committee of townspeople endorsed the selection unanimously."

Irini smiled slightly. " I should think that's hardly likely to comfort him," she said. " He has a great admiration for Manoli. He's very loyal to him."

" Manoli, Manoli, Manoli ! " he said, with a sudden flash of asperity. " I've already said there were perfectly adequate reasons why Manoli was not chosen. In any case, you may be quite sure that Manoli will have his hands full this summer. One is sorry enough for the poor chap as it is. It would be a dubious show of consideration to ask him to curtail all his operations when he has this whole tragic business to recoup."

"I suppose so, yes," she said softly.

Paul Pelacos folded his newspaper and pushed back his chair, but he paused at the door, as if he were sorry for his brief display of ill-humour.

"Irini," he said gently, "I meant what I said about your being lonely. And since Leigh will not now be with us this summer, I see no particular reason why you should stay here. The Teucers will be in the south of France all through July and August. You could go to them. Or London? I know your Aunt Grace would be delighted to have you."

She glanced at him quickly. The terrible Teucers with their ghastly cocktail parties and bickering drives in the old Renault, and Claude Teucer in his navy-blue blazer with the gilt buttons, and Aunt Grace's smothering kindliness and her interest in Girl Guides! Yet, for the first time in more than two years, the door to escape had opened.

Irini shook her head slowly. "Thank you, Daddy, but I think I should prefer to be here," she said, and because she was anxious to acknowledge his consideration she added: "You've been so sweet having Casalis build the *Astra*, I couldn't bear the thought of not being able to sail her."

"Ah, yes, you have the boat, haven't you?" He smiled. "If you change your mind, dear, let me know. The Teucers would only need a cable."

In the torrid emptiness of summer, Kalymnos lay in a dull, drugged torpor, like a town anæsthetised.

The truth of the town, its life and form and substance, had withdrawn to the distant coast of Africa; what remained was a lifeless effigy, its wax melting in the sun. Even the mountains had receded into a pale stipple of heat. At intervals one of the *depositos* would return with its freight of sponges, and before it sailed away again there would be a momentary stirring, a reminder that the realities lay elsewhere, that one day the drug of summer, of *kalokairi*, would lose its power to subdue the truth.

And then the *deposito* would sail away once more, rolling down to the urgent south, and the breakwater would be empty of its ships again, empty of everything except the idlers dozing in the shade of the lighthouse or fishing lazily from the rocks. At the town wharf, where the sponge boats had been moored, the ketches would come in from Kós to unload baskets of grapes and tomatoes and melons, or a caique from Rhodes with a freight of apricots, and Johnny and Mike and the others would rouse themselves from long siestas beneath the handcarts and drag the fruit wearily to the almost deserted market.

There were few people in the market, few in the streets. Every evening the tables of the coffee houses were put out along the water's edge, where a cool wind might breathe in from the sea ; but for the most part the tables remained unoccupied.

It was as if the people who could escape had already fled the plague of lethargy that infected the town. Those with cottages at Brostá or Myrtiés had moved across the island to find cooler winds ; those who were poor, and to whom the emptiness of summer denied both work and wages, had gone into the fields and hills and made their makeshift tents, and there, living with their families on the fish they could catch from the crowded sea, on the figs of the mountainside and the cool waters of the wells, they made their frugal, pastoral summer.

Kalymnos was a town stretched out in the sun, drained of both its life and its purpose.

On the first of May, Paul Pelacos had closed the big, white house and moved across to the smaller villa overlooking the bay of Brostá ; he spent ten days there and then, pleading urgent matters that demanded his attention, took himself off for a month's visit to Hamburg, Paris and London. His suggestion that his daughter should accompany him was made sincerely, but he was not unrelieved when she refused.

Irini had sailed the *Astra* around from Kalymnos and found a secure anchorage for it in the small, rocky fishing harbour at the foot of the cliff below the villa. Although she had taken up her painting again, she spent most of her time in the boat exploring the lonely islets of the wild coastline, sailing to Vathý or across to Leros, but most often taking the boat around Télendos, close inshore where she could see the caves and fissures and the empty desolation of secluded bays. Sometimes she would anchor the boat and take her clothes off and swim naked in the cool, hidden waters.

In her solitude she found a curious contentment, a sense of private satisfaction that she had never before experienced. The simplicity of the Brostá villa—its cool, dark quietness with the shutters drawn against the sun, and with old Savasti pottering in the kitchen and humming to herself—she found infinitely preferable to the more complicated refinements of the big house. And in the absence of her father there was an additional reduction to simpler values : the exhausting burden of the intricate relationship that had developed between them was for a time removed. For a whole month she could escape the guarded affections and those formal reticences of his which, in dictating his own mode of living, necessarily dictated hers. She loved her father, but she was afraid of him—afraid of hurting him, of offending him by in some way not conforming to the rigid pattern of his expectations. For a whole month she was free from all the nuances of filial behaviour imposed by his austere conventions ; she need not feel ill at ease, wondering if she were being gauche or unresponsive or intemperately restive.

Moreover, the placid procession of day following day—days blue and gold with the sea and warm with sunshine—helped to strengthen the link between her own solitude and the crowded urgency of the boats diving in African waters. In Kalymnos the link existed. Even the island's torpor was essentially a part of this distant adventure, as, in wartime, the women knitting woollen things at home are inseparably related to the soldiers' life in battle. By staying on the island she could retain a sense of unity with the boats ; she could see them and feel them and belong to them. In Cannes, with the Teucers, it would have all been impossibly remote, something happening beyond the rim of the world : the tidal wave in Yokohama reduced to dismissive headlines while the back of a spoon batters the fragile shell of the breakfast egg ; the atrocities of Kenya falling into a correct and ordered perspective behind Claude Teucer's golf swing.

There would have been no link. Nothing would have remained in which she could believe.

The *Okeanos* had taken her letter away, and there had been no reply, but she had not expected a reply. Perhaps one day another letter would arrive, with strange stamps on the envelope or brought in, with no stamps at all, by one of the *depositos*. She was content to wait until then, or until he returned in the autumn.

In the love she now had for Morgan she seldom thought of Manoli ; the memory of the night on the mountain top was dim, the pain and the humiliation had long since ebbed away. There had been the mountain top above Myrtiés too, looking across to Télendos, and it blocked out the shape of the other. Sometimes at dusk she would walk across the hilly trail from Brostá and she would sit beneath the pine trees above the bay to watch twilight's chromatic magic on the cliffs of Télendos, and she would think of him.

She was aware that what had begun had only begun, no more than that. He had gone away to Athens and Kós, and then he had been preoccupied by the preparation of the boats, and finally he had sailed away—and no summer would fructify the seed of spring. But he would come back in the autumn and it would be all resolved, and she was content to wait for him.

One Sunday in June she sailed along the coast westward from Brostá. It was a hot, calm day with light, fitful breezes from the westward that threatened to expire altogether if the day's heat became greater ; she had tacked the *Astra* to the westward so that running back home she might use the big spinnaker, the Ratsey spinnaker that her father had imported specially from England.

By noon the breeze was barely sufficient to make steerage way, and inshore the mountains concealing the monastery of Santa Katerina had receded into a pale shimmer of haze, but at the foot of the vermilion cliffs was a small secluded cove, two arms of sheltering rock around pale-green water and a narrow beach of grey shingle. Irini allowed the *Astra* to drift towards it.

It was not until after she had anchored the boat and rowed ashore in the little white dinghy that she realised the cove was already occupied. There were two small and rather primitive tents on the slope above the cliff, strung beneath the twisted branches of the fig trees, and on the beach a hearth of rocks in which a fire still faintly smouldered, and beside the fire were cooking pots and two water jars and a fishing rod. A stooped, elderly man with a heavy limp was gathering faggots on the hilltop. She was watching the man when she heard the movement behind her and she turned swiftly and there was the Vraxos woman, Manoli's mistress, smiling at her from behind a shelf of rock. Her hair was wet and she was wearing only a simple green cotton slip, the sort of garment the Kalymnian children wore, and as she came from behind the rock Irini saw that her feet were bare and her brown legs wet with the sea.

"I brought the boat in here," she said, after they had exchanged greetings, "because it looked so lovely, and I wanted to swim. I see you've anticipated me." She smiled.

"Yes," said Mina. "You can swim. You will not be disturbed." She laughed softly at Irini's quick, suspicious glance at the man on the hill. "It is my father," she said. "I can tell him you want to swim. He'll go away."

"Oh, no, don't bother, please. It doesn't really matter. It was awfully hot in the boat—no wind and the glare off the water. But I'm perfectly cool now. It's . . . it's lovely here. Are you . . . are you picnicking here or . . ."

"Not picnicking, no." Mina smiled. "In the summer we live here." She glanced towards the crude tents above the cliff. "In the summer the town has no work for my father. It is cheaper to live here."

"But how *can* you? There aren't any . . . any facilities." She was aware that her statement was exactly the sort of remark her father would regard as offensively gauche, but she had a sense of awkwardness, a feeling of embarrassment and guilt, as if she were slumming in an evening dress and tiara—and that was even more gauche, and snobbish into the bargain, and far more offensive!—and she was hideously conscious of the expensive sleekness of the little yacht anchored off the cove and of her own poplin shirt and linen shirt, and of the empty villa at Brostá with nine rooms and two terraces and a bathroom big enough to contain the two shabby little tents on the hillside.

"Facilities?" Mina laughed softly. The word seemed to amuse her and her eyes were warm and kindly as she looked at the younger woman. "We catch fish, and there are figs and nuts and grapes growing everywhere, and a spring of fresh water, and we get bread from the monastery, and——" She broke off suddenly. "I'm sorry—you must be thirsty. Come, you must taste the spring water. It is very sweet and cold. Are you hungry? I can make some food for you. Or there is fruit . . ."

"Thank you, no. I . . . I had some sandwiches, sailing along. But I'd love a drink of water." Irini had a sudden feeling of affection and gratitude towards this tall, grave woman, so quiet and kindly and so patient. So patient. That was it. they had this strange, rare affinity, the two of them, because her Lover also was away with the boats, and they had the same links running from the empty summer of Kalymnos to the busy shores of Africa. The two of them were united in this concord of patience, waiting for their men to return.

"It's quite lovely here," she said. "Your little boy must adore it."

"He is not here," Mina said quietly, leaning down to tilt the water jar. "He has gone away. There are only my father and I."

Something told Irini that the subject of the child should not be pursued. Was he not a cripple, or sickly? Doctor Telfs was involved in it in some way . . . she remembered Morgan's talking of it.

"You heard the terrible news about Manoli's boats, I suppose," she said.

"Yes." Mina handed her the water in a shallow earthenware bowl. "Yes, I had a letter."

"I feel so sorry for Manoli. He's such a good captain, and so careful for his men, and now they're beginning to talk against him . . . well, not against him, but they're saying that he's always been lucky and now his luck has run out."

"Yes," Mina nodded. "It's what my father says. They will all say it. Next season he will find it hard to get men to sail with him. They will not remember all the years when he was successful and good to them. They will only remember the three men who died." She shrugged. " It is a cruel island, this, and the cruelty creeps into people's thinking."

" Perhaps he will be tremendously successful," Irini said eagerly. She wanted the woman to know she was loyal to Manoli, that she too was anxious for him to succeed. " Then everybody might forget the other thing."

" Perhaps." Mina took the little bowl and refilled it.

" There's some talk about their not coming back now until November," Irini said. " Did Manoli say anything about it to you ? "

" Manoli ? "

" In his letter, I mean."

" Letter ? What letter ? "

" Oh, I'm sorry, I must have misunderstood. I thought you said you'd had a letter, and——"

Mina laughed. " Manoli has never written a letter in his life—not to anybody. No, it was Morgan who wrote to me."

" Oh, I see. I . . . I didn't know . . ."

The wind freshened in the middle of the afternoon and Irini sailed the *Astra* back to Brostá. It was not until she was stowing the sails in the locker of the boathouse that she realised she had forgotten to use the Ratsey spinnaker.

2

It HAD been in the mind of Stavros ever since dusk, but he said nothing of it to Mina, and after they had eaten the fish he had caught he sat with her on the rocks, watching the moon come up over the hills.

He was preoccupied by his decision and by the thought of the long walk in the darkness, and by remembering the stick he had cut and hidden in the thorn bushes. They were quite silent, sitting together, watching the moon. His daughter seemed to have her own thoughts, too.

The moon had lifted very high above the hills when he kissed her on the head and crawled into the shelter of the little tent, curling himself up on the soft grass and after a time breathing deeply so that she might think he slept. She sat outside for a long time watching the moon, and even after he had heard her go into her tent he had to wait until he could be sure she was sleeping.

When he got up and went outside, a quiet, pale darkness brooded over the mountains, and it frightened him a little, the stillness of everything, as if all the earth had died. It was a troubling thought that he would have to walk for three hours, maybe four, through this terrible, dark quietness. He went first to the patch of thorns and found the stick he had cut. He was glad he had kept it a secret from Mina because even when the pain was bad he had never walked with a stick before, but now it was necessary because it was like a knife all down one side of him and jabbing into his groin. And even with the moon to mark it, it was a rough, stony trail to Kalymnos, and it would take him all of four hours.

Stavros took the first incline slowly, testing the stick, finding the best way to hold it so that it would take the weight off his right side. Thinking about the stick made walking through the still, dark countryside less frightening; but after a while he got used to walking with the stick, and then the fear came back.

The moon had set by the time he reached Kalymnos and not a light showed in the sleeping town, but he struck a match at the window of the watchmaker's shop and the big clock inside told him it was ten minutes past three.

In the utter blackness left by the vanished moon the fear was greater than ever, and he had to sit down in the gutter for a long time because his legs were shaking so badly with the exhaustion of the long walk across the mountains and with the fear that ran through his body like pain. Pain and fear were the same things in the darkness.

It had been so long since he had been inside a church, ten years or even more, that he was scared at the thought of going into one : the smell of the incense and wax, and the eyes of the still, painted faces staring down at him from the darkness, and the little shapes cut out of tin hanging before the pictures and the icons—legs and arms and eyes.

Crouched in the black gutter, Stavros had to fight now against a desperate desire to go to the houses of his friends and to hammer on their doors so they would come out and go with him. It would be easier to do if they could go with him, because they would joke about his not having been to church for so long, and they would take him to the door and pat him on the shoulder. But George would be huddled in the big bed against the heavy warmth of Maria, and she would scream and yell and want to know what it was all about ; and Dimitri would be in his little room, dreaming of the big ships ; and Mike Grassis would be away somewhere on his summer living, sleeping on a beach under the stars with a cold fire beside him and his little boat drawn up near the rocks. Besides, it was a thing he had to do by himself ; he couldn't take anyone else along.

Stavros rose to his feet and took the stick in his hand and limped slowly down to the little hut behind the market, and he was careful to make no noise at all as he pushed the two envelopes under old Beanie's door. He could rely on Beanie to see that the letter to Manoli went on the next *deposito* that was sailing back, and that would explain some of the things to Manoli : why he had voted against him at the meeting of the town committee—that, and even some of the other things. But most of the things couldn't be explained to Manoli or to anybody else ; they could be explained only to God.

Walking along the dark, empty street, where the fish boxes were piled and a few nets were hanging on the sea rail, Stavros tried to assemble in his mind the things that had to be explained. Voting against Manoli because he had picked Christos ; hating Christos for going, and then hating Christos worse than ever for dying. It was funny that he had hated Christos most of all for dying, but that was because *he* could have died just the same as Christos if Manoli had taken him—anyone could die just the same

way as anybody else ; there wasn't any special skill about it—
and that would have been better than feeling the pain spreading
all the way through your body and down into the groin . . . and
there would have been the Government money for Mina, and
then maybe she wouldn't have had to take the money from Homer
Vraxos to send the boy away.

That was another thing to be explained, the way he had
agreed to her taking the money from Vraxos to send Nikolas
away, knowing that by doing that he had sanctioned his marrying
her. That was a terrible thing to have done, when he still
thought of Vraxos in the refugee place at Bodrum and still
wondered after all these years whether the bastard had betrayed
the secret of Elias the *papás* and the hidden boats. A terrible
thing, and very difficult to explain.

It had only been later that he had begun to think about it
and to realise how terrible it was. Because Vraxos wouldn't
take *him* away, that was certain ; Vraxos would still remember
how he'd been dragged out of the barn at Bodrum and thrown
into the pigyard. And then Mina wouldn't go, and what would
happen to Nikolas ?

Stavros went slowly up the wide steps to the church of
Saint Stephanos. There were a lot of strange, terrible things
to be explained, and then when that was done he would have
to pray very hard that Manoli's cruise would be successful.
God was in all the churches, it didn't matter which one you went
to ; but it was only Saint Stephanos who would be able to do
anything about Manoli's cruise.

The door creaked as he pushed it open, and it was very dark
inside, only the dim glow of the wick in the oil float above the
trays of candles, and the faint smoulder of secret, mysterious
things around it . . . an icon of embossed silver with a hole cut
out of the middle and the painted face of the Virgin looking out at
him through the hole in the silver . . . and on the frame of the
icon one shrivelled flower, dry and brown and brittle as a dead
moth . . . and the head of the Virgin like a face seen in a
coffin.

Stavros stood in the doorway, shivering and afraid and with
the pain burning his groin like fire—afraid equally of the thick

blackness and the dim, eerie glow under the coffined face of the Virgin.

He was about to go out again, shuddering in his terror, when he thought of the candles, and with a quick, sobbing groan he lurched across to the trays and began to gather the thin wax tapers into his trembling hands. First he took them all from the half-drachma tray because he had no money to pay for them and he felt better to take the cheapest ones, but then he realised that Saint Stephanos would understand why he could not make his explanations in this terrible, frightening darkness, and he went from tray to tray, taking them all, right up to the end tray with the thick candles that cost ten drachmae each and which only the rich people could afford to buy.

For half an hour he worked feverishly, no longer aware of any pain or fear, lighting one candle from another and filling every sconce he could find, until all the church was a glitter of light, until a hundred dancing pin points flickered on the rows of little blue-and-white Greek flags festooned from the pillars, and on the strong, soft face of Christ, and on the faces of all the saints and the prophets and the martyrs, and on the big picture of Saint Stephanos, embowered in ribbons of white silk and satin.

And then Stavros took all the candles that remained and put them in front of the picture of Saint Stephanos. There was a miniature sponge garden below the picture that some diver had made and left there; the sponges were mounted on a big rock with shells glued on and loops of pink seaweed, and Stavros could see all the tiny, fiery pricks of his candles reflected in the glossy curves of the shells. He went down on his knees before the picture of the tall, thin saint with the gentle womanish face. . . .

Although it was still dark, the cocks were beginning to crow on the hills when he left the church and began to limp slowly towards the rocks, and he was almost there when he remembered that he had left his stick behind.

3

THEY WERE sixteen miles off the coast of Tripoli, but the burning wind hammering them from the south had the smell of sand in it. The wind stung his eyes and made a stiff, gritty tangle of his hair, and it had a queer astringent taste in his mouth, like alum.

He leaned on the pipe of the frayed weather cloth, next to Manoli, watching the *Okeanos* circling in towards them, her high bow butting into the short seas as the engine slowed. There was a bleached, weathered look about the schooner, as if she had run down from Kalymnos through storms of dust, and her gear had a shabby, frayed appearance, as did their own.

It was no longer easy to remember how smart the boats had looked when they had sailed out together from Kalymnos, but that had been six months ago and now it was near the end of October. There were lots of things it was difficult to remember.

How many years ago had Christos died, and Costas? What ages had passed since that night off Matruh when they had eaten the *fooskas* and the lobsters with the garlic sauce and somebody had sung "*Thalassaki Mou*," and in the magic of that almost forgotten African night everything had seemed so exciting and wonderful?

Well, it wasn't that way any longer. It was brutal now and savage and hard. It was heat—heat that was in the copper sky and the wood of the decks and the water, heat that boiled beneath the skin and simmered in the brain. It was pus congealing in the corners of sunburned eyes and salt stinging in the broken scabs of sea sores. It was filthy foul food and sour water and agonising gut-aches. It was a never-ending monotony and tempers flayed raw by tension and confinement and the grinding sequence of laborious days. It was the exhaustion that came from hazard and hardship infinitely prolonged. It was everything you had ever known, everything soft and gentle and refined, rendered down into a stinking mess of sweat and filth and excrement and urine. It was faces falling away into bearded, sun-blackened caricatures with stained teeth and eyes burning in hollowed-out sockets and lips cracked open and caked with dried blood.

Faces? Had his own face changed as their faces had changed? There was no way of knowing; there was no looking-glass aboard the *Ikaros*. It was six months since he had seen his face . . . . that was another thing: he could no longer remember what he looked like.

They had lowered the boat from the *Okeanos* and Elias was climbing into it, swinging a canvas bag in his hand.

"More wiping paper from Zeffis, you'll see," Manoli growled. "Maybe some letters."

Would there be one from Mina this time? Irini would have written, but would there be one from Mina?

There were letters for both of them. Elias nodded as he began to undo the rope around the bag. There was paper from Zeffis too, plenty of it: declarations to be filled in on the sponges that had gone back, and papers to be fixed up about Christos and Costas.

"I sent the papers back last time you went," said Manoli.

"There's more." Elias grinned. "Zeffis always has plenty more when it comes to papers. Remember how Christos used to make the big joke about Zeffis and his papers? By Jesus! he'd laugh about it now, not even being allowed to stay dead but that bastard Zeffis's got to have more papers! Funny, eh?" Elias chuckled at the picture of Christos, sinking deeper and deeper into the earth under the weight of all the papers and the rubber stamps. "He's having a busy time, Zeffis," he said. "It's been a rotten year for all the fleet, not only us. Nine divers dead, counting our two, and thirteen paralysed. That was weeks ago. Maybe by now there's more."

Elias sat on the rail and watched interestedly as Manoli and Morgan sorted through the envelopes.

"There's one there from Mina," he said, and Morgan glanced up quickly, but Elias was looking at Manoli. "It's about what happened to Stavros. And one from Stavros too. He gave it to old Beanie to give to me before it happened."

"Stavros?" Manoli looked at him. "What about Stavros?"

"He's dead. He chucked himself in the sea one morning. Maybe it all sort of collected on top of him—he never did have much of a life, and his legs were getting worse on him all the time. The poor bastard went off his head at the finish. He walked right across from Santa Katerina and went into Saint Stephanos—and do you know what the poor crazy bastard does? He takes every candle in the church and lights 'em all up, fills the whole church with lighted candles. Next morning when old Calliope goes in she crosses herself and lets out a squeal you can hear at the Customs House because she thinks it's a miracle that's happened, see—everything lighted up, just as if it had been got ready for one of those rich weddings. Crazy, eh?"

Manoli was not listening. He had thumbed open the letter from Stavros, and he was frowning over it, running his fore-finger slowly along the lines of pencilling and mouthing the words to himself. When he had read it he stared for a moment at Elias, as if he were not there on the rail at all, and then he folded the two sheets of cheap ruled paper and put them back in the envelope.

"Well, what did he say?" Elias asked impatiently.

"Ah, he had some bug in his mind," Manoli said. He waved his hand dismissively. "Some bug he thought he had to explain to me. It doesn't make sense, not any longer. I guess it's like you said—the poor bastard was off his head."

"Off his head!" Elias laughed. "Would he have lighted up all those candles?"

Manoli shrugged, and slit open the flap of Mina's letter.

Morgan went up on the foredeck to open his own letters. There were two from Irini and two from Telfs and, surprisingly, one from Paul Pelacos—but there was none from Mina.

He had finished reading the letters when Manoli came along

the deck and sat down beside him. He must have been reading Stavros' letter again because it was in his hand, out of its envelope.

" What's the news ? " he said.

" I had a rather queer letter from Paul Pelacos," Morgan said. " It seems that Australian business didn't work out. It was a failure. They've abandoned the idea."

" Maybe it's different out there. Maybe it's harder."

" Pelacos seems to put it down to a difference in conditions and methods. There are the tides, and so on. I can see what he means. The Indian Ocean and the Arafura Sea, they aren't the same as the Mediterranean. And the boats are different. Pelacos appears to think they shouldn't have rushed into it, they should have taken more time and trained the men in the proper methods."

" Maybe. It was good bunch they sent out. Fine divers, all of them." He shrugged. " It's the way these things go. A lot of luck comes into things below the sea. Christos was the best diver in Kalymnos but the luck ran against him. There wasn't any reason he should have died. Another day he could have done it on his ear. He died, just the same."

" I still think they should have sent you. Perhaps it would have worked out differently if you'd gone."

Manoli looked at him for a moment and then his burned, unshaven face split into a sardonic grin.

" That's right," he said. " The big Manoli. Lucky Manoli. A winter off Crete for one man dead and a lousy hundred million drachmae of sponges. Over six months this summer and two more dead and the worst haul of sponges we've had in five years. Sure, why not send Manoli ? He carries the big recommendation."

" Well, that's why this letter from Pelacos is rather queer, coming from him. It's almost apologetic, as if he wanted to wipe it all out and begin all over again, and send you."

" Bah ! " said Manoli. " It's the way these things go."

" I can see why Pelacos is upset," Morgan said thoughtfully. " In a way his family *is* Kalymnos, and he's a sensitive man. I think it grieves him to see the island just rotting away. This

Australian idea did provide a solution that was bold and brave and audacious—it was a sort of gutsy thing to to. The alternative . . ." He spread his hands. " What is the alternative ? "

" There's work to do," said Manoli simply. " There's always work to do. One day we don't fish sponges. Okay, we fish something else. There's a whole world below the sea that people haven't looked at yet. You know, one day last year, in Alexandria, I got talking with a man, an Italian he was, some sort of a scientist. We got talking and we got drunk together, because he understood what was below the sea, too. He was a funny little man, all bald and brown and he wore short pants, and he had thin legs without a hair on them. But, by Jesus, he knew the sea. And do you know what he tells me ? "

" Go on," said Morgan.

" He tells me that one day people will farm the sea, way down under the water, just the way they do on land. Fish farms, and growing that alga stuff they feed cattle on—lots of things he says you can do." Manoli grinned. " It isn't any crazier than sponges, I guess. Maybe when there aren't sponges any more that's what we do, we go farming."

Morgan stared at him wonderingly. It was typical of Manoli to have this surprising information inside his head ; it was all part of the queer communion he had with the mysterious under-water world in which he had spent half his life. Like the evening off Derna when he had astonished him with his knowledge of the history of diving and for hours had talked to him—of how the two French salvage boats had come to Crete with their curious machines to pump the air, and of how Landy the Irishman had bought them for a song and sailed them to Symi to recruit a crew to go pearl fishing in Australia ; but Landy had died of a heatstroke during the first day's diving in Australia, and the Symi men were too scared to go down without him and they sailed the boats all the way back to their rocky little island in the Ægean. They'd been brave enough to sail the two little boats half-way across the world, but they'd been too scared to dive. It was a story Manoli loved to tell, particularly when he had

Symi divers aboard his own boats, because when they came back
the Symi men still wouldn't go down, not one of them, and the
captain's wife, whose name was Katerini Sizigos and who was
five months pregnant, scolded them all for their cowardice.
And she had put on the suit and helmet herself and gone down
and brought up two oysters and tossed them in the faces of the
men.

Manoli was staring down at the letter Stavros had written
to him, and then he glanced at Morgan and said, " You want
to get back to Kalymnos ? "

" Some time, sure. Why ? "

" To-morrow I send the *Elektra* in to Tripoli. We need
some meat and more stores. If you want to get back you can go
in with her, take an aeroplane back."

" But why should I ? It's only two more weeks and we'll all
be back." He grinned. " I've made a nuisance of myself for
more than six months—it would be a pity now not to see out
the distance."

" That's why I asked," Manoli said quietly. " I'm keeping
the boats out, another three months maybe."

" Three months ! But that will be way after Christmas . . .
winter . . ."

" That's right." He nodded calmly. " It'll be cold and
uncomfortable. The food won't be good even if we get fresh
supplies. It'll be a lousy three months, and maybe it'll be
dangerous, too. The men are tired and the gear's tired and the
boats are tired. That's why I asked. November December, that's
no time to stick out at sea in sour boats."

" I should go back," said Morgan doubtfully. " It will be
nine months. That's a long time."

" Sure," said Manoli, and yawned, stretching his big, bare
arms in the sun. " That's why I asked."

" When I came down it was only for a month, and I've stayed
six months. I should go back." Even talking about it made him
hungry to go, to turn his back on the barbarous cruelty of the
boats, on the demanding labours and primitive discomforts that
pounded all the subtle feelings of privacy and sensitivity, even
the simplest conventions of normal civilised behaviour into a

greasy paste, acrid and horrible. Three more months of it !
He had already lost the memory of his own face ; could the
memory of anything that was human survive another three
months of it ? And he could go now without any feeling that
he was deserting them. After the death of Christos and Costas
the obligation to stay with them had been profoundly compelling.
But the moral contract had been fulfilled. There was nothing
now to prevent his returning to Kalymnos, to walk again perhaps
with Mina, to pick up the threads of a quieter normality, to shape
from the notes he had made the book he must write, to talk with
Telfs, to bathe the senses in the civilised waters of the Pelacos
oasis, to explain to Irini what must be explained.

In May the compulsion had been to stay with the boats.
Now the pivot of compulsion was on the island. For more than
six months he had evaded the problem of Irini ; her letters made
it perfectly clear that he could not continue evading it ; common
decency demanded that he should talk to her, explain to her. And
Mina ? Could the torment of Mina, of *not knowing*, be endured
any longer ?

Yet there was something in the big man sitting beside him
that gave a pause to all these considerations. There was a
compulsion, too, in Manoli ; a more abstract thing, but greater
and darker, a force of infinite strength and power like the sea
itself that drew you to him and dragged you along with him
wherever he had to go, to help him in whatever he had to do,
to notch your own right to existence against his mark.

Could he go to Tripoli and take an air liner and fly across
the Mediterranean and look down from his leather arm-chair
with a luncheon tray balanced on his knees, searching in that
anonymous, rippled expanse of blue for the tiny speck of the
Ikaros ? Could he do it knowing what that speck represented ?
—heat and cold and sickness and hunger, the dirt in the sores
and the sores festering, the sour water swilling in the tanks,
rancid meat and rotten bread that made you gag on every mouth-
ful, Manoli's eyes, red-rimmed with fatigue and strain, squinting
into the glare as the bleached boats came back, and Manoli's
hands—clawing at the sea bed one hundred and eighty feet
below.

" I should go back," said Morgan, " but I suppose I'll stay. Why do you think another three months will make it any better than the last six months have been ? "

" I had some candles burned for me in Saint Stephanos," Manoli said, and grinned. " Maybe that kicks the luck round the other way. Two months we work to pay for what happened to Christos and Costas. Four months we work for not much more than what it costs to run the boats. Maybe now we have three months working for the big year. I need plenty sponges and I need big ones, strong ones. I need the big year, Morgan. I'll go down there ten times a day for the next three months, and if I have to tear every goddam sponge off the bottom of the Mediterranean with my bare hands, I'll have that big year ! "

" Well, let's get started," Morgan said.

Manoli looked at him for a moment, and smiled, and then he reached across and slapped his cheek softly.

" I got to have the big year," he chuckled, " because I got to have money. I got to buy *brika* ! "

And he went along the deck towards the diving gear, bellowing with laughter.

4

PAUL PELACOS had expected to find the big sponge room empty, but old Petros was there putting another coat of cream paint on the end wall, where the finish had not dried evenly.

The old man on the ladder and the smell of paint seemed to accentuate rather than diminish the empty bareness of the huge room, the wizened figure in spattered overalls giving scale to it, the paint smell establishing its emptiness. Pelacos, watching unobserved from the open doorway, realised dispiritedly that the old man on the ladder gave scale to more than the mere dimensions of the Pelacos sponge room. At the age of eighty years—or was it eighty-two ?—he persisted in his shabby,

unchanging continuity while all around him altered. His was
the only true reliability.

"*Kalispera*, Petros," he called from the doorway. The
shrunken face turned towards him, and Petros descended
laboriously from the ladder and shuffled across to him, squinting
his eyes at the thin, dark figure against the square of light; then
the dark simian face of the old man cracked into a smile of
recognition that revealed a single huge yellow tooth. Petros
had always looked the same to Pelacos, no older now in appearance, it seemed, than when Pelacos had been a schoolboy
coming to the odd-jobs man to have his toys mended or the
sprockets of his bicycle tightened. Even then Petros had
possessed only this solitary tooth, this gigantic gamboge mono-
lith rooted in the shifting terrain of his lower jaw, and in the
fluid recollections of Pelacos' childhood it had somehow come
to be part of his grandfather's collection of prehistoric bones and
flints dug up in the cave tombs of Damos, near the road to
Brostá. The tooth of Petros and the curious, dry fragments
on the shallow trays of the mahogany cabinet, they were all
related somehow; out of kindliness perhaps his grandfather
had presented Petros with one of his choicest specimens so that
he might be able to chew on his *barbunia*.

For sixty-five years Petros had executed the odd jobs of
three Pelacos generations, and if none of the jobs had been
particularly odd—for through all three generations nothing
really unorthodox had figured in the family demands—there
would be something startlingly astronomical in the number
of them. The autumn painting of the sponge room in preparation for the harvests that would be clipped and shaped through
winter and into the spring—Petros had been doing it for a
decade longer than his master's own lifetime! In the inexorable
recurrence, the ant-like persistency of the work, there was
something disconcerting, something humbling and humiliating.
There come times, Pelacos reflected, when all masters are
humiliated in the presence of their serfs.

"The room looks very well, Petros," he said. "Very well
indeed." He walked across to the empty packing case upon which
Petros had arranged his brushes and paint pots and removed them

to the floor and turned the case over and sat on it, tweaking the creases of his trousers.

"No, no, no! The old man was aghast. "I'll get a chair from the café next door. No, no, you must not——"

"Please don't bother, Petros. I'm perfectly comfortable here." He smiled gently so that the old man might be mollified. Petros was staring at him in a sort of horrified astonishment, as if he had never before seen a Pelacos seated upon a packing case—which, come to think of it, was quite probably true. He had no memory of ever having sat on a packing case before, and he was quite sure that neither his father nor grandfather would have permitted himself such an indignity. Pelacos smiled to himself. "I did not know you were working here, Petros," he said. "I had an impulse to come here when the room was empty."

Petros nodded. "It's different now, *Kérios*. It's hard to realise, *Kérios*, we had a hundred and sixty men clipping here last January." He winked with the wise, knowing familiarity of great age, and added darkly, "We'll be lucky if we have fifty this year, the way the boats are coming in. Thirty-two boats back and not a thousand okas of good sponges among 'em. I never remember a worse year, *Kérios*." It was a generalisation of age, Pelacos reflected, that swept away all the years he had known, years that were as bad or worse, in the pessimistic assurance that decay was inevitable, that all things tended to worsen, that nothing of the present or the future could ever shine as brightly as the past. "*Never!*" the old man said emphatically.

"I admit it has not been a very promising season," Pelacos agreed, "but we must not be despondent too soon, Petros. After the excellent prices last year there were many more boats out, you must remember that, and all the boats are not back yet."

"All but four of ours are," Petros said shrewdly. "Those other four, they've got to take some sponges!"

"Yes." The old man was right, of course. Half the fleet, or near enough to half of it, was already back: the boats still at sea would have to bring in some remarkable hauls if the season were to be saved from disaster. And could even one disastrous season be afforded? Would Hamburg overlook a disastrous season and be content to await something better? Would Cologne or Düsseldorf or Stuttgart or Coblenz? Would Paris or London or New York? The subsidy of time was something the world no longer granted. If something needed was not there when it was wanted, then an alternative was found, a substitute, a synthetic spun out of feverish, exigent need. There was no longer the time, nor even the necessity, to wait upon the favour of the seasons. The natural harmonies could be ignored. The world had thumbed its nose and turned its back upon the cosmos.

Pelacos had found much to think about since his return from Germany and France. In the black flowering of German industry, in the despairing delirium of France, in the feverish agitation of all Europe, he had for the first time in his life felt himself lost and bewildered and useless—pushed aside, as it were, by tumultuous things whirling along towards—— Towards what? Something too remote for his eyes to reach, too incomprehensible for his mind to imagine. All life, it seemed, was on an *autobahn*, and the fields on either hand were sown to the road's edge, machine sown, artificially fertilised, synthetically manured. There was only the tumult rushing on along the smooth concrete of the *autobahn*, and the fields on either hand were sown to the road's edge, contrived fields that allowed no chink of earth between where a man might loiter or a weed grow casually.

It had depressed him, the overwhelming feeling of not belonging to it; he had felt old and tired and obsolete, an object for amused curiosity, like his grandfather's cabinet of flints and bones.

And coming back to Kalymnos from that frenzied world— with the taut faces and calculating eyes, which by conjunction made calculating machines, with the pell-mell Gadarene rush down crowded slopes of steel and chromium and plastic and nylon and soda ash and plutonium—had awakened him to the very implausibility of his own being, of his dependence upon an archaic existence where men still wrestled nature with their bare hands, as if nature *mattered*: where fortune *had* to wait upon the twist of the seasons and the gloomy favours of the sea.

For a time the excited anticipation of the reports on the diving team they had sent to Australia had lessened the depression ; and then the cable had arrived to inform him of the failure of the experiment. Not until then, not until he had seen in the crumpled yellow cable form on his desk the dull grit of hopelessness and failure, had he realised how much it had meant to him, how much he wanted it to succeed.

" And there's another thing," old Petros was saying, standing before him with his gnarled arms swinging. Age seemed to have shrunk him downward, so that his arms appeared far too long for his body. Standing there, so small and wizened and brown, with the little simian face and the long arms swinging, he looked like a trained chimpanzee dressed up in painters' overalls. " We haven't got the men now, not the way we used to have, *Kérios*. They're all going away, *Kérios*, all going away. All leaving the island. This season none of them will make enough money to live through winter. They'll all go, too. The good ones, the young ones, they're the ones they take. Strong. They want 'em strong, *Kérios*. Next year, you see, it'll be hard to get divers, any sort of divers, good or bad. Engineers too. They can't get engineers even in Piræus now. You see." In his vehemence the great yellow tooth appeared to jiggle on the ancient jaw. " You only need one bad season and then the season after you won't have any divers to man a fleet. You wait and see, *Kérios* ! I watch 'em filling in their forms. They tell lies too, *Kérios*. They think I don't know." He sniggered cunningly. " They think Petros is too old and too stupid to understand. But I understand, oh, yes ! I see 'em filling in the forms. Writing down that they're farmers and labourers, just so they get permits to go to some other country. *Po-po-po-po-po !* Farmers ! Labourers ! "

" I'm not sure that one can altogether blame them, Petros," Pelacos said sadly. " What else is there for them ? "

" What *else* ? " The old man stared at him in astonishment. " When your grandfather was alive, *Kérios*, he wouldn't have asked what else. Nor the divers, for that matter. Why, they would have thrown someone in the sea if he said they were

farmers or labourers. They were proud men, *Kérios*, proud!
Not like now, snivelling around telling all those lies, pretending
to be what they aren't just so they can run away. They were
proud then!"

"It may not be so easy to be proud, Petros, when you are
also hungry," said Pelacos quietly. "I think the men to-day
are as good as they ever were, but I'm not sure that they have
the same chance to show it." *When your grandfather was alive*—
for thirty years they had been saying it. *When your grandfather
was alive* . . . Oh, yes, but it had been easier then to be so
many things—to be proud and expansive and generous and big,
to bestride the life of the island as if you had spawned it all,
to be charitable as Christ and omnipotent as a tribal god. Yes, it
had been easier then because there had been *time*.

All his life had been spent in the shadow of the legend of
the great Akilleous Pelacos, until he had sometimes come to
think of himself as a pygmy camped at the foot of some great
colossus, cringing for the night beneath its huge stone toe,
humbled by its impassive majesty. Even the people, the older
ones, still looked back to the time of his grandfather as to some
golden age of beneficence and plenty, as the ancients must
have looked back to the lost paradise of Cronus, as all the world
looked back wistfully to its vanished Edens.

He had been a great and patriarchal figure, proud of the fact
that there was no man on the island not known to him by name,
ordering feasts and festivals for the people like an ancient king,
showering the island with his bounty and his kindliness. In
the time of Akilleous Pelacos—yes, they would still tell you—
in the time of Akilleous Pelacos no man had suffered hunger or
want, no orphan was unsheltered, no child unclad, and at
Christmas and Easter the streets were abrim with his gifts. But
he had had *time*, time for everything : time to build the massive
fortune of the House of Pelacos, time to have the English
architect out to erect the vast and gloomy mansion that became
his palace, time to walk through its endless pompous rooms,
time to play the tribal patriarch and god, time to be benevolent
and philanthropic, time to go mountaineering in the Swiss Alps
in a deerstalker cap and ulster and tweed knickerbockers, time

to catalogue his knick-knacks and to quarry his flints and bones from the caves of Damos—time for *everything*!

But time was a compressible substance, and since then it had diminished, grown smaller and smaller and always more elusive, and neither the son of Akilleous Pelacos nor his grandson had ever been able to rival the leisured splendour and magnificence of his personality. Priam Pelacos—even the name he had given his son testified the old patriarch's lordliness—had tried and failed. Paul Pelacos had never tried. Instead, he had retreated from the intimidating shadow of the colossus, from its overawing grandeur, and he had built his own small castle and painted it white and put things into it that were selfish but beautiful.

In withdrawing from the colossus had he perhaps withdrawn too far? In withdrawing from the huge tribal legend had he perhaps created his own legend, a smaller thing, twisted and distorted? But if he had—did it any longer matter? There was no time for legends, for any sort of legend. There were no legends on the *autobahn*. For how long, he wondered, would the bearded, benevolent, slow-striding figure of Akilleous Pelacos have survived the rushing torrent of the *autobahn*? He would have been overthrown, his favourite stick of ebony smashed into fragments; in ten seconds he would have been trampled to death.

Time, that was it. Time had changed its character. It was no longer something placid and rewarding; it had become venomous and cruel. The Australian experiment had failed because they had wanted to do everything in a hurry and they had bungled it. Quickly, quickly, quickly! If it does not work we shall try something else. . . . Get out of the way, you've had *your* chance. . . .

Yes, he had had his chance, his chance to do something magnificent and audacious, something that surpassed in splendour anything that any Pelacos had ever done before. The Pelacos name ended with him. He had no sons who could embark on the bold adventure, the journey into this unpredictable to-morrow, but at least he could have been the architect of the adventure, renouncing his own heritage and all that the island meant to him, if necessary sacrificing everything he possessed, to send the Kalymnian people on their joyful, brave journey to a new future on the other side of the world. Old Akilleous Pelacos would have done it like Moses, carrying his patriarchy along with them; the grandson's way would have been more subtle, more civilised, more memorable. And in a distant continent the people, *his* people, would remember him as the last and the greatest Pelacos, the man who had sacrificed himself so that his compatriots might thrive. " One day men will turn their backs on the things they love and understand and they will fly to the moon "—how wonderful it had sounded nine months ago, when he had spoken to Leigh, how brave and flamboyant and audacious ! And later, dreaming about it, elaborating his own plans, how hungry he had become for the fulfilment of the dream !

And now they had bungled it, and there was nothing to foresee but the slow, stinking suppuration of a sore that would never heal, everything rotting away in a loathsome, gangrenous decay. The young men fleeing the island which had for three thousand years sustained and nourished them and their forefathers—lying to escape from it ! The old ones, the unwanted, embittered and hopeless, hating their miserable, poverty-stricken imprisonment. The fathers of large families resenting their own children because they bound them to the anguished torment of the doomed island. That was it ! The island was doomed. One bad season and all the life would drain out of it, and nothing would be left behind but the broken, unwanted fragments of the island's people, human potsherds tossed aside in the mad scurry of the *autobahn*.

" Yes, yes, Petros," he said, quietly, although he had no idea of what the old man was saying. " And now I must go." He lifted himself from the packing case and walked away slowly. Petros, his mouth hanging on the middle of a sentence that would never be completed, the yellow tooth standing like a monument, watched him go ; as the tall thin figure vanished through the doorway, he shook his head slowly.

Paul Pelacos walked out along the road to Lavassi and when he returned he took the steps to the higher level and came back past the big church of Saint Stephanos. Who would sell the icons this Christmas for Saint Stephanos? One of the domes and two of the walls were Manoli's, he reflected. Manoli! He was keeping his boats out for the winter. A risky business, but it was like Manoli to do it that way, to take risks when he wanted something badly. Perhaps he, Paul Pelacos, had been partly to blame for the bungling of the Australian experiment: had he sent Manoli, might it not have succeeded? Manoli had initiative and resource and a genius for adapting himself to the immediacy of a problem. Had he been influenced against Manoli, against his own sounder judgments, by his purely personal misgivings about the man? Perhaps he had. Had he allowed his decision to be swayed by that odious fellow Vraxos, with his spurious civic pride and his barely concealed enmity for Manoli? It was unlikely that he had, for he had been acutely conscious of the man's self-interest; yet how could one judge the subtleties of another man's influence when it ran concurrent with one's own secret desires and prejudices?

Paul Pelacos sighed. Well, it was too late now. The matter was over and done with. The file had been taped up and put away to gather dust on a shelf. Kalymnos would perish in a different manner.

At the top of the steps he paused and looked back at the church and then he went down towards the sea.

What a queer story that had been about the old diver, Stavros Cudakilis, lighting all the candles and then drowning himself. He had been one of the Pelacos divers, too, Paul recalled, remembering that frightful cruise of the *Seleni* and all the months of legal entanglements that followed. How curious that he could still see the face of the lawyer quite clearly—the way the man's eye twitched and the two big warts at the side of his nose and even the frayed cord of his spectacles—but could not longer remember what Stavros Cudakilis looked like. Would old Akilleous Pelacos have allowed him to die in such a peculiar fashion, he wondered, and without even remembering what he looked like?

Irini had set up her easel in a corner of the orchard by the old walnut tree, and she was doing a finished painting from one of the sketches she had made during the summer in Brostá.

He sat in the deck chair for a while watching her.

" Do you know if Doctor Telfs is still on Kós " he asked, after a time.

" I think he is, yes."

" You like him, do you not ? "

" Very much." She turned from the canvas.

" I think I shall go in and drop him a note. I should like to have him over for a few days to stay with us. There are some matters I should like to discuss with him." He rose and walked across to the easel to examine her painting with his head slightly on one side. " Very nice, my dear," he said, and then : " I am thinking of leaving Kalymnos," he added, and walked away.

5

MORGAN COULD feel the pain in his lips, and that made him yawn again and he tried to check it. He was forever yawning these days—each day had become a struggle against an over-powering ennui induced by poor diet and constant exposure to extremes of climate—and whenever he yawned it cracked his lips open again and the blood trickled down his chin. Nearly all the men had the same black gaps in their lips, and it hurt when the salt got into them, more than ever now that the water was getting cold.

It was queer how you didn't seem to notice the difference in the water until the wind scooped it up and flung it in your face. Or when the breeze would come across the sea in fitful squalls that set the loose gear rattling and then sigh away into agitated cat's-paws that ruffled the water into spreading fans all the way to the horizon ; the breeze would be warm but it would leave your skin chilled, as if the sweat had dried too quickly.

Three nights before a gale had come hard and stinging

from the south, filling the air with a red gritty dust so dense that the riding lights of the boats fifty feet away had been obliterated. Then the rain had fallen, quite warm at first and then suddenly cutting like ice. When dawn came all the boats were coated with a thick red slime, like congealing blood, and an albatross came in on silent wings out of a flat, slatey sky. For a long time it hung motionless above the boats with yellow, downcast eyes, as if it had some tidings to impart to them, and then it went away with a single slow beat of its wings, high above the small birds that were flocking southwards, skimming the crests of the waves.

It was after that that the skin divers had begun to complain about how cold it was getting. Even Dionyssos, who was the best of the skin men, had managed only seven dives that morning, and after each dive he would huddle, shivering, on the floorboards of the boat with his coat wrapped around him, and Morgan could see the black, ugly blotches on his flesh, around the eyes and mouth and just below the heart—the sort of blotches the men would get at the beginning of the season before they got accustomed to the cold deep currents.

" All right," Manoli said quietly. " Let's get started."

His words were for Morgan and Elias, but the men were suddenly tense and silent, their faces turned towards Manoli with a sort of bitter watchfulness, waiting to hear what most of them had guessed when the *Elektra* went in to Tripoli for the new stores.

There were more than sixty of them crowding the deck and the lower rigging of the big schooner, for only the boat boys had been left aboard the four *aktaramathes*, and it was something of a shock to Morgan to see them all assembled together—all the gaunt, bearded, exhausted faces, burned black as Berbers by the sun, and the suffering, suspicious eyes turned to the big man on the afterdeck.

The sun was within ten minutes of its setting. It no longer sank beneath the level line of the sea but went down attended by a liveried splendour of storm clouds, far to the southwards across the humped sand drifts of Africa. The angle of its light gave a theatrical look to the faces crowded above the tattered weather cloths. It was odd how many of them seemed strangers to him now.

Manoli hoisted himself up and sat astride the thick tiller and looked around at all the expectant faces. " Well, it's the twelfth of November," he said calmly, " and about this time we should be thinking of stowing the gear and heading back home." He stopped and looked around again, but there was not a movement or a sound from the ring of dark, expectant faces, and Manoli grinned.

" But if we go back now," he said, still speaking in a quiet, easy voice as if he were discussing the weather or the best way of splicing on a new block, " if we go back with all the crap we've taken we're all going to have a lean winter. What we've got so far won't cut up to much—maybe five million drachmae each man." He shrugged. " A little more, a little less. Whichever way it is it won't buy much fun at home this winter."

He looked away, again waiting for somebody to speak, staring to the northward past the bleached hulls of the anchored boats, as if he could see across the width of the Mediterranean to the rocky mountains of Kalymnos. The men watched him in silence, and one or two of them lowered their eyes to the deck, almost guiltily, as if they felt themselves responsible for the meagre, scraggy sponges packed into the hold below their feet.

Manoli turned to them. " So we're staying out," he said simply and grinned. " We're staying out here through winter. We're going to get sponges, lots of sponges."

Morgan was looking at Dionyssos and he saw the diver's fingers jump involuntarily to his chest ; and as Dionyssos made his cross, he saw Morgan looking at him and grinned sheepishly and shoved both hands in his pockets.

" While the weather holds we'll run all four boats," said Manoli. " And we'll run them hard." He hoisted his leg over the tiller and slid to the deck. He had said what he had to say. " We've got two barrels of retzina left," he added, almost as an afterthought. " Elias says we should keep one for Christmas."

Milos, one of the *skafendros* from the *Saint Stephanos*, scratched his head and grinned. " You keep that barrel, maybe it all sours up by Christmas. That's six weeks away. I noticed a peppery taste that last barrel. Maybe it gets as sour as that lousy meat we have to eat! We have both barrels now, all of us can get properly drunk!"

And that was all there was to it. Morgan watched with a lingering sense of astonishment as Manoli and Elias trundled the two blue barrels down to the hatch cover. Manoli had made no appeal to them, given them no encouragement. There had been no mention of the bad luck that had dogged them since the death of Christos and Costas, no promise of any future change in their fortunes. Manoli had simply told them, without pleadings or recriminations, what he intended doing, and the men had accepted it as a thing that must be done. And there they were, crowding around the two blue barrels, shouting and laughing and joking like children at a picnic!

It was neither the wine nor the thought of the wine that had loosened the faces of the men, drained them of that brooding cynical bitterness with which they had come aboard the *Okeanos* to hear what their captain had to tell them. It was the fact that the decision had been made for them, the doubt removed. For the time being Manoli's decision had emptied out of them the accumulated strains and tensions and misgivings; they were vessels to be renewed. This additional imposition of three more months of slavery, of a continuing and greater hardship, of a peril that would increase with every day it was protracted—all this for the moment was something that had become another man's responsibility. It would all come back, for most of them were already very close to the breaking point and the weeks to come would be a constant struggle, less against the sea than against the oppressive fears and tensions that lurked in their own exhausted minds and weary bodies.

At the moment they looked to Manoli, and Manoli was astride the main boom of the schooner, with a big tin can of retzina in his fist, and he was shouting "*Si-yia!*" to them, as if it was a challenge.

"He's built big that bastard," said Elias admiringly, and he gave half a finger to the engine wheel as the swell came up astern and kicked at them. They could feel the sea twisting them as it ran beneath the keel, and Elias took his eyes off Manoli to watch the upward stab of the stempost, waiting for the jarring thud of the *Okeanos'* towline when the swell reached the schooner. Beyond the roll of the schooner, across the black ridges of water, Morgan could see the anchorage towards which they were being towed—a bare and waterless harbour with ridges of white clay running down to the sea's edge.

Elias' fingers were very quick and deft on the engine wheel as he nursed the *Ikaros* along, trying to keep the strain off the towline because it was all frayed away and weathered. The swell had a nasty, curving bite to it and even with the big schooner hauling them in it wasn't easy to handle the *Elektra* with the rudder gone. The storm had not lasted ten minutes, but it had ripped away the rudder and the protective cages around the propeller that kept the air lines from fouling, and split the boom half-way down its length. And now they were running for a shelter where repairs could be carried out. It had all happened so quickly that the last two divers to come up were still sitting on the trestle by the foremast, wrapped in blankets and smoking the dry, stale cigarettes that had to sustain them in the absence of food.

Elias flipped the wheel and the jar of the towrope came soft and cushioned, and he turned his attention once more to Manoli.

" This damned rudder we've lost," he said, " maybe they think that'll give them a few days' rest, but he'll put the bastards on to one of the other boats and make them work twice as hard." Elias grinned. " I know him ! "

Manoli was down on his haunches before one of the divers, his eyes and fingertips searching the cold, wasted body for the telltale marks of paralysis, the black mottlings on the skin, the little lumps on neck and shoulders.

" The poor devils could do with a few days' rest," said Morgan sympathetically. " They're almost at the end of their tether, you know."

Elias smiled. " You give them a few days' rest now you might as well pack them up and send them home. You wouldn't get any more work out of them. They're scared already. What you've got to do now is drive them. Manoli knows."

" There's a law of averages," said Morgan. " That's why they're scared. And the way they are now, accidents could happen too easily . . . one little mistake . . ." He spread his hands meaningly.

" Sure, it's harder now. It's worse than when Costas and Christos went. It's not so bad when things happen quickly and suddenly . . . you get used to that. It's when a thing stays with you a long time. It's like a worm that gets into your brain and starts boring. You can't see from outside which way it's boring, or how far it's gone, or what damage it's done. This rudder we've lost, that's the way it happened : the worms were in the wood there, eating everything away near that topside pin— but you couldn't know that from outside." He braced his legs to the lift of the swell beneath them. " You've got to keep driving them," he said thoughtfully. " You let them stop, we start losing men."

Morgan knew that he was speaking the truth. There was something terrible and pitiable in the spectacle of the men fighting against the fear lodged immovably in their minds. They were constantly on the point of malingering, of exaggerating their condition of exhaustion, of feigning sickness, of inventing particular dangers in the waters below that did not exist at all. He could amost see their minds working as they tried to devise some reason, *any* reason, that might stop them having to go down again, to go again on that one particular dive that might, that just *might*, be the one that brought the crippling paralysis or death. And yet the astonishing thing was that not one of them ever did malinger. They thought about it. They never stopped thinking about it. But then they would move up along the diving lines to the forward ladders and the helmets would be bolted on, and they would go down again.

" Since we had to stop using the skin divers," Elias went on, " why do you think Manoli does all those dives himself ? When it's weedy or tricky, or there's a swell moving the couplings on the air lines, why do you think he stays down a few minutes longer than anyone else ? He drives the bastards, sure, and curses them, and spits in their eye for the crap they bring up . . . but you look at him now."

Manoli had finished his examination of the two divers and he was helping one of them, old Jacobus, into his sweater, and chiding him because he felt cold. Manoli himself was stripped to the waist, wearing only a pair of thin, striped cotton trousers rolled up above his knees. He was standing there in the cold wind, grinning and joking with Jacobus, his left arm lividly marked with the scars the shark's teeth had left. Morgan guessed that this too, was his way of making light of the cold that he knew was gripping the bones of his men and boring into their brains. Cold was a worm, too, like fear.

"The bastards are trying," Elias said morosely, "but they can't keep it up much longer. Not if we don't get sponges." His fingers stiffened on the engine wheel as the *Okeanos* began to turn slowly, heading close inshore past the neck of a narrow promontory where an Arab boy wrapped in a dirty sheepskin sat among his flock of scraggy goats watching them. When the anchor went down the boy fled, leaping from rock to rock and disappearing over the ridge. "We've got to get sponges," Elias said broodingly.

They hadn't been anchored ten minutes before the brawl began. It began in the waist of the ship, with two of the divers arguing about the best way the boom should be spliced, and in a moment they were standing face to face, screaming at each other like women and hammering with their fists.

Morgan began to move down the deck, but he saw Manoli looking at him and there was something in the big man's eyes that checked him. It was horrible to have to stand and watch the fight, because the two men stood toe to toe, not dodging or feinting at all, beating at each other's faces with their fists. And it went on until both faces were raw, bloody pulps and the men could only claw and scratch at each other, and then they fell together to the deck, moaning and sobbing.

Manoli leaned over the side and hauled in a pailful of sea water and flung it over their mashed faces.

And then he came down the deck to Morgan and Elias and said, "When we get this rudder fixed, we're all going back up there to Benghazi. That's where the big bastards are. They're there *somewhere*. I could smell them in May, and I can smell them now. They're still there."

When he had gone forward again to see about getting the work boat over the side so that the rudder could be looked at, Elias shook his head wonderingly. " I don't know what it is about him," he said, almost as if he was speaking to himself. " He's built big, that's all."

" You won't go back yet ? " Morgan asked Manoli. It was Christmas Day and they were seated together on the curved rail of the stern, waiting for the last man in the diving line to come up. The wind off the African desert was light but cold, and there was a desolate empty look to the sea. Morgan remembered the Christmas Day of the year before, with the kids in the streets blowing up their coloured *fooskas* and Manoli storming the café's patrons with his paper icons for Saint Stephanos and the smell of food cooking all the way up the hill to Mina's house and Manoli chasing Homer Vraxos along the clifftop near Saint Peter's.

" If the boats'll stand another month of it, I can," Manoli was saying with a grin. " We're making money now, and we're saving it, too. The men—another month and it'll cut up into a sizeable share, and that'll be three months they haven't been able to spend it on wine and beer and gamble it away. When we get back the bastards will live like kings ! "

Morgan nodded. It was hard to realise that thirty-five days could have made so profound a difference. It had been on the twentieth of November, eight months to the day since they had sailed out of Kalymnos, that they had come back to the Benghazi beds, the beds that had killed Costas and Christos. On that day Morgan had found himself almost believing in omens, for it had been a freakish day of warm sunshine and a calm, summer-blue sea, and on the first dive at sixty metres, Manoli had brought up twelve fine sponges.

It was part of the inexplicable mystery of the sea that in the very waters where, months before, they had searched unavailingly, the sponges began to come next day with the first

morning dives from the *Saint Stephanos*. It had delighted Manoli
that it was the *Saint Stephanos* that broke the run of bad luck, and
he had jumped around all day, playful as a child, and he kept
making jokes about Stavros and his candles. By midday all four
boats had been taking sponges, good sponges. In the weeks
since then there had been setbacks—gales would force them to
run for shelter, and all the boats were feeling the sea fatigue
and there was seldom a day without some mishap to gear or
rigging. In the storm that had split her boom, the *Ikaros* had
strained her stempost, and the pump was working most of the day,
and on the bottoms of all the boats the weed was thick as a
man's hair.

" You know, it's a funny thing," Manoli was saying, " but
if you asked the men to go back now, maybe they wouldn't
want to go. And it isn't just that they're greedy either, now that
the sponges are coming."

" I think I know what it is," said Morgan. " I think you
know it, too. That's why you kept at them, kicking them along."

Manoli laughed. " It's their job, and mine if it comes to
that, to go out and get sponges. It doesn't do them any good to
go back and have people think we can't get sponges. It doesn't
do them any good, and it doesn't do me. Maybe I've got a big
head, but I've been pretty lucky for a few years now, and I don't
like the idea of going back and having people think the luck's
run out on me. Maybe by the time we get back we have something to show them that makes them forget what happened here
in May. Next year they'll want to sail with me again, not look
around for some other captain." He paused and smiled meaningly
at Morgan. " Or run away to Australia," he said.

It was true as far as it went, Morgan reflected, but there was
more to it than that. The men were driven now by a queer sort
of stubborn enthusiasm. Their struggle had become a direct
contest with the sea, brutal and vicious and obstinate and un-
forgiving. They were cold and hungry and weary, but they had
become masters of the situation and they intended to make the
sea pay dear for what they had endured.

" You didn't decide to stay out only because of what people
might say in Kalymnos," Morgan said. " That day you made

the decision, that was the day Elias came back with the letters.
Yes, you told the men about it later, but that was when you
made up your mind. It was the day you decided you were going
to marry Mina."

"That's right," Manoli said quietly. "Maybe I'd have
decided that anyway, letter or no letter. Maybe I'd have decided
to stay out just the same. Once you turn your back on the
sea you can't face it again. If you let it lick you once, it's licked
you forever. Like Stavros." He reached down to scratch his
knee. "These scabs, once they begin to heal they get bloody
itchy," he said. "That letter Stavros wrote, did I ever show it
to you ? "

"No."

"It was full of some funny things." He glanced at Morgan
with a vaguely puzzled expression. "There were things he
told me, I never knew, things about Mina . . . things like that.
I suppose I just didn't bother to ask about them, and that Mina,
she's a deep one, she wouldn't say anything."

"Then it was because of Mina, really, that you decided to
stay ? "

Manoli's eyes met his for a moment, and then he stared
thoughtfully across the deck, without saying anything.

Morgan tried to picture Mina in the little cove at Santa
Katerina, but it was too far back in time now for one to seize
the significance of it. The picture was there, but the meaning
of it was lost. She would marry Manoli, of course—so far it
was only Manoli's decision, but it never occurred to him to doubt
that she would accept it. It was queer how the thought of it
could hurt him so much, even when that was the way he wanted
it to happen for Manoli. . . .

"No, not Mina—Stavros," Manoli said at last, turning to
him. "It was something he said in his letter. It's stuck in my
mind. 'There's nothing to be ashamed of in being beaten,'
he said, 'but it's a terrible thing to be beaten by a bastard.' "
Manoli looked away awkwardly, as if he were suddenly aware
of having disclosed the private soul of a man who was dead.
"It was full of funny things, that letter," he said quickly, and
then he laughed. " And then the poor bastard burning all those

candles ! I wouldn't have wanted him to think I wasn't grateful."

He lowered himself to the deck. " Here's Fortes up now," he said, with a sigh of relief, which, Morgan guessed, was not so much for the reappearance of the copper-helmeted diver as for his own escape from an embarrassing self-analysis. " Let's get those sponge nets over the side."

6

IT WAS five o'clock, the hour of *peripató*. Pelacos, Irini and Telfs sauntered along the broad walk, less inclined to talk than to watch the other people who walked, neither aimless nor purposeful, up and down the street and along the water front by the market and down behind the Customs House to the end of the breakwater.

The slow procession of the people in the golden afternoon possessed a queer sort of formalised rhythm, Telfs realised, as if all the townspeople had come out to perform this elaborate stylised ritual dance, to appease the day's urgencies and re-establish the proper pace of life. The women were out, too, in the evenings, walking together or in company with their men ; at dusk they would vanish again into the crowded mystery of their little houses with the great built-in shelf beds and the cook-ing smells and the clamour of children ; and in the *tavernas* and the coffee houses and around the gambling tables the men would reoccupy the town.

It was odd, this new insistence on the part of Pelacos that all of them should take part in the evening promenade—odd and rather sad in a way. All the stiff aloofness of the man had gone, and with it much of his air of assurance. He was no longer Paul Pelacos, the patrician of the town, wrapped in the tacit and comforting warmth of self-esteem, of the assurance of his own superiority. He was altogether a different man, respond-ing with a quick, shy eagerness to the greetings of those strollers who recognised him, pausing to talk to them, looking almost wistfully after some who passed him by without a glance, wondering who they were. It seemed as if Pelacos, having come to his decision to leave Kalymnos, had found a final, desperate longing to identify himself with those things on which for so many years he had deliberately turned his back.

They ended their *peripató* at the coffee house which Telfs usually shunned because it had a soda fountain inside and glass cases of sweets and syrups and cookies—it reminded him too much of an American drugstore. He didn't have anything in particular against American drugstores, but he didn't want them in Greece. Pelacos always took coffee there when Irini was with them ; if he was alone or in masculine company he went elsewhere. They took an outside table beneath the salt tree.

" Well, Telfs, now that you have had some time to think about what I said, what is your opinion ? " Pelacos said, and clapped his hands for the waiter.

" It's not for me to have an opinion," Telfs replied thoughtfully. " It's a big decision for anyone to make. It's your money and it's your life."

" My dear Telfs, the decision *has* been made. There will be ample money for the necessary building and for all the essential endowment. It can be a very big thing, something of which we need not be ashamed. There will be an adequate settlement remaining for Irini and more than sufficient to enable me to live quietly abroad, even perhaps to purchase a little villa in Hydra. There are some pleasant villas there and the view across the Gulf of Hermione is quite charming. As for Irini I am convinced she must go away from here. The island is crushing her. Her spiritual home, I feel, is Paris or London." He glanced affectionately at his daughter.

" Yes, but what if you do it all and go away into this self-imposed exile and then find, too late, that *your* spiritual home is still Kalymnos ? " Telfs asked pointedly.

Pelacos smiled. " My spiritual home, Telfs, will always be Kalymnos. But I have not the least intention of declining into a maudlin nostalgia, of spending my retirement repining something lost to me. When I was a younger man I had quite a flair

for writing. And for a good many years now I have harboured
a subdued ambition to write a real history of Kalymnos—a unique
story, Telfs, and a magnificent one, and somebody must tell it.
It will be something to occupy my mind, perhaps to possess it,
while I look across from Hydra at the Troezen peninsula. In
doing this I shall belong to Kalymnos more entirely, I shall be
closer to it than I have ever been while living here." He spoke
with an earnestness and a humility which Telfs found both
moving and impressive ; yet, had he not himself once harboured
a subdued ambition to sit down somewhere quietly and to write
about something ?

"Enough of that," Pelacos said briskly. "Is it feasible ?
That is the crux of the matter."

"Sure, it's feasible," Telfs said. "It's always feasible to
try. The Russians, you know, have spent years in research on
this underwater paralysis. They haven't got anywhere. They
know what causes it. They don't know how to prevent it."
He shrugged. "You've got to keep chasing these things."

"There is much to be found out about many things, Telfs.
We do not know yet what an aspirin really does to the body's
metabolism. But you must remember that the medical aspect
would be only one section of the laboratory's activities. There
would be all the scientific side, all the work of research into the
promise and prospects of this untouched world beneath the sea
—marine archæology, so many things. And what place more
fitting for its centre than this island ? We could make Kalymnos
the focal point of a wonderful human adventure."

"It could be important, yes. I wouldn't like to say it's a
way of saving the island."

"It is a way of saving *some* of it," said Pelacos. "Of saving
the best of it, perhaps. At least of giving it a new purpose, in
place of the old. And then there is the other aspect—the centres
at Brostá and Myrtiés. In the western Mediterranean there are
thousands now who are engrossed with this new world beneath
the surface of the sea. It has become an important form of
recreation, a craze—oh, much more than that, a new source of
adventure and excitement in a world where all the old forms of
adventure and excitement have staled. We shall give them

hostels and schools and clubs and boats, and we shall give them the Ægean. They can live here with every facility, they can seek the sunken city at Télendos. . . . They will bring money into the island, resuscitate it." He looked first at Telfs, then at his daughter, and his eyes were shining.

Telfs smiled to himself. There was a curious piquancy in hearing Paul Pelacos talk of finding a lost Atlantis. " Sure," he said, and grinned. " What you aim to do is to make this place a sort of capital of the undersea world. A sort of Washington, D.C., of Thalassia or Pelagia, or whatever you want to call it." He turned to Irini. " And how do you feel about it, Miss Pelacos ? Don't you have any objections to your birthright being thrown away on something that sounds as if it's come out of the mind of one of these science-fiction writers ? Or do you plan to be the first Princess of Pelagia ? " He chuckled.

" I think it's Daddy's decision," she said seriously. " At first, when I heard him telling you about it, I think I was sceptical. It sounded impossible, visionary—the sort of thing, as you say, that you might read about in a not very plausible book. Now I'm not sure. Now I think it would be rather wonderful. It seems to me to be something *worth* doing."

" Oh, yes, I've heard of crazier schemes that turned out in the end to make good sense." He glanced at Pelacos. " Have you worked out how much this scheme is likely to cost you ? "

Pelacos nodded. " Not to the last cent, but in general estimate, yes. To establish the laboratory, and the centres, construction work, equipment, personnel—approximately five billion drachmae, say two hundred thousand dollars in your money, American money. Another ten or fifteen billion in endowment. Let us say six to eight hundred thousand dollars in all."

Telfs whistled softly.

" I have adequate funds," Pelacos said calmly. " I have well-invested capital abroad, apart from our business here. I dare say the sale of property alone would realise that much money, possibly more. All this money has been derived from Kalymnos, either directly or indirectly. Some of it can be returned to the island."

It was a way, Pelacos reflected, of maintaining the descendancy —the true descendancy. The fish in the sea, the weeds on the hills, the eternally flowering forests of the sponges—they had their cycles and their seasons, but they had their descendancy fixed and inflexible. When he sat down to begin his book, he must have this theme fixed in his mind ; his history must spring not from the stale words set down by others but from the old Kalymnian rocks and its sea-beaten shore. It would have to grow out of the island itself, to which the people belonged as harmoniously and as inseparably as the rocks and weeds belong to the mountains, the fish to the sea. The Kalymnians would not seem some queer animals who came for a time to prance and posture and then were suddenly blown away and forgotten. Americans and Australians—they were the new races, the children among the nations, offering their aid and succour to this the oldest of the islands. It was their brave time, their singing time, but would time roll over them, too, as it had rolled over all the others—the Persians and the Romans, the splendour of Byzantium and Ottoman grandeur ? And would this trivial little thing of descendancy survive, this flimsy and half-forgotten little thread persisting through it all, this Greek thing that went on and on forever, enduring and everlasting ?

He could see the old madman, Stephanos, coming along the street towards them, hesitating and lost among the walking people, his vague eyes searching the passing faces for one face that might give him hearing. Could it be Paul Pelacos ? The lost, questing eyes seemed to be seeking him among the crowd, the mumbling mouth framing his name—Where is Paul Pelacos ? He will listen to me. It happened to him, too, the same way, except that he lost only two sons, and I lost five. . . . The ragged figure wandered slowly through the crowd, looking from side to side as if there was something he had lost—Where is Paul Pelacos ? He will understand. He will listen to me. . . .

And Paul Pelacos, watching the madman approach, had a sudden hope, anguished and sickening, that Stephanos would come to him.

The vacant eyes met his for a moment and turned away, unseeing ; the broken figure shuffled on towards the wharves.

"Poor devil," said Telfs, studying Pelacos curiously. "I took him up to Athens three years ago. I thought there might be something we could do." He shook his head. "Schizophrenia. We could have tried a leucotomy, I guess, but at the best it would have made only a genial, unsuffering animal out of him. I guess it's best to let him be the way he is. At least he's in Greece. You people don't give much attention to your lunatics, but you aren't ashamed of them, you don't laugh at them. Crazy people belong to places just the same as anyone else, provided you let them belong. Do you know, when I was a kid there was always a cretin or two in the neighbourhood, and every place you went had its village idiot. You don't see them any more. They're locked away, I guess."

"It's a terrible, pitiable story about Stephanos," Irini said. "He was a rich man once, before it happened, and now look at him. And there isn't anybody any longer who'll even listen to him. It's all he has left, to be able to talk about it, and nobody listens."

I would listen to him, thought Pelacos sadly, but he has no wish to talk to me. I would listen to him, and I would understand. "There really is no hope whatever of a cure?" he said.

"It's not in the book," said Telfs. "He's not a predictable cure, nor even a likely one, whatever you did. That leaves only the inexplicable factors. A shock maybe could restore his sanity, just the same as a shock robbed him of it. But where do you look up the formula for the particular sort of shock that would do it? The brain's a funny instrument. It's balanced on a razor-edge, and once its jiggled off balance it's not easy to get it back. With old Stephanos I'm not even sure it would be wise to try. It's been eleven, twelve years, and what he'd wake up to wouldn't be a funny story like Rip van Winkle." He shrugged. "Well—now, let's get back to this project of yours," he said.

"Ah, yes," said Pelacos absently. The bomb had taken the whole of the wall out, and the two faces were side by side in the fallen rubble, all powdered over white like plaster casts of people. And the other face, the face he had hidden away from everybody for seven years . . .

7

THEY COULD see the arms of the windmills on the flat tongue of Kós and the spray and surf boiling over the shallows, and the sea all the way across to Pserimos was dark and angry and slashed by whitecaps.

It was somehow fitting that they should come in on such a day, Morgan thought, with the wild sirocco bearing them home and all the air whistling and the sea singing them in with its deep, triumphant roar. The wind and the sea followed them, chasing them in, tumbling up astern of them, flinging spray at the gulls hanging in the cold rush of the day. To starboard the *Saint Stephanos* was prancing home in a smother of white, and the hull that had once been crimson was now a pale, faded pink streaked with rust and slime from the scuppers, and the curve of the bilge, when it rolled and lifted from the waves, was thick with a dark-green oily scum, like the coating on an old well. The *Okeanos* ran close to their port beam, so close that they could hear the thick thud of her bows hammering down into the seas and the hiss of the spindrift, flying almost across to the *Ikaros*. They could hear Elias singing at the wheel, and up on the fore-deck, by the heel of the bowsprit, the wind was flapping the trousers of the men clinging to the forestay and staring ahead for the first glimpse of Kalymnos. And when the bow of the schooner came sheering up out of the sea clear to the curve of the keel, the coated weeds shuddered and trembled like something alive.

There was an awkward, dragging swing to the big schooner as she wallowed home beside them, heavy with Manoli's *brika*.

Whatever had happened and whatever was yet to happen, Morgan realised, this was the moment essentially splendid. This was all experience purified and made magnificent: the weary ships shouldering home on the arms of a wild wind; the faces of the men clinging in the forestays, staring ahead through the spray, and all the tired, strained eyes alight with expectancy; and Manoli standing wide-legged on the deck with the tiller hooked beneath his arm, his face grave and calm, as if, in this richest moment of his triumph, he was possessed by an understanding of humility.

Cold sunshine broke through the clouds as they ran down from Point Cali, and it glittered on the mountains and the coloured scatter of the town and on the valley all the way up to Brostá, and it gleamed white on the high chapels on the cliffs.

The February kites were in the sky, tugging and dancing above the town, and as the boats ran in towards the breakwater the wild pealing of the bells of Saint Stephanos could be heard.

Manoli crossed himself, remembering Stavros and the candles, and then he looked at Morgan and grinned, and he was smiling as he took the *Ikaros* in.

Morgan, knowing what was to come, found his own sadness submerged in his joy for Manoli as the boats went in around the lighthouse, into the crowded harbour where the kites romped in the sky and the air swung to the clamour of the bells.

For a whole week one hundred and thirty men worked on the sponges which Manoli's boats had brought home, in the clipping room below Morgan's house and in five other sponge rooms through the town. The men from the boats clustered around the doors like possessive women, watching the steel shears snipping, and on the day of the sale they all went with Manoli to the salesroom, as if they were unwilling to relinquish what had been won so hardly from the sea.

They were fine sponges, the thick, strong sponges from Benghazi and Tripoli, and, coming at the end of a season which had seen a dearth even of medium-quality sponges, they brought every buyer in Kalymnos hurrying to the rooms.

Paul Pelacos walked with Manoli between the wired-in pens enclosing the heaped, tawny mounds, and occasionally he stopped and asked for a sponge to be tossed out to him and he squeezed it gently between his fingers and threw it back.

" They're all good," Manoli said and grinned. " I went down and picked them out myself."

" It would not surprise me if you had," said Pelacos. He glanced at the note-book in his hand. " You have one hundred and twelve bins. Let us say that ninety are the first quality, the balance mostly second quality, and nothing below third. I suggest that everything be regarded as one lot and that we bid as a single over-all purchase. On that basis I will be prepared to open the bidding at a million the oka. The third quality are not worth that price, the first quality much more."

Manoli glanced at him interestedly. " It suits me," he said, and jerked his thumb towards the salesroom. " They're hungry for good sponges in there. You open at a million, they might go high."

" I shall go higher," Pelacos said calmly. " Our boats had lean pickings in the summer."

" So did mine—in the summer."

" I hope you get a good price, Manoli, even if I have to pay it. You deserve it. It must have taken a lot of courage to keep the boats out, a lot of courage and perseverance. Now I want the sponges, *all* of them. I intend this to be my last season of buying, and I should like it to be a good one."

Manoli chuckled. " It will be the first time I've worked nine and a half months in a season for anyone, and it has to be for Paul Pelacos ! Well, let's go in and get started. I got to sell these sponges, and then I got things to do."

He was about to lead the way into the salesroom, but Pelacos checked him. " One other thing, Manoli," he said. " I wanted to say something to you about that Australian proposal, which unfortunately came to nothing. I wrote a letter to Leigh, perhaps he told you, but I did want you to know that——"

" That's slack water, Pelacos." Manoli cut him short. " That's slack water, and there's no point in fishing in it any longer. I know how you feel about it. Morgan explained it to me. We talked a lot about it. It wouldn't have made any difference, me going out, and besides I had things to do."

" It was so important to the future of this island, Manoli, and I cannot help feeling a sadness that it did not succeed."

" Life doesn't afford any time to be sad about things that can't be fixed by weeping. You're a smart man, Pelacos, and you've got education and I haven't, and I don't pay much attention to this business of philosophy. Down there off Tripoli at the end of the summer it looked bloody hopeless to me too. I'd spent six months taking peanuts, and I'd paid for them with the lives of two fine men. What was I supposed to do ? Sit on my tail and weep until someone heard me cry and came along to help me ? Come home with my tail between my legs so I could sit around all winter and watch the men starving who had dived for me, see them being driven off the island because they can't live here any longer ? I don't have any sort of philosophy about these things, and I don't have your education, but I know that *that* isn't the way it works. A friend of mine burned some candles for me—and candles maybe are better than philosophy if they're burned right—and then we all got together on the boats and talked it out. We went down and stayed down until we'd collected those goddam sponges there that you're going to start bidding for at a million the oka ! " For a moment he stared at the long line of sponge bins, and then he laughed. " Come on, let's go in and get started," he said happily. " I want to watch those faces—and yours."

PART FIVE

Vraxos

I

" It CAN all be done rationally," Tony Thaklios said. " It don't call for Manoli being impulsive or truculent or you being unreasonable," He enjoyed his role of go-between just for the opportunity of using the good words from his lexicon—*rationally, impulsive, truculent, unreasonable ;* that was a set of fine words for just one thing you had to get across—but he was sorry it had to be with Homer Vraxos. Vraxos had a way of turning his stomach somehow and making him feel depressed, and once you got depressed that was when the real words became elusive.

Besides that, he didn't like the look of Vraxos and he didn't like the smell of his room. He sat gingerly on the edge of the bed, and the bed smelled sour, as if the linen hadn't been washed in a long time. And there was a pile of rubbish in the corner that gave off a sort of stale, furry stink so you knew that if you rummaged around in it you'd find rat turds, maybe even a dead mouse. Vraxos was fastidious enough about his clothes—he was at the table pressing down on the big charcoal iron, getting the creases right in his checked pants so he could look smart as a whip at the *maskaras* at Brostá—it was a pity he didn't pay a bit more attention to sanitation. He was the sort of man who looked down his nose at the Kalymnian privies and was always shooting his mouth off about the hush-flush he'd had in Detroit, but if this room of his was any criterion—he dwelled happily for a moment on *criterion*—if this room was any criterion, Tony Thaklios wouldn't want to be caught short and have to go to his toilet !

There was another offensive smell, too, that the iron gave off, the steam off the damp pressing cloth ; it wasn't sour and it wasn't sweet, just sort of sickening.

"You got something dead in here, Homer?" Tony asked suspiciously. "There's a hell of a stink!"

Vraxos put the iron to one side and lifted his head, sniffing. "I don't smell anything," he said.

"Maybe you're used to it. There's a smell, all right. Some time you ought to try opening those windows, let a bit of air in." He nodded. "What I was saying is, there isn't any call for you being unreasonable."

"Manoli had plenty time to ask her to marry him. Maybe he gets what he's after without all the trouble, eh?" Vraxos leered at him across the table. "Then along comes some other guy who's willing to do it proper, taking into account she's no chicken and she's no virgin either, and Manoli sees this bit of nooky he gets for free slipping away from him and his nose goes out of joint. He had plenty time before."

"Maybe you'd like to come with me down to Mikali's, say all this to Manoli. He's waiting there. He wanted to come up here with me, but we talked him out of it. We didn't want no bother. These things can be negotiated without bother if people are reasonable." Tony smiled. "You say these things to Manoli, these things you just been saying, and we don't have bother on our hands any longer. What we have is justifiable homicide."

"He talks big," Vraxos said contemptuously.

"He acts big, too. Besides, this circumlocution is only wasting time. Manoli's going to marry her, and that's that. Okay, you paid for the kid to go off to London, arranged the permits and so on. You had expenses."

"I had plenty expenses, make no mistake about that!"

"Okay, Manoli takes over the responsibility for the kid now. You paid out money in the expectation of marrying Mina. Manoli pays the money over to you and that cleans it all up. No obligations. That's all we're discussing."

"He had plenty time before," Vraxos said stubbornly. "He wants her now, he's got to pay. He's got to pay plenty. I had big expenses. It's going to cost him a thousand dollars."

"It doesn't cost all that much to send a kid to London," Tony said softly. "Not even with the extras, it doesn't cost that much."

"Who paid it out, you or me? I'm the one to know, aren't
I? What about the incidentals? What about my feelings? Eh,
what about that?"

"We're discussing your expenses sending the kid to London.
We're not talking breach of promise."

"You tell him my figure's a thousand dollars. He doesn't
like that, maybe that's the time we talk breach of promise. He
can play it how he likes, but that's my figure. He's got the
money. The bastard cleaned up big on those sponges he brought
in. He's not short of a buck. He had plenty time before. Now
he wants the woman, so he has to pay for her."

Tony rose from the bed. "Okay, that's the way you want it,
I go down now and tell him." He paused at the door and
wrinkled his nose. "Why don't you open those windows?"
he said. "Blow this goddam stink out."

The door closed behind him, and Homer Vraxos smiled.
Manoli would pay all right. If he'd asked fifteen hundred,
Manoli'd still pay. The smile faded. He'd been a damned fool
not asking fifteen hundred: Manoli would have met it all right
because Manoli always had to be the big boy, doing it the big
way. The big-time wine buyer! The big-time wife buyer!

Vraxos smiled again. No point in being greedy. A thousand
gave him near enough to a hundred per cent clear profit on
his investment, and it freed him from a commitment he'd begun
to regret anyway. He'd got himself all snarled up some way,
working on that business of the diving team, making sure
Manoli didn't get picked on the Australian deal, and somehow
it had got into his mind that he wanted to give Manoli another
slap on the face while he was away. Well, it was still a slap on
the face—a thousand-dollar slap!

And then there was Stavros—there were all sorts of angles
tangled up in it—and it would have been nice to have that bastard
for a father-in-law just to show him that Vraxos hadn't forgotten
what happened in Bodrum. But Stavros had gone off his head
and killed himself, so there wasn't much point in that angle any
longer. Even the thought of Mina had curdled a bit, too.
Maybe thinking about Stavros and what happened at Bodrum
had twisted him up some way, so he had got to thinking of her

the way she'd been then, when she was just a kid and nobody had ever touched her. By Christ ! she had been a beauty then—just thinking about it made him hungry in the guts for her. But even when he'd paid out all that money to send her kid away, it hadn't made any goddam difference. You'd have thought a woman would be a bit generous for all that dough, and knowing he was going to marry her anyway as soon as the Church got itself untangled, but no, sir ! She wouldn't let him play around at all, although it was just fun and fooling.

No, he was well rid of the whole business—and five hundred dollars in pocket into the bargain.

Homer Vraxos was pleased with himself as he bent over the pressing iron, and then he frowned and put the iron to one side and began to scratch with his fingernail at a tiny mark on the cuff of the checked trousers.

2

AT THE point where the roads joined they took the thin, scribbly path through the fields, and they walked together in silence past small, walled plots where almonds grew and walnuts and olives, and then on through an orange grove where blossom and fruit hung together on the branches. Beyond the wall of the orange grove was a high rock ridge with three old windmills on the slope of it and at the summit the citadel that the Knights of Rhodes had built. You could still see the old shields carved into the yellow stone of the walls, but half the fortress had crumbled away and what was left had been painted white and pale blue and made into a chapel.

Off the main road, bustling with the Sunday crowds streaming up to Chorió for the dancing, there was a peaceful emptiness, and a tethered goat cropped the long grasses sleepily as if the drone of the bees in the orange blossom above had mesmerised it.

In the choice of this quiet, secluded place there had been no deliberation. They had gone out together along the crowded road with no fixed destination in their minds; when Mina had taken the path into the empty fields, it had seemed right and natural and there had been no need for explanation, and Morgan had followed her. What had begun in the places of calm solitude would come to an ending in a place of calm solitude, and it would all end quietly and gently, as it had begun.

She led the way up the rocky ridge past the windmills, climbing to the whitewashed steps and then through the archway to the old walls. Inside there was a small courtyard with a well and a twisted tree, and a ruined gateway through which you could look down on the Kalymnos-Brostá road. From the walls the whole length of the valley was visible—the white houses overlooking Brostá to the northward and the coloured houses of Kalymnos scattered around the blue bay to the south, hundreds of specks of pure colour laid side by side like a pointillist painting.

" It is beautiful, you know," Morgan said softly. " In some ways it's the most beautiful island in the world—beautiful, I mean, in a way you don't expect beauty to be. What's curious about it is that if you added to it the attributes we generally associate with beauty it wouldn't be beautiful at all." He turned and looked at her. She was seated on the coping of the well and the shadows of the overhanging branches made a soft pattern on her white head scarf. " I shall be very sorry when I go away from here," he said.

" You don't have to go. Manoli wants you to stay."

" Yes." He smiled at her. " Not now though, not really. I could stay when you were trying to escape from here, but now it's my turn. Perhaps I'll go to Nissiros or Astypalaia, and write to you about it."

It was curious, this spreading infection of escape, passing from one to another, changing people. He had come to Greece because he had been trying to escape—to escape from cities and grey faces and newspapers and the racket of radios, from polluted air and hurry and the dementia of society. And in Kalymnos he had found peace and beauty and he had fingered the texture of important things, and he had been content to stay until Mina's desire to escape had infected him. Now she could stay and he was obliged to go, and it all made logic in some twisted fashion because she belonged here and he didn't, and he could never really have taken her away because what existed between them was all complete within itself and it belonged here, too. It had all been made complete one afternoon in the little cove near Santa Katerina, and nothing could be added to it and nothing taken away.

" You must not worry about Nikolas," he said. " You could not be with him, you see, not now that he is to go to Switzerland, but they will look after him very well—better than you could— and in two years' time he will come back to you and he will be better. And then Telfs himself will be going to Switzerland late in the year for the post at Zurich, and he can see the boy. What you've got to worry about now is Manoli." He smiled. " I imagine that's quite a handful of responsibility for any woman."

" I understand Manoli," she said.

" Of course you do. You're the same sort of person. You both have the same sort of strength, but Manoli's is masculine and yours is feminine. I think you'll be very happy with him." He picked up a pebble and dropped it from the wall and listened until he heard it clatter on the rocks below. " You love him, don't you ? " he said.

" I love that part of him that can be loved, yes. There's another part of him that nobody can touch or affect. It belongs to *him*. You can respect it or admire it or hate it or resent it, but you can't do anything about it. Whatever you think, it doesn't alter it. It's a part of him that doesn't belong to you."

" You have it too, you know, Mina," he said softly. " There's a part of you that nobody can touch or affect, that belongs to you, a part that nobody can change. That's why you and Manoli are the only two people here who don't have to fly away from something that is haunting them, tormenting them."

It was true. Both of them stood unaffected by the restless tides of change, secure in the certainty of belonging, aware of what they were and of the things that surrounded them and of the things that had to be done. They were not complicated things ; they only seemed complicated when you examined them through the lens of your own tangled intricacies.

They stood apart even from their own people, from the poor devils who hadn't enough to eat, who couldn't find work and couldn't keep their children clothed, and who clamoured to get away, to escape, to go to America or Australia or some other place, to reach the Big Rock Candy Mountain. And they were separated by the width of all existence from people like Paul Pelacos, confronted suddenly by the picture of his own futility and turning away from it with his hands over his eyes. Or poor Irini, like a child lost in a dark wood, fearful of the shadows, trying to grope her way out into the light. "You don't have to go away to escape from it ; you can escape from it here——" that was what he had told her. But it hadn't been true. When he had said it to her, he had not been touched by the infection ; he had not then seen Mina Vraxos smiling down at him, with the platter of *smarithes* in her hands.

"The rest of us," he said, "are all running away from something. All of us like crazy guinea pigs, running up and down inside our cage until one day a man in a white coat comes along and doses us with chloroform and opens us up with a sharp knife to see what went wrong."

"But you're only running away from yourselves," Mina said quietly. "All of you. There isn't anything else to run away from."

"What about Nissiros ? Astypalaia ? "

"It was only myself I was wanting to escape from, not anything else. It is the same with you. You are only running away from yourself."

"And from you."

"Not from me, no." Her hand touched his lightly and moved away. "I shall still be there in the other place you go to. The part of me you think you are running away from is part of *you* now, so you are only running away from yourself. And when you run away from the little girl Irini it will be exactly the same, and that's why you must remember this."

"Irini ? "

" She came to me in the summer. She came in her boat to where we were living, and she is very sweet and lovely."

" She is, yes, but——"

" And she is a very lonely child, and she loves you. So before you run away from her you must be very careful not to make a mistake and hurt her. You must make her understand *why* you have to run away. It would be cruel to make her believe you are running away from her when you are really only running away from yourself."

" Yes, of course I understand, Morgan," she said, and smiled. " It's perfectly all right." How agonising it was to have to smile, to have to smile again and again as the awkward, laboured explanations came—to have to smile and nod and shake her head and to invent quick little reassurances so that it would hurt him less, having to tell her. Why didn't he say it quite quickly and brusequely and get it over : I'm sorry Irini, I'm awfully fond of you, but I don't love you, you see, and so I am going away. Why didn't he say it like that and walk off and leave her ? Then she would have no need to smile or to say things that had no meaning at all, no need to keep making these stupid little puffballs of words that blew away between them. She could go running through the crowds of people, past the music and the whirling dancers and all the houses, running up to the empty hills where she could be alone and her heart could break without her needing to smile and smile and smile. . . .

" It's my fault, Irini," he said earnestly. " I left everything hanging in the air, unresolved. I didn't want you to be hurt again, and I kept evading it. I ran away from it."

" You don't have to explain, Morgan. It's perfectly all right. I know what you mean. I'm . . . I'm not a schoolgirl. I think I've known anyway, through most of the summer, but I wanted you to come back so I could find out. That's what I meant in my letters . . . " She shook her head and smiled quickly and looked away, and Morgan's teeth bit thoughtfully on his lower lip as he watched her.

She was looking across the crowded tables to the packed swirl of the dancers on the threshing floor and all the other coloured rings of dancers beneath the olive trees, the men in masquerade and the girls in the old costumes that had a queer oriental look, so that each olive tree seemed part of a ballet setting, and it was strange that they were dancing to the thin, thumping Kalymnian tunes and not to a score by Stravinsky or Khatchaturian or Rimsky-Korsakov. . . . It was on this day, a year ago that they had walked together to Myrtiés.

" Shall I get some more wine ? " he said awkwardly. " We've had quite a lot already, but . . ."

" Yes, please," she said, not looking at him. " In the summer," she said thoughtfully, " I met Mina Vraxos. I was talking to her. I think I began to realise it then, but I kept writing the letters because I wanted to make sure."

" Mina ? This isn't anything to do with her, Irini. Mina is marrying Manoli."

" That isn't what I meant. It was meeting her and talking to her. It made me begin to understand what was wrong with me." Mina is marrying Manoli . . . he had turned and gone away from her and not looked back. And Jacques had gone away in the taxi she had paid for, and now Morgan was going.

" Irini, my dear, there isn't anything wrong with you," he said, pleading with her to understand. " It's me. It's the way things happen that we don't have any control over. We all go blundering through life, bumping into people and hurting them. It's because we're careless more than because we're cruel, but the hurt is just the same, just as cruel. Maybe it's crueller when it's carelessness. It's difficult to explain, Irini, but——"

" You mustn't try. You don't have to. That's what I said to you. Heavens, we can forget each other ! It's not hard. You'll find something new to interest you, and so shall I, and everything will take a new shape. Next month we shall be packing up anyway. Daddy has to go to London and Paris to wind up the business, and I shall go with him, and then for the summer I shall be in the south of France with friends of ours. The Teucers. They're awfully nice, awfully nice. . . ."

It was a self-deception that she allowed to drift away with all the other senseless puffballs.

"Look, we'll never get wine if we have to wait for a waiter,"
Morgan said suddenly. "I'd better go and fetch it myself."

"No, no, please don't bother. I've changed my mind. I
don't really want any more. I want to walk for a while, just
by myself. You do understand, don't you?"

"Yes. Shall I wait for you?"

"If you want to."

"Of course."

"I'll come back here in about an hour. And then I think I
should like to go home."

She had no idea how long she had walked, nor where she
had been, when she came to the field where the Gymnasium
girls were dancing beneath the plane tree. They were all in the
old dresses and their hands were linked as they circled in the
slow, stately dance, and they looked like figures from a frieze.
At the edge of the field there was a tiny *taverna* with pink walls
and beyond it a few cultivated acres, timidly nudging the austere
barrenness of the hills.

"Why, hallo, Miss Pelacos!" cried the voice from behind
her and she turned, and the fat little figure of the Vraxos man
was walking towards her with his hand outstretched and his face
beaming. "*Kaléss Apokryés*, Miss Pelacos." He gave the ancient
greeting with a Rotarian heartiness and then winked archly and
said, "And what's a pretty girl like you doing on a day like this,
walking around without an escort, without a beau?"

"I just wanted to walk," she said, and realised even as she
spoke that what she wanted to do more than anything else in
the world was to sit down somewhere and rest. The burden
of her mind had suddenly become more than she could bear,
and the cheerful urbanity of the old, yellow face smiling at her
pressed down on her like a leaden weight. She felt dazed and
exhausted. Her legs ached with the effort of supporting her
body, the burden, the weight of concern—everything. "I
wanted to walk," she said dully, "but now I think I'd like to
sit down somewhere."

"Why, sure!" Vraxos' brow was puckered with concern
for her. "You look tuckered out, Miss Pelacos. Come on,

we'll get a table. I know your father would expect me to take care of you. A table over at the *taverna* there and something to drink, some wine. What do you say?"

"I'd like to sit down. I don't think I want anything to drink. I feel a little dizzy even now. I've been drinking retzina."

"Ah, that stuff!" Vraxos snorted scornfully. "What you need is some of the real wine, the *krassi glikó*. That'll pull you together. Come now. Let old Homer Vraxos look after you." The yellow smile enveloped her, enfolding her senses.

What did it matter? The wine burning in her stomach only made a hot core in the leaden numbness, and everything else was vague, coming up close and drifting away, things half perceived as if a broken mist were spreading between her and what was happening. She was aware of things only dimly : of the clouds coming over the mountains from the southward ; of the Gymnasium girls going away towards the village, one behind the other, like a coloured ribbon twisting in the wind ; of her elbow knocking the carafe over and the dark wine running like blood across the table and Vraxos dabbing at her skirt with a big checked handkerchief ; of the red drops falling into the lap of her skirt and watching the yellow hand with the handkerchief rubbing, rubbing, rubbing. . . . She had no idea what he was saying . . . he was calling her " honey " now and not " Miss Pelacos ". . . . and he kept raising his glass and smiling at her and saying " *Si-yia, si-yia, si-yia !* " like Manoli on the night she had gone with him up the mountain. . . .

"I must go," she said thickly. "I must go back!"

She could hear the clatter of the chair falling behind her as she lurched away.

Homer Vraxos watched her go. She did not take the path towards Brostá. He watched the small, slight figure stumbling through the meagre fields where the plough had left its lumpy clods and up the first ridge of the empty hills.

He paid for the wine and took his hat and followed her.

When Stephanos saw the girl coming up the ridge his first inclination was to stop her, because she was alone and might listen to his story up here on the hills where there was no noise to interrupt and no other people to turn their indifferent eyes away.

In the village nobody had listened to him. And with all the clatter—the wine beakers clanging on the tables, the music, the voices singing and shouting, the people pushing past him, pushing him out of the way so they could jostle in closer to the dancing—it would have served no purpose if they had been willing to listen. It was not a simple thing to explain when there were lots of noise and interruption; it was something you had to concentrate on very particularly if you wanted to understand it.

That was why he had come away from all the crowding and the noise to tell what he had to say to the walls and trees and to the ants nesting in the warm, sandy crevices between the rocks.

The impulse to talk to her faded when he remembered what he had done to the big ants' nest in the hollow beneath the olive tree. What he had done to the ants' nest and what he had to explain were really part of the same thing, but nobody except himself could ever understand that, and if this girl knew what he had done to the ants' nest without understanding it, she might think it was a very terrible thing he had done.

Stephanos hurried off the path before she saw him and concealed himself behind a clump of aloes, and while he waited for her to pass he took out his big knife and began carefully to cut a small figure 5 in the soft prickly flesh of the smallest aloe he could find. The surface of the fruit would take only a very small 5, which had to be intricately cut out with the sharp point of the knife, but as the fruit grew the figure 5 would grow with it, growing bigger and bigger—just the way it had grown in his own mind. He often cut the aloes this way, always with the figure 5—because that was how many sons he had had before the bomb fell on them—and all over the island there were these figures hidden in the clumps of aloes, growing bigger and bigger, and there was nobody who knew about it except himself. Stephanos shaped the tail of the 5 more symmetrically and chuckled at his secret.

With the ants' nest it was different, because the thing you had to try to do was *not* to make the figure 5. You had to get as high as you could above the ants' nest, climbing the overhanging rocks or even swinging from the bough of a tree, and you had to wait for the right moment to drop the stone. And then you had to go down on your hands and count the squashed bodies of the ants. There were always more than five, often twelve or fifteen or twenty. In the big nest beneath the olive tree there had been thirty-two, maybe even more than that if he had searched more carefully in the crushed sand.

It was becoming complicated now, because the girl had not gone past the clump of aloes at all. She had stopped at a grassy bank right below him, and she was standing there, looking from side to side as if she did not know which way to go. She seemed to be ill or frightened. Then she lay down on the grass and closed her eyes. Perhaps she was tired and wanted to sleep. Stephanos squatted behind the grey-green screen and searched for a really small aloe upon which he might carve another 5.

He was glad now that he had not approached the girl, because she wanted to sleep, and because he had seen the figure of the man coming slowly up the hill towards them.

When Stephanos had completed the second 5—giving this one a handsome curly tail which pleased him—he peered again through the prickly barricade, and he could see that the man was kneeling on the grass beside the girl and he was stroking her forehead with his hand. Stephanos smiled to himself and nodded. He had been quite right then—she was ill and this man was caring for her.

The girl was either sleeping or unconscious, because she did not appear to pay any attention to the man's hand stroking her head, nor to the other hand which had begun to feel around her legs, perhaps to see if there was something wrong with them.

The man was becoming very agitated. Maybe the girl was dead, because she lay quite still, not taking any notice of anything that was happening. And something crazy had possessed the man too, as he crouched over the girl.

Stephanos pressed closer to the spiky screen of cactus, sucking his breath in as he watched the horrible thing beginning to happen.

"*Si-yia!* . . . *Si-yia!* . . . *Si-yia!*—it was a sound spinning around in her head, spinning in a whirlpool of wine, and the sound had the colour of wine in it and the smell of it, too, all mingled with the smell of the sea and wild thyme, and she could feel the weight of Manoli pressing down on her. She opened her eyes so that she could smile at him for coming back, and the figure was crouching over her.

Her scream seemed to come from somebody else as she pushed him away. He rolled over on the ground, moaning and clutching himself, and as she staggered to her feet everything became a horrible nightmare, because Stephanos the lunatic was there too, coming from behind a huge clump of cactus, with a long knife in his hand and an innocent, questioning smile on his face.

She fled down the hill, stumbling on the loose stones, trying to fasten the buttons of her blouse as she ran.

"You seen it, you seen it!" Vraxos screamed and he flung himself at Stephanos, hammering with his fists at the chest, trying to reach the idiotic smile on the face. "You seen it, you bastard!" he squealed. "You seen it all!" But Stephanos kept his head back, and the smile stayed there because Vraxos couldn't reach it with his fists. He stooped to one side, gasping with fear, and took the big stone up from the ground and lifted it above his head.

Stephanos saw the stone coming up and the smile faded, because this was the sort of stone you used for the ants' nests. Thirty-two there had been, and maybe more if he'd sifted through the sand. . . . That was why the girl had run away—she must have considered that what he'd done to the ants' nest had been a terrible thing . . . although it wasn't a terrible thing at all as long as you understood. . . .

The little fat man's scream was quite different from the girl's—more a cough or a choke than a scream, very sharp and quick, as if it had started out to be a scream but had been cut off short. Maybe the sound of the big stone falling to the earth had cut it off.

Stephanos stared at the figure sprawled at his feet beside the big stone, with the dark stain spreading down from his belly across the unbuttoned checked trousers, and then he looked at the knife in his hand, with the blood dripping off it like spilt wine dripping from the edge of a table. He began to count the drops as they fell—*one . . . two . . . three . . . four . . . five.*

Counting the drops, Stephanos saw it all clearly, and he began to weep quietly.

3

AT FOUR o'clock the storm reached Brostá. It came in gusty squalls sweeping in over the mountains from the south-west, scattering the dancers and causing the leaves of the olive trees to rattle together like dry seeds in a gourd.

Morgan watched them fleeing down the hills to the bus station, the women in their vivid old-fashioned dresses running with skirts and petticoats flapping and shawls streaming in the wind, and the weirdly costumed men bounding across the trampled fields of corn, flitting beneath the fig trees, leaping and yelling, calling to one another as they ran. It was the fantastic, delirious, make-believe finale to the day of *Kaloéri*. Salome and Mephistopheles and Scheherezade and an Evzone and a cowboy out of a demented dream trotted past him, all holding hands and singing as they ran ; a child dressed as Harlequin tripped on an olive root and sprawled among the flowers ; a tall figure hurried by with no face at all, only a blank, white cloth beneath a straw hat, and a girdle of dead, headless fish and yellow gourds bobbing as he ran. It was all fantasy commingled, spilling over, pouring down the hillsides, the wild colour draining into the steely funnel of light that hung between the earth and the thick clouds piling above the mountains.

Morgan walked around for the fourth time, although there was no point in searching for her any longer. Everybody had gone ; nothing remained in the fields but the littered papers blowing in the wind and a broken kite entangled and flapping in the bare branches of a plane tree.

At the bus station the fantasy had grown into a bizarre riot, men and women and children fighting and struggling to find places in the already overladen cars, the wind swirling lace petticoats and brocades and satins and silks, a drunken musician propped against a pink wall strumming a guitar, and a woman with a surly face squatted beside him, giving a huge brown breast to a naked baby. In the centre of the screaming, good-natured confusion Morgan could see the smiling face of Sergeant Phocas. The policeman had obviously abandoned all hope of dealing officially with the melee. He was smiling and nodding at everybody, giggling when somebody's buttocks became jammed in the door of a car, swinging his *kombolloi* contentedly.

Morgan pushed through the crowd until he came to him.

" Ah, she went back a long time ago," Sergeant Phocas said. " An hour, an hour and a half perhaps. Long before we got all these idiots who believe a car built to hold twelve people will take fifty if they scream loud enough ! "

" She probably saw the storm coming," Morgan said, relieved. " I'm glad she had sense enough to get away early."

" Had she been sick ? " the sergeant asked interestedly. " She did not look well, very pale and upset. Sick ? "

" Oh no, I don't think so. Not sick, no." He flushed slightly. " Perhaps a little tired—all the music and the noise . . ."

" I put her on her own in the big Fiat with old Vousalis," said the sergeant. " I told him to take her home. I thought she looked sick. Would you like me to get you a car ? " He giggled. " I can soon break up this menagerie."

Morgan's first impulse to be polite, to be fair and wait his turn, was checked by his continuing sense of uneasiness, by the new realisation burning in his mind. " As a matter of fact, I would," he said. " I'm a little worried about her. If I don't get away now, it might be hours."

" Why not ? " Sergeant Phocas beamed and skipped towards

the nearest car, shouting " *Bros ! Bros ! Bros !* " and striking the struggling figures across shoulders and buttocks with his delicate *kombolloi* of sea shells. It could not have been more effective had he used a knout. In less than a minute all the people were standing back smiling at Morgan, and the car was empty.

He climbed in beside the driver and said, " Can you take me straight to the Pelacos house ? "

But she had not gone back to the big white house, and the old housekeeper, Savasti, seemed surprised that he should have returned without her. " She should have been with you," she said disapprovingly, and added irrelevantly, " It was her best skirt and blouse she had on, the ones from Paris." She sniffed. " I told her the weather would change, she should take a coat. They always know, these young ones ! "

" But she left Brostá two hours ago. I expected she would have come here. Sergeant Phocas put her in the car himself, and told old Vousalis to bring her home."

" Vousalis ! " Savasti studied him frigidly across the starched blackness of her bosom. " Vousalis drinks ! " she snapped.

On the waterfront the knot of people was clustered by the dinghy steps, not far from the door of his own house. The wind was blowing hard into the harbour, and spray was beginning to lift against the lighthouse. Off the quay a faded sponge boat was moving slowly ahead with engine thudding, taking up the slack of the anchor. It was one of Manoli's boats, the *Angellico*.

Morgan ran towards the clustered men.

" What is it ? " he said anxiously. " What's the trouble ? "

" Ah ! " A small monkeylike figure with a single yellow tooth, a very old man whom Morgan could not remember ever having seen before, detached himself from the group and pushed up to him. " Her father thought she was with *you*," he said accusingly.

" Thought who was with me ? "

" Miss Pelacos. Miss Irini." The old man glared at him suspiciously.

" Well, so she was. What about her ? "

But the old man had turned his back on him and was holding

out his hands to the group of men, as if offering them an explanation that might satisfy them. Morgan took him by the elbow
and turned him round

"What is the matter?" he insisted. "What's happened?"

"What's the matter, eh?" Old Petros nodded wisely.
"That's the thing to ask when she comes back with pneumonia
or gets herself drowned out there! Maybe I'm to blame because
I happen to be doing some odd jobs on her dinghy, and they'll
say I should have stopped her going out. *Stop* her! She was
supposed to be with *you*, wasn't she? It's what I tell her when I
see her going out to the boat. As if I don't know better than a
squib young enough to be my great-granddaughter the way the
weather grows out of these waters. For eighty years I watch the
way that sou'wester comes up." He had turned again to the
other men, loath to relinquish his role of public informant and
oracle. "I say to her, 'Miss Irini, this is no day to take a boat
out sailing, not a little stick of a thing like that,' I say, 'not with
that sort of weather coming up out of Kós.' And for all the
notice she takes of me, I could have kept my mouth shut! Just
jumps into the dinghy and out she goes! 'You go get a sweater!'
I yell to her. 'I've taken the oilskins out of the locker!' I say.
'You get a sweater!' And she doesn't even turn round! Just
casts off the moorings cool as you please, and up with the sails
and off she goes, just like it's midsummer." He frowned and
nodded sagely. "Something wrong with that girl, you ask me,
something crazy! Doesn't even speak to me, as if I'm not there
at all. As if I don't know——

"Where has she taken the boat?" said Morgan urgently.
"Where was she going?"

"How do *I* know if she doesn't even speak to me?" the old
man complained. "Looks right through me as if I'm not even
there. That's where Manoli's going, to find out. And her
father with him, and by Jesus, he'll have plenty to say! If she'd
listened to me—I know this weather . . ."

But Morgan had begun to run along the quay towards the
Customs House. He could see the *Angellico's* anchor coming
out of the water and the clots of mud dropping away from the
flukes and the curved bow swinging and the black sea piling

along the breakwater with the white running through it, as if
sharp knives were slashing it open.

He ran fast, down behind the Customs House and out
along the breakwater, and the spray driving in off the rocks
stung his face as he ran. He had to get to the end of the breakwater before the *Angellico* went past, because Manoli would see
him and bring the boat in close enough for him to jump on to
the deck ; and he had to be aboard the *Angellico* when it brought
Irini back so that he could tell her. Tell her what a ghastly
mistake it had all been, that he'd been all tangled up in his own
mind, that he loved her, and he wanted her to marry him. But
he could not tell her now, pounding along the breakwater with the
spray burning at his face ; he had to be on the *Angellico* to go to
her and tell her.

"Manoli !" The wind seemed to take the cry from his
mouth and toss it away, but Manoli looked across to him and
lifted one arm from the tiller and made a gesture with his hand
that could have been a wave of recognition or a signal of
dismissal. Neither Elias, crouched in the bow stowing the
anchor cable, nor Paul Pelacos standing amidships with both
hands gripping the coaming of the deckhouse, appeared to have
heard his shout. In his brown hat and tailored gaberdine raincoat
Paul Pelacos looked incongruous against the frayed gear and
weathered timber of the boat.

The *Angellico* cleared the end of the breakwater by thirty
feet, rolling awkwardly as the first wave struck her and then
getting the measure of it and lifting with a quick, springy motion
that feathered the spray up from the bow and scattered it the
length of the deck. Morgan could hear the creak of her timbers
and the hiss of water along the faded planks as she went past.

"*Manoli !*" he screamed.

But Manoli did not look back. His big shoulders were
bunched against the push of the tiller and his legs braced into the
curve of the after-rail. A lumpy sea burst across the port bow as
he put the tiller up.

"*Manoli !*"

A seagull hung for a moment above Morgan's head, scrutinis-
ing him with impressive yellow eyes, and then it squawked

derisively and planed away downwind. Aboard the *Angellico* Elias was dragging on the halyards to get the black sail up, and Morgan could hear the muffled drumming and thudding of the canvas in the wind, and the deeper thumping of the thick bow shearing the waves aside as Manoli headed her down towards Cape San Giorgio.

Paul Pelacos crouched in the lee of the enginehouse watching the water drip from the skylight on to the soaked shoulders of his raincoat.

"That was Leigh on the breakwater, was it?" he asked dully. "I suppose he wanted to come."

"Wouldn't have been time," said Manoli curtly.

"Time? You mean . . ." Pelacos looked at him anxiously.

"The sea's kicking up. In another hour it'll be nasty. In two hours, less than that, it'll be dark."

Pelacos moistened his lips, and there was a taste of salt on his tongue, salt that had a flavour of engine oil.

"I think she has taken shelter somewhere," he said hopefully. "She is an intelligent girl, a good sailor."

Manoli grunted. A good sailor wouldn't have taken an eighteen-footer out in this sort of weather, not a boat that wasn't a work boat. The squalls were coming hard and flat across the water with a lot of sting and malice in them, and the sea was building. "That's not the sort of boat to be sailing in this time of year," he said disapprovingly. "That's for summer for having fun in. There's no fun in the sea this time of year."

"Oh, it's a very strong little boat, the *Astra*. Casalis is a fine builder. It has watertight compartments fore and aft, you know."

"Sure," said Manoli. "She'll be all right." The poor bastard was worried sick; there was no point in adding to his anxiety. Watertight compartments fore and aft and fancy sails imported from London, and the sea to sail it in comes in special bottles with labels on so you can see it's genuine. "If she's got around the point she'll run into the bay at Piso. That's where we'll find her, anchored there, manicuring her fingernails." He eased the tiller down to meet a big sea coming in and breaking.

The bow lunged into it and kicked away and Elias, clinging
in the forestays, looked back at him, shaking the water from his
eyes.

It was a minute or two later that Elias came aft in a series
of quick, running hops and stiff, watchful pauses ; for a moment
he stood alongside Manoli staring inshore intently, and then as
the *Angellico* lifted he touched his arm and pointed.

" There," he said softly.

Manoli could see the tiny wedge of white jabbing upwards
out of the dark sea, like a nick in the black face of the cliff.
" Jesus ! " he said, and whistled.

" What is it ? " said Pelacos uneasily. " Can you see something ? Can you see her ? "

" Sure," Manoli said. " She didn't make it round the point
after all. She's right inshore, not far off the rocks. Just below
that big cleft that comes down. Wait till we hit the top of this
sea. Now ! Look ! "

" But great heavens, she is *on* the rocks ! " Pelacos cried,
clutching him. " She is on the rocks ! "

" No, she's not. She's still sailing. There ! " They could
see the little triangle lifting in a swift, curving swoop, and then
it seemed to check and shudder and go flat on the water again.
" She's sailing," said Manoli, and for a moment his eyes shone,
as if he had seen something that had pleased him. " Not for
much longer though," he said. " The jib's gone, and even if it
wasn't she couldn't put about in that sea." He grinned at Elias.
" Okay, let's go," he said and pushed his shoulder at the tiller.
The *Angellico* gave a wild, swinging heave as the sea came up
behind her and then she was running towards the shore with the
waves boiling at the bow.

" But you cannot take *this* boat in there," Pelacos said desperately. " You will be on the rocks yourself, man ! "

Manoli looked at him for a moment and laughed.

" Mister Pelacos," he said, " I can take this boat anywhere.
But right now Elias is going to take her. I'm going up in
the bow. You better get down in that enginehouse, I think.
Things are likely to get a bit mixed up when we hit that loose
water."

Manoli gave Elias the tiller and went forward, scampering down the slope of the deck as the boat's stern lifted, and Paul Pelacos crouched in the stern, watching him as he pulled the blue sweater over his head and kicked off his sea boots and began to unbuckle the wide belt around his waist. When he had stripped down to a pair of white drawers, he took a coiled rope and made one end of it fast around his belly.

" What is he going to do ? " Pelacos asked, but Elias did not seem to hear him. His brown face was thoughtful and his eyes were on the surf lathering the inshore rocks. It had been eleven months, he remembered, since the engine had been overhauled. And in there, where the sea was coming back off the rocks, it wasn't going to be easy to look after the tiller and the engine wheel as well. The column of the wheel came out of the house at a forty-five degree angle, and he could reach it all right, even holding the tiller, but in there in the broken water it wouldn't be so easy, with the propeller out of the water half the time and that backwash piling off the rocks against the rudder. Maybe without two hands you wouldn't be able to hold off the kick of the tiller. It would have been nice to have another man aboard. One more man would have made a lot of difference.

He stared at Pelacos for a moment and said, " I guess you better do what Manoli says, get down there in that engine-house. You'll be out of the road. We're likely to be busy in a few minutes."

Pelacos nodded dumbly and lowered himself awkwardly into the dark cubbyhole, pulling his soaked gaberdine raincoat around him.

The *Astra* was no more than thirty feet from the outer edge of the reef, a fang of black, weedy rock jutting out from a wide, flat ledge which was alternately smothered by foam or streaming cataracts of water. The girl was still sailing her, crouched in the cockpit so that you could see only her small head with the hair plastered down like a skullcap and one hand reaching back to the tiller and the other dragging at the mainsheet. The torn remnants of the jib were twisted around the forestay, standing out stiff in the wind like pieces of metal, but the little boat was still sailing, still holding parallel with the lip of the reef. It was the

surge back from the rocks as much as the girl's determination
that was holding her off.

Manoli came aft again with the rope dragging behind him
from his belly. " Stay twenty or thirty feet away from her,"
he said. " We're deeper, that surge it'll take us in on her. And
for Christ's sake keep astern of her. If we blanket that sail of
hers she'll go straight in."

" We keep thirty feet off, you got to go over the side," Elias
said. " Maybe you catch that drag in on to the rocks."

" You got a better idea ? " Manoli grinned at him.

" I got no ideas. But you go over the side, I can't haul
you in. I got only two hands. We get in a bit closer and I'm
going to need twenty."

" The other end of this rope's fast to the forward bitts.
That's another reason I want you to stay astern of her, we don't
want the line fouled in the propeller. I can drag myself in on the
line, and her too. We won't worry about the boat. Pelacos
can buy her a new one."

" Who's going to buy *you* a new boat if this bastard goes in ? "

Manoli chuckled and went forward, but at the deckhouse
he stopped and turned. " Pelacos was right ! " he yelled admiringly. " The little bitch can sail a boat ! "

Paul Pelacos crouched in the dark, smoky stink of the engine-
house, fighting against his own misery and shame and the bile
retching up into his throat. Through the scuttle he could see
the soaked, sea-booted legs of Elias swaying to the movement
of the boat and behind the legs the whirling insanity of sea and
sky. Everything was shaking and shuddering inside the throbbing
frame of the enginehouse, and the fumes burned his eyes and
choked in his throat. It was as if all his senses were being pounded
into a pulp, into a meaningless, helpless mash, by the running
shudder of the timbers and the deafening explosive clangour of the
engine. " Slow her now ! "—it was Manoli's voice, drifting to
him from miles away, drifting to him along the sliding hiss of the
sea and the cry of the wind. The note of the engine softened, and
the great, greasy bank of metal shivered on its housing bolts,
and through a square opening in the slimed wood of the floor

he could see the thick mess of the bilge rolling its viscid rainbows from side to side. " Keep astern of her ! Keep astern ! " It came from a million miles away, from another world, from a world where men were not helpless and futile and useless. " Better do what Manoli says. . . . You'll be out of the road."—Old and futile and useless, pushed off the *autobahn*, pushed into the foul-smelling, reeling compartment of this enginehouse, where he would not be in the road ! It was his own daughter who was in peril, and there was nothing he could do about it ; if he tried he would only be in the road.

He put his head down on his knees and was violently sick.

Manoli went in head first, throwing the coiled slack of the rope ahead of him as he dived, and he could feel the churn of the sea tugging him back when the *Angellico* rolled away. He swam powerfully, putting all his strength into it before the slack of the line took up and began to drag at him. The sea was tugging all ways, and beneath him it seemed to be rolled up into tight, thick coils of water that twisted this way and that, and when the surge piled back off the rocks the coils wrapped themselves around him, trying to pull him down.

The yacht appeared to be hanging against the black wall of the cliff, just in front of a snout of reddish rock streaming with water, and as Manoli swam the picture of it flickered in his eyes in quick, disconnected stabs of vision : the water falling in cascades from the face of the rock and the bright-green weed rippling beneath it . . . her face, pale and wet beneath the tight, soaked cap of her hair . . . a width of froth, like soapsuds in a tub, banked up beneath the overhang of the rock snout, and mussels and sea urchins edging it like a decoration . . . her face above the varnished band of the coaming, the face of a young boy under the black cap of hair, a pretty boy, all puckered up with concentration, looking at the rocks . . .

Manoli reached up and groped for the coaming, and she turned her face and looked down at him, and she smiled as if she had been waiting for him to come, waiting a long time for him to come. It flashed across her face only for an instant, the smile, so that afterwards Manoli never could be quite sure whether she had smiled at him or not. It was a smile of wonder and rapture, like somebody seeing a vision, and then she turned her head away from him and deliberately pushed down on the tiller.

The yacht swirled round and down and hesitated for a moment, with the canvas flogging in the air, and then the wave came in and lifted it and hurled it towards the rocks.

Manoli could feel the weight of the boat rolling over on him, driving him under. If it had rolled the other way he would have lost her, but his hand was on her shoulder and he wrenched at her as he went down. He did not hear the splintering crash of the boat striking. All the sea seemed to be boiling and splitting apart, disintegrating into separate fragments of pain and numbness, of blindness and a dazzling brilliance; the cold kelp was coiling around his legs, and the knobs of rock bruising and battering him, and he had the sensation that his body was rolling away from him, a body flayed by the razor edges of the shells, rolling away from him across the streaming red snout of rock. And then the numbness came to choke him, deadening the agony of the rocks and shells, stripping the skin from his arms and back.

He held her tightly, hooked inside the curve of his body, to shield her from the rocks, and when the surge came he summoned every reserve of his failing strength and flung himself outward. He could feel the sea lifting them together, out and over the clot of soapsuds beneath the overhanging ledge.

Elias watched them come. They came slowly. Often they were smothered by the sea and he would be afraid that they had gone; but the wave would swing on, spiralling and kicking into the surge, and they would still be there, and the clots of foam drifting around Manoli would have a pink tinge, and Manoli would still be dragging on towards the boat, inch by inch. He'd taken the line over his shoulder and he was coming in on his back, dragging the rope in over his shoulder with his right hand and holding the girl on top of him with his left. Doing it that way, the poor bastard couldn't see that he was wasting his time. The kid had drowned already; you could tell the way her head was back, hanging loose from the neck and half the time under water. The eyes and mouth were open, too, and that was a sure way to tell. But Manoli still dragged on.

"Pelacos!" Elias shouted, but there was no sound or movement from inside the enginehouse.

"Pelacos!" he yelled, and listened for a moment and shook his head.

Elias eased the tiller so the waves would come abeam and roll the rail down to him, and the drowned body of the girl came in first, with Manoli clinging to the big ringbolt and pushing her in over the rail. She looked very small on the deck, lying there in the flooded scuppers. The sea had stripped most of her clothes off; she had only a brassière and a strip of her skirt clinging around her hips. And Manoli came in naked as the day he was born, and it was a terrible thing, seeing him come toppling in over the rail with the bloody face all blind and dazed and the blood pouring down his arms and shoulders so that it looked as if all the top part of his body had been dipped in paint—the same colour paint he always used for his own boats.

But he staggered to his feet and stooped over and lifted the girl and began to carry her up towards the stern, although he managed only two reeling, stumbling steps before he fell with her, and the two of them lay together on the wet deck, not moving at all.

Elias pushed down on the tiller and reached across to the engine wheel, and the echo of the exhaust crashed back from the cliffs as the *Angellico* began to turn away. There was nothing much to be seen of the yacht now, only a piece of the mast lodged in a rock crevice. It gave a crazy kick each time a wave broke.

To Elias, it seemed very quiet taking the *Angellico* back. When you considered quietness, you didn't take into account the noise of the wind and the sea because that was all a part of it, and you didn't consider the thudding of the engine because that was a part of it, too. What you took into account was the silence from the enginehouse, and the silence of the two naked figures sprawled so quietly on the deck beside the midships house. It was like sailing back with a shipload of dead people.

Maybe they *were* dead, both of them. There was no way of telling; he couldn't leave the tiller to go up and find out. Another man on board would have been handy, even if it was just to go and look at them and see if Manoli was still alive. The girl wasn't, that was certain ; maybe Manoli wasn't either, because there hadn't been anyone to go up and give him attention.

There was no movement from him, no more from the girl, and now when a sea came over the deck and washed across them it didn't run off into the scuppers all tinged with that pale-pink colour it had at first. Maybe that meant something, maybe not.

She'd been a pretty kid, the Pelacos girl. So small, and with that funny haircut of hers, like a boy's. She looked like a child, lying there against Manoli's huge, bloody body, and his big, torn arm thrown across her breast, as if he was still trying to protect her from the seas washing over them.

" Pelacos ! " He yelled the name not because he thought it would do any good, but because he had to do something to stop it being so quiet—but there was no sound from the engine-house.

4

" WE COULD do with more of that colour paper, maybe a string or two of the little flags." Mikali's tone indicated that his general approval of the decorations was qualified by an insistence on absolute perfection. " Just two more strings across the door there, you won't see the ceiling at all."

" Nobody sees your ceiling," said Tony Thaklios. " It's one of the things they stopped looking at way back. There's better things to look at. Besides, what you got to avoid is the pedestrian approach. We got to look for a *touch*, that's what's needed."

" A touch ? " Mikali repeated the word questioningly.

" Sure, a touch. Something novel. Something people remember and talk about. Like in Clearwater once—I had the catering for this wedding—I employed the moss."

" Moss ? "

" Sure. Had it spread all across the supper tables. You ought

to seen their eyes open when they came in. Boy ! " He chuckled.
" I can still see Calliope standing there in a starched white apron
trying to palm away a snail that came crawling out from behind
the wedding cake. That moss, that was a *touch*. People talked
about it a long time after."

" I never see moss around these parts," Mikali said sadly.

" It doesn't have to be moss. With Manoli and Mina it'd
have to be something else—sponges, I guess."

" The moss would look pretty," Mikali said wistfully. " That
would be a novel touch all right. I don't see anything novel in
sponges."

But Tony was lost in the pleasures of reminiscence. " Ah,"
he said, " I had a genius for that sort of thing, for touches.
All over Clearwater people used to talk about it. Maybe there
was a wedding and they'd get stumped for an idea and they'd say,
' You send round, get Tony Thaklios. He'll have an inspiration,
all right ! ' "

" If sponges is an example," said Mikali sourly, " the bastards
got short-changed."

" Best touch I ever had," said Tony, ignoring him, " was the
red rose. That was in Clearwater, a wedding, just like the moss.
But this time we used flowers, it was a wonderful season for
flowers, and there was one single rose left over, a beautiful
red rose, and that was when the inspiration came. I'd never
plan these things, you understand, the inspiration would just
come."

" Sure," Mikali said dubiously, staring at the ceiling.

" You know what I do with that red rose ? "

" I could make a guess, but it wouldn't be decent."

" I take that red rose and I drop it in the toilet, in the flush
bowl of the toilet. It was a nice bowl, pale green, and the red
rose there in the water looked beautiful. There was a whole
lot of talk about that touch. Nobody used the toilet all night
and they trampled all the flower beds down going to the big tree
in the corner of the yard."

" I'd be happy with a bit more of that colour paper and a
string or two of the little flags," Mikali said impatiently. " We
got this wedding to arrange. We got no moss. We got no red

roses. We got no pale green toilet bowl. We got no time to
listen to your life story." He sighed. " It's nice now with all
the tables pushed back against the wall and that space there for
the dancing. Like a night club. Now what we got to do is
finish it off nicely."

" This place looks like a night club," said Tony acidly, " and
I go off to Hollywood right now and take over from Clark Gable !
You want the novel touch I'll supply it all right, but I got to wait
for the inspiration. When you got a flair for things you don't
have to force it. You give it time, it comes. But what you got to
realise, Mikali, is this dump of yours has difficulties. Most
fellows would say "—he paused, selecting the word that most
fellows would say—" most fellows would say these difficulties
are insuperable. You put all the coloured paper and strings of
flags you like, it's still no Stork Club, no Copacabana. You try
to take a red rose into that privy of yours out there, it withers
as soon as it hits the stink. You put moss on the tables, it all gets
tangled up with fish bones. Okay, you want me to make a silk
purse from a pig's ear, the least I can do is try. We got the ceiling
fixed, so now we look for the right touch. You give me time,
I'll give you the touch all right."

" What you give me is a touch of the trots," Mikali said
tartly. " All I want is two more strings of little flags. What
I'll get is sponges. *Sponges !* When I go to the Belgian Congo
I never want to see a sponge again ! "

" When you go to the Belgian Congo, you take my advice
and stop worrying about sponges. You concentrate on making
some dough so you get that toilet fixed. I'll have the red rose
waiting for when you come back. Maybe we get the mayor
along to throw it in ! "

Telfs came from the police station with Sergeant Phocas
and walked along the broad walk to the café where Morgan
was waiting, and the three of them sat down together at a table
beneath the salt tree. Across from them five vermilion boats
from Samos, two *depositos* and three diving boats were loading
drums of water and gasoline and big coils of white air hose, and
each boat had a man aloft painting the rigging. Farther along

the quay, in front of Morgan's house, Manoli's five boats rode
at their moorings, gleaming with fresh paint. Because of the
wedding, each of the boats had a Greek flag flying.

" Well ? " said Morgan.

Telfs nodded. " It will be all right," he said. " I went
through the statement with Dimitropolis, and he'll put in his
own report. The file will have to be sent to Athens, but I'll go
up for a week and see it through."

" It is not easy for the captain to understand," said Sergeant
Phocas happily, " when a matter is not orthodox. He likes
things to have the proper pattern." He giggled and took out
his string of shells.

" Nothing has the proper pattern," Telfs said. " Because
there isn't a pattern to begin with. It's all made up of little threads
running together, but we haven't worked out a loom that can
handle them. We make bits of rag, that's all. There isn't a
pattern."

" I can see the captain's point of view, though," Morgan said
thoughtfully. " It is complicated. It isn't just the killing of
Vraxos. It's Irini's death, too—that's part of it." He shook his
head sadly. " It's . . . it's all sorts of things."

" All they're concerned with is Stephanos' killing Vraxos,"
Telfs said brusquely. " Whether it was self-defence doesn't
really matter. Stephanos didn't kill him anyway for the reason
he should have been killed ; the poor old guy killed him because
he was insane and didn't know what he was doing. That's all,
just as simple and uncomplicated as that. There were plenty
of complicated reasons why Vraxos *should* have been killed, and
he wasn't killed for any of them. He was killed irrationally by
a poor crazy bastard who had no more sense of purpose in what
he was doing than if he had swatted a fly that was troubling him.
If you go beyond that you get into deep waters."

" It doesn't make any difference that Stephanos is sane now ? "

" Only to Stephanos," said Telfs. " That poor devil can rot
away, very slowly, thinking how much easier it was when he was
crazy. They won't do anything to him. They don't have to.
He's done it to himself. But that's getting into the deep waters
I'm talking about."

" But it isn't easy to reduce it all down to one simple aspect," Morgan protested. " You can just say that——"

" It may not be easy," Telfs interrupted, " but it's wise. You start to look for a purpose in this thing and you go just as crazy as Stephanos was. You think of it as something done blindly by a blunt, unthinking instrument and you're closer to the truth of it—to the truth of most things." He stirred the sugar into his coffee thoughtfully. " Once you begin trying to sift the tangle you have to find a point to start from. So what ? Was it really Vraxos who was responsible for his own death, and who killed Irini and old Stavros ? If it was, we have to find the point where Vraxos begins to have a reason for it—that's if we want to look for reason and purpose in something that could be purposeless. But maybe it wasn't Vraxos. How do *we* know ? Maybe it was some other cause, something of which we're not even aware. . . ."

Maybe it was, Morgan reflected bitterly. His own self-deception and stupidity, his carelessness, his injustices and cowardice—had he been the blunt, unthinking instrument, blind and blundering and finally destructive ? How absurdly pre-occupied he had been by his own feelings towards her, how heedless of *her* true feelings—until it was too late ! " You can escape from it here ! " Well, she had escaped from it here, and chosen her own way of doing it, and perhaps, in a sense, he had driven her to it. We all go blundering through life, bumping into people and hurting them. . . . It's because we're careless more than because we're cruel, but the hurt is just the same—they were almost the last words he had spoken to her, and now there was so much he wanted to say to her and it was too late. . . .

" Stephanos is the simplest part of it," Telfs said, " because there you don't have to look for a reason. All the rest of it . . ." He shrugged. " God set out to make the perfect animal, but he got tired before the job was done and he never finished it off. Instead of making something big and fine and faultless he made a crazy little homunculus, all twisted up, with none of the parts working properly. You'd have thought when he put so much work into it he'd have finished it off properly."

" Do you remember, in Athens, the first night I met you ? "

Morgan said. " You told me to come down here to see God with the Byzantine face. The big God with the dark, hard face, that's what you said."

" Sure. The blunt instrument. It's the same all places, but they paint it here in simpler colours, that's all. And the light is clearer. It's easier to see." He turned to Phocas. " That's the way of it, isn't it, Sergeant ? "

Sergeant Phocas looked up with a start and giggled self-consciously. " I'm sorry," he said apologetically. " I wasn't listening." He giggled again. " I've been thinking about Manoli's wedding."

Telfs grinned. " That's what we should all be doing. All this other stuff is just gassing into the wind."

" Ah, Leigh, how nice ! " Paul Pelacos looked up from his desk and motioned him to the leather arm-chair and busied himself for a moment with the stack of papers on the blotter. " I am so glad you came. I have something extremely important I should like to discuss with you. I shan't keep you a moment."

" But I came to go with you to Saint Stephanos," Morgan said doubtfully, " to Manoli's wedding."

" Yes, yes, of course, of course." Pelacos continued to rummage among the papers, a frown of concentration on his face. His grey hair was a little dishevelled, and there was tobacco ash on the lapel of his jacket. Morgan had seen Pelacos only twice since the day of Irini's funeral, but each time he seemed to have aged a little more. And there was a vagueness about him, an uncertainty, that made it difficult to remember the man whom he had met on his first day in Kalymnos, the man in the raincoat twirling the gold key chain, so suave and self-assured, so *certain* of things. It was interesting that you never saw him now with the key chain in his hand ; had he lost it or forgotten that he had it ? The air of his earlier self-possession still clung to this study of his, to the pictures and the photographs and the books, to the bottles in the mahogany cabinet and the leather and the chintzes, but as he rummaged through the papers on the desk he gave the impression of being another person, a relative perhaps, who had assumed occupancy of the room and was not

quite certain where things were kept. Morgan half expected him
to look up from his papers and point out the Oxford photographs
on the wall and say, " A cousin of mine. They were taken when
he was at university in England."

" I find something intensely amusing in the thought of
Manoli's being married," Pelacos said, but he said it absently,
and it was obvious that he found neither intensity nor any
particular amusement in the thought. " Ah ! " His face
brightened. " This is what I have been seeking. I knew I had
left it here because I needed it for the figures and I completed
them only this morning."

" Look, I hate to be pressing," Morgan said, " but could we
talk about it as we walk down ? It's three-thirty. If we don't
go now, we shall never get *near* the church, let alone inside.
All the town will be there."

" But my dear Leigh, this will occupy no more than a few
minutes of our time. As we go down to the church we can
discuss it in detail, of course, but if you are to grasp it all it is
essential that you skim through one or two of these newspaper
clippings, and more particularly, run your eye over these figures
of the travel agencies."

" Travel agencies ? "

" Yes. You will find the figures most interesting, Leigh.
Not merely interesting—significant. Did you realise that travel
agencies nowadays are among the most important merchants
of all Europe ? Everywhere—London, Paris, Rome, Berlin,
Athens——"

" I'm sorry. I'm afraid I don't quite follow. I've never paid
much attention to——"

" One moment, Leigh. It is when you relate these agency
figures to this scheme of mine that you realise how formidably
the case is presented."

" Scheme ? The centre, you mean ? "

" The centre ? " For a moment Pelacos paused and turned
his gaze to the door, and for an instant there was a queer
expression in his eyes, haunted and tormented, as if he expected
the door to open and an apparition to appear. And then he
looked at Morgan and laughed lightly. " I am afraid I have

discarded that proposal altogether. We all have pipe dreams, Leigh, all of us. What I have in mind now is something different, something infinitely more practical. The other ? " He shrugged. " A Utopian fantasy, Leigh, an idealistic whimsy, like my talking to you once of flying to the moon. Do you remember ? Your friend Telfs, of course, saw its absurdity at the very outset. He defined it, I recall, as something germinating in the mind of a science-fiction writer. A shrewd chap, Telfs, a good brain."

" On the contrary, Telfs was considerably impressed, as I was," Morgan said. " Until he accepted that Swiss post, I think he harboured a wistful hope that you might allow him to take over the medical side of it."

The uneasiness flickered again in Pelacos' eyes, but he smiled and said, " Telfs has a streak of the visionary in him, too, you know. There would have been an initial appeal to that side of his character. However, he would have seen, as I did, its sheer impracticability upon closer examination."

" Perhaps. And the new proposal ? "

" Tourism."

" Tourism ? *Here ?* " Morgan looked at him blankly.

" Most decidedly here ! Why not ? An island of singular interest and unique beauty, a climate unrivalled in all the Ægean . . . " Morgan closed his eyes. It was impossible to believe that this was Paul Pelacos talking, talking as if he were quoting from a tourist brochure—" An island of singular interest and unique beauty ! " Only the night before Morgan had gone through the dark town with Telfs, and in the back streets the fires were burning beneath the vats in which the beef for the sponge boats was boiling—great chunks of beef, boiling in the salt and oil and butter fat. And all through the town these wonderful, dramatic nocturnal groupings that cried out for a Rembrandt to paint them : the wives in the head scarves, holding the lanterns aloft, and the men in their sea boots and jerseys and peaked caps, squatting round the vats ; and it was always an old man with pale sea-washed eyes who was stirring the meat with a long billet of wood and a young man packing it into the cans that would go in the boats to Alexandria and Benghazi and Tripoli. . . . For an hour he and Telfs had walked through the town watching them, never talking, overawed by something beyond the power of the imagination to grasp : the shadows, black and gigantic, moving on the flat walls of the houses, filling the crooked streets . . . the lamplight, deathly pale on the quiet proud faces of the women, and the fires, flickering red on the hard strong faces of the men . . .

"I am not thinking of just another tourist resort like all the others," Pelacos was saying. "Here it is possible to have something completely different, something of unique charm. One has always recognised the infinite possibilities of the Ægean, Leigh, but to what extent have these possibilities been explored ? We have Crete, impregnated with the dark, humbling enigma of Knossus. We have Rhodes. Rhodes is stately, and also rather humbling in its way. Mykonos ? Mykonos is pretty, Santorin is quaint and dramatic, Delos is possessed by an elusive magic that few people can be expected to grasp. Here, I think, we should strive for something charming and lively, something gay."

"Something gay." Morgan echoed the words numbly. Waiting for Telfs to come from the police station he had watched the men working on the Samos boats and there had been a sailor hung in the rigging sewing white canvas around the shrouds.

"My dear Leigh, it is what the people *want*. People are satiated with the gravities of the world. They are desperate for pleasure, gaiety, escape, for entertainment. You read these clippings and then run through the agencies' figures. You will see for yourself. Something lively and gay, that is what is wanted. I am visualising a casino—not necessarily large nor elaborate, but possessing charm, built out over the water perhaps —and good restaurants, possibly a cabaret. These would be merely the trappings. Most important would be the development of the island's natural charm : the beaches, a pavilion or two in the hills. Can you imagine what superb *plages* could be developed here with a little planning and imagination. Piso, Brostá, Myrtiés, Télendos . . . With good tourist hotels, by heavens, we could transform Kalymnos, Leigh ! "

"You could, yes." Morgan looked at him tiredly.

"I hope I am wrong in inferring to you a lack of enthusiasm," Pelacos said suspiciously.

" Since you ask me, I think I preferred the earlier proposal. I'm sorry you've abandoned it. It seemed to me to be something that had *scale* to it. It was grand and bold and it had . . . it had *purpose*." He rose suddenly and walked to the window and looked out to the orange grove where once Irini had stood in the dusk and offered him the Golden Apple of the Hesperides. " This other proposal, I don't know, it seems defeatist, sacrificial." He turned into the room. " There are so many tourist resorts, Pelacos. There is only one Kalymnos."

" But this new proposal is no more than an adaptation, an elaboration possibly, of the earlier one. We could embody something of that, its tourist aspects. Why not? It all adds to the variety and the novelty. . . ."

Morgan let him talk on, scarcely heeding him. Kalymnos as a tourist centre! The spiky heels of the women tourists trampling its guts out! The girls in their slacks and sunglasses staring at the old, black-shawled women as if they were creatures in a cage! The sailors in blue jerseys with Moby Dick printed across their chests, taking out glass-bottomed boats to display the wonders of the sea bed! . . . The man with Pan's face fleeing with his *tsabuna* into the secret hills because the tourists wanted rhumba rhythms and samba rhythms and Palm Court music in the afternoons. . . . And the tinkle of ice in the cocktail shakers and post cards and shawls embroidered garishly and the cabaret music drifting across to the sleek yachts anchored at the old moorings of the sponge boats, drifting across the waters that had sailed the galleys out for Troy.

And Pelacos could do it. That was the horrible, terrifying thing about it—he *could* do it! He had the money to do it, and he had the taste and intelligence to do it well. Money was a blunt instrument too, destructive and blind when it was used without purpose. Was Telfs right after all? Was it ridiculous to look for purpose in anything any longer? But where was the Paul Pelacos who a year before, in this very room, had talked to him with such dignity, such selflessness, of what had to be done for Kalymnos? Had all boldness gone, all audacity withered, so that the only solution to be found was this shameful escape into a sordid parasitism, into cabarets and cocktail bars and souvenir stalls ? The dark, bloody history of three thousand years, the enduring fibre of the island and its people, suddenly unravelled into pretty little tinsel threads ; the guts and strength and fortitude of it all twisted into . . . into *variety* and *novelty* ! Was this the way it ended, as Eliot said, not with a bang but a whimper ?

" I suppose you realise," Morgan said softly, " that what you propose could accomplish in two years what all the conquerors failed to achieve in two thousand. It could enslave Kalymnos, destroy it."

There was a pause, then Pelacos looked up from his papers with a vague expression of inquiry. " Forgive me, Leigh," he said apologetically. " You were saying . . . ? "

Morgan moved across and took up his raincoat from the chair. " I was saying it's gone four o'clock. I'm afraid you'll have to excuse me. The wedding begins at four-thirty."

" Ah, yes, the wedding." Pelacos smiled absently. " Do tender to Manoli and his bride my heartfelt wishes for their happiness and prosperity. Would you do that for me ? And if you could make some sort of apology for my absence . . ." He smiled quickly. " Pressure of business is as good a phrase as any, I suppose."

" Yes," said Morgan. He went out, closing the door quietly behind him.

In all the streets around Saint Stephanos the people were crowded, and the wide curve of stone steps leading up to the church was a packed mass of men and women and children, and even with the assistance of Sergeant Phocas and his intimidating *kombolloi* it was a difficult matter for Morgan to reach even the outer courtyard. Every window of the church provided precarious perching for the small boys of the town. They clung like limpets to the pale stone, swarmed strangely in every archway, hung in the branches of the trees like queer roosting birds ; and those unable to achieve the vantage points stood squirming below them, clamouring shrilly for information.

" I can get you as far as the door," Sergeant Phocas said bravely. " Inside you won't be able to move."

"It doesn't matter." Morgan shook his head. "I should have come earlier. I'll wait here."

"*Po-po-po-po-po !* " Sergeant Phocas rejected the suggestion with an emphatic twirl of his *kombolloi*. "And not even *see* what it looks like ! It's very pretty. I was inside before you came down."

He thrust his small figure determinedly into the crowd and Morgan followed him reluctantly. The interview with Pelacos had affected him far more deeply than he had realised : he was almost afraid to witness Manoli's wedding now lest it, like everything else, dribble away into the futile melancholy of anticlimax.

From the door of the church he could see neither Manoli nor Mina for the press of people packed shoulder to shoulder beneath the glitter of all the candles. Around the walls the candles flickered, and in the two huge, swinging chandeliers, the *polihélië*, the blaze was silver among the crystal and the wide, hanging ribbons of blue and white. Had it looked like this, Morgan wondered, for Stavros ?

It was obviously impossible to push through the crowd and even with the advantage of his tallness Morgan could see nothing of the ceremony ; after a minute or two his attention was seized by the picture of the watching women in the high gallery.

There were nine of them in the front row, all old women, all with the black Kalymnian scarves covering their heads and brought round in front to half-conceal their chins, their lined, leathery faces impassivly attentive as they looked down upon this latest renewal of a mystery which to them was no longer mysterious, which in labour and travail, in the pain and harshness and suffering which had marked the anguished gestation of their lives, had long since lost its power to mystify. They were all alike, these nine black-coifed women—alike in the posture of veiled chins, resting on the gnarled arms laid along the railing of the gallery, in their unblinking immobility, in the withdrawn secrecy that marked their engrossment, in the black-framed ovals of their similar faces, faces that saw it all with the impassive accuracy of the uninvolved onlooker. Yet, for all their resemblance one to the other, Morgan realised, they were different

beings, each possessing the special separateness of a unique knowledge, for what each one thought and saw was filtered down
through the soggy, compacted gauze of her own experience,
through the sad accumulation of her drained decades.

They had seen it all before, these nine women in black. They
had been watching it since time began, and they would be
watching it for all eternity . . . always watching it like this,
with the same still, unblinking, passionless absorption. If
something different ever happened perhaps they might turn,
one to the other, and their aged eyes might brighten and the
sibilant whisper of their comments might drift down to give
startling revelation to the people packed below. But in the
nine pairs of faded eyes there was no expectancy that anything
different would ever happen. Nothing ever had. Nothing ever
would.

In a sense, they were the chorus, the women of Canterbury.
In the withered black-veiled faces there *was* something alarmingly
medieval. They were from the paintings of Breughel, from the
woodcuts of Dürer, from the tumultuous crowds of Bosch.
They lived in the black-letter books, sucking their sustenance
from sad litanies. Morgan had the feeling that the nine women
—not just any women, but these particular nine—had been
there for centuries, silent above the jostling heads of the ever
altering crowds, looking down, seeing witches burned and
heretics racked, hearing princes praised and victors acclaimed,
seeing all the days of joy shrivelling into sadness and despair . . .
always looking down, looking down. . . .

It was not inconceivable that Pelacos was right after all,
that his solution in the end might prove the most merciful.
Kalymnos no longer belonged in the world : the medieval
women in the gallery personified its persisting anachronism.
There was no time for it, no room for it. Better to wrench it
without compunction from the wizened claws of the nine old
women in black.

From the body of the church there was a rising triumphant
note in the chanting priests and a murmur growing into a shout
of joy ; the two great glittering *polihélië* were set swinging
from their golden ropes above the unseen figures of Manoli

and his wife, and they were swinging in great, vivid arcs of silver flame and floating ribbons, swinging like silent bells. The people were pushing in closer, jostling, shouting, and all the arms were upraised and the handfuls of rice were flying through the air, thickening into a storm of white, bursting through the church like driven spray. The watching faces of the nine old women in black were fading, fading, fading . . . fading behind the white whirl of rice and swinging light. He could not see them any longer. They were gone.

Morgan turned and pushed his way out into the sunlight.

"Conch shells," Tony said proudly. "It came to me just like that." He snapped his fingers. "That's the touch, I said—conch shells!"

Mikali folded his hands across his aproned stomach and morosely studied the centrepiece of the decorations, a huge pyramid of sea rocks and sponges, surmounted by a single conch shell. He turned to Morgan. "Just looking at it, not taking sides, what would you say it was? Conch shells or sponges?"

"Well, I would have thought sponges. I must say it looks very impressive, whatever it is."

"Sure it's sponges," Tony said impassively. "But it's that conch shell that gives it the *touch*. It had to be something about the sea, being Manoli."

"Yes," Morgan said thoughtfully. Being Manoli it had to be something about the sea. Mina, too. It all went back to the sea. Manoli, Mina, Irini, even Pelacos.

"It's a fine, old-fashioned touch, that conch shell," Tony said with satisfaction. "Very old, the conch shell."

Morgan nodded. Just as old as the nine women in black. Older. "Very old, Tony," he said. "The Tritons used them."

"I didn't mean like that. When I was a kid, my grandfather used to have them all over the house and we'd hold them to our ears and you could hear the sea in them. You could hear the waves rolling. When I first listened to it, it made me cry, it was so wonderful. Very mysterious, that noise the conch shell makes."

"Everything about the sea lies at the edge of mystery," Morgan said. He turned towards the door. "They're coming now," he said.

They could hear the shouting and the music growing louder, and they went out into the waning, mellow light of the afternoon, the three of them together, and they could see the long column winding up the narrow street towards them, the musicians leading with their mandolins and fiddles and an escort of darting children scampering around them, and then all the crowd behind bringing Manoli and his wife to their party, and they were singing "Thalassaki Mou" as they came.

They stopped outside the door, the two of them side by side and the priests beside them holding the broad, flat basket of sugared almonds and the tray for the offerings to Saint Stephanos. Morgan stood to one side to watch them slowly filing up, one after the other to kiss Manoli and his bride. All of them—Elias and Tony and Mike Grassis and old Beanie and Dimitri and George and Mikali and Katerina and Petros and Sergeant Phocas and Katina Gravos and Tomás and Iannis the boat boy and all the divers and the seamen and their women.

And finally it was Morgan's turn to do it, and he walked towards Manoli, standing big and strong and proud in his badly chosen tie and white collar and new navy-blue suit, not looking at all absurd nor made ridiculous, as another man might have been, by the powdering of rice in his thick black hair and the tiered white wreath of waxen flowers askew on his head. For a moment Morgan looked at him, at the terrible half-healed wounds scarring the face below the absurdly tilted wreath, and then Manoli grinned at him and his teeth gleamed whiter than the flowers, and Morgan leaned across and kissed him.

"Long years, Manoli," he said softly. "Long years to you both," and he turned to Mina, to the face that was beautiful and proud and sad and joyful, a face that humbled him with its dignity and compassion, and he could feel it all choking in his throat as he put his lips to her cheek.

They were all wrong, all of them. Pelacos was wrong. And the nine black harpies in the gallery of the church, they were wrong, too. And he was wrong himself, and Telfs was wrong. Because this was something stronger than them all, some enduring fibre of human strength and dignity that was everlasting, immortal, unconquerable. This was the thing that went on.

5

THE ACTIVITY began long before dawn, so that it was difficult to believe that a night had intervened, that there had been any nocturnal pause of quiet in the town.

The farewell parties of the night before, the ripping and roaring through the streets, the singing from *taverna* to *taverna*, seemed so essentially a part of the departure of the boats that they became fused with the mysterious matutinal stirrings along the quayside and in the dark twist of the harbour streets. Before the sun came up to poise like a giant's golden playball in the clear sky between Kós and Pserimos and before a dawn wind rose out of Brostá to stir the skeletons of the February kites still dangling in the electric wires the restless town was awake to see the day come, as if in the communion of wind and sun they might read omens of the seven months to come.

Morgan, who had not reached his bed until two in the morning, was awake before five, and he dressed quietly, so that Telfs should not be disturbed, and went to the balcony overlooking the harbour. The dinghies were already moving between the boats, and in the quietness he could hear the slow splashing of oars and the mouse-like squeaking of ropes on thole-pins. On the quay below the balcony a boy with wide, sleepy eyes held a lantern high for Zeffis to examine his papers. There were five men with Zeffis, discussing the documents, and when one of them struck a match to light his cigarette Morgan saw that it was Elias. A gust of laughter from the group was quickly stifled, as if in fear of awakening the town. A boy in a dinghy swung himself into the chains of a grey-hulled *deposito*, whistling nonchalantly. The exhaust of one of the diving boats exploded in a stab of orange flame that changed into a pale-violet glow as the engine settled into its slow rhythmic beat. From the dense shadow beneath the salt trees, a drunken seaman reeled, singing in a voice thick with wine.

By daybreak there were many people already clustered at the sea rail, staring at the boats in their bright, brave finery with a preoccupied curiosity as if they were trying to puzzle out where they had come from in the night, as if they had never seen them before, as if there was a compulsion to examine every detail of every boat in compensation for the neglect shown them in the weeks of preparation and loading. It was, in a sense, the town's belated recognition that this sun which had risen upon a crowded harbour must set upon an empty one.

Morgan had never seen the harbour so full before. There were all the boats of Kalymnos, for the yards at Lavassi were empty now and the shingly beach behind the Customs House had been abandoned to the play of children and to women washing rugs, and there were the chartered boats from Symi, Rhodes, Patmos, Samos, Piræus, Hydra, Spetsae, Amorgos, Kós and Astypalaia to add to the numbers of the Kalymnian fleet. Until now had he, too, been no more than a casual passer-by, oblivious to the massing of this vivid armada—to the hundred coloured boats poised and waiting in the sunlit harbour ? It was their colour that made the most profound impact on the senses : the gaily painted blocks and shining rigging, the insouciant decoration of rudders and tillers and stemposts, the strakes and gunwales painted with the same joyous abandonment to pure pigment that one saw on fairground swings and circus merry-go-rounds, the hulls that were scarlet and green and blue and white and yellow and black and pink and purple and vermilion and brown and lavender and grey—boats painted with a childish passion for brightness, boats painted with arresting Bracque-like subtleties of unexpected harmony. With the blue-and-white flags flying from every mast and the childishly coloured prisms of the town behind, it was some fairytale flotilla assembled for romantic ventures. By nightfall they would all be gone, all of them. Nothing would remain but the mooring floats riding on the

empty sea and the flotsam of garbage crusted at the quay's edge
and the women in black veils afflicted with their burden of
patience . . . and all the boats would be running to the southward, running for the African beds . . . and this day's harbour
would seem a dream one had had or a morning of particular
bliss remembered from childhood.

Through the first hours of the day the excitement mounted,
and by midmorning it seemed as if all the people of Kalymnos
were crowded along the broad walk, and the harassed captains
of the boats pushed among them, shouting for missing members
of their crews, scouring the innumerable *tavernas* of Kalymnos
for divers reluctant to abandon the convivial securities that
retzina offered ; in the growing pandemonium men dodged
from *taverna* to *taverna*, gulping at the wine and running on,
shouting together as if it were a game, and infuriated captains
pursued them, and drunks were pushed laughing aboard the
boats, and Zeffis ran backwards and forwards like a man possessed
waving his sheaves of paper, and the women were clustering
around the boats and weeping already, and the men, clutching
meagre cloth-wrapped bundles in their hands, spoke to them
sheepishly, and there was a roar of laughter as six drunken seamen
rowed ashore in a purloined dinghy and scampered off to the
tavernas again, yelling as they ran.

To Telfs and Morgan, watching from the balcony, it seemed
impossible that such confusion could give way so suddenly
to the aching, watchful quietness that marked the blessing of
the boats. Surprisingly, all the boats were manned and a pale-blue
mist was adrift in the harbour above the slow-thudding exhausts.
The bearded priests were going from boat to boat with the holy
water and the crucifixes held above their heads, and the incense
smell was mixed up with the gasoline fumes, and all the sailors
and the divers stood with bared bowed heads on the decks
among the roped and crowded oil drums and coiled air hoses
and kegs of water and *galetis* and boiled beef, and the men were
crossing themselves, and all the way up the crowded, hushed
broad walk the ripple of hands fluttered.

For all its moving solemnity, it was an instant transcended
in poignancy a moment later when the first bells chimed from

Saint Stephanos and, as if in response to its signal, the women whose men were sailing donned the black head scarves of mourning which they would wear until their men returned, and, in the crowd below, Morgan could see Mina replacing the white kerchief with the black, and she was smiling across to Manoli, standing by the tiller of the *Okeanos*.

Morgan turned to Telfs, but he said nothing because there was something in the face of the American that told him more clearly than any words could express what Mina had meant to him also. And it told him more than that : it told him that Telfs as well as he was aware of the significant enrichment contained within this poised moment of peculiar, moving beauty—this separation from all other things of the women in black and their men and the boats that were waiting to go. This tiny island in the Ægean, for all its poverty and suffering, touched both men with its greatness. It enriched them, and it humbled them.

Manoli was grinning down at Mina from the afterdeck of the schooner, and then he waved to her once and turned away and called something to the crew. Morgan knew that he would not look back again. The arms of the windlass began to lift and fall and the *Okeanos* slid slowly from the quay, riding out on her tautening anchor chain. When she was in the stream and free, the four *aktaramanthes* followed slowly, and Elias was waving up to them from the tiller of the *Ikaros*, and the other boats were slipping their moorings and moving out, and all the Greek flags were snapping in the wind and the blue mist of smoke from the exhausts was spreading across the broad walk, blowing into the drawn faces of the weeping women. Manoli, in the *Okeanos*, was leading the fleet to sea.

Morgan could feel a prickling in his throat and his lips were dry and his eyes smarting. " You must learn to cope with your sense of ' reverence ' "—that was what Telfs had said to him. But this was the Kalymnian, the Kalymnian taking his boats out ! For three thousand years the boats had gone out. And now they were going out again. Going out and down to whatever there was to be encountered on the African beds, and the women were waiting as they had always waited, and the bells of all the churches were ringing.

Very softly Morgan spoke aloud : " One thing you forgot about. Continuity. It's the one absolute thing about humanity. It makes sense. If you believe in continuity, it doesn't matter much if you don't believe in God."

Telfs looked at him, then solemnly turned to the sea and the boats again.

Three times the *Okeanos* circled in the harbour, with her own boats and the others forming a long line behind her. They could see the tall, strong figure of Manoli at the tiller, and his cap was off and the wind was blowing in his hair. All the rest of them were possessed by dreams and delusions, by ambitions and plans as trivial and as vain as poor George's hunger for the calendar of the Nomikos Line or Mikali's dream of the Belgian Congo or Pelacos' pursuit of his mirages.

But there was the truth of it all—in the coloured boats circling in the blue and gold of an Ægean day and following Manoli out. Each boat made its three circles in the harbour while the men clung to the rigging and waved to the crowded houses on the shore.

The beating thud of a hundred exhausts swelled into a thunder that drowned the jangle of the bells, drowned the sobbing of the women who waved from windows and balconies and the white railing by the sea, drowned the hymns of the church choir singing on the breakwater, the chanting of the priests, drowned all things.

The Kalymnian was taking his boats out.

Below the balcony Mina was going away slowly through the crowd, moving towards the steps that would lead her to the empty house on the hill. From her right hand the discarded white scarf trailed.

The noise of the boats faded across the empty harbour, its thin echo coming back from the flanks of the bare mountains. And then there were only the bells ringing and the sound of women weeping and the quiet lap of the harbour waters. The leading boats, Manoli's boats, had hoisted their sails off Point Cali and all the sea was leaping with the rhythm of the south-bound fleet.

Morgan went inside and began to pack his bags.